PRAISE FOR

Praise for *A Killer's Alibi*

"William Myers' riveting new novel is not just a crackerjack legal thriller, it is also a wrenching portrayal of a whole range of father-daughter relationships, showing how they can damage, how they nourish, how they go dangerously off track. A story not to be missed."

—William Lashner, *New York Times* bestselling author

Praise for *An Engineered Injustice*

"About as close as one can get to . . . an exciting train ride, short of purchasing a pricey Acela ticket. Fast-paced, tightly written, and inspired by a real-life railroad disaster."

—*The Big Thrill*

"Excellent characters, proper full-on courtroom drama, and a mystery element that is unpredictable and highly intriguing."

—*Liz Loves Books*

Praise for *A Criminal Defense*

An Amazon Best Book of the Month: Mystery, Thriller & Suspense

"[In] Myers's impressive debut . . . the gripping plot builds to an ending that's a complete shocker."

—*Publishers Weekly*, Starred Review

"Talk about a mystery . . . I just couldn't put it down."

—*Fresh Fiction*

"Heart-thumping. This comes together making you want to race to the finish."

—*Night Owl Reviews*, Top Pick

"This intense debut legal thriller builds to a startling conclusion."

—*Stop, You're Killing Me*

"*A Criminal Defense* is an outstanding debut from a talented writer to keep your eye on."

—*Novel Gossip*

A KILLER'S ALIBI

OTHER TITLES BY WILLIAM L. MYERS, JR.

A Criminal Defense

An Engineered Injustice

A KILLER'S ALIBI

WILLIAM L. MYERS, JR.

This is a work of fiction. Names, characters, organizations, places, events, and incidents are either products of the author's imagination or are used fictitiously. Any resemblance to actual persons, living or dead, or actual events is purely coincidental.

Published by Thomas & Mercer, Seattle

www.apub.com

ISBN-13: 9781503903333
ISBN-10: 1503903338

Cover design by M.S. Corley

Printed in the United States of America

This book is dedicated to Wayne Chalmers, my father-in-law and friend.
We spent many a fun hour shooting the breeze, watching golf and football. I loved your devilish sense of humor. And your strength, even through your final, difficult days, was an inspiration.

Prologue

Eight are with him at the table. His three best friends: Vinny Itri, Dominic Ricci, and Geno Moretti. Four guys who work for his father: Bruno, Dave, Tomasino, and the guy everyone calls "Pits" because of his pockmarked face. And, of course, his father: Big John.

It's his twelfth birthday, March 15. Outside, the night is bitter cold, the South Philly streets covered in ice and snow. Inside, Alighieri's is cozy. And it's all theirs, Big John having persuaded the owner to close the restaurant for the private party—a big favor to grant on a Saturday night, as his father has reminded them all.

The older men amaze the boys with ribald stories, everyone guffawing over "Three-way" Wendy Mancini and "Pass-around" Patti Peregrino. The mobsters shift gears eventually and trade veiled tales of "jobs" they've done, the boys recognizing the word as code for one type of illegal activity or another.

They feast.

"My boy reaches manhood, we eat like kings," says Big John.

The waiters bring plate after plate, starting with the antipasti: meats, cheeses, and peppers; prosciutto, provolone, and Sicilian olives; stuffed portobello mushrooms; mussels; steamed clams in spicy marinara sauce; calamari stuffed with crabmeat. For entrées, the crew orders perciatelli Genovese, linguine and claims, penne alla vodka, fettuccini Alfredo, pork chops Milanese, and osso buco di vitello. Big John orders the special—pasta with Italian gravy and meatballs—and makes clear he expects his boy to order the same.

He does as his father suggests, though his mouth is really watering for the branzino.

His stomach full to bursting, he unbuttons his pants even before the waitstaff brings out the desserts: tiramisu, cannoli, semifreddo, tartufo. There will be no cake.

"Fuck cake and candles," Big John says. "This ain't a kiddie party. Right, boy?"

"Right," he answers.

The *real* dessert, he knows from Geno, will come later. Geno is the oldest in his group, having turned twelve the month before. His father, not as well-off as Big John, put out a big spread at home. Then, after everyone left, he took Geno to a motel near the airport.

"When I opened the door," Geno told him and Vinny and Dominic, "there she was, smiling on top and bottom." As Geno told it, he didn't let up until the sun rose, and the woman told him he was "amazing" and "the best" and "You're going to break some hearts in your time, that's for sure."

The waiters clear the table. The owner comes over, thanks Big John for hosting such a special occasion in his restaurant. No check is tendered or asked for.

He and his father walk outside, and his eyes water in the frigid air. He has on a heavy winter coat, long-sleeve shirt, undershirt, and wool pants his mother bought him for the occasion, but he's still freezing. Big John just has a fall jacket over a short-sleeve shirt, and it seems he could stand outside all night and not mind it one bit. It amazes him how tough his old man is. In so many ways, they couldn't be more different. Big John is five nine and weighs two hundred pounds, not an ounce of which is fat. His father's head is starting to go bald, but everywhere else he's covered with thick black hair, and he has a perpetual five-o'clock shadow. The old man has an overhanging brow, a fat nose, and a jaw so square it looks like his head was carved from a block of wood.

He, on the other hand, is 120 pounds soaking wet and has a thin nose and sharp jawline. The only things they have in common physically are their dark eyes, which turn into black pits when they're angry.

His friends pile into Dave's car to be driven home. The last to get in, Geno, glances back at him and gives him a thumbs-up. Earlier in the night, Geno had given him four Trojans, saying he'd be disappointed if he didn't use them all.

Bruno gets in the driver's seat of Big John's Cadillac, and his father takes shotgun. Tomasino waits for him to get in the back seat, then slides in beside him. He's thinking Bruno, Tomasino, and Pits will get dropped off, after which Big John will take him to the motel. But the car leaves their neighborhood with all the grown-ups still inside, and they make their way to I-95 South, then to Route 1 West.

He's starting to get nervous now, because he's thinking his father's crew are all going to be waiting around while he's with the woman. Maybe in the next room . . . maybe listening in.

What if I mess it up? Will she tell them? Will they laugh at me?

His father wouldn't laugh. Big John would be pissed if he didn't perform, especially if his men were there to hear it.

The drive goes on and on, the men seeming to grow quieter as they get closer to wherever they're going. After they turn off the main roads, they go from one winding country road onto another, a single lane in each direction. It is pitch-black—no moon, no stars, and hard to see outside—but he senses the roads are lined with farm fields.

Finally, they turn onto a dirt road. Up ahead, in the Caddy's headlights, he sees a second car, a dark sedan, pulled over to the side. Bruno pulls the Seville up behind it, and Big John orders everybody out.

The air here is even colder than in the city, and his eyes sting as soon as he gets out of the car. No one is saying anything, so he doesn't, either, simply follows the four men into the field, keeping his head down and using their bodies as shields against the wind. They walk for a while until he hears two voices ahead. Actually, three voices, but one sounds muffled.

Big John, Bruno, Tomasino, and Pits stop, and he stops behind them. His father looks back at him, waves him forward.

"Come on," he says in his gravelly voice.

His heart is beating a mile a minute as he steps forward. He knows what his father does for a living—sort of, at least—and he guesses what he's about to see even before the men move aside.

The man is on his knees, his hands bound behind his back, his mouth wrapped with duct tape, his face a battered mess. He is naked. There is a large hole in the ground to his left. To the kneeler's right, two men stand. One of them leans on a shovel. Watching them shiver, he realizes that it must've taken them hours to dig the hole in the frozen ground.

"Come up here, son," Big John says, grabbing his arm and pulling him closer. "You see this guy? He stole from me. And that means he stole from *you*. And from your brother and from your mother, too."

He looks at the man, who looks up, tears and terror in his swollen eyes. The man mumbles something through the tape, but it's indecipherable.

"The real reason he's here, though? I trusted him. He led me to trust him. You see, son, he was one of our own. And that means he didn't just steal from us—he betrayed us."

Big John stares into his eyes, and he can tell his father is looking to make sure that he's getting it.

He nods.

"You know what happens to a Judas, don't you?"

He nods again, and his father reaches into his jacket and pulls out a gun. He's seen it before. It's a .38 Special. A revolver with a cylinder that holds six bullets. His father told him all about it one night at the kitchen table. "You see this?" Big John had said as he cleaned and oiled the weapon. "Some people say dog is man's best friend. I say bullshit. *This* is man's best friend. You take care of this, it'll take care of you."

Big John holds out the gun now. And only then does it hit him what this is all about, what his father has brought him here to do. His jaw starts to drop, but he stops it. He takes a deep breath, then accepts the gun. For all the times his father has let him see the weapon, he's never let him hold it. He's surprised at the weight of it.

Big John nods at the kneeler, then steps back. Taking his cue, he moves up to the guy.

He can't hesitate, can't let himself think about this. If he does, he knows he won't be able to do it. He raises the gun to the back of the man's head and pulls the trigger. The recoil is stronger than he expected, and it pushes his hand and arm up into the air.

It takes all his willpower to keep his knees from buckling, to keep from throwing up. To keep from bursting into tears.

"Dirty Judas," he says. Then he calmly turns to his father and hands him the gun.

Big John's mouth spreads into a grin.

He watches his father put the gun back inside his coat, then reach out to pat his head. More than anything, he wants to smack away his father's hand. But of course he doesn't, just smiles as he tousles his hair.

"Now you're a man," his father says, reaching down to shake his hand.

He shakes with Big John, then with the other men as they move forward to take their turns.

"Good job," says Tomasino.

"Good man," says Bruno.

"Your son's got a heart of stone," Pits says to Big John.

Big John Nunzio is beaming now.

They all stand still for a minute, watching their breath turn to steam. Then his father, Bruno, Pits, and Tomasino lead him back to the Cadillac while the two other men kick the body into the hole and start shoveling.

He's numb the whole ride back. He tries to think about school, basketball, the girl with the red hair in homeroom whom he has a crush on—anything not to face what he's just done. But he can still feel the solid weight of the gun in his empty hand. The man's whimpers and the crack of gunfire resound in his ears. The smell of the man's fear is fresh in his nose, as is the ripe stench of his evacuated bowels.

Every now and then, his father glances back at him. After the third or fourth time, he says, "Hey, Dad, what was that veal Dave had? It looked good. You think Mom can make it?"

Big John smiles. "I'll find out what it was, bring some home for your mother to cook."

He smiles back, his guts roiling at the thought of eating anything ever again.

Later that night, his old man comes into his room, sits on the bed. He pretends to be asleep, acts like his father woke him up.

"You made me proud tonight, Jimmy. You knew what had to be done, and you did it. And you didn't hesitate, which looked good." Big John pats his knee, gets up, walks toward the door. Then he turns around. "It gets easier. What my old man told me my first time. And he was right. But I guess I don't even need to tell you that. You're a natural. You got the heart for it."

He waits for two hours, until long after Big John and his mom and his brother are sound asleep. Then he goes into the bathroom and throws up everything he ate that night. And when he's done, he crawls back into bed and cries himself to sleep.

1

Wednesday, April 10

Ten p.m. A half mile east of League Island Boulevard, a lone police car bounces its way down the cracked macadam that is Mustin Street, in the undeveloped part of the Philadelphia Naval Yard. Mustin bends into Admiral Peary Way, which is wider but not much better. To the immediate left lies the Delaware River. To the right, a giant building with a barrel roof that looks like an old airplane hangar.

"It's the goddamned middle of nowhere out here," says Lou Piccone, the older cop riding in the passenger seat. The whole plot, from Windy Point to the developed part of the Naval Yard, is a no-man's land.

I should be home in bed, not patrolling this godforsaken place with a rookie partner.

Past the hangar and a hundred yards down a service road, a pair of two-story brick buildings sits on a patch of ruined concrete that used to be a parking lot. The buildings have large factory windows. A gleaming Cadillac Escalade is parked outside the main door.

"What are you doing?" Piccone asks as Trumbull turns the car onto the service road.

"Those buildings are supposed to be vacant. That car shouldn't be there. Don't you think we should check it out?"

A minute later, Piccone unbuckles his seat belt as Trumbull parks the squad car. "All right," he grumbles, lifting his heavy frame out of the vehicle. He pulls out his flashlight, uses it to scan the interior of the Escalade. The black leather is spotless. The walnut woodwork shines.

"Should we call for backup?" asks Trumbull.

Piccone thinks on it. Whatever's going down inside the building can't be on the up-and-up. He's about to tell Trumbull to call for backup when he hears the sound of a woman sobbing.

"No time," he says.

He unholsters his Glock. Trumbull does the same, and they move toward the door.

Piccone sees that the metal doorframe is bent, and the left edge of the wood door itself is splintered, rendering useless the three dead bolts intended to secure it. "Someone kicked the shit out of this."

Someone strong.

Piccone pushes open the door and takes in the scene. The two-story structure contains one open room. Steel shelving occupies the back half of the building. Bags of white powder are stacked on the shelves. The front half of the room is laid out as a living area—a couch, chairs, lamps, end tables, a television, a small kitchen with an island.

On the large Oriental rug at the center of the living area, a young woman sits, crying and rocking a dead man in her arms. The woman and the corpse are covered in blood, which still drains from a gash in the dead man's throat.

"Why, Daddy? *Why?*" she wails as she cradles the body. "I loved him . . ."

"Drop the knife!"

It's only when Piccone hears Trumbull shout the words that he spots the man standing in the shadows. Piccone raises his gun and repeats Trumbull's command. "Drop it and kick it away from you! Hands behind your head!"

The man complies, and Trumbull steps forward while Piccone stays back, keeping his gun trained on the man. The younger officer walks behind the man, grabs his arms, and cuffs him.

"Watch the blood," Piccone says, seeing that the man is as covered with it as are the woman and the corpse.

Once the killer is cuffed, Piccone holsters his pistol and walks up to the perp. It takes a minute for him to register what they've just done, but when it does, he stops cold.

"Oh shit."

"What?" asks Trumbull.

"Not what. *Who.*"

Everyone in Philly law enforcement—at least everyone on the force longer than a month—would recognize the coal-black eyes staring back at him.

"Mr. Nunzio."

2

Thursday, April 11

"Daddy, where'd you put Harry's box?"

Mick's nine-year-old daughter, Gabrielle, looks across the breakfast table at him. Harry is a turtle Gabby discovered in their yard a week ago. She'd insisted that he and Piper let her adopt it.

"Harry and his box are locked in my office, where Franklin can't get to them," Mick says, referring to the family's Bernese mountain dog.

"Harry doesn't like your office," Gabby says. "Don't you know that?"

Bringing the plates to the table, Piper says, "Maybe Harry's changed his mind about where he wants his box, like you changed your mind about what color you wanted your room painted."

"I don't want eggs. I want French toast."

"You had French toast yesterday," Mick says.

"Yeah? I went to school yesterday, too. Does that mean I can stay home today?"

"You're so funny," Mick says. "Anyone ever tell you that?"

"You're not. Did *everyone* ever tell you that?"

Mick shakes his head, looks at Piper.

"Grandma's going to pick you up after school today," Mick says, knowing that Gabby enjoys spending time with Piper's mother.

Helen Gray had blossomed in the wake of her husband's debilitating stroke following the Hanson trial more than two years ago. She'd quickly rediscovered her passion for painting and was much in demand as a portraitist. She'd even set up an easel for Gabby, who'd taken to the brush—at least for the moment.

After picking at her eggs for a minute, Gabby looks up and points. "Who's that? He looks like he's hurt."

Mick follows her eyes to the small flat-screen TV they keep in the kitchen.

The news video, taken the night before, shows two police officers escorting a man in his late forties or early fifties. He's dressed in black slacks and a white shirt soaked with blood. The man has jet-black hair, a square jawline, and dark eyes. His hands are behind his back.

"Isn't that Jimmy Nutzo?" asks Piper, turning up the volume.

Mick listens to the morning anchor explain that reputed mobster James Nunzio was arrested for murder late Wednesday night inside a warehouse along the Delaware River waterfront.

"Sources within the police department have told *Action News* that Nunzio was found covered in blood and holding a knife used to kill a man found murdered in the warehouse. The victim is believed to be a member of a competing organized-crime family, and there are rumors that he was dating Nunzio's daughter, Christina, who was also found inside the building."

Mick glances worriedly at Piper. "Go brush your teeth," he tells Gabby. "It's almost time to leave for school."

Gabby casts him a dark look. "You never let me see anything good. It's not like I don't know what blood looks like."

"Go easy on your father, Gabrielle. He's only trying to protect you."

Mick and Piper listen as Gabby stomps up the steps, shouting behind her, "*I'm* not a turtle! You can't keep me in a shell."

Mick turns to his wife. "And . . . three, two, one . . ."

The bathroom door slams.

◆ ◆ ◆

Mick and Piper drop Gabby off at school and head down the Schuylkill toward the law firm's office at Fifteenth and Market Streets in Center City.

Piper turns to Mick. "I think the Dowd case is worth looking into."

Three years earlier, when the Hanson fiasco was crashing down around them, she and Mick had a come-to-Jesus talk. She told him that he'd spent all his life running away from the people he loved. That his behavior had led to his brother Tommy's self-destructiveness and imprisonment. That he was on the verge of losing her, too.

One thing she told Mick that he hadn't realized was that his move from the DA's office to his criminal-defense practice had hurt her deeply. She had always admired him as a prosecutor. He'd even brought her into his cases, practicing his openings, closings, and cross-examinations with her, asking her for ideas and input. She saw them as a team working to make the world a safer place. But then he switched sides and fought for the bad guys. Worse, he closed her out of his cases and spent less and less time at home. She'd felt abandoned, rejected.

As part of the devil's bargain they struck to win the Hanson case, Mick promised her that they would become a team again. In their personal relationship, he made good on it right away, taking a leave of absence to spend time with her and Gabby. It took a while, but he found a way to bring her back into his professional life, too. He set up the firm's own Innocence Project. He decided to devote a chunk of his firm's resources and time to helping win freedom for the wrongly convicted, and he invited Piper to spearhead the work. She jumped at the chance. Already her work had helped free two prisoners. She was coming to the office with Mick one or two days a week.

"Remind me of the facts again?"

"It happened up in Buchanan Township, southwest of Allentown. Darlene Dowd, age nineteen, was convicted of first-degree murder and sent away for life. She was tried for bludgeoning her father to death."

"Heartwarming. So, what's the basis for a retrial?"

"According to the questionnaire she filled out for the Pennsylvania Innocence Project, a witness came forward with important information but was scared off by the police chief. There's also a deathbed letter to Darlene from her mother claiming that this same witness knows where the murder weapon is—it was never found by the police—and that it proves Darlene didn't commit the crime."

"Okay," Mick says, aware that a law enforcement officer's hiding of potentially exculpatory evidence is a major malfeasance, often justifying a retrial. "What was the prosecution's theory of motive?"

"This is why I feel so strongly about the case. Darlene's father raped her repeatedly—from the time she was twelve years old."

"That is a pretty strong motive to kill your father."

Piper doesn't answer.

"The Pennsylvania Innocence Project passed on the case, I assume?"

"Elise Daniels called me Monday. The review committee rejected the case."

"Lack of resources again?"

Piper hesitates. "I'm not sure."

"She said the case smelled bad?"

"No. But I got the sense she was uneasy about it."

"Are you sure you want to look into it?"

"I want to look into it."

"Then we'll look into it."

An hour later, Mick is in his office finalizing a brief in a case involving two brothers who inherited their father's insurance firm, then used it to defraud clients by collecting premiums for policies they never bound. White-collar dirtbags, the both of them. Raised in privilege, neither believed it possible that they could end up in prison.

He hears a knock and looks up to see the firm's receptionist, Angie, opening the door. The look on her face is an odd mixture of fear and excitement.

"There's a woman here who says she's Rachel Nunzio."

"Rachel?"

She lowers her voice, looks behind her. "Jimmy Nutzo's wife."

"I assume she's here to see Vaughn." The year before, firm associate Vaughn Coburn had represented his cousin Eddy, an Amtrak engineer arrested for a train accident that killed, among others, James Nunzio's son, Alexander. For a time, Vaughn feared that Nunzio, notorious for his impatience and bloodlust, would exact his revenge on Vaughn's cousin long before Eddy had his day in court. In the end, with some help from Nunzio, Vaughn proved that Eddy and Alexander Nunzio were both victims in the crash.

"No," Angie says. "She wants you."

Mick takes a deep breath. "I see. Tell her I'll be out in a minute."

Angie leaves, and Mick leans forward and closes his eyes. Jimmy Nunzio is widely recognized as the most violent organized-crime figure in the history of the Philly mob. Born to a midlevel wiseguy, he maimed and killed his way to the top of his crime family's pyramid and became the Philly underboss to Giancarlo Moretti, head of the New York–based Giansante crime family.

Mick knows representing someone like Nunzio carries both large upsides and downsides. The notoriety of taking on such a case can attract other major clients. Winning the case brings public scorn—along with the client's appreciation. And losing . . . well, it's never good to disappoint the Jimmy Nunzios of the world.

In the lobby, Mick spots a woman sitting on the sofa. She turns to him and rises.

"Mr. McFarland," she says, extending her hand.

Mick takes it and studies her as they shake. Rachel Nunzio is stunning. Raven hair over an exotic, almost Egyptian-looking face. Large brown eyes, full lips, a perfect nose. On the taller side, maybe five seven, with a womanly figure.

He escorts the mob boss's wife to the larger of the firm's two conference rooms. They exchange small talk while Angie brings in coffee on a silver tray. Mick pours her a cup, waits until she takes a sip, then says, "This is unusual. I've never had a prisoner's wife visit my office even before a preliminary arraignment."

"Mine is an unusual family."

"So I understand."

Something flashes across her eyes—a mixture of darkness and amusement.

"The prisoner himself is supposed to call his lawyer," Mick explains. "Ask the lawyer to come to the station. It's his right to do so."

"My husband did call a lawyer from the station. His business lawyer. There were some pressing issues that needed to be addressed right away."

"More pressing than being arrested?"

Rachel smiles enigmatically. "My husband's arraignment is set for tomorrow morning at nine. He's asked that I hire you to represent him."

"Why not Vaughn Coburn? They have history."

"I expect he'll explain why when you meet him."

Mick nods. "How is your daughter doing? Christina."

"Not well. The EMTs said they had to pull her off . . . that man. And that when they did, she went completely limp. They had to carry her to the ambulance, take her to HUP. She's still there. The doctors tell me she's in shock."

"I'm sorry. It must've been awful for her to see—"

"To see her father slit her lover's throat?" Rachel Nunzio's voice is flat, matter-of-fact. Her face betrays no emotion. She seems an apt match for her sociopath husband.

"Before you hire me, we should talk about my fee—"

"Two hundred and fifty thousand dollars was wired into your firm's operating account an hour ago."

"How do you know the number of my operating account? Or what bank I use?"

Rachel Nunzio shrugs.

"I see." Already, Mick is feeling uneasy.

"What time should I tell my husband you'll be out to meet with him?"

"You can get a message to him, at the Roundhouse?" he asks, referring to the Philadelphia police headquarters building where Nunzio will be held until his preliminary arraignment.

She smiles.

Of course she can.

Mick escorts Rachel Nunzio to the lobby and sees her off. He returns to his office to find Vaughn Coburn in one of the guest chairs in front of his desk, waiting for him.

"I assume she was here to hire us," Vaughn says.

"She was . . . ," Mick answers carefully. He pauses, then asks, "Is there some reason you can think of that Nunzio would want to hire me instead of you? Was there bad blood between you, at the end?"

Vaughn thinks. "Not unless he was hiding it. Maybe he wants you because you're more senior than I am."

Mick, at forty-five, has ten years' more experience than Vaughn.

Mick nods, although he's convinced there's more to it than that. "What can you tell me about Nunzio? That isn't public knowledge, I mean."

Like most criminal-defense attorneys, Mick is already familiar with the history of the Philly mob. With its base in South Philadelphia, it operates throughout the southeastern part of Pennsylvania and southern New Jersey. From the late '50s through 1980, it was run by Angelo Bruno. Nicknamed "the Gentle Don," Bruno was known for his cool, businesslike approach. Bruno was murdered as a result of a dispute with the New York–based Genovese family and was succeeded by Nicodemo "Little Nicky" Scarfo. Famous for his temper and violence, Scarfo ruled the organization for ten years, until he and many of his top lieutenants were arrested and sent to prison. That led to a mob war, followed by the short reign of John Stanfa, who was backed by the Gambino family in New York. A group of younger mobsters disputed Stanfa's ascension and took control once Stanfa was arrested by the FBI. The organization slowly weakened until it became a vassal state of the Giansante family in New York. Over the past decade, under the leadership of Jimmy Nunzio, a protégé of Giansante don Giancarlo Moretti, the Philly organization had gotten back on its feet.

"I really can't think of anything," Vaughn says. "Except that he doesn't seem to fit my idea of a Philly wiseguy. Most of those guys live in row houses in South Philly. They operate out of local bars and scrounge up money by selling drugs or acting as loan sharks and bookies. They don't wear twenty-five-thousand-dollar Stefano Ricci suits."

"Nunzio is different?"

"He runs his business from a modern office at the Naval Yard. He has a fleet of cars and his own jet."

"What's a Philly wiseguy need with a jet?"

"And how can he afford one?" Vaughn thinks about it. "The last time I saw him, after Eddy's trial, I brought up his cars and jet. I suggested I thought he might be more than just some Philly underboss. He didn't say anything, but he smiled like he was agreeing with me."

"So the question, then, is what exactly *is* Jimmy Nunzio?"

"I guess we'll find out soon enough," Vaughn says. "*If* we're going to represent him. Are we?"

"His wife wired two hundred and fifty thousand dollars into our account this morning."

Vaughn raises his eyebrows. "That answers that."

Mick passes through security at the Roundhouse. He's ushered into the attorney-client meeting room, where he sits at the small metal desk. The room is standard-issue: low ceiling, cinder-block walls, chipped linoleum flooring. A place where arrestees sit numbly while their attorney explains the various stages of hell they'll be passing through before and after trial.

The door opens, and a guard escorts the city's top mobster into the room. Nunzio waits while his cuffs are removed, then thanks the guard and sits across the table. For a long moment, Nunzio says nothing. Mick can tell the crime lord is studying him, taking his measure.

Without saying a word, Nunzio reaches across the table, extends his hand. Mick takes it and the two men shake, their eyes locked. They release at the same time.

Nunzio smiles. "Good."

"Let's get down to business," Mick says. "You want to tell me what went down in that warehouse?"

Nunzio takes a deep breath. "When the time is right."

So that's the way it's going to be. Smart.

Nunzio reaches for a cup of water the guard placed on the table.

"Vaughn Coburn asked me to give you his regards."

"You can send mine back to him. He did a great job on the Amtrak crash. He's a straight arrow."

"Yet you chose to hire me, not him."

"He's not the right man for this job. You are."

Mick opens his mouth to ask why, but Nunzio speaks first.

"That was some stunt you pulled in the Hanson case. Using your wife to save your client."

"Everything Piper testified to was true."

It wasn't, of course. To the contrary, Mick had Piper commit wholesale perjury. But it was the only way for them to extricate themselves from the quicksand Mick had landed them in.

Nunzio smiles. "Maybe. Maybe not. Either way, you used her."

Mick's eyes narrow, his thoughts returning to the Hanson trial and the terrible events that precipitated it. Nunzio was right: he had used Piper. And not by accident, or on the spur of the moment, but as the culmination of a meticulously orchestrated plan. Nunzio had probably had too little time to uncover all the details, but Mick has no doubt that someone with Nunzio's resources could, eventually, get to the bottom of what Mick had done. That's the message Nunzio is sending him now: that their relationship is not as unequal as it appears, and that Mick isn't going to run the show.

"We're not getting off to a good start," Mick says.

Nunzio pauses, studies him. "I understand lawyers like hypothetical questions. Here's one for you. A man wakes up on an island. All he has is a gun, a saw, a hammer, and some nails. What does he do?"

"Seriously? This is how you want to spend our time?"

"Indulge me."

Mick leans back. "All right, your nickel. The first thing he does is find water, then food. Then he uses the saw, the hammer, and the nails to build a shelter."

Nunzio nods. "Now let's alter the scenario. A man wakes up on an island with a gun, a hammer, a saw, and some nails. But this time, there's another guy on the island with him. What does he do?"

"He uses the gun to make the other guy find the water and food and build the shelter."

Nunzio smiles. "I'd say we're getting off to a great start."

"I wasn't saying *I* would do that. It was your hypothetical, so I was envisioning you."

"It doesn't matter who you imagined in the story; the important thing is, it took you about two seconds to come back with your answer."

So what? Now he thinks we're birds of a feather?

"There's one thing I *will* tell you about last night," Nunzio says. "The reason I went to that building is that I received a call on my cell phone. I was in my office at the Naval Yard, and someone called and told me that my daughter was about to be killed at the Valiante family's heroin warehouse."

"And you knew the location of the warehouse?"

"Sun Tzu, Mr. McFarland. To win, the general must know his enemy as well as he knows himself."

Mick considers this. "Did you know your daughter was seeing Antonio Valiante?"

Nunzio doesn't answer.

"Is there anything you want to tell me about your daughter?"

Nunzio shakes his head. "That girl. She doesn't think. She feels."

Shifting gears, Mick asks, "Did you go alone?"

"Again, when the time is right."

Mick looks down at his legal pad. "Talk to me about Antonio Valiante."

Nunzio answers slowly. "Tough. Smart. And very careful."

"Not smart enough. Or careful enough."

It's Nunzio's turn to switch gears. "I want you to find out who called me."

"The police will be able to determine that easily enough. I'm sure they took your cell phone when they arrested you. They'll learn the caller's identity from his number, if they haven't already."

"I'm about a thousand percent certain the call was placed from a burner phone."

"Still, I'd think you'd be in a better position than I to find out who made the call."

"I'll be working on it, too. Absolutely. But it helps to come at a problem from more than one direction."

Mick senses there's more to this than Nunzio is letting on, but he doesn't push. "I'll do what I can."

Nunzio takes another drink of water, then says, "I understand you have a daughter of your own."

Mick's hackles go up.

"Relax, counselor. I'm just looking for common ground."

Anger in his voice, Mick says, "Our worlds overlap. That's it. You and I are not alike."

Nunzio smiles. "We'll see."

3

Thursday, April 11, Continued

It's three o'clock when Mick walks into the conference room. With the exception of his partner, Susan Klein, the whole firm is assembled. Associates Vaughn Coburn and his fiancée, Erin Doyle, sit next to each other on the far side of the large glass table. The firm's investigator, Mick's brother, Tommy, is on Vaughn's left. Piper, along with paralegals Andrea and Jill, and Angie, the firm's receptionist, are lined up on the near side of the table. Mick takes a seat at the end and asks about Susan.

"Doctor's visit," Angie says, looking away.

Mick watches her for a second, then addresses the group. "So, I just met with Jimmy Nunzio—"

"How'd that go?" Tommy interrupts.

Mick pauses. "We danced. He led."

Tommy smiles. "A new experience for you."

Though five ten, the same height as Mick, his brother is built like a brick and has prison tats sneaking up from underneath his collar. There's an edginess to him, even when he makes an attempt at humor.

"On the surface, this looks like an open-and-shut case," Mick says, ignoring Tommy's jab. "Police bust into a drug warehouse, find one guy dead of a slit throat, another guy covered in blood and holding a knife." He looks around the room. "But, of course, it can't be that simple."

"Why not?" Piper asks.

"Because the guy with the knife is Jimmy Nunzio."

"A killer," Piper presses.

"A capo," Mick says. "Guys at his level don't do the dirty work."

"Plus, he's smart," Vaughn says. "He's never been convicted of anything. Or even been tried."

"But . . . his daughter." Piper looks around the conference table.

"Exactly," says Mick. "All bets are off. Nunzio told me he went to the warehouse because he got a call that his daughter was there and that she was going to be killed."

"So . . . what? He lost his head and just rushed over without any backup, without a plan? Doesn't sound like him." Tommy reaches for one of the pastries sitting in the center of the table.

"I don't know. A man gets a call his daughter's in mortal danger, I think he's going to run to her as fast as he can."

"So, take it to the next step," Erin says. "He managed to get inside the warehouse. What happened that Tony Valiante ended up dead? Was there a fight, or did Nunzio take him by surprise and open him up before Valiante had time to react?"

"He wouldn't tell me what happened. Said he was going to wait until the time is right."

"Of course that's what he's going to do," Tommy says.

"So, what's the plan?" asks Vaughn.

Mick leans into the table. "The plan is we're going to try to find out who placed the call to Nunzio—and why."

"The why seems pretty obvious to me," says Tommy. "Someone wanted either Nunzio or Valiante dead. So he found a way to get them into the same room together."

"And the daughter?" asks Mick.

"Collateral damage," says Tommy.

"They're already comparing them to Romeo and Juliet," says Angie. Everyone turns to her. "The press. It fits, too. Think about it—two rival crime houses, the fathers hate each other, the kids fall in love."

"Anyone have the background on the Valiantes?" Mick asks.

"I did some research while you were visiting Nunzio," Vaughn says. "Antonio 'Tony' Valiante was the elder son and chief lieutenant of underboss Frank Valiante, second-in-command to Vincent Savonna of the Savonna crime family in New York. Of the five families, the Savonnas and the Giansantes are the most powerful. Since Nunzio is an underboss to Giancarlo Moretti, the Giansante don, he and Frank Valiante are natural rivals. They are also close in age. Nunzio is fifty-one, and Frank Valiante's fifty-five."

"Does anyone want to talk about the five-hundred-pound gorilla in the room?" asks Erin.

Everyone looks at her.

"A wiseguy underboss slits the throat of the son of another powerful mafia leader in New York—"

"War," Tommy says. "Frank Valiante's gonna come to Philly with guns blazing."

For the second time, Mick recalls the case of Vaughn's cousin, whom Nunzio initially blamed for killing his son. When it was over, Vaughn told Mick in confidence that Eddy had come within seconds of being burned alive by Nunzio's henchmen. Although Eddy narrowly escaped that fate, another man didn't. And a second man's death was equally gruesome: torn to shreds by dogs brought into prison as comfort canines.

"Depending how hard Nunzio fights back, it could be a bloodbath," Vaughn says.

"Will we end up in the middle of it?" asks Erin.

Mick considers the idea that Valiante's retaliation might include Nunzio's legal team. As a rule, lawyers are off-limits when it comes to mob revenge. But it was Frank Valiante's *son* Nunzio killed.

Will normal rules apply?

"I admit I hadn't thought of that. But it is worth thinking about, and I will. In the meantime, is there anyone here who has strong opposition to our representing Jimmy Nunzio, for any reason?"

Everyone looks at each other. Mick spots concern on some of their faces. But they all shake their heads.

"All right. Here's what I'd like to do. Vaughn, find out everything you can about Nunzio and the Valiantes. Tommy, reach out to your sources in the police department, ask them to keep an ear to the ground about the call to Nunzio. Dig up what you can about the daughter, too. Christina."

"I already know about her," says Angie, a South Philly native. "She's a party girl. Dances and drinks her way all around the world—on Daddy's dime, of course. In the papers, her nickname is the Queen of Clubs. Because she's always out clubbing."

"Any insight into why she'd be spending time in a dirty warehouse with a rival underboss's son?"

"Have you seen Tony Valiante? He's gorgeous. Was. And you know what they say—the heart wants what the heart wants."

Mick recalls what Nunzio said about his daughter—that she doesn't think, she feels.

"As for the crime itself," he says, "since Nunzio's keeping quiet about what happened, we're going to have to piece the puzzle together ourselves. Hopefully learn something that will help our client beat what otherwise looks like a slam-dunk case against him."

That seems unlikely, although it's hard for Mick to be certain. When he saw the cops pulling the mobster from the police car and walking him toward the Roundhouse on TV, Mick spotted something in the famous man's eyes that he hadn't seen before. The unflappable monster was visibly rattled.

Whatever happened inside that warehouse shook Jimmy Nunzio to the core.

4

Friday, April 12

Mick enters the Juanita Kidd Stout Center for Criminal Justice at 1301 Filbert Street, passes through security, and takes the stairs leading to the basement, where the preliminary arraignments are held. He enters room B-08 and takes a seat on one of the front benches. On the other side of the Plexiglas half wall that divides the bunker-like gallery from the well of the courtroom, a female public defender sits on the desk at the left. To her right, a young assistant district attorney, no jacket, waits at the prosecutor's table. Magistrate Delia Smick presides from the bench.

The defendants appear on CCTV, on a screen mounted in front of the defense attorney. Processed assembly-line fashion, the preliminary arraignments introduce a sad progression of disheveled miscreants sitting against a yellowed tile wall. With each prisoner, the magistrate first confirms the man or woman's name, then gives the same speech: "It is alleged that on such-and-such a date, you: entered the property at such-and-such an address and took two thousand dollars' worth of property/fondled the genitals of a minor/offered sexual favors to an undercover police officer. You are being charged with: burglary and related offenses/indecent sexual assault and related offenses/prostitution and related offenses." The magistrate then informs the defendants of their court dates, orders them not to have any contact with the person they raped/stole from/intimidated, including through social media. Finally, the magistrate sets bail: $500 for the man charged with possession of a controlled substance and $250,000 for the child rapist. "If you fail to show up, a bench warrant will be issued for your arrest, and the trial can proceed without you."

Once the magistrate is finished, the public defender gives her own spiel: "Hello, I'm from the public defender's office. I sent you a non-waiver form; did you sign it? Good. That means you are represented, and that no one can question you outside the presence of your public defender. 'Question' includes subjecting you to a lineup, lie-detector test, or blood test. If anyone does try to question you, tell them you are represented." The defender informs them that their phone calls will all be recorded. And finally she says, "Just because you meet someone in prison doesn't mean they're a prisoner; don't say anything to anyone in prison about your case."

Each defendant's arraignment takes about five minutes.

Mick has listened to six or seven of them when Max Pagano, a high-ranking assistant district attorney, takes a seat across the aisle from him. He nods at Pagano, who grunts back. Built like a bulldog—a muscular five-nine frame supported by bowlegs and topped by a bald head—Pagano is known as a fearless fighter.

The DA did well to pick Pagano to run the case against Jimmy Nunzio.

Three more arraignments—fifteen minutes—come and go before Nunzio is placed before the camera. The public defender and junior ADA leave their seats, and Mick and Pagano take their places.

Slurping from a giant Wawa cup, Magistrate Smick watches impatiently. Once Mick and Pagano are seated, she asks, "Are we ready now?"

Mick has appeared a hundred times before Delia Smick, a rough-edged native of the city's Kensington section. Delia's hair, once black, turned gray years ago but is back to black again now that her husband has passed and she's back on the market.

Mick glances at the TV screen. Nunzio looks back at him. His eyes are cold and black, his face devoid of emotion. Gone completely is the chagrin Mick spotted on the news the night the mobster was arrested. Nunzio appears composed, almost bored.

The magistrate, reading from her computer, asks Nunzio if he's Nunzio. When he says he is, she continues. "It is alleged that on Wednesday, April tenth, at a warehouse off Admiral Peary Way in South Philadelphia, you caused the death of Antonio Valiante by cutting him with a knife. You are charged with murder in the first degree . . ."

Mick waits until the magistrate has completed her speech, then tells Delia Smick that he's already given his client instructions about not talking to anyone or letting himself be questioned.

Turning to Nunzio, she says, "Because the charge is murder one, you will be held without bail. Following this arraignment, you'll be taken directly to the Curran-Fromhold Correctional Facility on State Road, where you will remain until trial. Do you understand that?"

"He understands, Your Honor."

Delia Smick turns back to Mick, annoyance on her face. She skips a beat, then says, "I assume you're not waiving the preliminary hearing, Mr. McFarland?"

In the preliminary hearing, the prosecution proffers its evidence to persuade the judge to bind the defendant over for trial. A defendant has the right to waive the preliminary hearing, but the right is rarely exercised because defense attorneys use the hearings to learn what they can about the prosecution's evidence. The prosecutors know this, so they offer up only as much of their case as necessary to move the case to trial.

"Of course not," says Mick.

The magistrate schedules the preliminary hearing for Monday, April 22, ten days hence, and the arraignment is concluded.

"A word?"

Mick looks over his shoulder at Max Pagano. "Sure."

Mick lets the prosecutor lead him through the waiting area and into the hallway. They board the elevator alone. Mick knows what's coming. When the doors close, Pagano starts in.

"We have your client dead to rights. You know that."

"Let's skip directly to sentencing, then."

"Funny."

Mick puts up a hand. "You're going to tell me I should get him to plead. Save time, money, spare my client and his family the embarrassment of a trial, yadda, yadda, yadda."

A smile spreads along Pagano's lips. "That's what you're expecting, I know. The standard pitch. What ten out of ten other prosecutors in my position would be saying. But here's the thing, Mick. I'm hoping your client will tell me to go pound sand. Actually, more than hoping. I *know* he will. There's no way Jimmy Nutzo's going to plead to anything. He thinks he's too smart for that. He's beaten the system his whole life, and he thinks he's going to beat it this time, too. He's not—because of me. But he won't see that until it's too late. I'm counting on it."

The elevator doors open, and Pagano steps out. Mick follows him, and they face off.

"Looking to bring home the trophy, eh?" says Mick. "Land the big fish nobody's been able to catch? Maybe make a run for district attorney?"

"Close."

"Well, good luck with that." Mick turns and walks away.

Fuck you, Pagano. You want a ball game? You got one.

Mick is at his desk after lunch when Susan Klein walks past. He catches her long legs and ash-blonde hair in his peripheral vision. Susan is a triathlete who has competed in several Ironman competitions. Running is her strong suit, and she consistently finishes among the top twenty women in both the Broad Street Run and the Philadelphia Marathon. Her blue eyes and strong jaw complement her athletic body and complete his picture of her as the perfect Nordic archetype.

She wasn't in the office yesterday or this morning. She's been missing a lot of time lately, he's noticed, which isn't like her. He decides to see what's up.

"Hey," he says, walking into her office.

Susan puts down her pen, looks up at him.

"You okay?" he asks. "You were out yesterday. Angie said health issues."

"I'm good," Susan says, waving him off. "So . . . Nunzio. When's the preliminary hearing?"

"It's scheduled for the twenty-second. Should be a quick affair. The DA will put on the two cops. They'll testify they found him covered in blood and with a knife in his hand ten feet away from a dead guy with a slit throat."

"Who's the prosecutor?"

"Pagano."

"Figures the DA would pick him. That guy doesn't back down for anyone. He give you the speech? Your client's dead in the water, plea now or forever hold your package—in prison?"

"Just the opposite. He's *aching* for a trial."

She considers this. "He gets a conviction, it's a giant notch on his bedpost."

"You want in? It's a big case, whichever way it goes. Lots of press."

She smiles wanly. "My name in lights?"

He studies her. "You seem tired."

She shrugs.

He gets up. "If you ever want to talk . . ."

Back at his desk a few minutes later, Mick stands by his windows, looks east past City Hall to the Delaware River, considers his partner. Susan graduated from Penn Law, five years behind him. At Penn, Susan was managing editor of the *Law Review* and valedictorian of her class. She was offered a clerkship with a court of appeals judge but wanted to try cases. She went straight to the US Attorney's Office in Philadelphia, where she became known for her no-nonsense attitude and her fiery brilliance in the courtroom. When word got out she was looking to go into private practice, Mick and his former partner, Lou Mastardi, literally raced to meet her and scooped her up.

Susan's personal life, as far as he could tell, had been less of a success. She'd made at least three bad boyfriend choices in the time he'd known her. Most recently, she'd been dating an Argentinian soccer player with the Philadelphia Union—an athlete famous for temper tantrums on and off the field. More than once, Susan had shown up for work wearing sunglasses or heavy makeup around her eyes, and he'd been sorely tempted to enlist Tommy to do some reconnaissance. He knew he would have to be careful to tell Tommy not to send soccer-boy a message without clearing it with him first.

5

Friday, April 12, Continued

It's just before 7:00 p.m., and Mick and Gabby are on the side lawn in front of a soccer net. Mick is guarding the goal as Gabby tries to kick the ball past him. In two weeks, the Radnor Soccer Club will begin its spring/summer season. It will be Gabby's second year with the sport, and she's determined to excel. She practices passing, dribbling, and attacking the net every day, both before and after school. At four foot one and fifty-nine pounds, she's a little small for a nine-year-old, but her tenacity more than makes up for it.

"Come on, guys," Piper calls from the front door. "Dinner's ready. Time to wrap it up."

"One last shot," Gabby says, spearing the ball past Mick and into the net.

"Hey, I wasn't ready."

"You snooze, you lose." Gabby picks up the ball and walks past Piper and inside. Mick carries the net into the garage.

A few minutes later, they're seated on the back patio. The temperature is in the low seventies, so Piper decided they would eat outside. Franklin has strategically positioned himself between Gabby and Piper, both of whom are notorious for breaking the rule against feeding him from the table.

"So, what are you painting at Grandma's house?" Piper asks.

Gabby chews a mouthful of salmon. "Grandma's painting an old man. His hair is completely white, and he has a mean look on his face. I'm painting Franklin," she adds, tossing him a piece of fish.

"Don't talk with your mouth full, honey," Piper says.

Gabby rolls her eyes. "Well, then don't ask me a question with my mouth full."

Mick smiles at Piper's own eye roll. "She's got you there."

"How was school today?" Piper asks, switching gears.

"Boring. Gym was fun."

"Who's Jim?" asks Mick. "You haven't mentioned him before."

"You're such a nerd, Dad."

"You really are," Piper agrees.

They continue trading jabs as they finish their meals.

The sun goes down, and the temperature begins to drop.

"I'm going in," Gabby says.

"Right behind you," Piper says.

Mick volunteers to clean up. He spends the next fifteen minutes clearing the table and loading the dishwasher while Piper pours herself another glass of wine and relaxes in the living room. Gabby retreats to her bedroom to do homework and text her friends.

After cleaning up, Mick joins Piper on the couch. She asks him how the arraignment went.

"As expected. No bail. He stays in county lockup until trial."

Mick pauses, knowing Piper can sense that he has more to say but is holding back.

"What?" she asks.

"When I met with Nunzio at the Roundhouse yesterday, he brought up the Hanson trial. He said it was quite a move we pulled at the end."

Piper sits up. "You don't think he'd try to look into it, do you? Jesus."

Mick shrugs. "I'm going to return the favor and find out everything I can about *him*, in case we need leverage."

Piper doesn't respond, but she sets her wine aside, a sick look on her face.

Around nine thirty, Mick walks upstairs and goes into Gabby's room. Sprawled on the floor at the foot of the bed, Franklin opens his eyes but doesn't bother lifting his head.

"You're late," Gabby says.

He's read to her almost every night of her life: *Not Now, Bernard*; *The Tiger Who Came to Tea*; *The Elephant and the Bad Baby*; *Lost and Found*; *Dear Zoo*; *The Story of Babar*; *A Sick Day for Amos McGee*; *Oh, the Places You'll Go*; *The Complete Adventures of Curious George.*

When Gabby was eight, she got into the Harry Potter books. Mick found that she could read them herself. But he still comes to her room and reads her to sleep. She's made it to *Harry Potter and the Goblet of Fire*, in which, for the first time, Lord Voldemort's physical appearance is described.

Gabby listens quietly as Mick reads the passages conveying Voldemort's skeletally thin physique, his white face, red eyes, and snake-like snout. When he's done, he sees a confused look on her face.

"I thought Voldemort would be handsome. He was good-looking when he was Tom Riddle, wasn't he?"

Mick considers her question. Before he has time to answer, she asks harder ones.

"Why was Voldemort so bad? Was he always bad?"

"Well . . ."

"Will I turn bad someday?"

"No!" Surprised at the vehemence in his voice, he leans over, hugs her. "You're a good person. You will always be a good person."

She looks up at him.

Is that doubt in her eyes? Does she already think she's a bad person?

He hugs her tighter, kisses her on the forehead. "Come on, it's time to go to sleep."

He tucks her in, places the book on the nightstand. When he gets to the door, he turns. Her eyes are already closed, her chest rising and falling with her breathing.

So innocent.

6

Monday, April 15

It's 8:00 a.m., and Piper and Susan are on I-476 North, heading toward the Lehigh Valley. The Darlene Dowd case is the second innocence case they've worked on together at the firm. As with the earlier case, they'll share the legwork, but Susan will prepare all the legal papers.

The two women are close in age, Piper being forty-three and Susan three years younger. It was awkward between them following Piper's revelations in the Hanson case. Piper sensed that Susan simply didn't know how to treat her. But their relationship has warmed over time, and Piper knows it's largely because of her work on the innocence cases. Susan has told her more than once that she is impressed by Piper's work ethic and her passion for winning freedom for people who don't deserve to be in prison.

For Piper's part, she admires Susan's strength. The woman is a fierce competitor. In their previous case together, she saw Susan stand up to—and dismantle—two senior male prosecutors. She expects that the same inner strength and willpower underlie Susan's success as both a triathlete and a trial attorney.

They talk awhile about Gabby, but when Piper asks Susan about her own life, she cuts her off and brings up the case. Piper knows Susan has been missing work lately. Angie thinks it has to do with Susan's father showing up after being absent for years. But Piper suspects there's more to it.

"I went over everything again last night," Susan says as she riffles through the file and pulls out the deathbed letter from Darlene Dowd's mother. Holding it up, Susan reads the letter aloud:

> I told you this so many times but Im so sorrie for what happened and for me not stopping it. Pleas find it in you're heart to forgive me. There is something you don't know that can help you get out of jail. Lois knows where the claw hammer is. And she saw you walking home that morning and that you didn't have blood on you. She told chief Foster but he wouldnt lisen. You have to find Lois!
>
> I am so sorry
> I will love you forever
> Mom

"I feel like a teacher," Susan says. "I want to pull out a red pen."

"Her spelling leaves much to be desired. But what do you think of the letter itself?"

"Sounds like some pretty explosive stuff. But the state Innocence Project passed on it?"

"The director wouldn't say why."

"They have a nose for bad leads, you know."

"I do, but given the . . . other stuff, I want to give her a chance." Piper has already told Susan about Darlene Dowd's sexual abuse at the hands of her father.

"I get it. And I hope there's something there."

"If Darlene's mother is right, the police hid a witness who might have helped exonerate her."

Darlene Dowd was convicted fifteen years prior and long ago exhausted her direct appeals. Her only hope is to win a new trial under the Pennsylvania Post Conviction Relief Act, which provides another avenue of redress in certain circumstances, including cases in which new evidence comes to light that the defendant could not have known about at the time of his or her trial, or in which the state wrongfully withheld evidence.

Half an hour later, Piper and Susan approach the State Correctional Institution at Muncy and spot the main building, a three-story brick-and-stone structure with a central bell tower. The rest of the sixty-two-acre enclosed campus consists of both permanent and modular inmate housing units.

"Looks more like a small college than a prison," Piper says.

"A small college surrounded by chain-link fence topped by razor wire."

Piper pulls the car into the visitors' parking lot, and she and Susan walk to the small building used as the waiting room. There, they enter their information into the logbook, hand over their driver's licenses, and receive their day passes.

They leave and cross the road to the visitation room. Inside, they pass through the metal detector and hand their passes to the guard in charge. The visitors' room is large, filled with rows of chairs and movable coffee tables. Piper chooses a set of chairs in the corner of the room, where she hopes they can have some privacy. Susan sits with her. They wait.

It doesn't take long before they see Darlene. Piper recognizes her—barely—from an old newspaper photo taken during her trial. The girl in the picture was nineteen. And although she was wearing conservative-to-dowdy clothing probably provided by her public defender, there was no mistaking her beauty. Young Darlene Dowd was a buxom girl with broad shoulders, a thin waist, and narrow hips. The shimmering blonde hair, bright-blue eyes, and sprinkling of freckles across her button nose evoked Rebecca of Sunnybrook Farm.

At thirty-four, after fifteen years of little exercise and a prison diet, Darlene's girlish figure is now long gone. Her belly and hips push out against her red jumper. Her once-glistening hair is dry and tangled. Her face is heavy. Her eyes are sunken and dull.

Darlene spots them and walks over as they stand.

"Darlene, I'm Piper. We spoke on the phone. This is my boss, Susan Klein."

Darlene cautiously shakes their hands, and they all sit.

Darlene says, "I know you explained on the phone, but I'm still not clear why you're here. I thought the Project wasn't taking my case."

"The Pennsylvania Innocence Project has declined, that's right. But our firm also handles innocence cases. We've overturned convictions for two inmates already. One had his case retried and won an acquittal. The other is set for trial in a few months, and we think we'll win that one, too."

"So this kind of thing really happens? People who were convicted and locked up can actually get out of prison? Even after years and years?"

Piper nods and smiles an encouraging smile. "One of the two men I told you about served twenty-eight years. The other, seventeen years. They were both convicted of murders they didn't commit. We found new evidence that wasn't available to them at the time of their trials, took it to a judge, and the judge let them both out."

"We read your mother's letter," Susan says. "If it's true that the police chief scared off a key witness, that could be enough to get you a new trial, too."

"Do you know who 'Lois' is?" asks Piper.

"It has to be our neighbor. Lois Beal. She and her husband lived right up the road from us. My mother was good friends with Lois. She was very nice. Her and her husband. When I was little, I'd visit their house sometimes, and they would give me treats. Cookies and milk. Or a candy bar. Sometimes, she'd make me a fluffernutter sandwich." Darlene smiles sadly. "I remember Lois coming to the farm the morning my father was killed."

"Did she say anything about seeing you that morning, before your father was found?"

Darlene looks from Piper to Susan. "I don't know. She could have. It was all so confusing. My mother was shouting at the chief to let her help me, he was shouting back, and the other officer was holding my arm. I was so upset. I felt like I was in a fog."

"How about the hammer? Did you hear anyone, including Lois, say anything about that?"

"I didn't even know for sure it was a hammer until I read my mother's letter. The police never found the murder weapon. The state's doctor, the medical examiner, testified at trial that he thought my father could have been killed by a hammer. But he couldn't say for certain."

Piper looks at her notes. "If you don't mind, I'd like to go through everything in chronological order. What can you tell me about your parents?"

Darlene thinks a long time on this. "My mother . . . was very quiet. She was kind. She liked it when everyone got along. I remember she was always cleaning. Or doing laundry. Or cooking. Or sweeping the porch. Always keeping busy."

"And your father?"

Darlene's eyes flatten; her body goes still. "He was strong, and had black hair and very large hands, always dirty. When I was young, he mostly ignored me. Went about his business, trying to grow things on our farm. He was always fixing things for other people, in his workshop. He was always criticizing my mother, telling her she missed a spot, or overcooked something, or undercooked it. Or that her dress made her look heavy."

"You said when you were young, your father ignored you," Piper says. "But when you got older . . ."

"You want me to tell you what he done to me."

Piper nods. "I'm sure that's the last thing you want to talk about. But it's all important in regards to what happened . . . or didn't happen."

"I talked to so many counselors about it—before the trial and after I was convicted and sent here. After a while, it stopped feeling like something that happened to me and more like it was just a story I was telling, over and over again. That was years ago, though. I haven't talked about it in a long time."

Piper sees worry flash across Darlene's eyes, so she reaches out and touches the woman's hand. "We can take this as fast or slow as you need."

Darlene looks away. Then she looks back at Piper. "A Pepsi would be good. Would you mind getting one? I don't have any change."

Susan fetches a can. She and Piper wait until Darlene takes a swallow. And then another.

"The first time it happened was the day after I turned twelve. He would never let me up in his workshop. He said it was dangerous because it was where he had his big circular saw set up and kept his other power tools. Then, the day after my birthday, he asked if I wanted to help him with a project in the shop. I couldn't believe it. It made me feel special."

She pauses again. Piper can see that she's steeling herself.

"So he took me up to the workshop and gave me a little tour, showed me some of his tools, explained what they were used for. And while he was doing this, he started brushing up against me. Like, he'd reach for a tool, and his hand would brush my chest. I was an early bloomer, and I had breasts by then. I told myself it was just accidental, his touching me, but at some level I knew it wasn't.

"That was as far as it went the first time, and for a couple times afterward. But then he called me up there and told me he was going to show me how to whittle a duck out of wood. So he sat down next to me on the bench and laid a block of wood on my thigh. He told me I had to grip the one end of the block firmly because I was going to whittle the other end with a knife. And to illustrate what he meant, he grabbed my thigh. He kept his hand there for a long time. I had shorts on, so my skin was bare. Then he told me I was going to have to make long, smooth cuts in the wood with the knife. And he showed me what he meant by slowly caressing my thigh.

"He said he wanted to make sure I understood what he was saying, so he asked me to do the same to his thigh. Again, I knew that something wasn't right, but I thought, *Well, he's my dad, he wouldn't do anything to hurt me.*

"We did the whittle thing a couple times. Every time, he'd move his hand—or my hand—closer to our private parts. One day, he just started rubbing me there, and had me rub him. He told me I was the prettiest girl he'd ever seen, much prettier than my mother. And he leaned over and kissed me. And then he took himself out of his pants, and . . ."

Darlene stops and excuses herself to go to the restroom.

Piper watches her, watches the guard search her before she goes into the bathroom. "This is awful," she says. "But we need her to tell her story."

"That's right. And we need to look her in the eye as she tells it. Our innocence project is just that—we can represent only someone who is actually innocent. Someone sent to prison for a crime they did not commit. So we listen to this part, watch her as she tells it. When we get to the killing, we'll have something by which to gauge her veracity."

Piper watches Darlene exit the women's room, get searched again by the guard. When she walks over and sits down, her face is set in stone. Piper knows Darlene needed time to build her resolve, prepare herself to retell, and relive, the horrors she suffered at her father's hands.

Darlene doesn't waste time.

"The first time he actually raped me was a week after he started with the whittling routine. He called me up to the workshop, but that time he didn't even bother to pretend what was going on. He just pulled me close to him, kissed me, and then took my clothes off, and his, too. He had an inflatable mattress laid out on the floor. That's where he took me."

Darlene's mouth quivers, but she presses forward. "When he was done, and we were putting our clothes back on, he told me how beautiful I was. That I was his special little 'sugar-pie.'"

Piper cringes at the pet name.

"I don't remember if he told me not to say anything to my mother, but there was no way I could've brought myself to tell her what we'd done. It was wrong and disgusting, and I knew it. I knew it would hurt her to find out, and I was also afraid she'd be really mad at me."

Darlene looks out the window, but Piper knows she's not seeing the fields outside or the hills beyond.

"In the beginning, he was calling me up to the workshop a couple times a week. After a while, it got less frequent. But over time, he got more businesslike about it. There was no more sweet talk, or calling me his sugar-pie, or telling me how beautiful I was. It was just, 'Get up to the shop, I'll be by in a few minutes.' If I wasn't naked by the time he showed up, he'd be angry and let me know it. By the end, I could tell he was disgusted with me—and with himself. But he kept doing it anyway. He said he couldn't help himself. Once, he broke down and cried and told me his own parents were terrible people, that they'd been terrible to him, that they didn't give him enough to eat or decent clothes to wear, and that they ignored him except when they beat up on him. He said everything we did was their fault. That I should hate *them*, not him."

"Did you ever meet his parents, your grandparents?"

"No. I never even knew where he was from. And I don't think my mother did, either. He just showed up one day and whisked her away from her own sorry situation. 'I was your mother's knight in shining armor,' he liked to say when we were all together. My mother would just smile and look away."

"Her letter suggests that she knew what was going on."

Darlene looks hard at Piper. "She pretended like she didn't. And I pretended like she didn't, too. But there were only three of us living on that farm. He never hid the fact that he was calling me up to the workshop. And sometimes he left their bed and came for me in the middle of the night. It was so obvious I can't believe my mother and I could look each other in the eye and act like nothing was wrong."

Darlene stops and takes a couple of deep breaths.

"They taught us to breathe like this in a class I took here," she explains. "It helps to calm you down."

"Take as much time as you need," Piper says. "There's no rush."

Darlene nods, but starts talking again. "She later admitted to me she'd known. Not at first, she said, but by the time I was thirteen. It wasn't until after I was in here that she told me. I had some choice words for her, told her to get out, and we had no contact for a while. Eventually, she wrote me a letter begging forgiveness. I tore it up. Some time passed, and I decided to let it go, like my counselors suggested. So I called her collect and told her she could come back."

Susan asks, "Did you ever think to tell anyone at school? A teacher? The nurse?"

A bitter smile forms on Darlene's lips. "He pulled me out of school shortly after he started abusing me. Told my mother the other kids were a bad influence, and it was best if I was homeschooled."

"What did your mother say about that?"

"That was the one time I ever saw her stand up to him. They fought about it for weeks. But in the end, she caved."

They sit in silence for a few tense minutes, Darlene sipping the Pepsi, Susan and Piper glancing at each other, preparing themselves for the next step. Finally, Piper asks, "Are you ready to tell us about the day your father died?"

Darlene nods.

"It had been almost a month since the last time he'd come for me. I'd been spending a lot of nights away from home by then. I'd fashioned a sleeping bag out of some old quilts, and I would lay outside in the fields, or by the stream. It was a beautiful night, I remember. No clouds and no moon, and the stars were brilliant against the blackness. It was June, but the temperature was comfortably cool. And it wasn't buggy. I slept well that night, and I woke up just after dawn. There was enough light for me to walk along the road, and it took me about twenty minutes to get home, a little after 6:00."

Darlene pauses. "I think I have to use the ladies' room again."

Susan buys another Pepsi while she's gone. When Darlene comes back, she thanks Susan, takes a sip, and sits down.

"I remember that I opened the back door. I only got one step in when I tripped over something big and fell to the floor. I thought, *What did I trip over?* The floor felt wet, and I thought, *How can there be water on the floor?* But I looked down and saw it wasn't water. It was blood. All over the floor. And all over me. And my father lying there, dead. I raced to get up, but I slipped and fell again. I remember I started crying."

Darlene takes a deep breath. "I ran up to the workshop and hid there. I don't know what made me do that—choose that place as my hiding spot after all the horrors that had happened there. But I did. It wasn't long before I heard my mother coming out of the house and shouting my name. She called for me over and over, but I didn't answer. She walked up the driveway toward the shop, shouting my name the whole time. But she stopped outside the door. She wouldn't come in. Wouldn't even open the door."

Bitterness hardens Darlene's face. And anger. Piper gives her time to work through it.

"Not long after that, the police showed up. I could hear commotion through the screen window. I wanted to leave the shop, but I couldn't move. Finally, one of the officers came into the shop. He found me and took me outside. My mother was screaming the whole time, telling the police to leave me alone, let her take me inside and shower me. At least let her hug me.

"But the chief wasn't having none of that. I remember him clear as day. Chief Sonny Foster. As soon as he got me to where everyone was standing, he made himself into the judge and jury and convicted me right there—I could see it on his face.

"After a while, the township detective showed up. The chief ordered him to take pictures of me, standing there, covered in blood."

"Let's talk about your statement. The one you gave to the detective."

"I remember that. He kept me in that little room all day and into the night."

"Did he read you your rights? The Miranda warning?" asks Susan.

"He gave me the speech about the right to remain silent."

"And to have an attorney?"

"That was part of it, but I was just too numb to really grasp what he was telling me. I don't think I even understood that I was under arrest until after I signed the confession and they put me into a cell."

"Can you remember *when* the detective gave you the Miranda warning?" Piper asks. She's learned that when a law enforcement officer reads a suspect their rights much later and in a casual tone—instead of Mirandizing someone immediately upon arrest, when the person is on guard—the warning's impact is often lost.

"Not exactly. We were in that room for a long time. He handed me a glass of water—it was the first time he was nice to me—then told me I had the right not to say anything."

"In your own words, tell me why you signed the confession if you didn't kill your father."

"That's something I asked myself a million times. *I* knew I didn't do it. But the detective was so sure I had, and he kept saying over and over that I did it. So after a while I began to ask myself, 'Is he right? Did

I do it and I'm just not remembering?' And when he said they found the murder weapon, and it had my fingerprints all over it—my fingerprints actually imprinted into the blood—that kind of sealed it for me. Fingerprints don't lie. And I thought a policeman had to be truthful. So I thought, *Well, I must have done it. Maybe I was in a trance, or sleepwalking.* I don't know, but I agreed to give them their statement. The detective got real nice again then, and he helped me with the wording. And then I signed it."

"Of course he didn't *have* the murder weapon," Piper says.

"Which the public defender told me later on," Darlene says. "Even after all these years, I feel like such a fool. It's probably the oldest trick in the book, for a cop—tell the suspect there's actual proof they did something when there's no proof at all."

Piper and Susan probe Darlene for more details about the confession and the morning of the killing, then excuse themselves to go the restroom. Once they are alone, Piper asks Susan what she thinks.

"I think it's still painful for her. Reliving the abuse."

"And her version of what happened the morning of the killing?"

Susan looks down for a moment, then back up at Piper. "She doesn't show nearly as much emotion when talking about finding her father's body as when recounting the abuse."

"I can understand that, for a whole lot of reasons," Piper says. "She was physically present for the abuse. It took place again and again over a period of years, and it scarred her deeply. If she's telling the truth about the murder, she wasn't there when it happened. Finding her father's body was a onetime event. And, to be honest, I wouldn't expect her to be that broken up about his death, given what he'd done to her."

Susan nods. "So what do you want to do?"

"I want to tell her we're going to move forward. Are you on board with that?"

Susan nods without hesitation. "Let's give her the benefit of the doubt."

Piper smiles. They return to Darlene, who stands.

"So?" Darlene asks.

"We're going to move forward with our investigation."

Darlene's eyes start to moisten, and Piper sees her fighting back the tears. Clearly the woman doesn't want to risk hoping too much.

"So, you'll get ahold of Lois?" Darlene asks. "She moved a while back, according to my mother."

"She shouldn't be hard to find," Susan says.

"Do you have any idea why your mother thought Lois would know where the hammer is?" Piper asks.

Darlene shakes her head. "She never said anything to me about the hammer while she was still alive."

Piper sees something flash across Darlene's eyes, but she can't tell what it is.

An hour after Gabby goes to bed, Mick is working in his home office. Piper walks in, carrying two glasses of wine. She hands one to Mick, then sits across the desk from him. He says, "Come on, let's sit on the couch," and they move to the sofa in the office.

He notices she's been quiet since she came home. Preoccupied. She picked at her food, then went upstairs while he cleaned up. He could tell she was processing whatever happened that day with the potential innocence client. That she's come into his office tells him she's ready to talk about it.

"How'd it go?" he asks.

"Susan and I agreed to move forward with the case. We told Darlene, and she was so happy she almost cried."

Piper looks away. They sit in silence for a while.

"You all right?" Mick asks.

"I reread the trial transcript when I got back to the office. Darlene's testimony from the sentencing phase. Her lawyer had her describe the things her father did to her in even more detail than she gave to Susan and me. He sodomized her. He used things on her. His own daughter. How could he . . . ?" Her voice cracks and trails off.

He sees her searching him for an answer, and he opens his mouth. But nothing comes out. There is no explanation for what Lester Dowd did.

7

Wednesday, April 17

It's just before eleven o'clock, and Mick is walking down the hall toward the firm's small kitchen to get some coffee when Angie comes up to him.

"Why the grimace?"

"That slimy detective is here," she says. "The one who was such a pain in the Hanson case."

"Tredesco."

"I parked him in the small conference room. Should I tell him to come back later?"

Mick thinks for a minute, decides it's better to get this over with.

Tredesco stands as Mick enters the room, steps forward. Mick side-steps him, moves to the end of the table.

"Have a seat. Take a load off."

The detective's eyes narrow, and Mick can see he's trying to figure out whether he's just been insulted.

"I'm down five pounds," Tredesco says.

Watching him, Mick decides the detective's gut gets fatter every year while his greasy black hair gets thinner. Mick's distaste for the man, though, has nothing to do with his appearance. Back when Mick was a prosecutor with the DA's office, he had the misfortune of working with Tredesco a few times. He learned afterward that, in one of their cases, Tredesco manipulated him into winning a conviction against an innocent young man. Later, in the Hanson case, Tredesco persuaded a key prosecution witness to perjure himself in hopes of sending Mick's client to prison for the rest of his life.

"Let's cut to the chase. What do you want?"

"Can you think of a more hopeless case for the defense? I sure can't."

Mick stares.

"I mean, the dead guy still pumping blood on the floor? Your client standing there with the murder weapon in his hand? The girl boo-hooing?"

"I've come to view your gloating as a harbinger of your inevitable defeat. Is that how you intend it?"

Tredesco's mouth remains fixed in a grin, but the smile disappears from his eyes. "This case will be different. You can count on it."

"You sound like Pagano."

"One thing I don't get. How in the world did a guy as smart and careful as Tony Valiante end up in a warehouse without his bodyguards?"

Mick takes note of the term "careful." It was one of the exact words Nunzio used to describe Valiante.

"Everyone knows he didn't go anywhere without two soldiers and his driver."

Mick reaches over to the center of the conference table, lifts a bottle of water from the serving tray. He twists off the lid and takes a swallow.

"I know what you're going to say," Tredesco continues. "Tony wanted some alone time with his squeeze, so he left his protection behind."

Mick takes another swallow and sets the bottle down.

"Everyone on the street knew they'd been seeing each other, behind their fathers' backs. Just like Romeo and—"

"Is there a point to all this? Or is this how you jack off now? By wagging your tongue?"

The detective smiles and waves a finger. "Ah, that famous wit of yours."

Mick starts to stand, but Tredesco says, "Okay, look. There's just some things I'm wondering about is all. You know this case is going to end up with a plea deal, so it can't hurt anything for you to give me a little heads-up on some of the minor details."

"Minor details?"

"Like, for instance, your client obviously went there to kill Valiante, but why use a knife? Why not just shoot him? He was carrying."

"You want me to help you out? How about you show me yours first? Tell me who placed the call to Nunzio's cell phone that night."

Tredesco shrugs. "Burner phone. Untraceable."

Mick nods. Nunzio was right about that.

"My turn," Tredesco says. "Tell me who your client called after the murder." Seeing Mick's unease, the detective smiles. "Oh, he didn't tell you? That he used *his* burner to place a call from the warehouse?"

Mick clenches his jaw but doesn't answer.

"Not going to answer me? All right, how about telling me what happened to Johnny Giacobetti?"

"What do you mean, what happened to him?"

Johnny G. is Nunzio's infamous enforcer. A sadistic giant once caught on videotape lifting two grown men off their feet and smashing their faces together.

"You know Nunzio's office is right there on the naval base, right? So I went there and spoke to building security about who might have seen him. The guard on duty told me Nunzio left the building around 9:30, and he insisted Nunzio was alone. Which is kind of funny, because the security guard in the building across the way says he saw Nunzio and his 'Hulk' running out of Nunzio's building toward the parking lot. But when the cops show up just after midnight, there's no Johnny Giacobetti. And no one's laid eyes on him since."

"Maybe he's on vacation. He probably gets three weeks a year, maybe even four, given how long he's been with Nunzio."

Tredesco shakes his head. "I'm disappointed. I give you the cell-phone thing, and you give me nothing back."

Mick stands. "Here, let me help you find the lobby."

Mick pokes his head into Jill's office. He knows Piper asked the paralegal to locate Lois Beal. They had expected it would be easy to track down Darlene Dowd's former neighbor. But when she moved ten years ago, she left no forwarding address. And she apparently didn't tell anyone where she was going.

"How's the search coming?"

"Not much luck. I found a couple of Lois Beals on Facebook, but one's nineteen and the other one's page shows her winning an award for working at the same company in Spokane, Washington, for the last thirty years, so it can't be her. A handful of Lois Beals came up on Google, but they're too young. A few on Twitter, but no pictures or information."

"It seems like it would be a common name. Which means that if you check Peoplelooker.com or Peoplefinder.com, you'll end up with too many candidates. I'd tell you to ask Tommy, but he's busy on the Nunzio case." He thinks for a moment. "Ask Angie for the contact information for Matt Crowley. He used to be with the United States Marshals Service, but now he has his own security firm. He's good at tracking people down."

Nunzio waits as the guard opens the door to the little room, where he can see that the attorney is already waiting for him. He likes the fact that McFarland doesn't stand for him and waits for him to extend his hand to shake. The attorney is a cool customer. Smart, too. Clever. A planner, a plotter. He can see it in the man's eyes, the way McFarland studies him the whole time they're together. Trying to figure out how to outmaneuver his own client, get the upper hand. It's what he does himself. All the time. What he's done as long as he can remember, with everyone.

"I'm surprised to see you," he tells McFarland. "My preliminary hearing isn't for another week."

"There are some things I want to ask you about. And a concern my staff has raised."

"A concern?"

"Is there going to be a war? Between you and Frank Valiante?"

Absolutely, there's going to be a war. We're laying our plans now.

"I hope not. War isn't good for anyone. Valiante knows that."

"But this was his *son* who died," the lawyer says.

"The Commission would never stand for an all out war."

"They'd have to approve it?" McFarland asks.

"Again, the Commission would never allow a war."

This time, though, they're willing to look the other way.

"So there's no chance my firm, my people, will end up in the middle of something?"

A 100 percent chance. Smack-dab in the middle. The lawyers, anyway.

"I wouldn't let that happen."

Nunzio opens his face to let McFarland study him, find the reassurance he's seeking.

"All right," the lawyer says. "Let's get to the case, then. One of the detectives paid a visit to my office today. He was fishing for information."

"And of course you gave him nothing."

"Duh."

Nunzio smiles. Few people have the balls to address him so casually.

"He asked about Johnny Giacobetti. He says the guard in the building next door saw both of you that night, running for the parking lot."

It's Nunzio's turn to stare.

"So you're not taking a position on whether he was at the warehouse with you or not."

"Did the guard see Johnny *in* the warehouse? Did he even see him getting into the car?"

"How about Antonio Valiante's bodyguards? What happened to them? The detective said Valiante always had soldiers around him. And you told me yourself that Valiante was very careful, and smart."

Nunzio shrugs.

"You know that, sooner or later, the police are going to put these same questions to your daughter."

"And she won't answer them. No one is obligated to talk to the police. Not even a witness to a crime. As you know."

Mick considers this. "The prosecutor could always empanel an investigating grand jury, which could subpoena Christina. If she refuses to talk, a judge could hold her in contempt, sentence her to up to six months in jail."

Nunzio feels his eyes narrow. "That's not going to happen. My daughter . . . She's not doing well. Her mother wants to fly her out of the country, to some chalet in Switzerland. She might even be on her way already."

"Unless you want to get on the stand yourself—"

Nunzio puts up his hand. "Also not going to happen."

"Then Christina's your only hope. She's the only one who can give the jury a narrative that might exonerate you." Mick pauses. "*If* there is such a redeeming story to tell."

There'll be a story, all right. And you'll hear it the same time the jury does.

Mick sighs. "Just keep me informed of everything the detective—and the DA—tell you."

They sit silently for a few more moments. Then, "Anything else, counselor?"

The lawyer shakes his head, stands. "I'll see you Monday morning, before the hearing. To prepare you."

"No need. I know what's going to happen. I'll meet you in the courtroom."

The lawyer signals the guard through the door that they're finished. The guard enters and takes Nunzio back to his cell.

Alone again, Nunzio sits on the bunk and shakes his head.

All these years doing what I do and the law never even got close. Then this shit happens. It was rotten luck the cops came up to the warehouse.

He knew he should've had Johnny pull the car in back; if he'd done so, the cops would've kept on going down Admiral Peary Way. Tony Valiante would still have been dead, and there would still have been a war, but he wouldn't have had to watch it happen from a jail cell.

Thank God for Rachel, and for Uncle Ham. Those two.

He smiles, lets his mind drift back twenty-eight years. He was twenty-three, a young buck; Rachel only twenty, a sophomore at Penn. They met at Smokey Joe's, him and his crew there looking to pick up pretty undergrads. Rachel and her Jewish girlfriends looking for a little danger, taking their chances with real men, not Ivy League pencil-necks. He bought her drinks, traded jabs with her, was impressed with her ability to go toe-to-toe with him. As smart as she was good-looking, and, man, was she good-looking. At the end of the night, she let him walk her back to her dorm room—something he'd done with a dozen girls before. Let him make out with her, too. Until she didn't. He crossed the line, and she stopped him. He crossed the line again, and she smacked him. Hard. *Him.* And she knew who he was!

That really impressed him. He backed off and asked her out proper, and they started dating. Then, he found out about Rachel's history. Her blood. That sealed it for him. He and Rachel were married. And it had been smooth sailing ever since.

Or at least until seven days ago.

He shakes his head again. Then lowers it.

"Christina, Christina. What am I going to do with you?"

But he already knows the answer.

God help me.

8

Monday, April 22

Mick sits at the defense table in Courtroom 306. To his right, Max Pagano is removing papers from his leather satchel at the prosecutor's table. The gruff ADA did little more than grunt his acknowledgment at Mick when he came in. Behind them both, a bulletproof Plexiglas wall separates the well of the courtroom from the gallery. Mick glances back, sees that the wooden benches are filled. The arrest of Jimmy Nunzio has caused a stir in Philadelphia, and everyone wants to see the show. Mick recognizes half a dozen members of the press, a handful of other criminal-defense attorneys, some junior ADAs, courthouse employees, and a handful of mob-o-philes from South Philly. Also present are a few guys Mick suspects are part of Nunzio's crew. Noticeably *not* among them is Nunzio's enforcer and personal bodyguard, Johnny Giacobetti.

A door to Mick's left opens, and Jimmy Nunzio is escorted into the courtroom by two chief deputies. His cuffs have already been removed, and he's wearing a form-fitting Italian suit—a remarkable sartorial upgrade from the jeans and T-shirts worn by most prisoners. Mick rises and shakes Nunzio's hand; then they both sit down. Nunzio turns his seat sideways, giving him a view of the entire courtroom. Mick studies his legal pad, noticing in his peripheral vision that Nunzio is scanning the gallery, taking in everyone present.

After a few minutes, the Honorable Marvin Montgomery, the judge who will preside over the preliminary hearing, enters and takes the bench. Fifty years old, pasty white and rail thin, Marvin is new to the criminal world, having spent his entire career at a large corporate law firm. He took the bench only a year before and, like many new judges, will have to spend his first years in criminal court before moving over to the slightly more refined world of civil litigation. The judge does his best to affect an air of cool control but doesn't quite pull it off.

The court crier has Mick and Pagano state their names, after which Judge Montgomery turns to the prosecutor, who offers up the death certificate for Antonio Valiante. Mick doesn't object, and Montgomery accepts the document into the record.

"Defense counsel and I have agreed on a stipulation, which I'll read," Pagano announces.

The judge asks, "Don't you just want to submit the writing into the record? How long is it?"

"It's short," Pagano says, launching immediately into the stipulation. "On Wednesday, April tenth, of this year, at 11:45 p.m., Antonio Valiante, aged thirty, was pronounced dead at the scene in a warehouse building located off Admiral Peary Way in South Philadelphia. The body was transported to the Philadelphia medical examiner's office, where the medical examiner determined to a reasonable degree of medical certainty that the cause of death was exsanguination—massive blood loss—from a wound to the decedent's throat."

Pagano hands the stipulation to the tipstaff and then says to the judge: "I offer exhibits C-1 to C-20, a series of photographs depicting the decedent and the crime scene."

"Objection." Mick stands. "Your Honor, I've already stipulated to the cause of death. There is no purpose to showing the photographs, which are gratuitously inflammatory."

"Inflammatory to who?" Pagano asks. "There's no jury here. I'm sure we can trust the court not to be overcome by emotion."

"With the stipulation, there's no need for the photographs," Judge Montgomery says. "The objection is sustained."

Pagano turns away from the bench while the judge is still talking. Pagano's rudeness is legendary, but Mick is still surprised to see him snub a sitting judge. Glancing at the bench, Mick sees that Judge Montgomery is none too happy with the prosecutor. Nunzio, on the other hand, is smiling.

"Call your first witness," says the judge, pretending not to notice Pagano's disrespectful behavior.

"The Commonwealth calls Jake Trumbull."

The patrolman is a big kid in his early twenties. Mick predicts Pagano will keep his testimony short and to the point, offering up as little detail as he thinks is necessary to persuade the judge to bind Nunzio for trial.

"Have you ever seen the defendant, James Nunzio, before?" Pagano asks.

"Yes."

"What was the date? What was the time?"

"April tenth. Between 10:30 and 11:00 p.m."

"Tell the court how you came to see the defendant, James Nunzio, on April tenth."

"Me and my partner, Officer Piccone, were patrolling east of the Naval Yard. It's that big area that hasn't been redeveloped yet. We were on Admiral Peary, and I noticed a Cadillac Escalade sitting outside a building that was supposed to be vacant. So I thought we should take a look, and we drove up to it."

"What happened next?"

"We got out and examined the Caddy. It looked brand-new. Then we went over to the front of the building. The door was all dented, and the wood frame was busted up. It looked like someone had kicked it open. There was light coming from inside, too."

"Did you hear anything?"

"Crying. A woman was crying. So we unholstered our weapons and went inside."

"And that's where you saw the defendant?"

"Objection. Leading." A pointless objection, Mick knows, and Pagano will simply rephrase because there's no dispute that Nunzio was inside the building.

Still, I'm not going to let Pagano cruise through this on autopilot.

Pagano casts him a nasty look.

"Where was the defendant standing when—"

"Objection. Leading."

"Really?" Pagano snarls.

Mick smiles inside. *Pagano's pissed. Good.*

"Gentlemen . . . ," the court admonishes both of them.

"Just tell us what happened when you got inside. What you saw and what you did."

"The first thing I saw was the girl on the floor, holding the dead guy. She was crying."

"Was she saying anything?"

"Like, 'Why? Why?'"

"Did she say, 'Why, *Daddy*?'"

"Objection!" Mick's on his feet. "Putting words in the witness's mouth."

The judge sustains the objection and tells Pagano to continue.

"Did the woman say anything other than 'Why? Why?'"

"She did say, 'Why, Daddy?' And she went on about how she loved him. The dead guy, I mean."

"So it was the decedent she loved, not her father?"

Mick doesn't glance at Nunzio, but he feels the gangster's eyes darken. He stands. "Objection."

"Sustained. Keep to the point, counselor."

"How was the woman holding the decedent?"

"She was sitting on the floor, and she had him, like, leaning up against her. His head was tucked into her shoulder, and she was rocking back and forth."

Pagano pauses. It seems to Mick that he's waiting for Trumbull to say something more, something the prosecutor and the cop had rehearsed.

"The blood was still coming out of his throat. There was a giant slit. A gash."

Pagano smiles slightly, and Mick knows Trumbull gave him what he was looking for.

"What did you do, or see, next?"

"I started to go over to her. That's when I saw a guy standing in the shadows. Him," he adds, nodding at Nunzio. "He had a knife in his hand, and I ordered him to drop it. My partner started yelling, too. When he dropped the knife, we had him put his hands behind his back. Then I cuffed him."

"What did you do with the knife?"

"Me? Nothing. I didn't touch it. That was for CSU."

Pagano pauses a moment. "Did you notice any blood on the defendant?"

"Are you kidding? It was all over him."

Mick glances at Nunzio. His face is stone.

"Nothing further, Your Honor," Pagano says.

Mick considers how to handle the direct examination. There was no mention of Johnny Giacobetti, despite what Tredesco said about the security guard seeing Giacobetti and Nunzio racing out of Nunzio's building on the night of the murder. Mick knows that's because Pagano has no idea how Johnny G. fits into this yet. Pagano also didn't touch upon the cell-phone call that apparently caused Nunzio to show up in the first place—another thing the prosecutor hasn't decided how to fit into his narrative. Not that Pagano needs to bring any of this up; he's presented more than enough evidence to persuade the judge to hold Nunzio for trial.

Judge Montgomery looks at Mick. "Do you have any questions?"

"Just a few."

To send a message to the press.

"After you cuffed Mr. Nunzio, I assume you checked him for a gun."

"Absolutely."

"Did you find one?"

"Yes. Tucked into the back of his pants. A nine-millimeter."

"A Sig Sauer P938 Nitron?"

"I guess."

"So why would he have used the knife? Why not just shoot the decedent and skip getting covered in blood?"

Pagano doesn't bother to stand. "Objection! Calls for speculation."

"I withdraw the question, Your Honor."

Turning from the bench to the witness, Mick says, "Did you *ask* Mr. Nunzio what happened in the warehouse?"

"It was obvious what happened."

"Was this a case of self-defense?"

"Self-defense?" The officer's voice is thick with incredulity.

"Do you know whether Antonio Valiante attacked Mr. Nunzio first?"

"How could I know that?"

"Uh . . . by asking."

Trumbull stares. Then a light bulb goes off in his head. "After I cuffed him, I read him his rights. So we couldn't ask him anything."

"How long after you handcuffed him was this?"

"I don't know, maybe ten minutes."

"Ten minutes during which you could've asked him for his side of the story."

"Well . . ."

"So, what happened after you read him his rights?"

"My partner was asking him if he was all right. If he needed water."

Mick glances at Pagano, who rolls his eyes. They both know what had happened: Piccone, the older cop, recognized Nunzio and knew to treat him with respect.

"Let me get this straight. A young woman is weeping on the floor as she holds the bleeding body of her lover, but your partner is spending his time taking care of Mr. Nunzio?"

"Well . . ."

"Sounds like Officer Piccone thought maybe the situation wasn't as *obvious* as it seemed to you."

"Objection!" cries Pagano again.

The judge leans over the bench. "This isn't trial, Mr. McFarland. You can score all the points you want, but you already know the prosecution has made out its *prima facie* case."

Mick thinks for a moment. "Officer Trumbull, is there anything else you remember that sticks out in your mind? Anything you noticed, anything you saw?"

"Saw, or noticed?"

Mick does a double take. "Either."

"There was one thing that seemed odd. It smelled like pasta. In the warehouse. There were no dishes out or anything, but it smelled like they'd just had dinner."

Mick glances at Pagano, sees him look away.

Another thing he hasn't figured out.

After the preliminary hearing, Nunzio waits for his attorney in the holding cell. He enjoyed McFarland's sparring with the cop, but it was all grandstanding; there's no question he's going to face a jury. He looks at his hands and shakes his head. *Damn.* If he'd had more time to think before the cops showed up, he'd have used the knife to stab his own hands, make it look like he'd sustained some defensive wounds. Self-defense is what it's all going to come down to at trial. Still, it could've been much worse.

If I hadn't seen the cops' headlights through the busted doorframe . . . The thought makes him shudder.

The guard opens the door, and the attorney enters.

"You had a little fun out there," Nunzio says.

"The cop will be better prepared at trial," Mick says. "All of Pagano's witnesses will be."

Nunzio shrugs.

"Have you given any thought to a plea?"

"There will be no plea. I want my day in court."

"You're going to trust your fate to a jury? Twelve people you've never met? Most of them having grown up hearing stories about you?"

Those would include the most notorious tale: of him locking his cheating fiancée and her lover—his own boss—inside a coffin until they both starved to death. That yarn has an element of truth to it: He *did* seal his boss and the woman inside the box. But not in a fit of jealous rage. It was a fully sanctioned hit. The higher-ups wanted that guy gone. And the woman wasn't his fiancée but a floozy he started nailing *after* she was already seeing the boss. He eliminated them both as part of a carefully calculated plan to advance. It didn't hurt that it enhanced his image as a hair-trigger hood.

"Let go, let God." He smiles.

"I don't think you're taking this seriously enough."

He shoots to his feet, leans into the lawyer's space so their faces are inches apart. "I know the stakes. Believe me. I'm taking this as serious as hell. And you better be, too. Don't think that just because they caught me dead to rights, I'm going to roll over. I'm not. And neither are you. I expect nothing less than the fight of your life. Because that's what this *is*!"

He feels his heart pounding in his chest, the rush of adrenaline, the reddening of his face, the darkening of his eyes—physiological reactions, partly instinctive but mostly deliberate now. Tools he uses to manage people through fear. It's working: McFarland's trying to act nonchalant, but he can smell the man's fear.

Good. He needs to understand who the boss is. Who's really running the show.

"I don't like the way you're talking to me," the attorney says. "I won't be threatened."

The two men square off.

Neither moves until the deputy steps up to the bars. "Everything all right in here?"

"Peachy," Nunzio answers, his tone cold. Then, when the deputy leaves, he breaks the ice by offering up a smile, one of his warmest. "I don't want to threaten you, Mick. We're on the same side. You're the best lawyer in town, and that's why I hired you. I just need to know you're going to go to bat for me. That you'll keep an open mind and figure out a way to beat this thing."

McFarland exhales, takes a step back. "I'm going to do my best. I *always* do my best for my clients, always look for a way to win."

"That's all I needed to hear."

◆ ◆ ◆

Mick leaves the holding cell and walks into the hallway feeling as though he's just been whipsawed. Nunzio's reputation for emotional volatility is well deserved. As he turns toward the stairwell, he sees Max Pagano talking heatedly to a man who looks like another attorney. Wearing a dark-blue suit, the man appears to be in his midforties and is tall and strongly built. Mick passes Pagano and the second man just in time to hear Pagano say, "Or you could just stick it up your ass."

Pagano slams open the door that leads to the stairs and disappears. From behind, Mick hears a voice calling his name. He turns and sees the lawyer Pagano was talking to. The man approaches him and hands Mick his card. It identifies him as Assistant US Attorney Martin Brenner. Mick gets it now, what was going on between Pagano and Brenner. As is fairly predictable for a case involving the arrest of a high-level mobster, the feds are going to try to take it over in hopes of turning Nunzio against his New York overlords.

"Can we talk?" Brenner says, taking a step closer. His dark-blue eyes are intense, and his strong frame radiates the energy of a tightly wound spring.

"Sure, but I can tell you up front that Nunzio's never going to flip."

"I wouldn't be too sure. His bosses are facing a war, thanks to him. They have to be pissed as hell."

"If you're suggesting he agree to be conscripted into witness protection, I just don't see Jimmy Nunzio letting you move him to Iowa to sell fire insurance." Mick taps the lawyer's business card. "And why am I being approached by the Philly office? I'd have expected this to come out of the Southern District of New York."

"Nunzio's a Philly boy. We get first dibs."

"Not buying it. But even if I did, this is a nonstarter. He's not going to turn. You're wasting your time."

Brenner smiles. "We'll see."

9

Wednesday, April 24

It's just before 9:00 a.m., and Piper and Susan Klein are headed back to the Lehigh Valley. They have a full day ahead of them. First, they're going to meet Melvin Ott, one of the Buchanan Township police officers who showed up at the Dowd farm the day of the killing. Then, they'll head up the pike to meet former police chief Sonny Foster, the bad guy in Darlene Dowd's version of events. Finally, they're going to the office of Ken Galbraith, the lawyer who represented Darlene the first time around.

Piper is the one who spoke to each of the men and set up the meetings. She's explained to Susan that, of the two law enforcement officers, she wants to talk first to Melvin Ott because he seemed the most forthcoming over the phone. He agreed to the meeting right away, unlike the ex-chief, who had to be talked into it. He actually laughed when she told him she was considering taking on Darlene as an innocence case at the firm. The lawyer, Galbraith, was open to speaking with Piper but didn't want to talk about the case over the phone.

Piper pulls the car into the parking lot of the Perkins Restaurant on Hamilton Street in Allentown. She and Susan enter the restaurant and look around. A large-framed man sitting in a back booth waves them over. He has graying hair and deep wrinkles from too much sun.

He appears to be in his early sixties. He rises to meet them, extends his hand.

"Mel Ott," he says.

"I'm Piper McFarland. We spoke on the phone. And this is Susan Klein, an attorney with our firm."

Piper and Susan slide into the bench seat across the table from the ex-officer. On the table is a porcelain mug, silverware, and a plate picked clean. Ott has already eaten.

The waitress, a bone-thin woman with wiry red hair, comes over with two menus. Piper and Susan order coffee but decline breakfast, which seems to annoy the waitress.

Piper is quick to get out of the way that she is not an attorney, but that she spearheads the innocence cases at the law firm run by her husband and by Susan. This seems to surprise Ott, but he warms to Piper as she engages him by asking about his life and family and career in law enforcement. Once he's talking easily, she gets down to business.

"So . . . Darlene Dowd," she says.

"Darlene Dowd." He nods and repeats the name. "One of the sorriest cases I ever worked on. What her father did to her. I almost can't blame her for what she did back to him."

"Then you think she did kill her father?"

"What I think is that the jury who convicted her didn't have all the evidence. There was a witness who should've been allowed to testify. She was a neighbor of the Dowds."

Piper glances at Susan. This was starting out better than she expected. As friendly as Ott was over the phone, she still thought she'd have to pull teeth to get potentially exculpatory evidence. She decides to let him run with his story and gives him the opening to do so.

"What do you remember about that morning?" she asks.

"Well, I'd just come into work when the call came in from a woman who said she'd found her husband dead on the floor, that there was blood all over from a head wound. I got the address, jumped in my car, and drove straight to the farm. On the way, the chief, Sonny Foster, called me on the radio, said he was on his way, too, and that he'd called out our criminal-investigation team. We had a detective, John Cook, and a crime-scene technician, Dave Fonseca. I pulled into the driveway just before Sonny. We approached the woman—Cindy Dowd—who was walking around in a circle outside the house, crying and pulling at her hair.

"We asked her where her husband was, and she pointed to the back door and said he was in the kitchen. We walked to the door, which was hanging wide open, and there he was—his body was—right inside the doorway. It was a holy mess, let me tell you. His head all bashed in, brains and bone and gore spilling out. Blood everywhere.

"Cindy told us that she'd woken up, gone downstairs, and found her husband dead. She said he was facedown, and when she turned him over, she got blood on her hands and her slippers."

The waitress returns with coffee, and Melvin Ott pauses to let Piper and Susan stir in their sugars and milk. Piper takes a sip, then asks how Darlene came into the story.

"A neighbor, Lois Beal, showed up. She told us she'd seen Darlene walking past her house around six, a half hour or so after the sun came up. She told us Darlene often spent the night in the fields because she liked to sleep outdoors, under the stars. Sonny looked at me, and I could tell he wasn't buying that a teenage girl would choose to sleep on the ground.

"Sonny asked Cindy where Darlene was. Cindy said she didn't know, and Sonny gave me another look. I could see his gears were turning. Just about then, our crime-scene guys showed up, along with some other patrolmen. Sonny sent them inside the house and told me to go up to a big shed we saw on the property and report back to him with what I found. Well, I went inside and there she was, looking right up at me. Darlene. She was huddled in the corner, covered in blood.

I helped her to stand up and walked her outside. As we got closer to the house, her mother tried to run up to her, but Sonny held her back.

"I brought Darlene to where everyone was standing—Sonny, Cindy, Lois, and some patrolmen. Sonny smiled and said, 'Well, well. Look at what the cat dragged in.' And I knew that, in his mind at least, the case was solved. He told me to fetch the technician to take pictures of Darlene; then he had the detective take her to the station."

"And that's where she gave her confession?" Susan asks.

"After about eighteen hours."

Ott grits his teeth, and Piper can see he's not comfortable with this part of the story.

"Sonny had John Cook let her stew for three hours before they went in to talk to her. She must've been mighty uncomfortable sitting there in clothes covered in blood. It was a small room to begin with, just enough space for a table and some chairs. And I'm sure it got closer as the day wore on. Our office has air-conditioning, of course, but Sonny kept the door to the interrogation room closed, and the window open to the outside air. And I remember it being unusually hot for June.

"I didn't go in the room, but the mic was live, so I could hear what went on from the outside, and I watched through the window. Darlene denied that she'd killed her father, but Sonny and Cook weren't having it. Cook used all the usual methods to gain a confession. He kept insisting that she'd done it. He lied about finding evidence proving it was her. Finally, he just wore her down, and she agreed to a confession. It took her three or four drafts, with him coaching her as to the details, before she gave him something he was satisfied with. He had her sign it. Once she'd done so, he booked her, took her clothes as evidence, and locked her in the cell until her preliminary arraignment.

"A few weeks later, Lois showed up at the station. Detective Cook was on vacation, so she asked to talk to the chief. I know this because I happened to be in Sonny's office when the clerk brought Lois back. She told Sonny and me, again, that Darlene couldn't have killed her father that night because she wasn't at home, that she'd seen Darlene walking past her house, *toward* her own house about 6:00 a.m., and that she had no blood on her. By then it had been established that Lester Dowd died between 3:00 and 5:00 a.m."

Ott lifts a mug and takes a sip of coffee before continuing.

"Lois told us she often slept on the front porch of her farmhouse. Sometimes when she did, she'd wake up in the morning to see Darlene walking down the road past her house. She told Sonny and me that once Darlene hit puberty, she developed a habit of wandering off and spending the night in the fields or down by a small stream that ran through the nearby woods. Lois said she'd asked Cindy about it, and that Cindy told her the girl was born for the outdoors, didn't like living under a roof."

Ott pushes his coffee to the side and sighs deeply.

"We came to learn later from Darlene's lawyer that the real reason she spent her nights away from home was because she was being abused by her father." He shakes his head. "I sat in at the sentencing phase, when Darlene testified about all the things her father had done to her. I still can't wrap my head around it. How a father could do that."

Piper waits a moment, then says, "We met with Darlene at the prison, and she told us that she had spent the night in a field down the road and that she'd gotten home a little after six in the morning. She said she'd entered the house through the back door, the door to the kitchen, and tripped over her father's body. She said she'd started crying and tried to get up, but slipped in the blood. That's how she explained the blood that was all over her. She testified she panicked and ran and hid in her father's workshop, thinking that the killer might still be around. A short while later, she heard a commotion down at the house, but she kept herself hidden in the workshop because her clothes were bloody, and she was afraid the police would think she was the killer."

"That's what she said in court," Ott says.

"But Darlene's attorney never put Lois Beal on the stand to corroborate her testimony that she'd been away from the house at the time of her father's killing."

Piper lets the sentence hang in the air.

Ott nods. "When Lois was done repeating her story, Sonny told her to get the hell out of the station and keep it to herself."

Susan frowns. "And that's all it took to get Lois to bury what she knew?"

Ott sighs again. "Sonny and Lois had a history—what kind, exactly, I'm not sure. When he kicked her out, he told her if she didn't go away, he'd look into her background. He said he had some buddies in the FBI who owed him a favor, and he'd give them a call."

"And that scared her?" asks Piper.

"The look on her face—I've never forgotten it. She turned white. Then she turned around and walked out of the station. That was it."

"But what was Sonny's motive for keeping Lois from telling what she knew about Darlene?"

"Apart from his not liking Lois, his motive was twofold, I believe. First, he was certain from the start that Darlene was guilty. Second, he was the kind of cop who was always right."

"A great combination."

Ott nods, and they sit quietly until Susan says, "And you let all of this happen. Why?"

The ex-cop lowers his head. "This is where I start to feel like shit. I'd just joined up with the township police a few months earlier. I was a deputy out in Westmoreland County for twenty-two years. My wife is from here, though, and when her mother got sick, she felt she needed to come back. I agreed to relocate, but it took me a year to find a job, Sonny Foster being the only one who'd take a chance on a fifty-year-old new-hire cop. So I didn't want to rock the boat with him on the Dowd case, even though he wasn't playing it straight. All of which is just a roundabout way of saying I was a chickenshit. I got no better answer for you than that. I should've stepped in and stopped Sonny from scaring that woman off."

"You think Lois Beal's testimony would've made a difference at trial?" Piper asks.

"I don't know, but I think Darlene and her lawyer should've had the chance to find out." He looks away, then back at her. "And I got the sense that there was even more to it than Lois told me and Sonny. You know, we never found the weapon that killed Lester Dowd. I've been thinking for years that Lois Beal might know where it is."

Piper glances at Susan. If Darlene's mother was right, Lois did indeed know the whereabouts of the murder weapon.

"Do you know where Lois is now?" Susan asks.

"No idea. She moved away after her husband died, but I never tried to find out where. Never had a reason to."

"Would you be willing to put all of this in an affidavit we can use to get a hearing on a petition for a new trial?" Piper asks. "Would you testify at the hearing?"

He takes a deep breath. "Yeah, I'll do it. I was in law enforcement for close to thirty years. I never fudged on evidence. Never manufactured it, or held it back, or helped anyone else do it, either . . ."

"Except this one time," says Piper.

He looks down.

"Except this one time."

Piper's cell phone rings as she and Susan drive to their second stop, the home of former police chief Sonny Foster. She presses the button on her steering wheel, and the call is put through to Bluetooth.

It's Melvin Ott.

"Hey, listen. I've been thinking about this since you left. There's one thing I forgot. Lester Dowd had been at an all-night poker game run out of Elwood Stumpf's barn. The game was a once-every-other-month thing, and it brought in enough of the locals that the pots got to be pretty big."

"Did something happen at the game?" asks Susan.

"Rumor is that Dowd got into a shouting match with the guys at his table. They accused him of cheating. And he did walk away with close to a thousand dollars—we found it up in his workshop after the murder. It got heated. If Elwood hadn't stepped in, it would've come to blows."

"They listened to Elwood?" Piper asks.

"Everyone listens to Elwood; he goes six foot six and close to three hundred pounds."

"Why would the poker thing have anything to do with the chief not wanting Lois to testify?" asks Susan.

"I'm not saying for sure it did. But the thing is, one of the guys at the poker table was Richie Foster. Sonny's brother."

Piper glances at Susan. "The plot thickens."

"Now, Richie was a no-account. He'd been arrested on DUIs more than once and even served time for something or other."

"And you think Sonny Foster may have been trying to protect his brother," Susan says. "By locking in Darlene as the suspect."

"Protect himself, more likely. Sonny was up for reelection at the time, and it was going to be close. His opponent was a good man, well liked. Career law enforcement, clean-cut, the whole nine yards. Any scandal could have swung the election his way."

"Such as having a low-life brother who got into a fight at a poker game with a guy who ended up dead a few hours later," says Piper.

"Again, I'm not saying for sure this factored into Sonny's motivation," Ott says.

"But you're suspicious enough to raise it with us," Susan says.

"When I heard the rumors—this was about a month after the murder—I went to Sonny and asked him about it. He waved me off, saying he already knew all about that. He said he had personally questioned Elwood and some of the men involved in the poker game. He said it did get heated, but not to the point that anyone seemed ready to kill. He said if it came out, it'd give Darlene Dowd's attorney a bunch of smoke to blow in the jurors' faces. He told me to drop it, and I did."

Once more, Piper hears self-reproach in Melvin Ott's voice. When she hangs up, Susan turns to her.

"I think it's more with him than just feeling Darlene didn't get a fair trial."

"You're saying he saw fire behind the smoke Sonny Foster was worried about?"

Susan nods, turns back to the road ahead. "I think we shouldn't offer up that we know about the poker game when we talk to the chief, at least not at first. See if he volunteers it."

Piper agrees, and they drive on in silence.

Twenty minutes later, Piper pulls into the driveway that leads to Sonny Foster's large log home. The uneven driveway is dirt, grass, and gravel, and Piper's Range Rover bounces up and down.

Sonny Foster clearly saw them coming; by the time they reach the house, he has descended the porch steps. Piper takes him in as she climbs out of the car. Now seventy years old, the retired chief is a square-jawed man with a military-style haircut—white hair buzzed close to the head. Tall with broad shoulders and no gut, he strides confidently toward the car, extending his hand as he approaches Piper. His fingers are thick, and his grip is strong and dry. Susan joins them, and he shakes her hand as well, then invites them to join him on the porch. His wife—thin and pretty and polite—brings out lemonade and iced tea as they make themselves comfortable.

"The Innocence Project . . . ," he says, arching his left brow as he pours for the women.

"Our law firm's own innocence project," Piper says.

"You don't believe Darlene Dowd killed her father?"

"We're still in the investigation stage," Susan says. "Trying to learn as much as we can."

"Trying to find loopholes, free a woman who bludgeoned a man's brain out."

"Not loopholes," Piper intercedes. "What we're looking for is evidence of actual innocence. Proof that a blameless person was sent to prison."

"You won't find such evidence in that case."

"But we can't know that until—"

"Darlene Dowd was found covered in blood. Her father's blood. She had the strongest possible motive. And no alibi—"

Piper cuts in again. "But she *did* have an alibi. She wasn't home at the time of the murder. As Lois Beal told you at the scene, and again later when she came to your office."

"Lois Beal." He spits out the name. "Pie-in-the-sky liberal who moved here from who-knows-where with her tree-hugger husband, the two of them pretending to be farmers."

Piper opens her mouth, but before she can get anything out, Sonny continues.

"Lois Beal, who just happened to be best friends with Cindy Dowd? She would've wanted nothing more than to help clear Cindy's daughter."

Sonny Foster takes a sip of lemonade, sets the glass on the table, and waits.

"That might all be true," Piper says. "But it doesn't justify scaring Lois away, preventing her from acting as a witness for the defense."

"I didn't *prevent* Lois Beal from doing anything. She could've walked right from my office directly to the public defender's office, which was all of a block away, and told Kenny Galbraith her tall tale."

Piper glances at Susan, who steps into the fray.

"So you're not denying that Lois Beal came to your office to impress upon you that she'd seen Darlene Dowd walking *toward* the Dowd farm after the time of the murder with no blood on her?"

"You mean that she'd claimed to have seen her, in dim early-morning light, from thirty yards away."

"All good points for cross-examination, chief," Susan says. "But no excuse for intimidating a witness from coming forward."

Piper sees Sonny Foster shutting down. She decides to pivot before he ends the meeting.

"I understand you searched the Dowd farm after the murder but never found the murder weapon," she says. "Wouldn't that indicate that the killer left the scene and took the murder weapon with them?"

"We searched the farmhouse, the workshop, and the surrounding land. But the Dowds' farm was a hundred acres. Darlene could've buried the murder weapon anywhere."

"If she were trying to hide her involvement in the crime, why not take a shower, clean off the blood?" Susan asks. "Why not go to a stream and do it? Bring a change of clothes."

Sonny Foster exhales. "Darlene's lawyer made all those same arguments at trial, and the jury didn't buy them. They probably thought she just wasn't thinking clearly after the murder. Beating someone to death tends to have that effect on a person."

Piper pauses, then decides it's time to bring up the chief's brother.

"Were there no other suspects?" she asks.

"None," he answers.

"No one who bore a grudge toward Darlene's father?"

He smiles. "Few people liked Lester Dowd. He was a sour, mean-spirited SOB. But being disliked is very different from being hated to the point that someone wants to kill you."

"He was liked enough to get invited to Elwood Stumpf's poker games," Piper says.

Foster sits up. "So that's where you're going with this? Let me tell you a few things. First, and of least significance, men didn't get *invited* to the card games, they just showed up. If they had the money to put down, they got to play. Second, the game Lester Dowd attended that night had nothing to do with his killing."

"We've been told he was accused of cheating at that game," says Susan. "So it could have had everything to do with his murder."

"There was never any proof that Lester cheated."

"But the other players *thought* he'd cheated. And he took them for a thousand dollars."

"I spoke to Elwood Stumpf personally, and to some of the men in that game, and—"

"Including your brother?" asks Piper.

Sonny Foster's eyes darken. Then he laughs.

"Richie? You think *Richie* killed Lester Dowd?"

"We think you were up for reelection—"

"Enough!" He smacks his hand against the table. "That girl killed her father. It's as simple as that. My brother was an alcoholic and a stoner. He was entitled and thought the whole world owed him, yes. But one thing he was *not* was a killer. Hell, Richie didn't have the ambition to kill someone."

Piper homes in on the fact that Sonny speaks of his brother in the past tense. As if sensing this, suddenly deflated, he says, "My brother passed about five years ago. He was in and out of rehabs most of his life. He'd do something destructive, then make a big show of repenting, dry out in rehab. He'd be sober for a while, then crash and burn all over again."

With that he stands, signaling the meeting is over.

"Look," he says, "you seem like good people. I'm sure you have the best of intentions. But you're wasting your time on Darlene Dowd. If ever a man deserved killing, it was her sick son-of-a-bitch father. But the law is the law, and people can't take it into their own hands."

Piper and Susan thank the ex-chief for speaking with them. As they're getting into Piper's car, Sonny Foster shouts out to them.

"When you talk to Lois Beal, why don't you ask her where my brother got his pot? Where most of the stoners in the whole county got their weed?"

Piper parks the car on Linden Street in Allentown, in front of a three-story brick building that has a brass placard announcing it as the home of Galbraith and Stevens. Piper and Susan climb four stone steps to a pair of heavy wooden doors that open into a quiet lobby. The furniture is traditional—dark woods and wing chairs and a Victorian-style couch. They introduce themselves to the receptionist, who invites them to take a seat.

"Did you ever consider practicing in a small-town firm?" Piper asks Susan.

"I never wanted to be a ham-and-egger. I think that's what Grisham calls them. Lawyers who do wills and divorces and some small-potatoes contract work. For me, the big city was always the lure. Glass office towers. The highest-paid and best attorneys. And, of course, I wanted to do criminal work, and trials. All of which is why I went to the US Attorney's Office in Philadelphia."

"Why did you leave? Go into private practice?"

Susan's face transforms in the blink of an eye. "It was time," she says. Nothing more.

Surprised by the reaction, Piper immediately switches topics.

"From what I read in the transcript, it looked like Galbraith did a good job at trial. He made some points against Sonny Foster and the detective, especially about the ordeal they put Darlene through to secure her confession. And in the sentencing phase, he really went to town on the horrors Darlene's father inflicted on her."

"In other words, no basis for an ineffective assistance of counsel claim," concludes Susan. "What do you think he can give us that's not in the transcript?"

"I don't know. Probably nothing. But I want to see his reaction to what we've learned about Lois Beal. And the idea that she might know where the murder weapon is."

Piper senses someone approach. She looks up to see a wiry man of middling height dressed in gray slacks and a white shirt. No tie. She rises, and he smiles and extends his hand.

"Ken Galbraith," he says, taking first Piper's hand, then Susan's. "Let's go back to the conference room."

Once they're seated, Piper thanks him for meeting with them, then opens her satchel and passes him the deathbed letter sent to Darlene by her mother, explaining what it is.

Galbraith reads and then rereads the letter.

"'Lois' is Lois Beal, who was the Dowds' closest neighbor," Piper says. "And a good friend of Darlene's mother. She went to Chief Sonny Foster, told him she'd seen Darlene walking toward home *after* the time of the murder, no blood on her. But Foster pressured her into not coming forward. Threatened to look into her background, apparently."

Galbraith stares at her, looking like a man dazed by a horse kick to the head. He rereads the letter again.

"Her letter says 'hammer,' not 'murder weapon,'" he says. "That jibes with the pathologist's testimony. No one knew for sure what the murder weapon was, but the injuries were consistent with blows from a hammer."

"And she doesn't just say 'hammer,'" Piper says. "She says '*claw* hammer.'"

"So either Cindy Dowd *saw* the hammer or talked to someone who did," concludes Galbraith.

Piper's chest floods with adrenaline. "Did Darlene's mother ever tell you about Lois Beal or the hammer?"

He shakes his head. "Not a word."

"Why would that be?" asks Susan. "Chief Foster pressured Lois Beal to keep quiet about seeing Darlene that morning, and Lois obviously told Cindy Dowd that. So why wouldn't Cindy come straight to you, her daughter's lawyer, and tell you that Lois Beal knew the location of the hammer?"

Galbraith shrugs. They sit in silence until Susan answers her own question.

"There is only one reason I can think why Cindy wouldn't tell you about it," Susan says. "And that's because the hammer would inculpate someone she cared about more than she cared about Darlene."

"But who in the world would she feel a stronger need to protect than her own daughter?" Piper asks.

They look at each other. Piper realizes they all know the answer.

"I guess there is only one person," she says. "Herself."

Galbraith nods. "So once Cindy was on her deathbed, and safe from prosecution . . ."

"She was free to tell Darlene about the hammer," Susan says.

Galbraith sits up. "Wait a minute, though. What we're saying here is that Cindy Dowd killed her husband, then told Lois about it. Why would she do that, and risk Lois turning her over to the authorities?"

"Cindy would have to be very certain that Lois wouldn't go to Chief Foster again, like she did about seeing Darlene that morning," Susan says.

"You said the chief scared off Lois Beal by saying he'd look into her background," Galbraith says. "That implies Lois was carrying a secret. Maybe Cindy Dowd knew Lois's secret and threatened to reveal it if Lois told the police about the hammer."

"My head is spinning with all this," Piper says. "So many unanswered questions."

"Seems to me there's only one person who can answer them," Galbraith says. "Where's Lois Beal?"

10

Wednesday, May 1

Mick is in the firm's lobby, reviewing his calendar with Angie, when Susan walks in and brushes past them without saying anything.

"She okay?" Mick asks Angie quietly.

"She has a lot going on with her father in town."

"I thought he fled the country."

When they were first getting to know each other, Susan told him that when she was a teen, her father left her mother for another woman, a foreigner, and followed the woman to Europe.

"He was living in London," Angie says. "But his second wife died, and now he's back. He told Susan he wants to rekindle their relationship."

"When's the last time she saw him?"

"Like, eight years ago."

"Unbelievable." He can't imagine abandoning Gabby, not seeing her for years at a time.

"She's been ducking him," Angie says. "She told me if he calls to say she's on the phone."

"Has he called?"

"A dozen times."

"And she doesn't call him back?"

"She did once. Told him she'd meet him for lunch."

"How'd that go?"

"She stood him up."

I don't blame her.

When Angie leaves, Mick walks to the office Piper uses when she's at the firm. He sits just in time to hear Angie buzzing through and telling Piper that Matt Crowley's on the phone. Piper hits the "Speaker" button and tells Crowley that Mick's with her.

"Sorry it's taken me so long to get back to you, but I've had a heck of a time tracking down the mysterious Lois Beal."

"But you found her?" Piper asks hopefully.

"Good news, bad news," he says. "It took some finagling, but I was able to unearth her Social Security number, which I used to track her down."

"That's great! Where is she? What's she doing?"

"This is where we move into the bad-news part. Lois Beal's in Albuquerque, New Mexico. And she's not doing a thing. Hasn't done a thing since she died—over sixty years ago, at the age of nine."

Mick and Piper look at each other. "So the Dowds' neighbor was using Lois Beal's identity as an alias?"

"Her husband, too. Jason Dell, age eight, died on March 7, 1957."

"They were on the lam," Mick says.

"They were hiding from something, at the very least," Crowley says. "And since they were hiding together, chances are that whatever it was they'd run from was something they'd done together, too."

Piper exhales. "So now what?"

"This is where we move into the expensive part. Basically, we'll have to scour the news for two people, a man and a woman, who disappeared in the early 1970s, the same time when Lois Beal and Jason Dell showed up in the Lehigh Valley, presenting themselves as husband and wife. Given that Dell's obituary in 2009 reported his age as sixty, this means he was in his early twenties when they disappeared, and probably she was, too."

"That also assumes they disappeared from wherever close to the time they moved onto the farm," Mick says.

"Yes, assuming that's true."

Piper okays Crowley to launch the next phase of the search, then ends the call and turns to Mick. "When does the law thing start to get easy?"

He laughs and laughs. After a few seconds, she joins him.

They're still chuckling when Tommy walks into Piper's office, dragging the weight that's present whenever the three of them are together—the sins and secrets they've all carried since the Hanson case.

"Did you talk to your cop buddies about the Nunzio case?" Mick asks.

"A bunch of 'em. Tredesco was telling the truth about the phone used to call Nunzio to lure him to the warehouse—it was a burner, untraceable. Nunzio's phone was a burner, too, as were all the numbers he called himself. Dead ends all around."

"Was anyone willing to tell you what the prosecution's thinking is on the case?"

"One, a detective assigned to the DA's office. He says Pagano can't figure out what happened to Johnny G. and Valiante's bodyguards. What really has him going is why Nunzio—who had a gun—didn't just shoot Valiante."

Mick nods. "Exactly what I asked the arresting cop. Maybe Nunzio wanted to send a message. You mess with my daughter, you're not just going to die, you're going to die slowly."

"And the bodyguards?" Tommy asks. "I still don't believe Tony Valiante was running around without his protection. But if the muscle had been there when Nunzio and Johnny G. busted into that warehouse, you know there would have been a fight. Blood and bodies."

"Maybe they cleaned the blood up," Piper says. "Johnny G. and Nunzio. Then Johnny took the bodies away."

Tommy shakes his head. "The crime-scene guys went over that place with a fine-tooth comb. They used luminol to check for traces of blood. Other than Valiante's, they found nothing. And no signs of a struggle."

Mick considers this, then switches gears. "Have you found out anything about the daughter? Other than she's a party girl?"

"Just that she really was seeing Tony Valiante. Had been for a couple of months, at least."

"That must've pissed their fathers off to no end," says Mick.

Piper says, "So it really was a Romeo-and-Juliet thing."

"I've been looking into her schooling," Tommy says. "Neighborhood Catholic schools while the Nunzios lived in South Philly. Then private schools on the Main Line once Jimmy hit the big time and moved to Villanova. From there, she got her undergraduate degree from the Wharton School at Penn. Honor student. On the soccer team. Joined a sorority."

"You should talk to some of her sorority sisters," says Piper. "Outside her family, they're the ones who'll know the most about her."

"Way ahead of you," Tommy says. "One of them agreed to meet me for lunch. She works in the provost's office at Penn."

"Piper should go, too," Mick tells his brother.

He knows a twentysomething Ivy Leaguer will be more likely to open up to an attractive middle-aged woman than a hard case in his forties with prison tats creeping out of his collar.

Tommy shrugs. "Sure, why not?"

An hour later, Piper is in the back seat of a cab next to Tommy, heading west on Walnut Street. In her peripheral vision, she sees Tommy glance at her, then back at his cell phone.

Time has partially chipped away the wedge the Hanson case drove between them, but they are nowhere near as close as they used to be. They still see each other frequently, of course, at the firm, and at her house when he comes over to visit, but long gone are their shared soul-searching sessions. She misses that, but every time she brings it up, Tommy denies that there's any distance between them.

"So, what sorority did she belong to?" Piper asks.

Tommy pulls a small notepad from his jacket pocket. "Kappa Alpha Theta."

"Isn't that the one Tiffany Trump was in?"

"No idea."

The cab stops at the light on Thirty-Fifth Street, and Tommy tells the driver they'll get out. "We'll go down Locust Walk. She's going to meet us at a Mexican place on the corner of Thirty-Sixth and Locust."

Tortas Frontera sits immediately off Locust Walk, a small place with five or six tables scattered around a brick patio. Inside, giant chalkboards list the offerings under the headings "Molletes" and "Soups and Salads" and "Cazuelas." They pick up their food and go back outside. They're digging in when an attractive young brunette walks up to the door and looks around. Tommy stands and waves her over.

"I'm Tommy McFarland," he says. "We talked on the phone."

Piper sees a wary look cross the young woman's eyes. To compensate, Piper stands and smiles broadly. "Hi. I'm Piper McFarland. I work with Tommy."

The woman warms a little and accepts Piper's hand, introducing herself as Amy Lewis.

"Are you hungry?" Piper asks. "I'd be happy to go inside and get something for you. We figured we'd sit out here. It's such a nice day."

Amy glances at Tommy, then says she'll go in and pick up the food herself. When she returns, Piper does her best to engage her in small talk, asking about her family, where she was raised, what she studied at Penn. She's about to broach the real subject when Amy beats her to the punch.

"Fascinating as I am, I know you guys aren't here to talk about me." Turning to Tommy, she adds, "You said you work for Christina's father. I know they've been in the news because of . . . that thing with her boyfriend. So you piqued my interest. I checked out your firm and learned that your brother does in fact represent Mr. Nunzio. My question is: Why do you need to know about Christina?"

"We're just looking for some background," Tommy says. "We're trying to get a sense for what might have happened in the warehouse that night."

"Why not just ask Christina and her father?"

"It's not as simple as that," Piper says. "Unfortunately. The rules of ethics kind of bind an attorney if his client tells him something, but not necessarily if the attorney learns the information from another source."

Amy looks from Piper to Tommy. "Sounds kind of dumb, but whatever. So, what do you want to know?"

"Just what kind of girl Christina was, how she got along with people, that sort of thing."

"Christina was great. A lot of fun."

"A party girl?" Tommy asks.

"No more than anyone else. And she worked a lot harder than most of us. Christina's the kind of girl who volunteered for everything. The sorority would decide to throw a party or run a charity event, and Christina would be the first person to raise her hand to organize it. She'd get other people to help, and it would be a roaring success, whatever it was. We elected her president of the sorority two years running. She declined in her senior year because she became president of the Panhellenic Council—that's the executive board that oversees all the sororities."

"I read that she was on the soccer team," Tommy says.

"She was the *captain* of the soccer team."

"What was her relationship with her father like?"

Amy's eyes darken. She takes a breath. "Complicated."

"Meaning?"

"We didn't know who her father was, at first. Who he really was. When we found out, it blew some of us away. It blew *me* away. I mean, he'd show up from time to time, and he always seemed very serious. But a lot of the fathers were like that, especially the ones that ran big companies. Then, one day, one of the girls ran into our house with a newspaper that had a big story on him, and we found out he was, like, the *Godfather*, but of Philadelphia. And we were all, like, holy shit."

"Did anyone say anything to Christina?"

"A couple of us did. Well, we didn't come right out and say it. We just said, 'Hey, Christina, did you see that story about your dad in the *Inquirer*? And she was, like, 'Yeah, ho-hum.' And that was it."

"Getting back to their relationship . . . ," Tommy says.

Amy pauses. "We got the impression that he was kind of smothering. You know, like, overprotective. He'd come by, and they'd go into her room and close the door. We could hear them arguing. Especially when we were juniors and seniors—that's when me and Christina and Bailey and Lucy got an apartment together. Then he would leave, and we'd ask what it was all about. She'd say her dad didn't 'get' her. And we all had fathers, too, so we knew that meant he was being controlling."

"Controlling is different from overprotective, isn't it?" Tommy asks.

"Yeah, but it was both. The thing with Tim Long proved how bad he could be."

"Tim Long?"

"He was the captain of our football team. He and Christina were an item from the time they were sophomores. By the time we were seniors, he must've gotten tired of her. He started dating this other girl one day, out of the blue. It broke Christina's heart. Her father got wind of it and had Tim beaten to a pulp. I mean, I went to see Tim in the hospital, and his face was so mangled I couldn't even recognize him. He never came back to school after that. It caused a major rift between Christina and her dad. They had a huge shouting match, which I overheard. It was hard to understand everything they said, but Tim's name kept coming up. I'm sure Christina was reaming him out for beating Tim up. She'd probably hoped she could get back together with him."

"Did you reach out to her about it?" asks Piper.

"I tried, but she brushed me off. I think it was too painful for her to talk about."

Piper thinks for a minute, then asks, "Did anyone ever think of going to Christina's father and talking to him yourselves? Try to get him to ease off a little, let her sprout her own wings?"

Amy tilts her head. "Are you serious? Try to talk sense into Jimmy-effing-*Nutzo*?"

◆ ◆ ◆

Mick looks up from his desk as Tommy leads Piper into his office. They sit and explain what they learned from Amy Lewis.

Mick processes it, then asks, "How does an honor student and the hardest-working girl on campus turn into Little Miss International Party Girl?"

"Seems like she's rebelling," Tommy says. "Trying to break away from her father."

"Why doesn't she use her degree from Wharton to get a high-powered job in New York, Chicago, LA? Make a life for herself?"

"Maybe he doesn't want her to make her own life," Tommy says. "Maybe he wants her close to him, where he can control her. So she fights back by jet-setting around the world. And when that doesn't piss him off enough, she starts dating his archenemy."

"It doesn't feel right," Piper says. "There's something going on between those two, for sure, but I don't think it's just him trying to control her."

"Or protect her?" Mick wonders aloud.

"That, either," she says.

Angie buzzes Mick on his speaker.

"You're not going to believe this," she says.

"What?"

"It's Jimmy Nunzio. I think he's calling from his jail cell."

Mick glances at Tommy, then at Piper. They both have the same sick look on their faces. He lifts the receiver.

"I want you down here. *Now*," the mobster tells him.

The line goes dead.

"At least in jail, he can't kill you," Tommy says with a shrug.

"You sure about that? Last year, he had *two* guys killed in jail. And in case you've forgotten, they were both lawyers."

Mick doesn't have to wait long. The guard ushers Nunzio, already uncuffed, into the attorney visiting room while Mick is still draping his jacket over the back of his chair.

"Mind telling me how it is you can call me from your jail cell?"

"Let me make something very clear to you, counselor: my daughter is off-limits."

Mick sees the menace in the crime lord's eyes. He realizes their dance has entered a dangerous phase.

"You want me to represent you, I need to know as much as I can about the players. That includes your daughter."

"Christina is not a 'player.' She's a civilian, as are you—so far. Which means she's not to be used or placed at risk."

"Placed at risk? Did you really just say that? You smashed your way into her boyfriend's building, thinking it might be fun to kill him right in front of her. Maybe you did it to teach him a lesson for bringing her into things? The same way you taught her college boyfriend a lesson for cheating on her? Either way, you had to know it would cause a war. And if Frank and Angelo Valiante are the type of guys I think they are, one of the targets in that war will be Christina."

Nunzio stares at him.

"Or maybe that *wasn't* the plan. Maybe you got the call tipping you off that Christina and Valiante were there together, and you raced over to talk sense into them, break them up before somebody got hurt. You were only trying to protect her. But things got out of hand, and Antonio ended up dead. Is that what happened?"

Nunzio sighs. "I think I can be forgiven for wanting to protect my daughter from someone like Antonio. As for what happened . . ."

"Yeah, I know. When the time is right."

Nunzio studies him for an uncomfortable moment. "Is it so hard for you to believe that I went there to protect my daughter? Haven't you ever heard of Occam's razor? Sometimes the simplest solution *is* the solution."

"I don't put a lot of stock in simple solutions. I find they rarely tell the whole story."

Looking tired, Nunzio takes a seat across the table. The two men sit in silence until Nunzio says, "My wife and I were blessed with two very sweet children. Alexander . . . I knew from the time he was a toddler that he wasn't suited for the business. We'd walk down the street, and he'd stop and pet every dog we passed. I'd take him to the park to teach him how to throw a baseball, but all he did was look at the birds, chase butterflies. He wanted to be a writer. He studied literature in college.

"As for Christina—you couldn't imagine a lovelier little girl. Always wanting to help out with the chores, with her brother. Interested in everything. And so much energy."

Mick watches as Nunzio's eyes get a faraway look in them.

"And then she grew up," Mick says.

Nunzio nods but doesn't answer.

"Maybe you need to give her some space to be her own person."

"'Be her own person,' says the father of the nine-year-old girl. Wait until you're the father of the nineteen-year-old girl."

Mick's heart skips a beat. He doesn't like that Nunzio knows how old Gabby is.

What else does he know?

"You can't control her forever."

"Maybe not. But I can protect her. Or try to. Isn't that my first duty as her father? To protect her? Isn't that your first duty to Gabrielle?"

Hearing his daughter's name rolling off the murderer's tongue brings Mick's blood to a sudden boil. "If the reason you went to that warehouse was to protect your daughter, you really fucked up. No disrespect."

Nunzio's eyes widen momentarily.

"You keep talking to me like that, counselor, and you'll find out what it means to fuck up."

Back in his cell, Nunzio lifts the picture of his daughter and stares at it. Christina was in fourth grade at the time. Her olive skin as smooth as silk. A smile that melted his heart. She'd sit in his lap when he came home from work, fall asleep to the TV. Such simpler times. Good times. When he and Rachel and Christina and Alexander still lived in the little row house in South Philly. Before he started to move up in the family. Before he met Uncle Ham and his business—his real business—took off and he bought the giant stone house on North Spring Mill Road in Villanova.

He thinks back to his conversation with the lawyer. Stupid to have let his guard down like that . . . to wax nostalgic. But he saved it in the end by mentioning McFarland's daughter's name. That made the lawyer good and mad. And a little afraid, off-balance—the whole reason he'd ordered McFarland to come and see him.

11

Wednesday, May 1, Continued

It's 9:00 p.m. Frank Valiante sits behind his giant mahogany desk. He's a big man, going 220 in the summer, 240 in the winter. Thick silver hair, black-framed glasses. He watches his second son, Angelo—a short, thin bundle of nerves—pace the floor of his office, hands waving in the air. Frank can't help thinking how different the boy is from his older brother. Antonio was a thinker, a planner. The apple that didn't fall far from the tree.

The war with Nunzio and his crew is now a foregone conclusion. But it didn't have to be that way. Sure, with Antonio moving in on Nunzio's territory, there was inevitably going to be a problem between them. But the smart thing for Nunzio to have done would've been to approach him personally and try to work something out, divide things up. And Nunzio's smart. Everyone knows that. All business.

But this wasn't business. This was Nunzio's daughter. That's the only explanation for his killing Tony. And he'd have probably gotten away with it—as far as the law was concerned—if the cops hadn't shown up and caught him in the act.

Then why did Nunzio call him from the warehouse, say what he said? Why strike the deal—suggesting their children should be off-limits—if he was going to break the promise as soon as he made it?

None of it makes any sense. But it doesn't matter. Nunzio's a dead man. The only question is how soon Valiante will make that happen. For Angelo, it can't come soon enough.

"No more waiting," says Angelo. "It's been three weeks."

"I'm laying the plans."

"Tony would have hit back before he was even cold. He's rolling in his grave, Pop."

He casts the boy the look, the one that tells him to shut up. "Listen to me. I'm working on getting someone into the jail to take out Nunzio. But it's going to take some time, and it's got to be the right guy. Remember, Philly's still Nunzio's backyard. He's sure to have people inside that prison. We don't do this right, he'll get tipped off."

"What about his family? Starting with the daughter? I want her to die slow. She set Tony up, I'm sure of it."

Frank nods. It's as good an explanation as any. He has no idea how Tony came to be mixed up with Nunzio's daughter. What the hell was he thinking?

"The time comes, you can take care of her yourself."

"Damn right, I will. And that Jew bitch wife of his. I'll fuck them both before I gouge their eyes out and slit their throats."

"In the meantime," the older man says, "I want to start in on his crew. I'm going to take out as many of them as I can. Starting with his gorilla, Giacobetti. That'll send a message."

Angelo nods but doesn't seem quite as sure.

"And still no word from Sabatino and the others?" Valiante asks, referring to Antonio's driver and bodyguards.

"They gotta be dead."

"Or he turned them."

"No way. Tony handpicked those guys. Sabatino grew up with us."

"Then how do you explain the cops found no evidence of a struggle? They're as loyal as you say, there'd have been a fight."

"I don't know, Pop. I'm pulling my hair out." He stops pacing for a moment. "If Nunzio walks, I swear I'll go out of my mind."

"How could he walk? The cops caught him dead to rights."

"I heard some things about his lawyer."

"Like what?"

"Like he got some millionaire off for killing his girlfriend. The cops caught him in the act, too. But this lawyer, he put his own wife on the stand with some cock-and-bull story, and the case just went away."

"What do you mean it went away?"

"The DA dismissed the charges."

"Sounds like the fix was in."

"We can't let that happen with Nunzio."

"Get me more on the lawyer. He's that good, maybe we add him to our list."

"I got no problem with that."

"I gotta make some calls," he says, signaling it's time for Angelo to leave his office.

He watches his son turn to go, then shouts after him, "Hey! When you kill Nunzio's bitches, I want it on video. I'll smuggle it into the jail, get it in front of Nunzio. I want him to see how they die."

12

Thursday, May 2

Mick is in his office, buried to his shoulders in suppression motions. He'll spend all afternoon and most of the next day in hearings, trying to persuade wary judges to exclude clearly relevant and damning evidence gathered by police because it was taken in an unconstitutional manner. A criminal-defense attorney expends as much effort safeguarding procedural fairness—keeping the other side honest—as working to keep defendants from imprisonment. Indeed, many of his clients have committed the crimes they're charged with. Admittedly, seeking to exclude relevant evidence improperly secured by the police can cause substantive injustice. But the larger gain—protecting everyone's right to a fair trial—is, in Mick's eyes, worth the price.

Apart from his belief in constitutional protections, of course, his core duty is to battle for his clients regardless of their guilt or innocence. A particular client isn't entitled to win. But they do have the right to expect that their lawyer will fight like hell for them. So when the police browbeat a suspect to the point that he'll confess to anything, Mick files a motion to exclude the confession. When the police bust into someone's house without a proper warrant and find evidence of a crime, he runs to court waving the Fourteenth Amendment.

In the Nunzio case, he's filed a motion to exclude all the evidence the police found inside the warehouse: the knife, the blood, even the body. He'll lose, of course; the smashed doorframe and the woman sobbing created "exigent circumstances," justifying the cops' decision to enter the warehouse without a warrant. And once they were lawfully inside, anything in plain view was fair game for seizure and use at trial.

He leans back in his chair and considers Nunzio. He doesn't feel good about representing the crime lord. He's represented mob guys before and didn't have a problem with it. But there's something about Nunzio that isn't sitting well with him. He feels like he's getting played. Nunzio is clearly withholding critical information that he's not ready to trust Mick with. But what could be more important than his freedom?

"Uh, Mick?"

He looks up. Angie is standing in the doorway, an odd look on her face. She moves inside and closes the door.

"Susan's father is in the lobby. I told him she's not here, but he says he wants to talk to you."

"Where's Susan?"

"She called and said she had a doctor's appointment and might not be in. Should I tell him to leave?"

Mick sighs. "No, no. I'll talk with him. I just need a few minutes to finish something up."

Five minutes later, Mick walks into the lobby to meet Leonard Klein. The man is tall and blubbery, with watery blue eyes and loose jowls. His thinning white hair is fashioned into a ponytail. He's wearing tan pants with a pink button-down shirt. The pants are too baggy, the shirt too tight.

Mick extends his hand and receives a sweaty handshake with a quick release.

"Let's go into the conference room," Mick says. Then to Angie: "Would you mind bringing us some waters and coffee?"

"Please, no coffee for me," says Klein. "Though a spot of tea would be much appreciated."

Mick exchanges glances with Angie and escorts Susan's father to the conference room.

"So I understand you're back from England," Mick says.

"Possibly for good, I'm afraid. My wife, Ava, passed a few months ago, and it's been a terrible strain on me living in our home—all of the memories just kicking me in the balls from the time I wake up in the morning. You can't imagine how hard it is to lose one's spouse."

Like your wife did when you walked out on her and Susan?

"You have my deepest sympathies," Mick says.

"But apparently not my daughter's. She wasn't expected at the funeral, of course, but a card would have gone a long way."

"Is there something that *I* can help you with? Is that why you wanted to talk with me?"

"I suppose I was looking for some enlightenment as to why my daughter refuses to see me."

Mick doesn't answer.

"I mean, circumstance has accorded her a golden opportunity to reunite with her own father. You'd think she'd jump at the chance, instead of putting me off."

Mick stares.

"One would also expect that, as an attorney, she'd enjoy helping help me with the, uh, legal issues being stirred up by Ava's children. I can't tell you how disappointed Ava would be to learn they're contesting her will. We were together for how many years now? To hear them tell it, I'm little more than a gold digger. If they have their way, I'll be out on the street."

So he's looking for money.

Mick feels an overwhelming urge to smack Leonard Klein in the face.

"Maybe Susan's having a difficult time reconnecting with you because you've spent so little time together since . . ."

"Oh, go on and say it: since I left. I've no doubt she's been beating that dead horse for years. Just like her mother. That woman—she all but drove me out of the house with her constant harping about responsibilities and the need to bring home as much bacon as I possibly could, regardless of the cost to my own happiness. The constant pressure I was under, the injuries to my self-esteem, meant nothing to Candace."

Mick clenches his jaw, envisioning Susan as a young girl, crying and terrified as her father packed his bags and turned his back on her.

Angie brings in the beverage service. Susan's father wastes no time placing his tea bag into a cup and pouring his water. While his tea steeps, he helps himself to two or three of the madeleines—butter cakes—on the serving tray.

"One thing Ava told me when we first met," Klein says after he's washed the cakes down with his Earl Grey, "is that Americans live to work, while Europeans work to live. It's a rat race on this side of the pond. You can't deny it. Our side is more civilized."

Our side?

"Susan told me you were a dentist. In Scarsdale. A very successful dentist."

Leonard Klein rolls his eyes. "Well, I suppose it depends on how one defines success. I certainly made enough money. But I was miserable. With Ava, I was freed of the need to debase myself with drudgery; her family owns a department store."

Ah . . . freeloading all this time, then.

Mick begins to tap his thumb on the conference table.

"It's not like I didn't intend to reach out to Susan earlier. Many times, I thought of arranging a visit, or calling. But life does have a way of interceding, doesn't it? I'm sure you understand."

"I understand perfectly." He rises and waits for Susan's father to do the same, then leads him to the lobby.

"It was great to meet you. I'll tell Susan you stopped by. I'm sure she'll be happy to hear it."

Happy that she was somewhere else.

He opens the door, watches the man make his way down the hall.

"What do you think of him?" Angie says as he turns toward her.

"I don't need to spend any time thinking about him. He does enough thinking about himself for all of us."

13

Friday, May 3

Working at his computer, Mick notices the light for Susan's phone line illuminate, indicating that she's back in the office and is placing a call. She never made it in the day before, so he didn't have a chance to talk to her about her father. He waits until her phone line darkens, then walks to her office.

"Hey." He smiles. "Do you have a few minutes?" She waves him in, and he takes a seat across the desk from her.

"So I assume you heard your father showed up yesterday?"

She nods wearily. "He left a message on my cell afterward. And Angie told me all about it when I came in this morning. I'm sorry you had to endure him."

Mick's not sure what to say to that.

She leans back in her chair. "He's only here because he wants something from me. Money, for starters. And help fighting his wife's kids in the battle over her estate."

"Yeah, I kind of picked up on that."

They sit in silence until Susan says, "I was ten when he left. In fifth grade. I cried myself to sleep for weeks. I could hear my mother weeping in her own bedroom. Sometimes she'd call me in, and we'd cry together. It wasn't long, though, before she toughened up and realized I needed her to be strong for both of us. She hadn't worked in years, but she went out and found a job. Sold the big place in Scarsdale, found a nice little house for us to live in. Made new friends, built a new life.

"When I got older, I asked her how she did it, where she found the strength. She told me plenty of women get left by their husbands. Some fall apart. Others rebuild. 'It all comes down to how you see yourself,' she told me. She said she wasn't raised to be a victim, and she refused to act like one. She told me she didn't see herself that way, and she'd never let anyone else see her as a victim, either."

Susan pauses. He waits, watching her eyes take her somewhere else.

"And your relationship with your father, after he left?"

"I wrote him letters—once we found out his address. Someplace in England. An *estate*, my mother called it. His wife's parents' place at the time, before she inherited it."

"Did he write back?"

"A few times, the first year. Two or three sentences."

Mick nods.

"But I kept writing, once a week or so, then every month, until I was thirteen. I sent pictures, too, from our Polaroid."

"Phone calls?"

"Long distance to England was expensive, but my mother would call once a month and put me on the phone with him, or try to. Most of the time he wasn't there, according to his wife. I stopped calling when I turned thirteen."

"What happened when you became a teenager?"

"Boys happened. My interest in them."

"And it all went downhill from there?" He smiles.

She doesn't smile back.

After a while, she says, "I tried again in college, to connect with him. I'd write long letters and get back a hundred words. Short discussions of some cause he and his wife were involved in. Vague promises that he'd see me the next time he was in the States."

"Did he ever come back? Did you get to see him?"

"Once. A month after I'd graduated from Bryn Mawr, his wife was being given some award in Philadelphia for donating money to some cause. He tagged along, and I met the two of them for dinner at Le Bec-Fin."

"How'd that go?"

"I never met people who could talk so much without saying anything. It felt like they were blowing words into the air to fill up the space between us."

"Did you get much of a word in?"

"What would've been the point? All I knew about was me. And I wasn't who we were talking about."

Mick exhales. "Lovely." He looks away, then back at Susan. "So, where do things stand now?"

A bitter smile. "The shoe is on the other foot."

"Payback," he says.

She shakes her head slowly. "I wouldn't treat him this way if he came to me because he was in pain. Because he needed a shoulder to cry on . . . because he needed his daughter, after all."

But, of course, that's not why Leonard Klein was here.

"I'm going to tell Angie that if he shows up again, he's to be turned away."

"I'm good with that," says Mick. He pauses, then reaches over the desk and pats her hand. She doesn't remove it, but he can sense that she's not comfortable with the gesture.

They switch gears and talk a few minutes about matters of firm administration until Angie buzzes through, looking for Mick.

"Are you expecting a call from Martin Brenner? He says he's a US attorney, and he's calling about Jimmy Nunzio."

"I'll give you my office," Susan says, shooting up from her chair.

Mick motions for her to sit back down.

"No, I want you in on this. Angie, tell him I'm on a call, but I'll hang up and will be with him in a few minutes."

He turns to Susan. "Tell me about Martin Brenner. I assume you worked with him while you were with the US Attorney's Office, or knew people who did."

More than a few times since Susan came to the firm, Mick has squared up against her former colleagues; each time, he's gone to Susan for inside information on them. Within the bounds of ethics and respect, she's accommodated him. He expects the same of her now. To his surprise, though, Susan offers up only a few descriptors that would describe every AUSA he's ever known: ambitious, smart. A stickler.

"Come on," he says. "You have to give me more than that."

He watches her struggle for a few moments, then lets her off the hook.

"One word. The word that best describes him."

She stares. "One word? Relentless."

He studies her face but can't decipher the look she's giving him.

Hitting the button for the blinking line, he says, "Mick McFarland. You're on speaker because I have my partner with me. You know Susan Klein, I believe."

There's a pause at the other end; then Brenner's voice beams: "Susan! Hello! How are you?"

"Martin," Susan says, her voice flat. Then, a little livelier: "How are Kathy and the kids?"

"Great. Duke has started high school, and Tabitha just turned ten last week."

"I hate to cut short your stroll down memory lane," Mick says, giving Susan a wink, "but can we cut to the chase?"

Brenner answers immediately. "Nunzio. Have you approached him about working with the good guys? Help us bring down his bosses."

"I told you before—that would be an exercise in futility."

"What about his daughter? We could always bring her into it. Nunzio certainly understands that."

"Nunzio's family is never going to talk to you. And you can't compel them to."

"No, I can't. But a grand jury can subpoena her."

"You can't be serious."

"She'd have to testify in detail about what went down in that warehouse."

"What's your endgame here, Brenner? You know Nunzio will never turn, and you know his daughter would go to jail before she'd testify against her father. So what's this really about?" Mick pauses. "Is this just to get your name out there? Is it politics? Because if it is, starting something that goes nowhere will only make you look bad."

He turns to Susan for confirmation that Brenner's ambition is what's propelling him, but finds her staring at her desk.

"We could work together on this, Mick, Susan," Brenner says. "The three of us. Ride Nunzio like a Sherman tank, mow down the New York mob. What do you think, Susan? It'd be just like old times. Remember the Zelonis case, the congressman we nailed for shaking down all the local businessmen? The O'Brien case? We took down the whole family on that one."

Mick looks at Susan and sees she's not enjoying Brenner's glory-days routine.

"Hello?" Mick says loudly. "Aren't you forgetting something? Susan and I run a *defense* firm. We don't work with the government to prosecute people."

Mick hangs up and looks at Susan. "What a horse's ass."

She doesn't disagree.

"Do you think I got through to him?"

She stares at him. "Remember the word, Mick."

He stares back blankly.

"Relentless," she says.

As Mick leaves, he tells Susan that she should come to him if she wants to talk about her father. Later, in his own office, he thinks about Susan, and about Darlene Dowd, and, finally, about Christina Nunzio. Three daughters. One abandoned, one abused, one subjugated by her father. He leans forward and lifts the framed 3-by-5 photo of Gabby in her soccer uniform, taken the year before. He spends a long time looking at the picture.

"I don't get it," he says aloud. "I just don't get it."

14

Wednesday, May 8

Angelo Valiante sits in the driver's seat of the stolen Ford Taurus. The car is a bland gray and otherwise unremarkable, a vehicle that will not draw attention to itself. The plates have been switched out with another car's.

To Angelo's right is Dominic D'Ambrosio, Angelo's buddy since they were kids.

"Are you sure about this?" Dominic asks. "Broad daylight? A public place? No one does this shit anymore."

Angelo turns to him. "We're sending a message."

The car is parked next to the building at One Crescent Drive, just behind the sign for PNC Bank. The location is a perfect vantage point to spot people entering and leaving the next building down—a four-story glass building with a big Philadelphia 76ers sign on top. It's where Jimmy Nunzio keeps his headquarters.

Normally Angelo would have someone else drive. But he wants total control over this situation. Wants to be certain he'll be able to make a quick getaway.

"Let's get some fresh air in here," Angelo says, opening the sunroof to the mild seventy-two-degree air.

Overhead, the sky is a bright, cloudless blue. A beautiful morning in May.

The unmarked police car—a blue Chevy Impala—turns from South Broad onto Crescent and parks next to One Crescent Drive. From the passenger seat, Detective Scott Weaver sees a couple of cars sitting six or seven spaces down—a red Mini Cooper and, ahead of it, a gray sedan.

"I can't believe Nunzio keeps his office in the same building as the Sixers," Weaver says to the driver, Donny Donoghue. Weaver is the more senior of the two men, having almost twenty years under his belt compared to Donoghue's five years with the department.

Donoghue shrugs. "I can't believe we have to sit here hoping the giant's gonna show."

"Tredesco got a tip he's here," Weaver says with a shrug. "What you gonna do?"

"Wasted effort, you ask me," Donoghue says. "Johnny G.'s never going to talk. Assuming he's even in the country. I'll bet he's in Italy right now, splitting some chick down the middle with his giant Johnny G. horse cock."

Weaver looks at him and winces.

"What?" says Donoghue. "The guy's like six six. He's got to be proportional."

"How much time you spend thinking about this? You're starting to worry me."

"I have to take a piss. I'll go into this building. Be back in a minute."

"You just went before we left the station."

"I've been pounding coffee all morning."

"You have the bladder of an eighty-year-old. You keep this up, you're going to have to start wearing Depends."

Donoghue starts to open his door, but closes it as soon as he sees the two men leave the 76ers building. One is thin and wiry. The other is huge.

"Holy shit," Donoghue says. "It's him!"

Just as he says the words, the gray Taurus at the end of the block pulls out and crosses South Thirteenth Street, heading for Johnny G. and his companion.

"Whoa, something's going down," Weaver says. "Come on, let's go."

They both exit the Impala and stride toward the Taurus, which is now stopped in the middle of Crescent Drive. The front doors of the Taurus fly open. Two men rush out, guns drawn.

"Police!" Donoghue and Weaver shout simultaneously as they begin to run, drawing their service weapons.

One of the men from the Taurus, the passenger, turns and fires at them. The driver keeps moving toward Giacobetti and the other guy.

Weaver hears Donoghue grunt, turns to see the younger man go down.

"Motherfucker!" Weaver cries as he fires on the sedan's passenger, hitting the man in the shoulder and chest. The passenger goes down, but not before getting off a final shot, which strikes Weaver in the hip. As he falls, he sees Johnny Giacobetti slowly sink to his knees, blood spreading like red ink on his white shirt. A final shot from the driver of the Taurus causes a spray of blood from the side of Giacobetti's head. The giant falls over, his face contorted in rage.

Struggling to get to his feet, Weaver spots the Taurus's passenger writhing in pain on the ground. He turns to see the driver of the Taurus walking toward him. The driver fires his weapon, and Weaver's abdomen explodes in agony, sending him back to the ground. Lying with his legs spread, he presses his belly in a futile effort to quell the pain—and stanch the blood.

He sees the shadow on the ground just ahead of him and looks up to see the driver pointing his gun.

The last thing he sees is a brilliant flash of light. The sound of the gunpowder's ignition doesn't reach him in time for his brain to process it.

It's just before noon when Mick looks up to see Vaughn rushing into his office. Tommy, right behind him, lifts the remote off Mick's desk and turns on the large flat-screen TV hanging on the wall. Anchorman Jim is talking to a female beat reporter named Maggie, who is standing in a grassy area about a hundred feet from Crescent Drive. A dozen marked and unmarked police cars are parked around the four-story glass-fronted building that Mick recognizes as the home of the 76ers. Scores of uniformed cops and detectives swarm the area, which is cordoned off with yellow police tape.

"According to sources inside the police department," reports Maggie, "an eyewitness standing approximately where I am now saw two men leave the glass-fronted building across the street. At the same time, a pair of men exited a gray Ford Taurus and moved toward them, firing their weapons. Two Philadelphia police detectives exited their own vehicle, which, as you can see, is parked farther up Crescent Drive, and exchanged gunfire with the men from the Taurus. In the melee, both of the officers were killed, as was one of the men leaving the building. The occupants of the Ford Taurus, one of whom was injured, escaped in the car. They are currently at large and considered extremely dangerous."

Anchorman Jim asks, "Do we have the names of anyone involved at this point?" The anchor's eyes sparkle, telling Mick that he already knows the answer.

"In fact, Jim, one of the two men from the building, the one transported by ambulance, is believed to be Johnny Giacobetti, enforcer for reputed mob boss James Nunzio. This is leading some in the police department to speculate that the attack is in retaliation for Nunzio's alleged killing of rival mobster Antonio Valiante."

"Any word on Giacobetti's condition?"

"We know only that he suffered multiple gunshot wounds."

Mick lowers the volume and tells Vaughn to get down to the hospital. "Tell everyone that you're Giacobetti's lawyer. He's not to be interviewed by the police."

"Sounds like he's all shot up," Tommy interjects. "You think he's going to be able to talk?"

Mick glances at Vaughn, who says, "I spent plenty of time with that giant. Something tells me that bullets are more likely to piss him off than kill him." With that, he's out of the office.

Mick turns to his brother. "Care to bet how long it's going to take before I hear from Nunzio?"

Before Tommy can respond, Mick's cell phone rings. He picks it up.

"You heard?" Nunzio asks.

"I heard."

"Get down here."

Angelo Valiante races the Taurus up I-95 North. Bleeding under a blanket in the back seat, Dominic moans.

"Don't worry," Angelo shouts over his shoulder. "We'll be home before you know it. Get you all fixed up." He knows it's bullshit. Dominic is bleeding out. Probably won't make it another ten miles. If he could stay in the area and take his friend to a local hospital, things might turn out differently. But that can't happen, for obvious reasons.

Angelo's phone rings. He knows without looking who it is. He takes a deep breath, lifts the phone to his ear, and answers.

"What the *fuck*?"

"Pop—"

"Two cops, dead!"

"Listen, they—"

"The heat this'll bring down on us—"

"They came out of nowhere. They surprised us."

"You did this thing out in the *open*? You outta your mind?"

"It was a message—"

"It was a message, all right. That we're a bunch of meatheads who kill cops!"

"The cops don't know it was us."

"*Everybody* knows it was us."

"I got the giant, Pop. I saw his head explode."

"Really? 'Cause I'm hearing he's not dead. Which means you just grazed him."

"That's impossible."

"Just get back here. Make sure you're not pulled over."

"Pop, listen. I—"

But the line is already dead.

Frank Valiante slams down the phone.

"Unbelievable."

He sits back hard in his chair, presses the sides of his head with his palms. After a minute, he leans forward, reaches into his drawer, pulls out a bottle of Johnnie Walker Blue and a tumbler. He fills the glass, throws it back, fills it again, and takes a long swallow.

How in hell am I going to fix this mess?

His favorite son, dead. The younger son racing away from an unauthorized botched hit. And to top it all off, two dead cops. Things couldn't have gone worse. He looks at the phone, racking his brain for who to call and what to tell them when they pick up. But no answer comes.

Until the phone rings.

He looks at the number, and hope sneaks into his chest.

"I heard." The voice on the other end is a familiar one. As old as dirt, it belongs to a man he's known for more than two decades.

"Angelo." One word. All he needs to say to the old man.

"Amazing how two kids sired by the same parents, raised in the same house, can turn out so differently," the old man says.

"You got that right."

He asks after the old man's health.

"Still aboveground."

They laugh; then the old man gets to his reason for calling.

"I have some news, from inside the company. About your friend."

"Nunzio? What'd you hear?"

"He's placed an order."

"A plane? Safe passage for his family?"

"Vans."

This puzzles him. "Vans?"

"Very special vans. Armor-plated. Bulletproof glass. Six of them. Each with seating for nine and a driver."

Valiante sits back, looks up at the ceiling. "He's planning a raid."

"Don't know the details."

"Will you be able to find out?"

"Maybe. Maybe not. But sooner or later, I'll find out the delivery date for the vans. That should help."

"Soon as you hear anything, let me know."

"As always. And . . . as always . . ."

"I'll be glad to send your payment, my friend."

He and the old man go way back. For years, he'd heard rumors about a company that would move anything, anywhere, for a price. They'd even supply vehicles—cars, trucks, boats, even airplanes. He asked around about it and eventually found someone who knew someone. He made a call and arranged a get-together. That's when he first met the old man. From what he could gather, the old man was a mid-level player, basically someone who took requests and fielded them to higher-ups. Since that initial meeting, Valiante had called the guy a dozen times and made deals to move drugs, cash, and people—some living, some not. He'd developed a rapport with the old man, and they'd enjoyed more than a few raucous meals together. One thing he'd learned was that if the old man promised he could get something done, it got done.

Obviously, Jimmy Nunzio knew about the old man's company, too, and had made arrangements for the use of specialized vans. Lucky for Valiante, the old man got wind of it and gave him the heads-up.

He smiles. *Nunzio thinks he'll have the drop on me. But I'll be waiting for him, and be ready.*

◆ ◆ ◆

Nunzio follows the guard down the hallway leading to the interview room. The guard's name is Butch Doyle. Butch has a wife and two kids and a mortgage he's struggling to pay. He has some gambling debts, too, but those have been taken care of, thanks to Nunzio's intervention.

Butch opens the door for Nunzio. He enters and sits across from Mick McFarland.

"How are things with you and yours, counselor?"

"Not why I'm here."

He feels his blood start to chill in response to the lawyer's disrespectful tone, but he fights it, forces himself to smile.

"No small talk. Straight to business. I can respect that."

"What happened outside your offices today . . . ," the lawyer begins. "Does this mean the war's started?"

"That? That was just distant thunder."

"But the storm is coming."

The lawyer's response is more a statement than a question. McFarland's been around the block. He knows how the business works.

He nods.

The lawyer stares at him, then asks, "How did the cops know to be there?"

That had been her idea: tip off the police that Johnny G. was in the building. The cops would send a car, provide added security in case Valiante tried something. A lot of good it did. Still, not a bad idea.

"Not a clue," he says, seeing in McFarland's eyes that the lawyer doesn't believe him.

"I sent Vaughn Coburn to the hospital to act as Giacobetti's lawyer. I assume you approve."

"I approve."

"I assume you'll pay."

"Take it out of the retainer."

The door to the interview room opens, and Butch brings in a pitcher of water and some glasses.

The guard leaves, and Nunzio pours two glasses. "Water okay for you?" he asks the lawyer. "Or would you prefer a Coke?"

He sees a wary smile form on the lawyer's lips.

"What else do you have the guards doing for you?" McFarland asks.

"Just little favors. In return for the little favors I do for them. The way the world works, counselor. 'Mankind is governed by tokens.' Louis the Fourteenth."

"That's why you bought Coburn the Porsche? After the Amtrak case?"

That's exactly why he gave the kid the Carrera. He smiles, but the ice is returning to his veins. This time he doesn't fight it. He leans forward, lets the darkness seep into his eyes.

"You make sure Coburn keeps the cops away from Johnny. Make sure, too, that your man doesn't ask questions I'm not ready for Johnny to answer."

"That's between them. Attorney and client, just like you approved."

"I'm not fucking with you here, counselor. Giacobetti knows to keep his mouth shut. But he might be doped up from painkillers and forget his place. I don't want anyone from either side taking advantage of that. Understood?"

"I hear you. Now let's talk about this war that's coming. What can you tell me?"

That it's all being planned out to the smallest detail.

"I can't tell you anything. It's not me who's going to start it."

"You must have some idea what Valiante's likely to do."

He shrugs.

"And what about your own plans? I don't see you sitting around, waiting to be attacked."

That's exactly what we'll be doing.

He thinks of the vans. Another one of her ideas, along with the rest of the plan to take care of Valiante.

Brilliant. Frighteningly so.

"What else *can* I do? I can't just attack Valiante. The Commission would never authorize that."

Except that it already has. Valiante's boss, Vincent Savonna, has gotten too big and too smug. This will bring him down a peg, level the playing field. She was right about the war being inevitable. Right, too, that it was best sparked sooner than later.

"I want your assurance that my people won't be placed in harm's way," says McFarland.

Not all of them. But you, certainly.

"I'll do everything I can. But, like I said, I'm not the one who's going to launch it."

"If representing you is going to put my family in danger, I want to know it now."

"Not to worry." Nunzio leans back in the chair. "I've already impressed upon my people how important it is that your family be kept safe. So long as you are part of the team."

Mick starts his Mercedes and exits the prison parking lot, turns onto State Road. A few minutes later he's on I-95 South, processing his meeting with Jimmy Nutzo. *So long as you are part of the team.* The murderer's words make clear that any decision by him to withdraw as Nunzio's counsel would endanger his family. Nunzio does it every time they meet, one way or another—threatens his family. The delivery is subtle. The message is anything but.

When Mick returns to the office, Angie tells him the district attorney has filed the Information in the Nunzio case, the document setting forth the charges being brought against Nunzio. Under the rules, the Information has to be filed at least five days before the scheduled date for the formal arraignment, which must be no later than twenty-one days after the defendant is held for court at the preliminary hearing.

The primary reasons for an arraignment are to make sure the defendant is advised of the charges and to have his attorney enter an appearance. Because there is no need for either in Nunzio's case—Mick having entered his appearance and explained the charges to Nunzio—Mick has already filed a waiver of appearance at arraignment with the clerk. Arraignment is also the point at which the prosecution typically produces its discovery. While ADA Pagano could have waited the additional five days until the actual arraignment in order to produce his discovery, Mick's happy to learn from Angie that the prosecutor's case materials have already arrived.

"The medical examiner's report and photos are also here," Angie says. "I put it all in the big conference room. Tommy is in there now, looking through it."

He walks directly to the conference room, where he finds his brother leaning over the table, looking at the autopsy photos. The rest of the materials—the autopsy report, the 75-49 (the detective's report), the CSU report, the 75-48s (the incident reports prepared by the responding officers), and the property receipts for the items taken from Nunzio on his arrest have all been carefully arranged on the tabletop.

"Any surprises?" he asks.

Tommy hands him three of the autopsy photos. Two are close-ups of Valiante's wrists, the third of his ankles. Each of the photos shows deep lacerations.

"Plasticuffs," Tommy says, handing him a crime-scene photo showing two cut pairs of plastic handcuffs.

"He was bound?" This stuns Mick, who sees it as very bad news for Nunzio, because it would eliminate a self-defense argument or even a heat-of-the-moment scenario.

"And judging from the wounds, he was fighting like hell to break free," Tommy says.

"But he wasn't bound when the police arrived," Mick asks. "Was he?"

"Not according to the incident reports," Tommy answers. "Or the crime-scene photos." He hands Mick a couple of pictures showing Valiante's body lying facedown, the position the police left him in when they pulled him off the weeping Christina.

"So, was he bound when he was killed? Or had he been freed by then?"

"The ME couldn't tell."

Mick stares at the photos. "And why would Nunzio uncuff him?"

They look at each other.

"This case is getting crazier by the minute," says Tommy.

Mick leaves the office at 4:00. Ever since the Hanson case, he's made it a point to come home early whenever he can steal the chance. One of many changes that have saved his marriage and deepened his relationships with both Piper and Gabby. The reason he's going home now, though, is that his meeting with Nunzio has made him uneasy. He feels the need to see his wife and child, make sure they're safe.

Franklin is lying on the front lawn as Mick pulls the car past the house and into the driveway. As he puts the car into park, turns off the engine, and unbuckles the seat belt, he sees the big Bernese get to his feet and walk toward the car. He climbs out and pets the dog.

"Come on, boy," he says, leading Franklin around to the back patio, hoping to find Piper reading or working there, her usual habit on beautiful afternoons such as this one.

"Hey," she says, looking up at him, "I thought I heard your car."

"Where's Gabby?"

"Still at soccer practice."

"Oh, right," he says, remembering that he's home early.

Piper is sitting at the cast-iron table, which is strewn with transcripts and other papers.

"The Dowd case?" he asks.

She nods. "I spent the day reading the appellate briefs her attorney filed. Now I'm rereading the trial transcript."

"Any revelations?"

"Just confirmation of what we already know." She summarizes the overwhelming evidence offered against Darlene, including a strong motive as a result of her abuse at the hands of her father, and the lack of any alibi or other exculpatory evidence.

"So, on the evidence, the jury did the right thing. And so did the appellate courts."

"On the evidence *presented*, yes. But not based on what we know now."

"So what's the plan?"

"Before we file our petition for a new trial, I want more information on that poker game and the men involved. And I want—no, need—to talk with Lois Beal. Based on the letter Darlene's mother wrote and what the ex-cop Ott told me, I'm certain Lois is the key here. She may really know where the murder weapon is, after all."

"You better hurry up finding her," he says. "Your clock is running; you had sixty days to file your petition, starting from when Darlene Dowd received that letter from her mother."

Piper exhales, and he hears the stress in her voice. "I know. I have Tommy going up there tomorrow to track down as many of the poker players as he can, and to generally look around and turn over stones."

He nods, looks at his watch. "It's five o'clock exactly. You want some wine?"

"Absolutely."

He brings out two glasses of white—Sancerre for her, Chardonnay for him. They move from the table to the outdoor sofa. He loosens his tie, and Piper curls her legs up underneath her. They sip in silence. Then Piper looks at him.

"Something happened today, with Gabby," she says.

"What?"

"They were playing soccer in gym class. The teacher called and told me Gabby tripped one of the other girls."

"That's ridiculous," he says, feeling his face redden. "Gabby would never deliberately trip someone."

He watches Piper pause. "The teacher said it wasn't the first time."

"That's bullshit." He's sitting up now. "I want to talk to this teacher. Who is it? And what's the other girl's name?"

"Miss Kendrick is the teacher. The other girl is Vanessa Coolidge."

"Alice Kendrick? Well, there you have it. She's a kook. And we both know Vanessa and her parents. They're a bunch of whiners. Remember the stink they raised when Vanessa didn't get to play Mary in the Christmas play? I mean, it was a fourth-grade play, for crying out loud."

Piper opens her mouth to respond, but before she can say anything, he continues.

"This infuriates me. Doesn't it make you angry, too?"

"Well, of course. If they're wrong about it."

He stares at her. "If?"

"Let's talk to Gabby when she comes home from practice. See what she has to say."

"She'll say she didn't do it. Because she wouldn't."

"Why don't you fire up the grill?" she says, pivoting. "I bought some good-looking swordfish steaks. And I've been soaking one of those wood planks in the sink."

He takes her cue and drops the subject. "I'm gonna need this," he says, lifting his glass of wine.

He changes out of his suit, feeds Franklin, and preps the meal. In addition to the fish, he'll serve rice and Gabby's favorite salad—hearts of romaine with shredded cheddar, Caesar dressing, and raisins. Franklin plants himself in the kitchen the whole time, hoping Mick will drop something.

From the kitchen, he hears a car pull into the driveway. Two of Gabby's close friends are on the team; their parents and Piper take turns driving the girls home after practice. The front door opens and closes, and he hears Gabby's footsteps on the stairs. She'll change out of her uniform, do some homework, and come down when dinner's ready. What he wants is to go upstairs immediately and ask her what happened in gym class. But he knows that's a conversation Piper will want to be part of.

Mick has just set the dinner plates on the table and is turning to go back into the house to call upstairs for Gabby when she beats him to the punch by making her entrance.

"I made your salad," he tells Gabby.

"Fish *again*?" she says.

"Stop rolling your eyes," Piper says, eliciting another eye roll.

"How about some chicken with that sweet barbecue sauce? You never make that anymore."

"I made it a couple weeks ago," he says.

"Just eat," Piper says.

They chew for a few minutes; then Mick asks Gabby how school was. "And I don't want to hear it was boring," he adds.

"Then don't ask." She smiles at her own comeback.

"So, you played soccer in gym class?"

"Waste of time," she answers. "I'm, like, the only one who knows how to play. Half those girls are too fat to run. Or too lazy."

Mick wills himself to wait as Piper tries to tease the tale out of Gabby, although he'd prefer to ask her directly.

"How about Vanessa? She's pretty good, isn't she?" Piper asks.

"She tried to trip me," she says.

He glances at Piper, then back to Gabby.

"Trip you?"

"Vanessa doesn't know anything about soccer. All she does is try to get in my way when I dribble down the field. As if she could ever get the ball from me."

"So, what happened?" he asks.

"What happened is I had the ball and was almost at the net. She stuck her foot out to trip me. But she's so clumsy that she leaned back too far, lost her balance, and ended up on her fat butt!"

Gabby leans her head back and smiles wide, her mouth full.

Mick smiles back, then glances at Piper. *I told you so.*

15

Thursday, May 9

Tommy pulls his F-150 from the two-lane road onto the paved quarter-mile driveway dividing Elwood Stumpf's farm. The farm is a two-hundred-acre spread in Buchanan Township.

The wide driveway suits the bright-red barn, silo, and outbuildings and the white two-story farmhouse, which all appear to be immaculately maintained. The vast fields are dotted by scores of grazing black-and-white Holstein cattle.

"Looks like Elwood's done well for himself," Tommy says aloud.

He was given Stumpf's address by Melvin Ott, the retired copper Piper and Susan met with. Over the phone, at least, Ott seemed eager to help him track down the guys who'd been at the poker game with Lester Dowd the night he was killed. Ott didn't think that any of the other players who had accused Lester of cheating, including Chief Foster's late brother, Richie, could have been the person who actually killed Dowd.

"But you never know where the trail will lead," the ex-lawman had told Tommy.

Tommy parks the truck in front of the barn and gets out. As he'd expected, it only takes a minute before someone exits the barn to check him out.

"Looking for Elwood Stumpf," he tells the boy who emerges, who looks to be in his twenties, lanky but with giant hands and arms corded with steel-cable muscles—the type of guy someone might underestimate when picking a fight.

The kid looks him up and down and asks, "About what?"

"Oh, this and that," he answers, seeing from the look on the kid's face that he's not happy with the answer.

"You don't want to tell me, just say so."

"Just did," Tommy says, surprised at how quickly he slips into the old tough-guy role, the one that served him well in prison—and helped to get him there in the first place.

The kid turns, squaring off.

Tommy raises his hand. "I didn't mean to give offense."

The kid tells Tommy to wait where he is and walks back in the barn. A few minutes later, an older man exits. Elwood Stumpf looks to be in his early seventies, a big old boy, well over six feet and going at least 250, 275. He walks like a man used to having others get out of his way. Elwood's crew cut is white, and his hair is thin enough that Tommy can see his bright-red pate beneath it. He has dark hawk-like eyes sunk into a heavy face. Those eyes, Tommy can see, are taking his measure as he approaches.

Elwood Stumpf plants himself directly in front of Tommy. "State your name and your business."

"Tommy McFarland," he says, handing the man his card, which identifies him as an investigator with the law firm of McFarland and Klein.

The big man glances at the card. "And your business."

"My firm is looking into the Darlene Dowd case," he says, watching for a reaction. Stumpf's eyes show that it takes a minute for him to make the connection.

"The girl who killed her father."

"Maybe not," Tommy says.

"How you figure? The police caught her dead to rights. A jury convicted her."

"Juries don't always get it right."

"Sure, just ask anyone in prison."

Tommy holds back a smile. "I heard the night Lester Dowd was killed, he was at one of your poker games. Won a lot of money and got himself accused of cheating."

"Accused don't mean he did it."

"Not saying otherwise. But if someone thought he cheated, they might just get angry enough to do something about it."

Elwood tilts his head. "Like beat a man to death with a hammer?"

"Was it for sure a hammer? I thought the police never found the murder weapon."

"Now, how would I know something like that?" Elwood answers, taking a half step forward.

Tommy takes a half step back, puts up his hand, apologizes. "I'm not looking for trouble."

"A dog not diggin' for wasps sometimes finds 'em anyhow."

This time, Tommy can't help smiling. He appreciates the man's toughness. Elwood Stumpf must've been a fearsome sight in his youth, and he's not a man to fool with now. He reminds Tommy of some of the hard cases he knew in prison.

"Look, I think we got off on the wrong foot here, and that's my fault. It's just that we have a client who's rotting in prison for something she probably didn't do, however much her father deserved it."

Stumpf stops his advance, but his body language doesn't change. "I know what Lester done to the girl. Most others from around here do, too, and most everyone would agree with you that Lester Dowd had it coming. That doesn't mean we want some Philadelphia law firm coming up here and digging into our business."

Tommy nods that he gets it. "Not trying to make your business into our business. But if someone other than Darlene Dowd killed her father, then that person, not her, needs to pay for it. She way overpaid for her old man already."

Elwood casts him a hard look. "What exactly do you want to know?"

"Just the names of the men playing poker the night Lester Dowd was killed."

Another hard look.

"We heard the chief's brother, Richie, was there. Lester, too, of course. Any others that you can remember?"

"That was fifteen years ago, and I was having those poker nights every other week. Hard to separate one time from the next."

"Did you give their names to Chief Foster back then?"

Elwood looks confused. Tommy suddenly knows for certain that Sonny Foster never questioned anyone about the game, despite having told Ott that he had.

"I see," Tommy says.

"Do you?"

Tommy looks away, then looks back at Elwood.

"I'm wasting my time here, aren't I?"

The big man smiles. "Depends. You want to learn something about cows, I'll talk your ear off. Come inside the barn. I'll show you how I'm using recycled newspaper for bedding. Keeps the cows warmer than straw. It also decomposes faster than straw. And no need to worry about the ink; most of your magazines and newspapers these days use soy-based ink, which is completely safe for the cows."

Tommy raises his eyebrows. "You're quite the innovator."

Elwood Stumpf's face turns to stone. "I'm going to go into my barn now. When I turn my back, that's the last time I expect to see you."

Driving away, Tommy dials Mel Ott's phone number. Ott had promised to look into who might've been at the poker game that night.

"I struck out with Elwood," he says.

"Didn't I say you would?" Ott says. "He's rough timber, that one."

"Have you come up with anyone?"

"I made a few calls. The only one who admitted to being there that night is Tim Powell. He's a real estate agent, works for RE/MAX."

"I passed a RE/MAX going out to Stumpf's farm. That the one?"

"That's it."

"I think I'll pay Tim a visit."

Tommy hangs up and wonders why no one wants to own up to having been out at Elwood Stumpf's place. Nothing wrong with a bunch of guys playing a little poker every now and then. *Is* there?

The RE/MAX office, housed in a three-story redbrick house, looks to Tommy like any other small-town real estate office. A clutter of desks and chairs, copy machines, filing cabinets topped with real and faux plants, and real estate signs, all sitting on low-grade industrial carpeting over creaky wood flooring.

As soon as he walks in, two agents rise to meet him. The one closest to the door gets to him first. The second one, farther back, sits down with a sour look on his face.

"I'm looking for Tim Powell," Tommy says, shaking the man's hand, which goes limp at the mention of the name.

At the same time, the agent in the back stands and approaches him, a broad smile on his face.

"Tim Powell," he says, extending his hand. He's a pear-shaped man, bony shoulders over wide hips. His hair, though still blond, is receding in front. Tommy can tell he'll be bald down the middle in another ten years.

Powell leads Tommy back to his desk, clears off a plastic guest chair, and gestures for Tommy to sit.

"So, you looking to rent or buy?"

"Neither," Tommy says. "Mel Ott told me he talked to you earlier, about the poker game at Elwood Stumpf's place the night Lester Dowd was killed."

The sour look returns to Tim's face. "He didn't say someone was going to come asking about it."

"Can you remember anyone else who was there besides you, Lester, and Richie Foster?"

The agent leans back and rubs the side of his face. "Man, that was a long time ago. Fifteen years."

"So, you'd have been what, twenty-five, thirty?" Tommy studies the photos on Tim's desk. "Looks like you have two boys in high school. Fifteen years ago, they would have been toddlers, right?"

Tommy sees the agent squirm in his seat and realizes he's hit a nerve. But why? He glances at the desk again, sees a picture of Powell and his wife taken when they were both younger.

And it hits him.

"It's funny," Tommy says. "I went up to Elwood's place just an hour ago and asked about that night and who was out at his farm. He wouldn't give up a single name. Mel Ott called around and had no more luck than I did. No one wants to remember the game. And I'm thinking, why not? What's the big deal with some good ol' boys getting together to throw down a few cards?"

He stops and watches Tim Powell struggle to keep his composure.

"And you know what? I'm thinking maybe it wasn't just poker going on at old Elwood's place every other week. Maybe it wasn't just cards that were getting thrown down. Maybe Elwood, smart businessman that he is, offered up other entertainment as well."

The agent leans forward and, half whispering, says, "You want to keep it down?"

Bingo.

Tommy leans forward and quietly asks, "How many women did old Woody bring in for those games? How many men paid for them?"

Powell leans across the desk even farther. "Come on, this is my place of business. I can't be talking about this here."

"I'd be glad to stop by your house."

Tim Powell sighs and speaks in a near whisper. "All right. Look, it was just a few girls, three or four. Woody would have them brought in from that strip club in Allentown. They'd walk around with no tops on, maybe give out a blow job here or there, if someone paid for it. That's all."

"That's all." Tommy repeats the words. "So why the secrecy?"

"You serious? We got small-town values 'round here. We—"

Tommy raises a hand, and Powell stops. "I can keep my mouth shut," Tommy says. "Just tell me who else was there."

Powell shakes his head. "I didn't even know most of those guys. A lot of them were older, in their fifties at the time. Elwood's friends. They were the regulars."

Tommy gives him a hard look.

Powell closes his eyes, takes a deep breath. "The only two I knew were Buck Forney and Dave Hillman, the mayor. Well, he wasn't the mayor then, but he is now."

"Forney. That name sounds familiar."

"Forney Chrysler/Dodge. You probably saw signs coming up here. He has them on all the major roads. As for the guys my age, you're right that Richie was there, Richie Foster. So was Dale Forney—Buck's his father. Dale was a couple of years behind me in high school . . . No, wait, that's wrong. Dale wasn't there that night, but he usually showed up."

"Who accused Lester Dowd of cheating?"

"That was Buck Forney and Dave Hillman and a couple of the other old guys. And Richie, too. Yeah. In fact, I think he was the loudest of the ones that got upset at Lester."

"Just how pissed off was Richie Foster? Did he seem angry enough to want to hurt Lester? Did any of the others?"

At this, Powell looks taken aback. "Are you serious? Is that where you're headed with this?"

"Not sure where I'm headed yet."

Powell leans forward again. "Like I said, I wasn't friends with the older men at that table. So I can't vouch for any them. As for Richie, he was a lot of things, and he did blow his top from time to time, but that guy wouldn't hurt a bug. He didn't have it in him."

"What's *it*?"

"Come on, you know what I mean. Richie had zero killer instinct. He'd have spent his life sitting around smoking dope and counting butterflies if he had the chance."

Tommy chews on what Powell's told him. "You say Buck's son, Dale, *wasn't* there that night, but he often did attend? What's Dale Forney like?"

"Well . . . he wasn't quite the stoner Richie was, but had about as much drive. If his old man didn't own that dealership, Dale probably would've ended up serving mocha lattes at Starbucks."

"Dale works at the dealership?"

"Since high school. That's how he came to know Darlene."

Tommy sits up. "Wait. What do you mean, he knew her?"

"They dated. He didn't tell the old man, of course. He'd have gotten no end of shit about screwing around with another employee. Not that Buck Forney didn't do the same thing himself every chance he got."

Twenty minutes later, Tommy parks his truck outside the showroom at Forney Chrysler/Dodge. The dealership is a good-size operation, twenty or more acres packed with vehicles grouped by model: Chrysler 200s, Jeep Wranglers, Dodge Darts, and lots and lots of Dodge Ram pickup trucks. The showroom building is a glass-and-steel structure that looks brand-new. Tommy walks inside, hurries to the service desk before any of the salesmen can approach him. He asks to see Buck Forney, which causes the pretty receptionist to tilt her head. Being the big boss, Buck must not get called to the sales floor very often.

"Can I ask what this is in reference to?" she asks.

"Darlene Dowd."

Too young to know the name, she gets a puzzled look on her face.

"He'll know," he says.

She tells him to take a seat, and he watches her speak into the phone, her hand over the receiver so he can't hear what she's saying.

A few minutes later, a tall man with broad shoulders shows up. He has thick hair, dyed red-turning-to-orange, and a mouth blazing with brilliant-white caps. Like Elwood Stumpf, he appears to be in his seventies, and he walks with the confidence of a self-made man.

"Impressive dealership," Tommy says.

"Let's go upstairs, to my office," Buck Forney says. He leads Tommy down a hallway to an elevator, which takes them to the second floor. Buck's office is spacious and well appointed. The walls are paneled with built-in bookshelves holding silver-and-crystal dealership awards. The ceiling is drywall with recessed lighting. Buck's leather-topped desk is large and ornate. Overly so, to Tommy's eye.

Buck walks behind the desk and motions for Tommy to take one of the visitor chairs.

"Darlene Dowd," Buck says. "Sweet girl. Tragic case."

Tommy waits for Forney to offer more. When he doesn't, Tommy explains the law firm's involvement with Darlene and his own role as investigator looking for leads that might help prove Darlene's innocence.

"But she wasn't innocent," Buck says. "That's why she was convicted. Why she lost her appeals."

"New evidence has come to light," Tommy says, studying Forney's face for a reaction. Something does pass across the older man's eyes, but it moves too fast for Tommy to read it. "There was a witness who saw Darlene walking toward her house that morning, no blood on her, *after* the time when her father was shown to have been murdered."

"I sat in on some of the trial, and I don't remember any such witness."

"Because she was scared away from testifying."

Tommy pauses and waits for Buck Forney to ask the obvious questions: Who was the witness, and who scared them off? But he doesn't ask. So either the older man knows or he doesn't care.

"Did you know Lois Beal?" Tommy asks.

Buck sneers. "Peacenik. Her and her husband both. Renters who showed up out of nowhere and tried to fit in. Never quite made it."

"What's your take on Sonny Foster?"

"Good man. Damn good man."

Meaning: My good friend. My damn good friend. Like Elwood Stumpf?

"How well did you know Elwood Stumpf, at the time?"

Forney's eyes darken. "What's he have to do with Darlene Dowd?"

"He ran the poker game that Lester Dowd was at the night he was murdered. Lester; the chief's brother, Richie; and if I'm not mistaken, Dave Hillman, who's now mayor, were there. And you."

Buck Forney clenches his jaw. "Lots of guys went to those card games."

"Yes, but it was only a few of them who called Lester on cheating. As far as you know, was he cheating that night?"

"He was. And we were right to call him on it."

"Did it come to blows?"

"Not even close."

"Got bad enough that Elwood himself had to come to your table, calm things down, though."

"Woody overreacted."

"He doesn't seem to me like the type of man to overreact."

"You talked to him?" Forney asks.

"Right before I came here."

Tommy sits back, watches the wheels turn in Buck Forney's head as he tries to figure out whether it was Elwood who ratted him out as one of the guys who got in Lester Dowd's face that night.

"So, where was Dale that night?" Tommy asks. "I'm told he was one for the card games, but he didn't show that time."

This rattles Buck Forney—no mistaking the look on his face. Tommy sees it and gives him no time to gather himself before pressing forward.

"Maybe he was with Darlene. They were dating, least that's what I hear."

Buck leans forward, his face red, temples throbbing. "I don't know where you're getting your information, but you've been fed a line of—"

"Dale *wasn't* seeing Darlene?"

"That was just a rumor that went around after Lester Dowd was killed. I asked Dale myself if it was true, and he said it wasn't."

"I'd like to ask him myself," Tommy says.

"Well, he's not here. He's on vacation this week."

"You have his cell number? I can give him a—"

"Look, I don't know what you're up to, trying to get that murderer out of jail. But you're not dragging me or my family into it. We run a business here, and we depend on the goodwill of our community. You do anything to damage our reputation, and I'll have my own lawyers, my *New York* lawyers, hit you so hard you'll wish you'd have stayed in Philadelphia."

As soon as he pulls out of the dealership, Tommy is on the phone to Angie back at the office. He explains the situation, then tells her to call Forney Chrysler/Dodge and ask for Dale Forney.

"If they say he's on vacation, say you decided to buy both cars you looked at, but you need to talk to him right away. Ask for his cell number."

He hangs up and waits. Angie is back on the line in five minutes with the number. He thanks her, hangs up, and dials. Dale Forney answers on the third ring.

"Dale. My name is—"

"I know who you are. I saw the 215 area code for Philadelphia, and I just met with my dad."

"Ah. So you're at the dealership, after all. Not on vacation."

"I'm not going to talk to you, so don't waste your time coming back."

"I wasn't planning on going back to the dealership. I was thinking more along the lines of going to your house. Talking to your wife about your relationship with Darlene Dowd."

Nothing on the other end. Then Tommy hears a sigh—the sound of resignation.

"I don't want to stir up trouble for you," Tommy says. "But we need to meet. If you can think of a place we can get together in the next half hour or so, I'll be there."

Dale Forney suggests the East Penn Diner in Emmaus, but says he doesn't want to meet until after work. "If I leave now, my old man will get suspicious."

"He watches you that close?"

"He watches everyone that close."

They arrange to meet at the diner at 5:30, an hour later. Tommy makes his way there and pulls into the parking lot. He leaves the truck and walks into the diner, taking a booth at the back. He's hungry and decides to have something to eat. The waitress tells him the chicken potpie is good, so he puts in an order. He catches the waitress taking in his size, glancing at the prison tats on his neck, trying to figure out whether he's trouble. Maybe hoping he is. She's good-looking, tall, and shapely, with thick brown hair that's pinned up. He decides to have some fun with her.

"What time you get off work?" he says.

"About ten minutes before my husband picks me up."

He smiles. "I don't see a ring."

"He's cheap," she says, and they both laugh.

"If I was married to a good-looking woman like you, you'd have at least two carats on your hand."

"Says the man who pulls up in an old F-150."

He nods with a smile, conceding the point.

She turns and walks away with his order, but glances over her shoulder and smiles, wiggles her tush a little more prominently than when she first came to his table.

Dale Forney shows up at 5:30, sharp. Tommy knows it's him because he Googled the man while waiting for his food. Dale's a little shorter than his father but has the old man's broad shoulders. Unlike Buck, his hair is still red, though it's starting to fade to gray. The biggest difference between father and son is that Dale doesn't carry himself with the same confidence. That fits the son's reputation, as told by Powell.

Tommy waves to Dale, who walks to the booth and slides in across the table.

"Thanks for meeting me."

"As if I had a choice, with you threatening to go to my wife about me and Darlene."

"Sorry about that. I don't like to be a hard-ass, but sometimes my job requires it."

"And what exactly is your job? To barge into people's lives, open doors that were closed a long time ago and should stay that way?"

He nods. "In some cases, yeah. That's exactly what I do."

"Well, it's not fair."

Tommy studies Dale for a moment, decides not to beat around the bush.

"Were you with her that night?"

His eyes widen. "Is that what she told you?"

Tommy opens his hands.

"Well, she's a liar if that's what she said."

"You were dating her."

"We went out exactly two times. It went nowhere."

"Did she tell you about her father? What he was doing to her?"

"No. But . . ."

Tommy leans in. "But what?"

"The girl had problems."

"Care to explain?"

Dale sits back. "Why are you asking *me* this? My dad said your law firm represents her. So you should already know."

Dale has figured out that Tommy's asking his questions because Darlene hasn't told her lawyers about anything that happened between them. Tommy decides to switch directions. "Tell me about Elwood's poker games. I spoke to Tim Powell, and I already know about the girls."

"Boy, you sure get around, talking to them all."

"Tell me about the card games."

Dale closes his eyes, rubs his mouth with his hand. "I hated poker nights. The old-timers chewing tobacco, getting drunk. Taking the girls out back to have their dicks sucked. And that smelly old barn. Nothing like that nice dairy barn Elwood has now."

"Seems Mr. Stumpf has come up in the world."

"Way up. His farm was a dump when his father left it to him. Literally. Elwood's old man couldn't farm for shit. Finally faced up to it and decided to let people pay him to dump their old cars and farm equipment—hell, anything—on his land. When he died, the county forced Elwood to clean it up, said he had to either farm it or sell it. He found a way to pay the mortgage doing neither."

"The poker games?"

"It was small potatoes the first few years. That's what my dad told me. But Elwood started bringing in the girls and the booze, and more players started showing up."

"Including guys like your dad and the current mayor. Men with money."

Dale laughs. "Men with money, sure. But not my dad, or that shit-head Dave Hillman. Neither one of them had anything back then. But they were hungry, like Elwood. Them and some others. They all started working together to help each other out. My family's been here for a hundred years, and my dad used his connections to drum up business for Elwood. He returned the favor by lending my dad seed money to buy an old gas station, which he turned into a used-car lot."

Tommy sits back and takes it all in. Dale Forney, it turns out, is holding a lot of stuff inside, probably has been for years. And now he's like a balloon with a hole poked in it.

"My dad got bigger. Elwood got bigger, too. About five years after Darlene's father was killed, Elwood brought in dealers and roulette wheels, and a lot of the people who showed up weren't playing against each other anymore—they were betting against the house. And the house always wins."

"Where'd he get the money to expand like that?"

"No idea. I asked my dad once, but all he said was that Elwood had an outside investor."

"So old Woody was pretty much running a casino."

"That's exactly what he was doing, right up until he had enough money to buy cows and build that big new barn to put them in. And . . ."

Dale catches himself and stops cold.

"And?"

"And nothing. I've said too much already."

"Getting back to Darlene Dowd, I—"

"No! Not getting back to Darlene. There's nothing to get back to." Dale slides out of the booth and stands to leave. The anger gone from his voice, he says, "I've given you all I have. Please tell me you're not going to come to my house."

Tommy shakes his head. "I won't. Just tell me one thing more. Do you think Darlene did it?"

Dale pauses for a long moment and seems to look inward. "Would you blame her?"

Tommy watches Dale walk away, seeing him as a puppy still on his old man's leash—and chafing under the collar.

He doesn't notice the waitress walk up from behind him.

"That didn't look like it went very well," she says.

"Didn't expect it to."

She smiles. "Well, maybe your evening will take a turn for the better. Seven o'clock."

He furrows his brow.

"When I get off," she says.

"Ah. And what about your husband?"

"He's a guest of the state right now," she says.

He feels his face change and sees that she's noticing.

"I say something wrong?" she says.

"I knew some guys when I was inside. Spent their time chewing their hearts, worried their old lady was stepping out while they were locked up. I felt bad for them."

"Wow. A con with a conscience."

"I guess you don't get turned down very often," he says, noting the surprise on her face.

"I'm usually not the one doing the asking." She slides in the booth across from him. "So tell me how you ended up in prison. You get blamed for something you didn't do?"

"No. I deserved it."

And a whole lot more. For some things, a man can't pay enough.

He watches her study him, trying to peer behind his mask.

"Well, if you change your mind, you know where I work."

He grabs the check, and they stand at the same time.

"Just get me a hall pass from your husband," he says.

"Not likely."

"No, I suppose not."

They linger for a moment, until he turns away.

A mile down the road, he calls Mel Ott, shares what Dale Forney told him about how big Elwood Stumpf's gambling adventure became.

"I knew there were card games at his barn. But I was never let in on the details," Ott says. "I certainly was never invited to attend. I'd just moved to the area the year before the Dowd murder, so I was the farthest thing from homegrown around here. Even after I'd been here for years, people still saw me as an outsider. They weren't mean about it, or even standoffish. I was just different from them."

Tommy glances in his rearview mirror and sees two pickups moving up behind him, fast.

"Sorry, I have to hang up," he tells Ott.

"Call coming in?"

"No. But I've a feeling someone's about to send me a message."

The two trucks, both Ram 1500s, one blue and one red, close in fast. He presses hard on the gas, creates some distance, but not for long. In a few moments, the blue truck is on his ass, and the red one pulls up next to him, on his driver's side. He glances over. He's not surprised to see the kid he took for Elwood Stumpf's grandson.

The kid lowers his passenger-side window, shouts for Tommy to pull over. Tommy responds by slamming his brakes, which causes the driver of the blue Ram to veer hard to avoid rear-ending him. In his rearview, Tommy sees the driver struggling to maintain control of his truck. He runs off the road and crashes into a ditch.

He glances at the grandkid, who has slowed and fallen back beside him. The boy's face is beet red, his eyes on fire. Again, he signals Tommy to pull over.

Tommy shakes his head, turns the wheel, and slows again, thinking, *You don't want this, kid.*

When both trucks are stopped on the berm, Tommy waits for the kid to open his door, then leaves his own truck at the same time.

"Let me guess," he says. "You and your friend are supposed to send me a message. Mind my own business."

"Something like that." The kid's smile tells Tommy he's probably the type who enjoys kicking dogs.

"Okay. Well, I hear you loud and clear," Tommy says in a bored voice. "So, you can be on your way, report back to old Elwood that you did your job."

The kid holds out his hands, knuckles up. "See these? Not a mark on 'em. Thing is, I go back with my fists looking like this, my granddaddy's gonna know I didn't send no message at all."

"I'm really not in the mood—"

Before he can finish the sentence, the kid fires his right fist, which lands hard on Tommy's face. He steps back, shakes his head to clear it, thinking, *Not bad. I was right about this kid.*

He raises his fists, waits for the next attack. It comes quickly, but this time he ducks out of the way and comes up with a right cross that sends the kid back two steps.

The kid feels his nose, confirms it's broken, and starts in again. Tommy takes a glancing blow to the head but pays the kid back with rabbit punches to the face and a left-handed battering ram to the solar plexus that doubles the boy over. He steps up to the kid and finishes him off with a descending blow to the head.

"When you tell your granddaddy that you delivered your message," he says, "tell him all those black-and-blue marks are my signed return receipt."

He walks back to the truck and climbs in. He looks at his face in the rearview, sees the skin under his left eye already starting to darken.

"Man, I'm getting too old for this shit."

He puts the truck in gear and drives off.

16

Friday, May 10

Mick glances at Piper in the passenger seat.

"I don't know what you're getting so upset about," she says. "Miss Kendrick simply told me what she saw and what she was told by the other kids."

A glance in the mirror tells him that his face has the look it gets when he's angry: pursed lips, flared nostrils, flat eyes.

Piper persuaded him that she alone should meet Gabby's gym teacher, Sharon Kendrick, in hopes of getting to the bottom of what happened with their daughter on the soccer field. She had a sit-down yesterday with the teacher, who was pleasant and reasonable and had no apparent agenda against Gabby or in favor of the other girl, Vanessa. When Mick got home from work, Piper said Sharon had told her the same thing in person as she had over the phone the day before: that Gabby tripped Vanessa Coolidge.

Mick's refusal to accept the teacher's story had carried over into this morning, along with his anger.

"So Sharon took the side of the girl who said Gabby tripped her when, in fact, it was the other way around."

"But that's the question: Who tripped whom?"

"It's not even a question for me. Gabby told us what happened. I don't care what Sharon Kendrick thinks."

She sighs, clearly unable to understand why he's having such a hard time with this. "It's not a big deal. Even if Gabby did trip her. Kids do stuff like that sometimes."

"Gabby's a good girl. Not the kind of who'd deliberately try to hurt someone else."

"Mick, please—"

"I don't want to talk about this anymore. We're just going to have to agree to disagree."

"Look, all I'm saying . . . Oh, never mind."

They ride the rest of the way to the office in silence.

"Any word from Giacobetti?" Mick asks. He and Vaughn are sitting across from each other at Mick's desk. In the shootout at the Naval Yard two days earlier, Nunzio's enforcer suffered a gunshot wound to the chest that just missed his heart, as well as an oblique wound to the side of his head that left him severely concussed. He was admitted to the trauma unit at Presbyterian Hospital and remained there until he checked himself out after just two days, against medical advice. The first thirty-six hours were touchy—heavily dosed on morphine, Giacobetti passed in and out of consciousness, talking and mumbling whenever he was half-awake. Much as Nunzio had feared. Fortunately, Vaughn Coburn and Erin Doyle took turns guarding his bedside until Giacobetti was off the morphine, recovering from the concussion, and in full control of his wits.

"Nothing since he left the hospital," Vaughn says. "He's already back underground."

"Good. I want him out of sight."

"You're worried the US attorney will subpoena him before a grand jury, make him testify?"

Mick nods. "I don't want Martin Brenner near him—at least not until Nunzio is ready to tell me where Giacobetti's going to fit in his endgame."

Mick sees Tommy standing in the doorway. He does a double take at Tommy's black eye but doesn't say anything, waiting to see if Tommy mentions it first. He doesn't, just enters and takes a seat.

"Has your source given you anything more on the prosecution?" Mick asks Tommy.

"Just that Pagano's chomping at the bit to bring Nunzio to trial, and he's worried that Frank Valiante's gonna get to Nunzio before Pagano gets his verdict."

"Taking Nunzio down would be a huge feather in Pagano's cap," Mick says.

"You thinking he's planning to make a run for the DA's job in four years if Devlin loses?" asks Tommy.

Devlin Walker, Mick's adversary in the Hanson case, is running against the incumbent. The race has been a bitter, hard-fought battle, so close that either man could take it. If Devlin wins, he'll likely hold the job for at least two terms. If he loses, there'll be an opening for another challenger to step up and take the crown.

"Absolutely." Mick thinks a minute. "Has your source told you how Pagano's going to handle the mysterious call Nunzio received, the one that caused him to go to the warehouse?"

"Anything they can't explain they'll call one of the great unanswered questions that don't matter and have nothing to do with Nunzio's guilt."

"For him it's an unanswered question. We'll call it a hole in the prosecution's case."

"We can argue that Nunzio was set up," Vaughn says. "That he was drawn to the warehouse by someone acting on Valiante's behalf."

"And things didn't turn out like Tony Valiante and his men thought they would. Yeah . . . ," Mick says.

"But if it was a trap," Tommy says, "why wouldn't Valiante have had his bodyguards there? To make sure things didn't go wrong."

"And on Nunzio's end," Vaughn asks, "why did he use a knife when he was carrying a gun?" He pauses. "And what's up with the plasticuffs? Why were they cut off?"

Mick nods. "There's no way to explain what went down that doesn't put Nunzio in prison for life. So *he'd* better try before we go to trial."

"What's he waiting for?" Tommy asks.

"Good question."

"Are you sure he's even going to give you his story?" Vaughn asks.

"Any other client would let *you* tell *him* what the story is," says Tommy.

"That's the rub in this case," Mick says. "Jimmy Nunzio's used to calling the shots."

"He's also used to not having his ass in the wringer," Tommy says. "But this is a whole different ball game."

Mick looks from Tommy to Vaughn. "I already told this to Piper, but I think there's something going on here that Nunzio isn't letting me see. Something he doesn't trust me with. Something big."

"Did I hear my name?" Piper asks, walking in.

"We're talking about Nunzio," Mick says.

"What's up?" she asks.

"Basically, nothing. We're in a holding pattern, for now." He turns to Tommy. "What did you learn up north?"

"That's what I need to know, too," Piper says.

Vaughn excuses himself, and Piper moves from behind Tommy to take a seat next to him, noticing his black eye.

"What happened to you?" she asks.

Tommy chuckles as he tells her about Elwood Stumpf's grandson, then leads into what he learned from Stumpf, Buck and Dale Forney, and Tim Powell. When Tommy gets to the part about Darlene and Dale, Mick sees Piper's eyes widen.

"This is the first I'm hearing about Darlene having a part-time job or a boyfriend," she says. "None of it was even mentioned in the trial transcripts."

"Something happened between those two—Dale and Darlene," Tommy says. "Dale said she didn't tell him about what her father was doing to her, but he said he knew Darlene had 'problems.'"

"What did he mean by that?"

"I don't know. He shut me down. Said we should ask her."

"That's exactly what I'm going to do," Piper says.

"Another road trip to Muncy," Mick says.

"Yep," she agrees.

"What about the mayor?" Mick asks. "You said the real estate agent told you he was at the poker games, too."

"I'm getting to that." Tommy tells them he didn't meet with the mayor but called him on the way back to Philadelphia.

"I dialed 411, got the number for the mayor's office. A guy answered the phone, asked me who was calling. When I told him, he said the mayor was out of the office on a fact-finding mission. Overseas."

"Seriously?" Piper says. "The mayor of Allentown, Pennsylvania, on a junket?"

"What I said. And he goes, 'Sure. He's meeting with Putin, learning how to hack the internet, interfere with elections.'" He stops, and they all look at him. "That's when I figured out what was up, and I say, 'It's you, isn't it?' He says, 'How can it be me? I just told you I was in Russia.' Then he hangs up."

Mick considers Tommy's story. "This isn't making sense to me. Elwood no longer has his card games. The whole 'casino' thing's over. The girls and the liquor are all in the past. So why would he feel threatened that you're snooping around, threatened enough to sic his goon on you? And why would Buck Forney care? Or the mayor?"

Tommy considers this. "Only one reason. They're up to something else now."

"Find out what."

◆ ◆ ◆

Max Pagano takes in the mobster's New York office. It's old-school: wood paneling, dark drapes and carpet, a giant mahogany desk. And the air is thick with stale cigar smoke. He's been waiting for ten minutes, two of the capo's thugs hovering behind him.

"So, Boston clobbered the Yankees last night," he says, to get a rise out of the goons.

"Fuck you."

He smiles to himself.

Another five minutes pass before Frank Valiante enters and takes his seat behind the desk. He takes his time lighting a cigar, takes a couple of deep drags, then seems to notice Pagano's presence.

Pagano leans forward. "The reason I'm here—"

The goon to his right cuffs him hard on the side of the head.

His hand flies to his ear and rubs it. "What the fuck!"

Another blow, this time to the left side.

He's boiling now, but manages to hold his tongue.

"That's not how these meetings begin," Valiante says. "The way it works is you start by saying, 'Thank you, Mr. Valiante, for agreeing to meet with me. Thank you for taking some time away from your very important schedule.' You sprinkle in a lot of 'sirs.' Then, when you're finished, I stare at you for a while, study you like the cockroach you are. Then I say, 'Tell me what you need.' Then, and only then, do you petition me."

Pagano glares. "You can't just hit a district attorney." Sensing another blow, he quickly adds, "Okay! Wait. I'll start again." He works

his way through the obligatory mantra, then waits as the mobster takes another few drags from his cigar.

"So," Frank Valiante says, "how can I help you?"

"It's about Nunzio. I want to take him to trial. I'm sure I'll get a guilty verdict. He'll spend the rest of his life in prison."

Valiante leans forward. "See, that's the thing. He's going to spend the rest of his life in prison no matter what you do. His *very short* life. I'm going to see to that."

"I know, I get it. That's really why I'm here. I just want you to wait a little while. Until after the trial. It's set for October, and—"

"That's five months away. I'm not giving that pig five more months of sunshine. He killed my son!"

Pagano came ready for this. "What if I can move it up?"

"How you gonna do that?"

"Get Nunzio and his lawyer to agree."

"Why would they do that?"

"Because Nunzio, overconfident bastard that he is, thinks he's gonna walk. The sooner he has his trial, the sooner he's out. In his mind, anyway."

"How do you know he *won't* walk?"

"Are you serious? He was caught ten feet from a blood-pumping corpse, holding the knife that killed him."

"Blood-pumping corpse? That's how you describe *my Tony*?" Valiante nods to the thug on the right, who cuffs Pagano again, on both sides of his head.

Pagano jumps out of his chair, furious, but the goons push him back down.

His head spinning, his ears hot with pain, he strains through the fog to hear Valiante's words.

"Listen to me very carefully, you Philly insect. I'm gonna do what I'm gonna do when I'm gonna do it. If you can squeeze in your trial before it happens, good for you. But I ain't waiting for some jury to hand down a piece of paper says 'guilty' on it."

Exactly one minute later, the goons deposit Pagano on the sidewalk next to his car. He slowly makes it to his feet and climbs in. He sits until the haze in his head clears, which takes . . .

He's not sure how long it takes.

Half an hour later, Pagano's on the turnpike headed south. He places a call to McFarland's office.

"Change your mind, Pagano?" McFarland says. "Looking for a plea?"

"Kiss my ass."

"Then what do you want?"

"How would your client feel about moving up his trial?"

There's a long pause at the other end. "How soon are you looking at?"

"This is May tenth. How about the middle of June?"

He hears McFarland laugh at the other end. Then he stops laughing. "You're serious?"

"As a kick in the nuts."

"You think Valiante's going to move on Nunzio sooner rather than later."

Pagano rubs the side of his head. "More than *think*. I was just with the motherfucker."

Another pause. "You met with Frank Valiante? You've got balls, I'll give you that."

"Goddamn basketballs, what they are. What's your answer?"

"I'll talk to him."

Pagano rubs his ear. "You'd better hurry."

17

Wednesday, May 15

It's just after 7:00 a.m. when Susan climbs into Piper's Range Rover. Susan took SEPTA from Center City to the station in Wayne, where Piper is now picking her up. They're headed for the women's prison in Muncy to see Darlene Dowd again.

Piper waits for Susan to buckle up, then hands her a small envelope. "Here," she says. "It's from Darlene."

Susan accepts the envelope, telling Piper she received a letter, too. "It's in my briefcase. I brought it for you to read once we get to the prison."

"She's pretty effusive in her thanks," Piper says as Susan removes the letter and begins to read.

"'This is the first time in years I've thought about the future . . . felt so hopeless for so long that all I could do was struggle through day by day . . . so glad God brought you and Susan into my life.'"

Piper listens to Susan read, taking note of the flatness in Susan's voice.

"It makes me feel good to bring hope to someone who's suffered through so much," Piper says.

She glances at Susan, sees her force a smile as she puts the letter away.

They drive for a while, Piper trying to engage Susan by repeating what she's shared about Dale Forney and everything else Tommy learned from his trip to the Lehigh Valley. Susan nods and makes the odd comment here and there, but Piper can tell her mind is elsewhere. She gives up for a while, asking Susan instead how things are with her father.

"The same," Susan answers. Nothing more. Then she pulls out her iPhone and begins scanning her emails.

Piper takes the hint and drives in silence until they reach the exit that takes them to I-80 West, where she pulls into a gas station to refuel and grab some coffee and snacks. When she comes back to the car, she finds Susan editing a legal brief. She hands a coffee to Susan, who glances up from the brief only long enough to accept the cup.

Fifteen minutes after they've started west, Susan's phone buzzes, the sound indicating she's received a text. Piper sees her glance at the screen and click it off. A minute later, another text comes in. Susan ignores it as she did the first. The phone rings, and Susan clicks it off. It rings again, and Piper feels Susan's stress level rise.

"Everything okay?" Piper asks.

"Fine. Just work."

Piper sees Susan shut off her phone. She wants to say something but bites her tongue.

Susan gets back to her brief, or pretends to. They drive along another ten minutes or so.

"Are you still seeing Armand?" Piper asks, referring to the Argentinian soccer player.

"We're done."

"Oh. Was it amicable?"

Piper glances to her right. Susan is staring at her.

"I don't mean to pry."

"He was an asshole."

Piper doesn't know how to respond to the acid in Susan's tone.

"They're all assholes," Susan says.

"What's the saying—you have to kiss a lot of frogs?"

"I'm not fourteen."

"Jeez. Shoot me for trying."

She hears Susan exhale. "I'm sorry, Piper. I just have a lot going on right now."

"Okay. But, you know, if you ever need to talk . . ."

"Thank you. But this is stuff I have to sort out myself."

Piper offers a sympathetic glance, then turns her eyes to the road and keeps them there. She's known Susan for eight years, but the woman is still a puzzle to her. As smart and gorgeous as she is, Susan seems to have a knack for finding the worst men. Piper's met a few of Susan's beaus—a couple of athletes, a successful businessman, even a race-car driver—all strong, all good-looking, and every one of them afflicted with an overabundance of self-involvement. The type of men chosen by a certain type of woman: the type who needs to fix something broken, or fill something lacking inside themselves. But Susan has never seemed that type.

Still, who can ever tell what's going on inside another person's head? A professor Piper had in college used to joke that everyone has two sides: the outside and the dark side. She saw her own dark side a few years back, learned what she was capable of when Jennifer Yamura was killed and David Hanson was tried for her murder. She learned what Mick was capable of, too. It still makes her shudder just to think of it. And it scares the hell out of her that Jimmy Nunzio seems to know the ins and outs of the Hanson case. That psychopath could destroy everything if he really looked into it, unearthed the crimes covered over by Mick's legal maneuvering. Mick says that's one of the reasons he's intent on learning as much as he can about the mobster; he might need something to hang over Nunzio's head.

How many secrets does a person end up hiding over a lifetime?

"You want me to move the trial date to *when*?" The Honorable Gene Braverman is a big man with thick dark hair and a five-o'clock shadow that typically makes its appearance just after breakfast. He's reputed to smoke five cigars a day, and his voice sounds like gravel.

Under normal circumstances, no defense attorney would agree to rushing the date of a murder trial, because they'd want as much time as possible to prepare and investigate. Mick ran Pagano's request by Nunzio, expecting the capo to reject being hurried to trial. But his client surprised him by agreeing—more than agreeing. He pushed for it.

Mick immediately pushed back, telling Nunzio that the cards were stacked against him, that his only hope was the sudden appearance of some sort of dramatic and favorable evidence, something no one could envision. Which is why it was better to delay the trial as long as possible. Nunzio simply shook his head and ordered Mick to ask the court to move up the date. Mick agreed only after Nunzio signed a written approval.

Consequently, Pagano and Mick broached the issue with Braverman, the homicide supervising judge.

"To June seventeenth, a little more than a month from now," Max Pagano responds.

The judge looks at Mick.

"The defense is in agreement," Mick says.

"What, you're both so confident you're going to win the race you can't wait to get your horse to the track?"

"We have all the evidence we need to move forward," Pagano says.

"The sooner the case is tried, the sooner Mr. Nunzio can rejoin his family and move forward with his life," Mick says.

Braverman looks from one to the other. "I want to see both of you in chambers. Ten minutes." He bangs the gavel and leaves the bench.

Mick glances at Pagano, then back into the gallery. The courtroom is unusually crowded for a motion hearing. Pagano must've leaked that something big was going to happen with the Nunzio case.

Ten minutes later, Mick is sitting next to Pagano in front of Braverman's desk. The judge's chambers are fitted out with modern office furniture and are bathed in bright light, thanks to two walls of floor-to-ceiling windows. To Mick, the space seems ill-suited to Braverman, who looks like he belongs in a dark, smoke-filled study.

"What's really going on here?"

Pagano leans forward. "It's like we said, Your Honor—"

"Cut the crap, Pagano. I smell gamesmanship."

Pagano leans back, shrugs.

"Let me guess: The DA is hungry for the conviction. He wants it to boost his poll numbers if you win, but he wants the verdict soon in case you lose, to give himself time to recover by November."

"We can't lose this case, Judge. Nutzo was caught with the knife in his hand."

"I know the facts." He looks to Mick. "Your turn."

"The DA's afraid Valiante's going to get to Nunzio before the trial."

"*Get* to him? You mean kill him in jail?"

Mick nods.

"I see. And you're afraid of the same thing, so you want the trial moved up to get your client out before that can happen?"

"Something like that," Mick says.

"I think you're both nuts. You've only had a month to build your case," he says to Pagano. "And"—turning to Mick—"without commenting on the merits, your client has about as much a chance of walking as a catfish."

"We don't see it that way, Your Honor," Mick says.

The judge looks from Mick to Pagano and nods. "All right. You two are so eager for your day in court, I'll advance the trial to June seventeenth. But hear me on this," he adds, leaning forward, "once I enter my order, that's it. I'm not changing the date again unless somebody dies. And there's only one somebody I'm talking about here. You understand me, Mr. Pagano? Mr. McFarland? Good. Let's go back to the courtroom, and I'll make this official."

Back on the bench, Judge Braverman rules on the motion, and the reporters all start tapping the new trial date into their iPhones. Mick isn't even out of the courtroom when his phone alerts him with the Philly.com news headline: RUSH TO JUDGMENT.

Mick waits for the crowd to clear, then walks into the elevator. Pagano, right behind him, waits for the doors to close. Then he turns to him.

"Oh, look. It's almost noon. My associate is down at the clerk's office, filing the notice that we'll be seeking the death penalty."

Mick steps back. "You son of a bitch."

Pagano smiles. "Nunzio *is* going to be killed in jail. But it won't be by a shiv in county lockup. It'll be upstate, by lethal injection."

The elevator doors open, and Mick hangs back until Pagano leaves. The last thing he wants is to be the one to tell Jimmy Nutzo that the state is planning on killing him.

Piper spots Darlene as soon as she and Susan enter the large visitors' room. Darlene stands, and Piper sees a light in her eyes that wasn't there the first time they met. Darlene walks toward them, arms extended, and gives each a hug. Piper glances at Susan and sees that even she's moved by Darlene's open display of affection.

"Did you get my letters?" Darlene asks.

"Yes, we did. We both did," Piper says. "We were very touched."

"I meant every word." Darlene's eyes tear up. "The two of you have literally changed my life. I feel like my faith in people has been restored."

Piper glances at Susan, who says, "Let's sit down."

They position themselves around the small, round table, and Piper says, "The reason we wanted to meet is to go over some things our investigator learned—"

"You found Lois?"

"Not yet," Piper says, seeing some of the light go out of Darlene's eyes, "but we're working on it. We'll find her," she adds, touching Darlene's hand.

Piper tells Darlene what Tommy learned about the poker games at Elwood Stumpf's place, including that her father was there the night he was killed.

"I knew he was at the card game. It was a regular thing. He went about once a month."

"So did a lot of the other locals," Piper says, watching Darlene closely. "Like Tim Powell, who's now a real estate agent, and Buck Forney, who owns the local Chrysler dealership."

At the mention of Buck and the dealership, Darlene's eyes narrow slightly. Piper takes note of it and waits for Darlene to say something, but she doesn't. Piper looks at Susan, who's looking back at her. They're both thinking, *Not a good sign.*

"We also learned that Buck's son, Dale, was a regular at the poker games, but he wasn't there that night."

Darlene stiffens at the mention of Dale's name but, again, offers nothing.

Piper exhales. "Darlene, we know about you and Dale—"

Darlene's eyes widen.

"There was something going on between you."

"Were you with Dale the night your father was killed, instead of by yourself in some field?" asks Susan.

"Our investigator asked Dale, but he wouldn't answer," Piper adds.

Darlene deflates. She sits still, with her eyes closed, for what seems to Piper a very long time.

"It was over between us by then. Not that there was much to begin with," Darlene says. "Can I have a Pepsi?"

Susan fetches a can from the vending machine.

Darlene takes a sip, then sets down the can. "I wanted to get away, leave home for good, but I didn't have any money. So I took a part-time job at the dealership, at the customer-service desk. It was just three days a week. I saw an ad for it in the paper. Of course, Dale worked there, too." She pauses and takes another sip. "He was very nice. He always said nice things to me. Like that my eyes were pretty, I had a nice smile. His father said things, too, but he creeped me out."

"Did you start dating?" Susan asks.

Darlene laughs—bitterly, it seems to Piper.

"We never made it to actual dating. We spent some time together. He took me to a movie once, on a night I knew my father wouldn't be home. He'd have freaked out if he knew I was with a boy."

"But he approved of you having a job?" asks Susan.

"He thought I was bringing all the money home for the family. But I lied to him about how much I was making, and I kept some for myself. My bus money, I called it."

"Why didn't things go further between you and Dale?" Piper asks, though she's sure she knows why.

Darlene shakes her head. "I wasn't ready. I thought I was. But he went to kiss me one time . . . I turned away, even though I wanted him to kiss me. I knew then that I needed more time. He was very kind about it, told me he was patient. He said to let him know if I ever wanted to go out with him." Darlene looks at her lap, then up at Piper. "Is this bad? Any of it?"

"No," Piper says. "But if you had been with Dale at the time of the murder, well, of course, that would be an alibi."

They sit quietly for a moment, and Piper sees Susan studying Darlene.

"Did you tell Dale about what your father was doing to you?" Susan asks.

"God, no! I didn't tell anyone. Did Dale say I did?"

"No," Piper says. She leaves out that Dale told Tommy that Darlene was messed up.

"If you find Lois, I won't need another alibi witness," Darlene says. "Right?"

"We'll have to see what she has to say," Susan says.

Darlene nods and gets a faraway look in her eyes. Piper can see the hope draining out of her, and it breaks her heart.

On the way back, the car is quiet until Susan says, "She's lying."

"About what?" Piper asks.

"I don't know. But she's holding something back."

Piper thinks for a minute.

"When she was talking about Dale Forney, saying how kind he was, she sounded like she was still sweet on him. Do you think she could be protecting him?"

Susan considers this. "If you're asking whether I think Dale was involved in the murder and she's helping to cover it up . . . no. She might still have feelings for him, but I can't imagine she'd keep herself locked up for something a casual date did. Not now, and not back then, either."

"She was pretty screwed up," Piper says. "Her father was a monster to her. Dale was kind. Maybe he did know what was going on, and he did it to save her."

"But she didn't tell Dale what her father was doing to her," Susan says. "She and Dale both said so."

"Maybe he found out on his own."

"I think you're grasping at straws," says Susan. "You want to believe she's innocent. I get that. So do I. But we have to go where the evidence takes us."

Piper gives Susan a curt nod. "We have to go where Lois Beal is."

18

Monday, May 20

It is just before 8:00 a.m., and Mick is in his office, editing an appellate brief. The phone rings, but Angie isn't in yet to pick it up. The caller ID shows that the call is local, from a 215 area code. The brief is due today, and he hates being interrupted when he's concentrating. But the call could be from a panicked client. He lifts the receiver.

"Mick? Martin Brenner. Have you reconsidered my offer to bring Nunzio in from the cold?"

He sighs. "Why are you wasting my time?"

"Let me have an hour alone with him."

"You must be joking."

"I'm serious as hell about this. Nunzio could be the key to bringing down the whole Giansante crime family."

"I'm going to hang up now, and—"

"Don't test me!"

Mick is startled by the heat in Brenner's voice. His own hackles rise, and he growls, "Don't you test *me*. Nunzio's not going to talk to you. Not today. Not tomorrow. Not ever."

"Then I'll bring in his daughter and that freak Giacobetti and make them tell me what went down in the warehouse."

"They don't have to talk to you, and you know it."

"They will if I haul them before a grand jury."

Mick's heart races. Brenner *could* convene a grand jury and subpoena Christina and Johnny G. to testify. They'd be legally obligated to answer his questions, or face contempt charges and possible imprisonment. And no matter what they did or didn't do, he could charge them as co-conspirators or accessories after the fact. This is the main reason Mick has wanted Giacobetti to stay underground—at least until Nunzio is ready to tell him what Giacobetti's role will be in Nunzio's endgame.

"That has you thinking, doesn't it?"

"Martin, you have to know that neither Nunzio's daughter nor his enforcer will turn on him, no matter what you do. They're hardwired not to do that. And as for Christina . . . don't you think she's suffered enough?"

He hears Brenner chuckle on the other end. "What I think is that our little Queen of Clubs would sober up at the thought of spending a year in jail."

They go around and around, neither budging, until Mick suddenly hangs up. He sits for a minute, then places a call to Max Pagano. He asks Pagano if Brenner is still pressuring him about taking over the Nunzio case.

"He hounded me for a while," Pagano says. "But I haven't heard from him in a couple weeks. I guess he got tired of hearing me describe all the sex acts I'd engage in with his mother and sisters if he kept it up."

Mick shakes his head.

Pagano's a piece of work.

"What I don't get is why the feds are coming at us out of Philadelphia instead of New York on this."

He senses Pagano thinking, trying to decide what to say.

"Look, I made some calls about that myself," Pagano says. "First, I called a friend at the US Attorney's Office in Philly. Someone very high up. He told me they give Brenner a lot of leeway because he gets results. He's undertaken some prosecutions everyone thought were long shots and won big. You remember those congressmen who got sent up a couple years ago? And the bigwigs at GSK? That was all Brenner's work. I called another friend in the Southern District of New York who told me that when Nunzio was first arrested, there was a lot of buzz about trying to bring him in, use him against Moretti or some of Moretti's other underbosses. But the word came down from on high to nix it."

"On high?"

"Washington."

Mick does a double take. "DC?"

"No, fucking Seattle."

Mick hears the line go dead. He sits back in his chair, his head spinning with questions. Who was the Justice Department protecting by stopping the effort to turn Nunzio? Nunzio? His boss, Moretti? But why protect them? And if Washington quashed the New York investigation, why was Brenner being allowed to move forward in Philadelphia? It's one thing to accord leeway to a good prosecutor. Another thing entirely to disregard the attorney general.

Mick is still stewing a half hour later when Angie appears in his doorway.

"We have a problem," she says.

"Oh?"

"I just got a call from PBI," she says, referring to the Pennsylvania Bar Institute, an organization that holds continuing-education classes for attorneys. Most of the speakers are lawyers brought in to discuss topics in their areas of expertise. Susan speaks on panels three or four times a year on various issues related to criminal defense.

Angie comes in and stands in front of Mick's desk. "Susan's panel for today is already on stage, but she's nowhere to be found."

Mick is shocked. Susan enjoys the CLE presentations, and it's a point of pride for her that she's recognized as an authority among her peers. Susan is also hyper-responsible, the kind of person who would never fail to honor a commitment.

"I'll call her," he says, lifting the phone. He dials her cell number, but the phone goes immediately to voice mail. He dials her apartment number and is treated to an endless dial tone.

"What's going on with her?" he says to Angie, though he thinks he knows. Piper told him about her conversation with Susan on the way to see Darlene Dowd, including how Susan shut Piper down when she asked how Susan was doing. And Susan's claim that she needed to work things out for herself.

"I'm going to her apartment. Call PBI back and cover for her. Say she's sick as a dog. Hundred-and-three-degree fever. Shingles, meningitis, bubonic plague, whatever."

"How about I say the dog ate her homework?" Angie calls, but he's already out the door.

A few minutes later, Mick is in a cab headed for Old Town and Susan's condo in the north building of Society Hill Towers. It takes him a full minute to persuade the scowling woman behind the front desk to buzz Susan's apartment. It takes almost as long for Susan to answer. She's not happy to learn that he is in the lobby. She reluctantly agrees to let him up.

Susan answers her door in rumpled pajamas and turns away as soon as he's inside. He follows her down the hall. He can't believe what he sees when he enters the living room. The whole place looks like it's been ransacked. The white leather sofa and chairs have all been ripped open, their stuffing pulled out. Her one original oil painting has been slashed, up and down, left and right. The top of her cherry desk has been carved up, the drawers pulled out, their contents strewn across the floor. On Susan's glass-topped dining table are piles of smashed porcelain—the remains of her dishware. As with her desk, all the kitchen-cabinet drawers have been pulled out. He doesn't ask about what's been done in the bedroom.

Susan lowers herself onto one of the torn couch cushions, lifts a plastic cup, and takes a sip. A tea bag hangs over the edge. He sits carefully on one of the ruined chairs on the other side of a tinted-glass coffee table, the only thing that hasn't been trashed.

"My God, Susan. What happened?"

"Vandals." She looks away from him as she says this.

He casts her a disbelieving look.

"Or robbers. Who knows?"

He shrugs. "Susan, come on. I'm your friend."

Susan closes her eyes, then opens them and looks directly at him. "Leave it alone, Mick. Please, just drop it. If you are my friend, that's what you'll do. It's what I want."

He stares at Susan for a long moment. He doesn't know what to do.

No, I do know what to do. Pry the information out of her.

He leans toward her. "I'm pretty damned sure you know both the who and the why of this."

She doesn't answer.

"Have you called the police?"

"No."

That seals it for him. The only reason she wouldn't report it is because she has a relationship with the guy who did it.

"Why are you protecting him?"

"You don't understand."

"So please explain it to me."

She stands and heads for the bedroom. "I asked you to leave, Mick. So leave."

She slams the bedroom door behind her.

He stands, stares at the door. He starts to move toward it, then stops, reaches into his jacket pocket, and pulls out his iPhone. He presses the camera app and takes pictures of the damage.

Minutes later, Ubering back to the office, he calls Tommy and tells him everything.

"It's that soccer player," Mick says. "I know it. The Argentine. Armand Romero. Everyone knows he's a hothead. Susan told Piper they broke up. I'm guessing Armand's not happy about it."

Tommy agrees to look into the guy, find out where he hangs out, buddy up to him at the bar. "If I can't win his trust, maybe I'll take a more direct approach."

"Okay," Mick says, worried, as always, that some act of violence will land his brother back in prison. "But don't do anything stupid."

Frank Valiante hangs up the phone, fuming. Twice now he's told his boss, Don Savonna, about his discussion with the old man from the transportation company. There's no doubt that Nunzio is planning to launch a direct assault against him. That Nunzio has gone so far as to order a fleet of bulletproof attack vehicles for the job. But Savonna refuses to believe it, claiming that neither Nunzio nor *his* boss, Don Moretti, would dare to make such a move without the Commission's approval. And Savonna himself won't approach the Commission for permission to take out Nunzio in retaliation for Nunzio's murder of Antonio.

"It's a terrible loss," Savonna said. "And an inexcusable thing to do. But the Commission doesn't want a war right now. And that's what would happen if you hit Nunzio. You know how much Moretti loves him."

"Does he love him as much as I loved my *son*?"

"Watch your tone, Frank. I know you're upset. But there are limits."

He apologized, of course; a don was a don.

But there is no way he's going to sit back and wait to be attacked. He'll find out where Nunzio is going to stage his army, catch the bastard preparing to launch an unsanctioned war. Then he'll attack first. He'll have to, and no one will be able to blame him. Not Savonna, not Moretti, not the Commission. Nunzio's army will be eviscerated, his wife and daughter dead. Antonio will be avenged. And Philadelphia and South Jersey will be wide open.

He reaches for the phone and calls the old man.

"Hiram," he says when the old man answers.

The old man says, "Frank!" There's warmth in his voice. "You have good timing. I was just about to call you."

"You know the where and when of his attack?"

"One week from today. Monday, the twenty-seventh. That's when he's planning to hit you. This weekend he's assembling his troops at a place he owns in the Poconos."

"How solid is this?"

"Have I ever been wrong before?"

He smiles. "Not once in fifteen years, my friend."

"So, what do you want to do?"

"Those bulletproof vans you told me he ordered . . . you got any more?"

A pause at the other end. "That's a special order. Vehicles like that have to be fitted out. It takes time. Costs money. Of course," he chuckles, "the more money, the less time."

"How much money to get them to me by Saturday?"

"Uh, hold on."

The old man puts him on hold for close to five minutes, then gets back to him with an amount that takes Frank's breath away.

"That much for six vans?"

"Six bulletproof attack vans."

He closes his eyes. Sees his dead son's face, followed by the sneering mug of James Fucking Nunzio.

"Get it done."

19

Wednesday, May 22

It's just after 4:00, and Tommy is at the desk in his cluttered office, reviewing property records, copies of old newspaper articles, and photos. He compares two pictures, one of a woman in her fifties, one of a girl aged eighteen from her high school yearbook.

"You're the same person," he says aloud. "I know it."

Matt Crowley, the guy Piper hired, learned that "Lois Beal" was an alias stolen from a dead child, as was the case with Lois's husband. Tommy figured that Lois probably dropped her alias after she left the farm following her husband's death in 2009. So anyone looking online for Lois Beal would hit the same dead end as Crowley. He racked his brain trying to figure out a way to track her down and finally hit upon the answer when he remembered that Buck Forney had referred to Lois and her husband as "renters who showed up out of nowhere." Renters. That was the key.

The law firm subscribes to Westlaw, which has various public-records databases, including ones that list property owners. So he punched in the address of the Beal farmstead and found that from the late 1960s through 2010, it was owned by Jeffrey and Heather Warden. Searching through other public-records databases, Tommy learned that Jeffrey inherited the farm from his father, Edwin, who had been raised on the farm before moving to Georgia in the late 1940s. Born in 1950, Jeffrey would have been about Lois Beal's age, and any sibling he had could have been, too. But Jeffrey was an only child, and he remained in Georgia his whole life, so he couldn't have become Lois Beal's husband, "Jason Dell."

Jeffrey's wife, however, Heather Corbett Warden, had a brother and two sisters. The brother died in Vietnam in 1970. The elder sister moved to California, where she went into politics, eventually serving in the state senate. And then there was the younger sister, Megan. Born in 1950, Megan was nineteen years old and a sophomore at Berkeley in 1969 when she disappeared with her boyfriend, a student radical named Bobby Moffat, the two of them having committed a terrible crime.

Tommy holds up Megan's picture from her high school yearbook and compares it to an old newspaper photo of Lois Beal, taken at a pumpkin festival held at the Beals' farm in 2003, the year before the Dowd murder.

"Oh yeah, it's you."

He gets up and walks to the conference room, where Piper has the Darlene Dowd file spread over the conference table.

"I think I found her," he says. "Lois Beal."

Her eyes brighten. She smiles and stands. "That's fantastic. Where is she?"

"Georgia, if I'm right."

"We can fly out first thing tomorrow morning. I'll call Susan."

"No, let me go down first. Do some reconnaissance. Figure out the best way to approach her."

"Why do you need to do that?"

"Because if I'm right about who she is, who she *was*, there's a good chance she won't want to talk to you."

Piper exhales. "Then she's in hiding. Like we thought."

He nods. "Give me a couple days. It's Wednesday, so plan on coming down Friday or Saturday."

"How bad is it—the reason she's running?"

"Bad."

They stare at each other for a moment; then he turns to leave.

"Tommy?"

He turns back. "What?" A little edge to his voice.

"Nothing."

He walks back to his office, sits behind the desk. He knows Piper wants things to go back the way they were before the Hanson case. Their friendship began just after she married Mick. Piper reached out to Tommy while he was in prison, writing him every week, encouraging him, giving him hope. Once he was out, she invited him into her family, even more than Mick did, helped him rebuild his life. But then came the death of Jennifer Yamura, David Hanson's lover, and it changed them all.

"People," he says.

The whole race of us. Hopscotching from one fuckup to another.

His mind jumps to Susan. He wonders what on earth is going on with her.

Someone smashes up her apartment, and she doesn't call the cops? Doesn't even want to admit to Mick what's happening?

He leaves his office, walks to the kitchen, brews a cup of Starbucks French Roast on the Keurig. He walks back down the hall, pauses at the threshold of Susan's office. She's at work today but in a foul mood, according to Angie.

"Hey," he says, walking into the office, doing his best to sound upbeat.

Susan looks up from her computer screen without raising her head. She doesn't say anything.

"I just told Piper I think I found Lois Beal."

"You're not here to talk about the Dowd case, Tommy."

He stares.

"I'm sure Mick told you what happened. But some things are private, okay?"

"I just thought—"

She raises her hand, signaling him to stop.

"Private, Tommy."

"You're the boss," he mumbles, turning away.

"Thank you for closing the door on your way out."

He returns to his office. "Hell with this," he says, grabbing his helmet off the couch.

Thirty minutes later, he's inching down I-95 South on his blue-and-silver Road King Special. It's sixty-five degrees, sunny and dry, great conditions for a ride. Or it would be, were it not for the traffic. Rush hour down 95 is a slog. But he has somewhere to be.

The Philadelphia Union are playing the Colorado Rapids at Talen Energy Stadium in Chester, a little more than twenty miles southwest of Center City. The game starts at 7:30. He'll get to Chester by six, buy a ticket, hang out for a while, grab something to eat from the Chickie's & Pete's inside the stadium, or maybe the Q Barbeque, then watch some soccer. Along the way, he'll talk to some people, maybe some cops assigned to the stadium, find out where the Union players go for drinks after the game. With luck, by midnight he'll be sitting next to Armand Romero, talking about the game, about his Harley, about fishing or hunting or whatever the fuck else the guy's into. Then he'll give Armand a chance to complain about his uppity lawyer girlfriend. What it's like to date a female attorney, how good she is in the sack, maybe how he needs to put the bitch in line every now and then. Show her who's boss. Then, later, when the bar closes, he'll follow Armand to his house or apartment. When he gets out of his car, Tommy will be there to show soccer-boy what happens when you go up against an ex-con hard case who doesn't go in for the woman-beating routine.

Yes, Susan, he thinks, *some things are private. Even from your friends. So I won't ever tell you why Armand doesn't come around anymore.*

"That is not going to happen," Nunzio says calmly. "Christina is not going to be subpoenaed, and neither is Johnny."

Mick McFarland has just told him about the federal prosecutor Brenner's threat to haul his daughter and enforcer before a grand jury.

"And you're going to make sure that doesn't happen . . . how?"

"You're the lawyer. That's your job."

"Any idea why the New York feds decided not to move against you?"

Nunzio shrugs, but he knows they were told to leave him alone by certain powerful government officials who owe him.

The lawyer taps his pen on his legal pad, says, "Let's switch gears. Under the new schedule, your trial is less than a month away. Are you ready to let me in on whatever story you're planning to run with?"

"Next question."

More tapping of the pen. "Do you at least want to tell me about the plasticuffs? If your narrative is built around a self-defense tale, you'll have a hard time selling it to the jury if they think Valiante was bound when his throat was slit."

"What is it they say? Truth is stranger than fiction?"

Admittedly, that part is tricky, but he's working on an answer.

McFarland shakes his head, frustrated.

Nunzio smiles, enjoying parrying with the lawyer. "You play chess?"

The lawyer's eyes flatten. "That's what this is to you? A game?"

He jumps to his feet, sweeps the lawyer's briefcase and legal pad off the table.

"My life is no game!"

He pounds the table, brings fire to his eyes, shoots it at the lawyer. He leans over the table, gets in the lawyer's face, lets him watch Jekyll turn to Hyde. It takes him back to the night "Jimmy Nutzo" was coined. It had been a month since his father was killed, and he'd taken over the crew. Most of the men under him were older, some by decades, and he was having a hard time keeping them in line. They weren't taking him seriously enough. One guy in particular, Donny Ricci, seemed to recoil at taking orders from him. One night, he was in his cramped office behind the bar—the old place. He waited until after closing, when all his guys were hanging out, playing pool, throwing back a few. Then he stormed into the bar area, picked up a full bottle of Bud, and smashed it against the side of Donny's face, screaming, "The next time I hear one of you motherfuckers called me Jimmy Nutzo, I'll cut out all your fucking tongues!" He stormed back into his office and slammed the door. As he'd expected, it was a lot easier from that point on to keep the crew in line. Even Donny, once he got out of the hospital, treated him differently. Also, as he'd expected, the nickname stuck. Jimmy Nunzio became the smooth-talking mask from which "Jimmy Nutzo" could spring at any moment.

He closes his eyes, takes some deep breaths, sits back down.

"This is no game to me. I promise you. I asked about chess because I figured maybe we could play someday, after this is all over."

"All over?" The lawyer looks confused. "Jimmy. Mr. Nunzio. When this is over, chances are . . ."

Nunzio puts up his hand. "I know. I know what you're going to say: chances are I'll be upstate. But I can't let myself think that way."

"I get it," McFarland says. Then he switches topics again. "Do you have any better sense as to when the war with Frank Valiante will come? And in what form?"

Sunday. In the form of white attack vans.

"I wish I did."

"Tell me honestly. Is this something you want? War?"

He smiles. "The greatest generals are those who win without fighting. Sun Tzu."

McFarland is staring at him now, trying to see behind his eyes.

Good luck with that.

Frank Valiante, his son Angelo, and three other top lieutenants stand around the conference-room table. The surface is covered with Google satellite photos showing a large building positioned in the center of a ten-acre clearing in the woods. A number of smaller buildings, log cabins, sit at the periphery of the clearing, adjacent to the woods that surround it for miles.

"The place was a luxury resort," Frank says, repeating the information he was given by the old man. "The owners fell on hard times a few years back, and Nunzio bought it for a song."

"I'll bet he got it for a steal," Angelo says. "I'll bet the owners didn't *fall* on hard times, he pushed them."

Frank stares at his youngest son, hears the hate in his voice. Angelo will never get over Nunzio killing his brother.

That's good. He'll need that hate to get this job done right.

"My source tells me Nunzio's going to bring his whole crew together at this place over the weekend. His plan is to come at us in force on Monday. He ordered six bulletproof vans to move his guys in."

He pauses, lets that sink in, watches Angelo and the others look around the room at each other.

"Problem for Jimmy Nutzo is that we're going to have our own vans—and hit him first." He leans over the largest photograph, a 36-by-40-inch printout of a satellite photo of the property. "I planned it all out. We'll have six vans. A driver and nine guns in each. The back windows will all be tinted. That's important, because the drivers are going to drive the vans empty onto Nunzio's property, park them in a circle right on this big lawn. Nunzio's guys will go apeshit, attack the vans with everything they have, thinking all our guys are inside the vans like sitting ducks. It'll be like Indians surrounding a wagon train. Except that when Nunzio's guys go after the vans, our guys will surprise them—run out from the woods and mow them down. They won't know what hit 'em."

Frank looks up and smiles. His guys are smiling, too, liking the visions of Nunzio's men getting cut to pieces, blood spraying everywhere, the air filled with screams and curses and moans. It makes him feel good, too, settling things this way. The way of his grandfather. Before the business got so civilized and political and you had to crawl before a Commission with your hat in your hand, begging for permission to do what needed to be done.

He looks at Angelo. "Then, once you're done with his crew, you go for the wife and the daughter."

"He's going to have them there?" Angelo asks in disbelief.

"He's going to have his whole family there. His lawyer, too, and *his* family."

"Stupid son of a bitch."

"Remember, I want the wife and daughter brought back alive. I want their deaths on film for Jimmy to watch. Once we get our guy into that jail, he'll make sure it's the last thing Nunzio sees before he dies."

Frank looks around the room, lifts his beer, waits for the others to do the same.

"For Tony," he says.

"For Tony!" the others shout.

20

Saturday, May 25–Sunday, May 26

Piper stands next to Mick, watching the children play.

"Gabby lucked out," he tells her.

"We all did. It's a perfect day for this," she says, looking around at their backyard, full of children searching for goodies, the "treasure hunt" portion of the program they put together to celebrate Gabrielle's tenth birthday. The kids had already done the hula-hoop relay, the three-legged relay, played on the jungle gym and the mini zip line. When done with the treasure hunt, they'll assemble around the piñata to take turns trying to break open the purple-and-yellow donkey.

"When did kids' parties get this elaborate?" Mick asks.

She shakes her head. "It was after my time, that's for sure." She watches the kids scour the yard, but her mind is on the Dowd case and the plan to interview Lois Beal.

Tommy called late Thursday and confirmed that the woman he found was Lois. "She lives on St. Simons Island, Georgia," he'd said. "I'm ninety-nine percent certain it's her." He also reminded Piper again that Lois was sitting on a big secret—something that could send her to prison—and she was just as likely to shut them out as to share what happened the day Lester Dowd was murdered.

"I thought about approaching her myself," he said. "But I think she's more likely to open up to you and Susan than to me."

She called Susan with the news, and they booked a flight for that evening to Jacksonville, on American Airlines. Piper told Susan the later flight would give her time to handle Gabby's birthday party; Susan said she had things to do and was fine with the evening flight as well.

"Thinking about tomorrow?" Mick asks.

"Was I zoning out? I guess I was." She nods. "Yeah, thinking about Lois Beal."

"I hope it pans out the way you're hoping."

"You don't think it will, do you?"

He pauses, takes a sip from his Blue Moon. "I just take the innocence claims of prisoners with a grain of salt, that's all. I've been around the block too many times."

"I know," she says. "I just really want her to be innocent. After what her father did to her. All the years she's spent in prison. I feel like her life was taken from her before it even started."

"I hope she's innocent, too. And if so, I hope you and Susan can persuade a judge to let her out."

Piper smiles wanly. She looks at the picnic table, where a bunch of the kids are spreading their "treasures"—small toys and trinkets she'd bought and hidden around the yard for them to find.

Gabby comes up to them, says it's time for the piñata. Mick escorts her to the candy-stuffed donkey hanging by a rope from a tree branch. He calls one of the other girls up and places a blindfold on her. He hands her a stick and spins her around, then nudges her in the direction of the donkey. The other kids shout and cheer as she swings the stick wildly.

Piper's heart aches to think that Darlene Dowd was not much older than these kids when her father started raping her.

"Come on, Lois," she says quietly. "Come through for us. Come through for Darlene."

It's 5:30 when Mick pulls the Audi out of the driveway. Piper is riding shotgun, and Gabby and Franklin are squeezed in the back seat. It'll take about forty-five minutes to get to the airport, giving Piper more than enough time to make the 7:30 flight.

"You know it's still my birthday," Gabrielle says from behind them.

"I know, honey," Piper says, turning around. "I wish I didn't have to go."

"We'll do something fun when she gets back home," Mick says over his shoulder.

He sees Gabby's arms crossed in the rearview mirror. She's not buying it.

Mick pulls up next to Terminal B and pops the trunk. Piper gets out and opens the back door while he retrieves her suitcase. He moves up beside her as she leans in, gives Gabrielle a big hug, and pets Franklin's head.

"You be good for your father," Piper says. "Do something fun together."

"Don't worry about us." Mick leans down and winks at Gabby. "We won't get into *that* much trouble."

Gabby rolls her eyes, lifts her iPhone, and starts playing a game.

"Have everything you need?" he asks.

"I think so."

"Good luck." He gives Piper a kiss and a big hug, then watches her walk into the terminal.

Mick has Gabby back home at 7:00, and they decide to eat pizza and watch a movie. Gabby goes upstairs to change into her PJs as Mick orders the pizza.

"I say we watch *Harry Potter and the Half-Blood Prince,*" Gabby says, coming down the stairs. Mick walks into the living room, carrying a Blue Moon for him and a Coke for her.

"But we're still reading the book," Mick says.

"*You're* still reading it. I finished a long time ago."

"Hey, that's against the rules. When we read a book together, it means we read it together. You can read another book on your own."

"Sorry, Charlie," she says.

The pizza comes about halfway through the film, and father and daughter gobble their pie on the couch, taking turns tossing small pieces to Franklin, who climbs onto the couch beside them—something Piper would never allow.

When the movie ends, Gabby persuades Mick to let her watch the next film in the series, *Harry Potter and the Deathly Hallows, Part I.* Gabrielle makes it through part of the film, but finally surrenders to sleep around 11:00. Mick carries her to bed and tucks her under the covers. Piper would have insisted Gabby wake up and brush her teeth.

"Happy birthday, sweetheart." He leans over and kisses her on the forehead. Then he walks to the small bookcase across the room, selects *The Deathly Hallows*, and returns to the bed. He finds the chapter that more or less corresponds to the scene during which Gabrielle fell asleep and begins to read.

He's back downstairs in his study when Piper calls at 11:40 to tell him her connecting flight from Charlotte just landed. They talk for a bit, Piper reminding him that Franklin isn't to climb on the furniture and soliciting his confirmation that Gabby brushed her teeth before she went to bed.

They exchange good-nights and love-yous, and he hangs up.

When the phone rings again, just after 1:30 a.m., it wrenches him from a sound sleep. He fumbles to find his cell phone on the night-stand, where it is charging.

"Piper?" he says, his eyes still shut.

"The war's on. Get ready to leave. Your wife and daughter, too."

He recognizes the voice, but it takes him a moment to place it. When he does, he springs out of bed.

Nunzio. Calling from prison.

"Piper's not here," he says.

A pause at the other end. Then, "Where is she?"

He hesitates.

"Look, I'm trying to save your ass here."

"What the—"

"I have intelligence that Valiante's planning a massive attack. Against my family. The word is that he might be going after my lawyers, too."

"You said we wouldn't end up in the middle of it."

"It's not as easy for me to deliver on my promises as it used to be, given where I am."

"Piper's in Georgia, on a case. So's my partner, Susan, and my brother, Tommy."

"And Coburn and his fiancée?"

"They're on vacation. Barcelona."

"They'll be safe. All of them. This is a local thing Valiante's planning."

"Then I'll take Gabby to—"

"You'll go where my men take you. Get dressed and pack some bags. They'll be there any minute."

The line goes dead. At the same time, Mick hears the front door open. He runs downstairs to find two large men in dark clothes entering the house.

"What the hell?"

The two intruders look at each other, then back at him.

"Didn't you get the call?" asks the larger of the two.

"I'm not going anywhere with you," Mick says.

"Aw, jeez. You gonna make this hard?"

The other man, slightly smaller and with more intelligence in his eyes, says, "The whole point of this is to protect you and your family. Get yourselves dressed, and let's go. Please."

Mick thinks. If these two goons are determined to take him and Gabby, they're going to do it. Fighting will only delay the inevitable. And he doesn't want to do anything that will upset his daughter.

"Give me a few minutes," he says, then turns and goes back up the steps.

Mick sits in the back seat of the Cadillac Escalade. Gabby is wrapped in a blanket, her head on his lap. He dressed her as gently as he could, to keep her from waking. She stirred a few times but remained asleep, even as he carried her to the car.

Quietly, he leans forward and sees the driver looking back at him in the rearview mirror. "I need my cell phone," he says. "I have to tell my wife what's going on. And my brother and my law partner, too."

Nunzio's thugs forced him to turn over the iPhone before they got in the car. The driver glances at the wiseguy in the passenger seat, who tells Mick to hold on a minute while he makes a call. He listens in as the guy explains to someone on the other end that Mick wants to make some calls. The goon hangs up.

"You can make one call," he says, reaching into his jacket pocket for Mick's phone. He turns around and hands Mick the cell. "One call."

Mick dials. After a few rings, he hears Tommy's sleepy voicc ask who's calling him.

"Tommy. It's me, Mick. Frank Valiante's on the attack. Word is he's going after everyone, maybe even us. Nunzio's lawyers."

"Damn."

"Where are Piper and Susan?"

"We're all together. I picked up Piper and Susan at the airport last night, drove us all to Saint Simons Island, got us a suite with three bedrooms at Ocean Lodge. We just got here about half an hour ago. Susan and Piper are in bed."

"All right. Listen, Nunzio told me—"

"Wait. He called you from jail? How—"

"He's Nunzio, that's how. He told me he doesn't think you guys are in danger because you're a thousand miles away. I think he's probably right, but I want you to be careful anyway. Tomorrow, tell Piper and Susan what's happening." He pauses. "Are you carrying?"

"No. I flew down. I can probably get my hands on something, though. What about you? You don't have a gun, do you?"

"No, but I won't need one. Nunzio's rounding everyone up, taking us somewhere to wait this thing out."

"What? You mean they *have* you?"

"Gabby and I are—"

"They have *Gabby*?"

"I'm not happy about it, either."

"Piper's gonna blow a gasket. She's going to want to fly back there as soon as I tell her."

"I know she will, and you have to stop her. Persuade her not to. I feel a lot better with the idea of you, rather than Nunzio's goons, looking out for her and Susan." The driver's eyes are on him again, in the rearview. The guy riding shotgun is turned around. They didn't like the "goons" thing.

Too damned bad.

"I don't like this at all," Tommy says. "Valiante's guys tried to take out Johnny G. in broad daylight, and they killed two cops doing it.

That tells me Valiante's crazy for vengeance, and he doesn't give a shit about collateral damage."

"I hear you. Get that piece and keep Susan and Piper close. Don't let them out of your sight. And if you see anything that raises your hackles, hire a private security firm to look out for all of you."

They talk a few more minutes before the wiseguy in the passenger seat says, "That's long enough," and holds out his hand. Mick and Tommy wish each other luck; then Mick signs off and hands over the phone.

"I didn't appreciate the pejorative reference," the driver says in a thick South Philly accent, surprising Mick with his vocabulary.

Mick glares at the man, then looks down at Gabby, still asleep on his lap.

What is he going to tell her tomorrow when she wakes up and asks where they are? Suddenly he's filled with anger. His involvement with Nunzio has put his daughter in danger. He'd like nothing more than to rush to the jail and wring the mobster's neck.

What were you thinking, killing a man right in front of your daughter? And not just any man, but the man she loved. What kind of monster does that? And what kind of idiot are you that you'd kill the son of another underboss as connected and bloodthirsty as you?

Something pulls him from his thoughts. He realizes it's the guy in the front passenger seat, now turned fully around and looking down at Gabby.

"What?" Mick asks.

"I said, they're all such angels when they're asleep."

He stares at the guy, furious at him for talking about Gabby, even more furious at himself for having exposed her to someone like him. Gently, he pats Gabby's head, pulls the blanket up over her shoulder.

"Some of them are angels even when they're awake," Mick says.

◆ ◆ ◆

Angelo Valiante walks into the conference room and sits across the conference table from his father. It is almost 3:00 a.m., but he's not the least bit tired. He's too excited by the imminent destruction of Jimmy Nunzio's crew.

"I just got off the phone with our guys in Philly. Your guy was right," he tells his father. "Nunzio's taking all his people to the mountains. They picked up his brother and his family about an hour ago. This afternoon, he had a whole convoy of guns escort his bitch wife. Johnny G. was with them. A couple hours ago, they even picked up the lawyer."

"The lawyer," his father repeats. "So he must be in on the planning. Which means he's not just a lawyer—he's Nunzio's consigliere. And that makes him fair game. What about the daughter?"

"No one knows where she is."

"She'll be there. My man was certain of it."

"I heard she was out of the country."

"Probably bullshit. Nunzio trying to keep her hidden so the cops can't question her about the warehouse."

Angelo looks down at the satellite photo of the resort. "I can't believe he has no fencing around this place. No gate. Arrogant prick. Thinks he's untouchable."

"I guess he never figured on having to use it for something like this," his father says.

Angelo thinks about this. "Did your guy tell you where Nunzio plans to attack us?"

"He said Nunzio didn't share that information with his contact at the company," Frank says. "My guess is he plans to divide his forces. He's got six trucks, so I'm thinking his plan is to send each to a different place, shoot it up, wipe out everyone there."

"You think he's planning on coming here, to the office?"

"Absolutely. The house, too. Some of our distribution centers, certainly. The places most important to us. The places where we have the most men. The places he thinks you and me will be at."

He feels his head start to burn. His heart pounds. "Well, too bad for him. Because the place I'll be at is in the Poconos—on top of his daughter and his wife."

He sees his old man staring at him. He knows what he's thinking.

"Pop. Don't worry. I've got it under control."

But his father continues to stare.

Mick watches through the windows as the Escalade progresses up I-476 North to 22 East, 33 North, 209 North, 402 North, and, finally, 590 toward Hawley, Pennsylvania. The drive lasts two and a half hours, and it's close to 4:00 a.m. when they pull off Welcome Woods Road onto a tree-lined driveway. The driveway continues for a quarter mile, opening onto the grounds of a large resort. The main building is a two-story stone-and-log structure. A wide, circular driveway leads to the front steps. A porch runs the length of the building, its roof supported by thick log columns. A second-story balcony sits atop the porch's roof.

Other buildings—log cabins—are positioned along the periphery of the clearing, backed by the thick forest that surrounds the grounds. A parking lot sits well away from the lodge. It is empty save for a few cars and, oddly, Mick thinks, six white Ford vans.

The Escalade comes to a stop in front of the porch steps, and the wiseguys get out of the front. The one from the passenger seat opens Mick's door, and Mick gently scoops up the still-sleeping Gabby.

Mick pauses to take in the scene. Large men in dark clothing stand guard or patrol the grounds, their flashlight beams cutting the darkness as they speak in hushed voices. In the middle of the lawn, three men are huddled around a giant figure—Johnny Giacobetti. Sitting nearby are two dogs Mick recognizes as English mastiffs. Overhead, thick white clouds race beneath a full moon. The chilly air is thick with menace. The whole thing has a surreal feeling.

"Mr. McFarland." A woman's voice.

He looks to the top of the steps and sees Rachel Nunzio. Curvaceously statuesque, with thick black hair over dark eyes. As stunning as he remembers her.

She smiles. "Welcome to our little retreat."

He doesn't smile back.

"Is that what you're calling this?" he asks once he reaches the porch, keeping his voice low so as not to disturb Gabrielle.

Unperturbed, Rachel smiles again. "She's adorable," she says, glancing down at Gabby. "We'll do our best to make this fun for her."

"Fun?"

"I'm sorry your wife and law partner won't be able to join us. Not to worry, though. My husband is certain they're not in any danger."

"Unlike us," he says, and her face darkens just a bit.

"This place used to be a resort," she says. "It actually still has a front desk. Your rooms are on the second floor, overlooking the grand lawn. It's a lovely suite."

"How long are we going to be here?"

"That's something you'll have to ask my husband."

She leads him into the great room, a vast space with thirty-foot cathedral ceilings, a massive stone fireplace, hardwood floors, club chairs and worn leather couches, and a deer-antler chandelier. The air carries the subtle scent of pine needles, and everything is polished, waxed, and shining.

"This is Mr. McFarland," Rachel tells the pretty young woman behind the reception desk. "And his daughter, Gabrielle. They're in room 204."

The receptionist smiles and hands Mick a heavy, old-fashioned room key. He takes his leave of Rachel Nunzio and climbs the wide wooden staircase to the second floor. Opening the door, he finds a large bedroom with a separate sitting area and fireplace. The four-poster bed—as big as a Buick Regal—is covered with a thick white quilt and six feather pillows. High-backed wing chairs sit on either side of the fireplace. The wide-plank flooring is covered by an oval area rug.

He carries Gabby to the side of the bed farthest from the door and gently lays her down. He looks around the room, wondering whether the Nunzios have it wired for sound or video. He wouldn't put it past them.

There's a small minibar with assorted liquors and snacks. He's surprised to find a bottle of Pappy Van Winkle 23. He opens it and pours a finger into a tumbler. The bourbon tastes of apples, cherries, oak, and tobacco, and has a long caramel finish. He pours some more and takes another swallow as he walks onto the small balcony.

He leans over the railing, watches another Cadillac Escalade pull up and unload a family—two parents, a pair of twin boys about Gabby's age, and an infant. The twins are asleep on their feet. The father seems nonchalant, but the mother is visibly upset. In the distance, he sees Johnny Giacobetti striding across the lawn, talking into a walkie-talkie. The two enormous dogs trot beside him. In the distance, another Escalade makes its way down the long driveway.

He turns back to the room, to Gabby. "What the hell have I gotten us into?"

21

Sunday, May 26

It is 6:30, and Tommy is brewing a pot of coffee when he hears the quiet knock on the door to the hotel suite. He opens it to find a muscular, bald man in a short-sleeve shirt. The man's arms are covered in tattoos.

"You Tommy?" the man asks.

"Yeah. Dave?"

The man nods and hands Tommy a brown paper bag.

"Tell Lenny I owe him one," Tommy says.

"He already knows," Dave says as he leaves.

Tommy closes the door and pulls the pistol from the bag. He turns around to find Piper standing in the doorway of her bedroom.

"What the hell?" she says.

"You better wake up Susan," he says, sliding the pistol back into the bag.

"What's going on?"

"Get Susan," he repeats.

He waits until Piper knocks on Susan's door and enters, closing the door behind her. Then he walks to the kitchenette, lays the bag on the counter, and pours three cups of coffee.

Susan and Piper are out of Susan's room before he even has time to pull the creamer from the fridge.

"Someone brought you a *gun*?" Susan asks.

"Is Lois in that much trouble?" Piper asks.

"This isn't about Lois. It's about Nunzio."

Susan and Piper exchange glances.

"I got a call from Mick last night," he says, seeing Piper's eyes widen. "Nunzio phoned him and said the war with Valiante's heating up. So Nunzio's bringing everybody in. Mick called me from a car—"

"You're saying he's got Mick?" Susan asks, looking confused.

"It's okay. He and Gabby—"

"Gabby?" Piper's face drains of blood. "Nunzio has Mick and Gabby, too?"

"Nunzio thinks Valiante is going to go after Mick?" Susan asks.

"I have to get back there," Piper says quickly, her voice cracking.

"Nothing's going to happen to Gabby or to Mick," Tommy says, trying to calm them down even as his own anxiety rises. "Nunzio has an army around them. Around everyone."

"This is crazy!" Piper is pacing now. "I'm going to call him," she says, turning for her bedroom and iPhone.

"You won't get through," Tommy calls after her. "They took Mick's cell."

"Then we have to call the police!" Piper shouts over her shoulder on the way to her room.

"This really is nuts," Susan says to him. "Are we in danger, too? Is that why you had that gun brought here?"

"Nunzio told Mick that Valiante isn't going to come after us down here. Still, I thought I should be ready. Just in case."

Piper returns, holding up her iPhone. "What should I tell the police?"

"That's the thing," Tommy says. "What *can* you tell them? We don't know where Nunzio's taking everyone. If the cops go to the jail and ask, he'll just say he doesn't know what they're talking about."

"Would Nunzio retaliate against Mick and Gabby if Piper called the police?" asks Susan.

Tommy's chest tightens—something else to worry about. "I don't know," he says, watching Piper lower the phone. "Look, I think the best thing for us to do is just get our business done down here as fast as possible and go home. The threat should be over by the time we get back."

"I can't believe this," Piper says, her eyes still wide with fear.

Tommy walks around the counter, takes her hands. "Let's just get this done. Talk to Lois Beal, see if she'll help you. Then, when Mick calls us with the all clear, we'll go straight to the airport and fly home."

He watches her take a deep breath and straighten her back. She nods.

"It's not even seven yet," he says, "so we have a couple hours before we should try to meet with Lois. Drink some coffee. I'll make us all some breakfast. While we eat, I'll tell you the tale of Megan Corbett, a.k.a. Lois Beal, a.k.a. Terri Petrini. Then you'll know why it's gonna be an uphill battle getting her to testify for Darlene Dowd."

◆ ◆ ◆

"Daddy? Where are we?"

Mick opens his eyes to see Gabby sitting up in bed next to him. Her eyes are filled with wonder—and worry.

"It's for your birthday. A surprise your mom set up for you since she couldn't be with us," he says, hating how easily the lie rolls off his tongue. He'd worked it out last night. A story to tell her so she wouldn't be afraid.

Gabby rushes to the balcony, opens the door, gazes out at the great lawn. "The yard is really big!"

"We're going to have a fun time," he says, walking up behind her. "There's a lake out back, and I saw canoes. Maybe we can hike in the woods."

Gabby dresses excitedly, and he throws on a pair of jeans and a sweatshirt. They make their way down the stairs. Gabby pauses to take it all in, craning her neck to look up at the ceiling far above, then scanning the great room, her eyes stopping on the giant fireplace and the antler chandelier.

"What *is* this place?" she asks, awe in her voice.

He reaches for her hand. "Let's go outside and see."

They walk across the porch and down the steps to the lawn. In the middle distance, he sees Johnny Giacobetti and his large dogs. Gabby sees the dogs, too, and makes a beeline for them. He follows and sees her slow down as she gets closer to Johnny G. She stops and waits for him to catch up. Giacobetti watches them approach, his face unreadable. Mick studies the giant but sees no sign that his relatively recent wounds are slowing him down.

"Hold out your hand," Mick tells Gabby as she approaches one of the dogs. "Fingers closed. Make sure he's friendly."

"She," Giacobetti says. "That's Loki. She's a bit—a girl," he says to Gabby.

Gabby reaches out, her hand tiny on the mastiff's giant head.

"What's that dog weigh?" Mick asks.

"About two hundred. A little less than her brother." He turns to Gabby. "His name is Thor."

Gabby looks at Thor, then Loki, then up at Giacobetti.

"Is *everyone* here really big?" she asks.

Mick looks down. "Come on," he says. "He has work to do. Let's look around."

They make their way to the rear of the building. A hundred yards from the back patio is a lake that looks to Mick to be a half mile across. A stone's throw from the shore is a diving platform, about twenty feet square. Half a dozen canoes sit on the pebbled beach.

"You can use the canoes."

Mick turns to see Rachel Nunzio approaching them. She's wearing a white blouse over tan pants and calf-high boots. Her dark hair is tied back.

"I wouldn't suggest swimming, though. It's a little early in the season, so the water's still pretty cold."

"What do you think? Want to go canoeing?" Mick asks Gabby.

She nods her head vigorously.

"We also have games. Horseshoes and bocce ball."

"How about soccer?" Gabby asks. "Do you have any soccer balls, and a net?"

Rachel smiles. "I think we can dig up a net and a ball." She turns to Mick. "Are you hungry? You can have your breakfast on the porch, or in the dining room. Or even in your own room, if you want."

"I think we'll try the dining room," he answers. He thanks Rachel and leads Gabby around to the front of the lodge. As they get close to the stairs, he sees a car pull up, a white 3-series Mercedes. The driver and a woman Mick presumes to be his wife get out of the sedan. The rear passenger doors open and three kids—two boys and a girl—jump out. Mick recognizes the man but can't place him. He wonders why that family was allowed to arrive in their own car.

There are ten tables inside the dining room, most of them occupied. He spots a couple sitting at a table across the room. They look to be in their late forties. The woman, an attractive redhead, seems familiar to him. He studies her face, and it hits him who the man in the Mercedes was. His name is Malcolm Crowe. He's a well-known movie director living on Philadelphia's Main Line.

What the hell is he *doing here? Surely Crowe isn't one of Nunzio's guys. Why would Nunzio think a movie man had to be protected from Frank Valiante?*

The question preoccupies him throughout breakfast, as does the nagging sense that he knows the redhead. When Gabby is finished, he takes her to the woman's table.

"Hello," he says. "I don't mean to interrupt. My name is Mick McFarland. I'm one of Mr. Nunzio's attorneys. Have we met before?"

The woman smiles and stands, as does her husband.

"Not that I remember," she says, shaking his hand. "I'm Alecia Silver."

"Ah, the author. I'm sorry I didn't recognize you." He's read some of her books. Steamy legal thrillers.

"No need to apologize. People know authors' names, but there probably aren't more than ten writers the typical person would recognize on the street, Stephen King and John Grisham counting as two of them."

Alecia's husband introduces himself as an attorney with one of the city's large defense firms. "And, of course, I've heard of you," he says to Mick. "I think every lawyer in town has."

Mick smiles, unsure how to take the remark.

"It's lovely here, isn't it?" Alecia says. "How generous of Rachel to invite us all for the weekend."

"When did you arrive?" he asks.

"Friday evening. We had a great time yesterday. Canoeing in the morning. Tennis in the afternoon. Dinner and the firepit at night."

"We arrived late last night," Mick answers. "I hope we have as much fun." He introduces them to Gabby and takes his leave.

Back in the great room, he hands Gabby the key to their suite and tells her to go upstairs and use the bathroom. "I'll be up in a minute." As she climbs the stairs, he catches sight of Rachel Nunzio by the French doors that open onto the back terrace. She turns and watches him approach.

"So, I just met Alecia Silver, and I saw that Malcolm Crowe is here as well, with his family. What gives?"

"Alecia is such a lovely woman. And Malcom's films are a bright spot for the city, don't you think?"

"What the hell's going on? You have me and my daughter woken up in the middle of the night and brought to this place against my will, under threat of mob war. At the same time, you lure celebrities here as invited guests? Do these people know you're putting them at risk?"

"But they're not at risk. Nor are you, so long as you're here. That's the whole point."

"But *you're* under attack!"

She smiles, but her eyes are steel. "This isn't the Alamo, Mr. McFarland. We are not under siege."

Piper sits quietly in the front passenger seat of Tommy's rented Lincoln Town Car, still processing what he's told her and Susan about Lois Beal. She wouldn't have believed it had Tommy not shown her Xeroxes of the old newspaper stories about the crime and ensuing manhunt. She wonders what she's going to say to persuade Lois to take a chance on coming forward for Darlene Dowd. She also wonders how she's going to persuade Susan not to turn Lois in to the authorities. They fought about that over breakfast, Susan insisting she was obligated as an officer of the court and former assistant US attorney to report Lois to the FBI. Piper and Tommy argued against it, but all they won was Susan's grudging promise to hear Lois out before she did anything.

The drive from Ocean Lodge to Lois's house is only fifteen minutes down Frederica Road. Frederica is a two-way road separated by a double yellow line, shaded by oak trees hung with Spanish moss. On one side of the road, Piper sees a jogging and bike path abutting a golf course.

Piper takes a deep breath as Tommy turns onto Militia Hill Way, a shaded private road off Frederica. He pulls the car into the driveway of a yellow stucco home with a red terra-cotta roof and a porch with white pillars and banisters.

"Here goes nothing," she says, opening the door. Susan exits the back, and they walk together onto the porch while Tommy waits in the car.

Piper knocks gently on the door. After a few moments, a petite woman with white hair and kind eyes appears in the screen.

"May I help you?" the woman says.

"We're looking for Lois Beal," Piper answers.

The woman's face registers fear, but she quickly recovers.

"There's no one here by that name," she says.

"How about Megan Corbett?" Susan asks.

The woman's eyes widen, and she seems to falter.

Piper says, "We're not with law enforcement, Lois."

"Though we know why you'd be worried if we were," adds Susan.

"We're here about Darlene Dowd," Piper says. "We're with a law firm, and we're trying to free her. We're hoping you can help."

Lois's eyes dart from Piper to Susan and back. She exhales and opens the screen door without saying anything. Once Piper and Susan are inside, she closes the outer door and screen door behind them, then leads them to a small dining room table.

"Would you like some iced tea?" Lois asks. "I just brewed some."

"That would be lovely," Piper says.

Lois disappears into the kitchen and returns a few minutes later with a pitcher and three glasses. She fills the glasses, then sits and takes a sip of the tea. Piper is impressed with her self-control.

"I suppose I always knew someone would come knocking at my door, sooner or later," she says. "Though I didn't expect it would be lawyers about Darlene."

"You figured it would be the FBI," Susan says. "Coming to arrest you for the armored car. The killings."

Lois lowers her head, closes her eyes. When she opens them again, they are wet.

"I expect this means Darlene's mother has passed," Lois says.

Piper nods.

"It's been so long since Lester was killed . . . fifteen years, I think. Ten years since I moved here after my Bobby died—that's how I still think of him, how I always did. I never thought of him as Jason Dell. I didn't even like that name." She sighs and shakes her head. "I'd almost forgotten the promise I made to Cindy."

"We'll get to that," Susan says. "Can we talk about 1969 first?"

Lois hesitates. "I suppose it's always best to start at the beginning." She takes a minute to gather her resolve. "I had just turned nineteen. I was young, impressionable, and idealistic—like everyone I knew. Fervently against the war and the generation that had caused it. Certain that my own generation was going to change the world."

She pauses and smiles. Sadly, it seems to Piper.

"And I was hopelessly in love. He was beautiful. Tall and strong, with big shoulders and long brown hair and blue eyes as deep as wells. And charismatic. That was my Bobby Moffat. God, but I fell so hard for him. I believed every word that came out of his mouth like it was gospel. So when he said that to fight the man the cause needed money—a lot of it, and fast, and we were going to get it by robbing an armored car—I was all in."

She shakes her head. "Ten thousand years ago, on the other side of the world. I read a story once that began that way. And that's how it seems now, looking back on it. Most of the time. Sometimes, though, at night, sitting on my porch, I can close my eyes, and it feels like I never left that place, that time."

Susan leans forward. "Tell us what happened with the robbery."

Piper shoots her an angry look, then turns to Lois. "When you're ready."

Lois closes her eyes. "It was supposed to be easy. No one was to get hurt. One of our group had a cousin who worked for Brinks. He knew the exact route of the truck, knew when it would be most full of money. He even knew the two guys who'd be in the truck. Most important, he told us that it was Brinks policy never to engage in a firefight with would-be robbers. So when our guys pulled their guns, the two guards were supposed to capitulate."

"But they didn't," says Susan.

"It was awful. We were in an old station wagon as big as a boat. I was the driver. I pulled in front of the armored truck when it stopped for a bank pickup. We waited until the guards came out of the bank with the money sacks and opened the back doors of the truck. Bobby and the two other guys—Dylan and Jake—jumped out of our car with their guns drawn and ran to the back of the truck. The guards were supposed to put up their hands as soon as they saw the weapons, but one of them went for his own gun. One of our guys—Dylan, not Bobby—shot him dead, right through the head. The other guard stood there, begging them not to shoot him. Bobby was afraid Dylan would kill the man, so he shot the guard in the leg to put him down. Dylan and Jake grabbed the money bags, they ran back to the car, and I took off. We found out later that both men died."

Lois squeezes her eyes closed and pinches the bridge of her nose. She exhales loudly.

Piper leans across the table, pushes her glass toward her. "Have some tea."

Susan asks, "How did you end up at the farm in Pennsylvania?"

"That was a long and twisted ordeal. The draft was on, and a lot of our friends were skipping out to Canada. Some were staying in the States, though, under false identities. We knew people who could make fake IDs. Bobby's draft number had already been called. He'd had an ID made, and even had one for me in case I wanted to go with him. We used those IDs and headed to the Midwest. We were there for almost a year. Then we decided to skip to Canada, after all. We lived in British Columbia, then Alberta, and then, when we were feeling a little safer, in Montreal, Quebec. But we got homesick. So Bobby got in touch with his fake-ID guys and had really good ones made. Two sets for each of us."

"Two sets?" Piper asks.

"Lois Beal and Terri Petrini for me. Jason Dell and another name I can't remember for Bobby."

"You go by Terri Petrini now," Susan says.

"Yes."

"When did you first contact your sister?"

"Early on. I couldn't bear the idea of talking to my parents, but I wanted to get word to my family that I was okay, while letting them know that they wouldn't hear from me for a long time. Heather was older than me by five years, but we were close, so I reached out to her. Then, once Bobby and I decided to come back to the States, I called her again. That's when I found out about her husband's old family farm. She said Jeffrey was renting it out to tenants on a month-to-month basis and that he could give them notice and open it for Bobby and me. I know she got into a big row over it with Jeffrey, but he eventually relented."

There's a rap at the door, and Lois jumps.

Piper smiles. "Relax, I think I know who that is."

"There are more of you?"

"Just one."

Piper walks to the front door and comes back with Tommy. She sees Lois staring, not knowing what to make of him.

"Hello," Tommy says solicitously, reaching out to shake Lois's hand. "I'm Tommy McFarland. I just came in to use the restroom."

Lois points him down the hallway.

"He looks rough," Lois whispers.

"I'm married to his brother," Piper says. "He's safe."

Tommy returns and heads for the front door again, but Lois calls after him. "You can stay, if you'd like. There's iced tea."

Tommy takes a seat at the table, and they wait for Lois to bring him a glass from the kitchen. She hands it to him, and he pours from the pitcher as Lois continues.

"So. I've told you how Megan Corbett came to be Lois Beal. I suppose it's time to tell you about Darlene and Cindy Dowd. And that monster."

22

Sunday, May 26, Continued

Mick and Gabrielle have been paddling a canoe around the lake for an hour when she tells him she's getting tired. He paddles them back to the small beach behind the lodge, Gabby waving to the other boaters they pass. When they started, Mick was wearing a light jacket, but he's taken it off. It's almost 11:00, and the temperature is nearing seventy degrees, a little warmer than usual for the Poconos in late May. He gets out and pulls the canoe on shore, then lifts Gabby so her feet won't get wet.

They're walking to the lodge when he hears a chopping sound in the air.

"Look, Daddy!" Gabby says.

He follows her gaze to a white helicopter slowly lowering onto a helipad that he hadn't noticed before. Rachel and some men are positioned near the helipad, waiting. He and Gabby stand together and watch the chopper as it touches down. The blades slow and then stop, and then a rear door on the pilot's side opens up. A young woman exits first, followed by a very old man so thin and frail he looks to Mick like he could be blown over by a mild wind. The woman is tall and athletically trim, with long legs and long reddish-brown hair. She's wearing jeans and high boots and a jean jacket over a light sweater. Something about her long legs and the way she moves reminds him of a doe. He wonders about her eyes, which are hidden behind sunglasses.

Rachel hugs the old man, then turns to the young woman. They embrace.

"Christina," he says, wondering how long it's been since she and her mother have seen each other.

"Christina?" Gabby repeats.

"I think that's her name."

He watches as Rachel, Christina, and the old man walk arm in arm from the helipad toward the far side of the building. Behind them, two men carry Christina's and the old man's luggage.

"Come on." He takes Gabrielle's hand and guides her to the path on the other side of the building. They walk around front, where he's surprised to find a baseball game in progress on the great lawn. There are bases and a backstop, even a pitcher's mound. The players aren't wearing uniforms, only jeans and T-shirts. The batter hits the ball solidly, the aluminum bat cracking its hollow twang, and he hears people shouting and clapping. He turns to the porch and sees twenty or more people sitting around tables, watching the game. Gabby tells him she wants to watch, too, and they make their way to the porch and take seats at a small table.

It's surreal to be watching a baseball game played by a pack of arm-breakers, number-runners, and hit men. Thirty of them, at least. Some are standing in the field, and others await their turn at bat on folding chairs set up as benches. More are standing around watching. What strikes him is that most of them aren't playing like they're having fun. There's no joking around. No clapping or smack talk or whistling. They look like men carrying out a work assignment. He scans the porch, wondering if anyone else has picked up on it. If they have, they're not showing it.

After two innings, Gabby tells him she's bored. They set off looking for a soccer ball and net. They ask the woman at the reception desk—not the same person as when they checked in last night, but also young and attractive—and she says she'll find out. She calls someone on the phone, has a short conversation, and hangs up.

"The baseball game will be over in about thirty minutes. They'll clear away the bases and chairs and set up a net for you. Do you need more than one soccer ball?"

He tells her one should be enough and asks for directions to the walking paths in the woods.

She pulls out a paper map of the grounds. "Some of the trails continue beyond our property. You'll know you're getting close because we have yellow stripes painted on the trees at our boundary lines. Don't go beyond those trees." She smiles and keeps her voice light, but he sees a warning in her eyes.

It's all a big show, he thinks. *The baseball, the leisurely canoeing, everyone seeming so happy. But who is the show for?*

He thanks the receptionist, and they walk out to the trails. These begin as gravel, then turn to chipped wood, then to dirt and rock. They spot some deer and even come across a turtle making his way across the trail. Gabby lifts the turtle and gently places it under some foliage, and they move on. He's enjoying the air and the woods and forgets for a moment why they're there.

"Is it thirty minutes yet?" Gabby asks.

"You're not having fun?"

"I need to practice."

When they get back to the great lawn, a net has been set up. Soccer balls are lying nearby. Elsewhere on the lawn, children are hitting cricket balls, throwing horseshoes, or just running around, their parents standing by.

"Defend the net," Gabby says. "If you can."

Mick positions himself in front of the net as Gabby dribbles for a few minutes, then starts practicing her attack. She starts from the center, then moves to the side for her attacks. He reaches, lunges, and dives, but he's no match for her speed. She gets the ball past him almost every time. He gets up from a dive, huffing and puffing.

He dusts himself off and hears, "You'll never get better doing that."

It's a woman's voice. He looks up to see Christina Nunzio, now in tight-fitting workout gear and bright-yellow sneakers, walking toward them.

"Attacking is the most fun," Christina says to Gabby. "But you need to spend time on your footwork."

Close up, Mick is surprised by Christina's striking beauty. Her wide-set almond eyes are a deep, liquid brown. She has generous lips and olive skin like her mother, but her cheekbones are higher, her jaw line sharper. She's the type he'd expect to strike an attitude, like a runway model, but her smile is mild and open—disarmingly so.

"It's nice to meet you, Mr. McFarland," she says. "My mother pointed you out to me." She turns to Gabby. "And our young soccer star here must be Gabrielle."

Gabby smiles shyly, nods. "I like Gabby."

"Then I shall call you Gabby." Christina picks up the ball. "Want to do some drills?"

Gabby says yes, and Christina backs up a few steps. "One bounce and return," she says, tossing the ball to Gabby, letting it hit the ground once before it reaches her. Gabby kicks the ball back to Christina. They repeat the drill a few more times.

"Okay, no bounce," Christina says, tossing the ball directly at Gabby's right foot. Gabby kicks the ball back to Christina, who tosses the ball again.

Mick watches as Christina runs Gabby through more iterations of the drill, having Gabby knee the ball before kicking it back, then feint left and right before kicking it back. As they're doing this, a man brings Christina a half dozen yellow cones. Christina positions the cones in a straight line and has Gabby dribble a ball from one end to the other, circling the cones as she does so. She has Gabrielle repeat this drill a number of times, then positions herself about ten yards from the net.

"Now see if you can dribble it past me."

Gabby tries, but Christina effortlessly steals the ball from her, turns, and kicks it into the center of the net. Again and again, Gabby tries to dribble past Christina, but every time, Christina steals the ball from her with almost casual effort.

"Your footwork's amazing," Mick says.

"It's been so long. I forgot how much I loved the game." Christina turns back to Gabby, who looks at her with awe. "Okay, now you can have some fun. I'll defend the net. You attack."

The first few times, Gabby fails to get the ball past Christina, who tells her not to lean over the ball. Gabby kicks again, and this time, the ball sails past Christina's extended arm and into the upper-right corner of the net.

"I did it!" Gabby beams, turning to Mick and pumping her fist.

He and Christina laugh at Gabby's showboating.

Mick watches as Christina lets Gabby attack the net a few times. He sees a resemblance in them. Not so much in their physical appearance, but in their open earnestness and determination, and in their obvious love of the game. He can envision Gabby growing up to be like Christina Nunzio.

He hears someone approaching and turns his head to see Rachel.

"It's nice to see my daughter smile again," she says.

Mick returns his gaze to Christina. Despite her genial demeanor, he knows how badly she must be hurting. He admires her for her strength.

They watch their daughters play awhile longer, then Christina ends the practice, and she and Gabby walk up to them.

"You're really good," Gabby says to Christina once they're all together.

"I played a little in college," she answers.

"She was captain of the team," Mick says.

"Because I worked hard," she says to Gabby. "And that's the lesson. If you want to be the best, you have to work harder than everyone else. Work harder"—she turns to her mother—"and be smarter."

Mick thanks Christina, then walks toward the lodge with Gabby. He glances back, trying to reconcile the two versions of Christina Nunzio. The Queen of Clubs party girl versus the overachieving college student and athlete getting all As, even while president of her sorority.

What happened to you, Christina?

"I knew Darlene since the day she was born," Lois says. "Bobby and I had been living on the farm thirteen years by then, and I had just turned thirty-four. Cindy and I were close, and she turned to me for help with Darlene—which I was more than eager to give. Bobby and I decided not to have children of our own. We couldn't bear the thought of one day being hauled away in front of our children."

Piper sits across the small table from Lois Beal, born Megan Corbett and now using the name Terri Petrini. Reliving her involvement in the armored-truck robbery and her years on the lam was clearly exhausting for Lois, so Piper suggested they break for a few minutes. She, Tommy, and Susan walked outside to discuss what Lois had told them.

"The killings weren't planned," Piper said to Susan, who still insisted that they needed to call the authorities. "And Lois didn't hurt anyone. She wasn't even armed. She was just the driver."

"If I had a dime for every time I heard some defendant make the same argument when I was a prosecutor—"

"It was fifty years ago!"

"All right. Let's go easy," Tommy interceded. "Even if we think the feds need to be called, there's no need to drop a dime on Lois *right now*. Let's hear what she has to say about Darlene. Then we can go back home and roundtable this."

Piper understands that Susan was a federal prosecutor, but she's been a defense attorney for eight years now. *So why,* Piper wonders, *is she so eager to turn someone over to the authorities?* Mick says Susan has always been a stickler when it comes to legal ethics, and she would certainly blow a gasket if she ever found out how Mick had used her in the Hanson trial to suborn Piper's perjury. But is a fifty-year-old crime a reason to destroy someone's life?

Lois begins leading up to what happened to Darlene Dowd's father.

"Darlene was the sweetest girl," Lois says. "She spent a lot of time at my house when she was little. But when she got to be a teenager, she didn't come by as much. When she did, she seemed remote. Moody. I chalked it up to adolescence. Cindy never told me differently—until after the killing."

"Tell us about Cindy and Lester," Susan says.

"Cindy was younger than me, by more than a decade. She was a good woman, and smart, but no education to speak of. She was raised in Appalachia, and some of the stories she told me about her life growing up . . . you'd think she was describing the third world. I'm talking *poor*, and I don't mean city poor, where everyone has a car and a color TV. I mean poor as in your house doesn't have heat or running water. She was always terrified of ending up back there. That's one of the reasons, probably the main reason, she never stood up to Lester."

"How did she end up with him?" Piper asks.

"Lester was an army buddy of Cindy's brother. After they both returned from service, Lester came to visit the brother, share stories, drink, look for trouble. The fact that Lester thought he'd find more fun in Appalachia than at home tells me that where he came from must've been god-awful. He was always complaining to Cindy about what a bastard his daddy was. And his uncles, and his brothers, and even his mother. But he never gave her any details.

"Anyway, Lester invited Cindy to come away with him, and she took the chance. For a few years, Lester worked odd jobs in the

Carolinas, Virginia, and Maryland. Then he got injured in a car crash caused by the drunk son of a wealthy man with lots of insurance, and the settlement earned him enough money to move north and buy the small farm in Pennsylvania."

Lois looks away, and Piper can tell her mind is drifting. They sit quietly for a moment. Then Piper breaks the ice.

"Are you ready to tell us about the night Lester Dowd was killed?"

"Ready as I'll ever be, I guess." Lois exhales, braces herself. "We had a big screened porch. When the weather was warm, I enjoyed sitting out there during the day, drinking iced tea and reading. Lots of times I'd sleep out there, too. I loved the sounds of the crickets and cicadas and bullfrogs at night, and in the morning, waking up to the birds.

"Every now and then, once Darlene got a little older, I'd wake up on the porch and see her walking along the road toward her home. I asked Cindy about it. She said Darlene was one for the outdoors, that she loved sleeping under the stars. I asked why she didn't just put up a tent on their farm. It didn't seem safe for a teenager to spend the night alone in some field. But Cindy passed it off, not worried about Darlene's safety. I thought there might be more to it, but I didn't press. I wished I had once I found out about what her father had been doing to her. Maybe if I'd have pressed the issue, Cindy would have opened up to me."

"So you think she knew all along?" Susan asks.

Lois sighs. "All along? I can't say. But at some point, she figured it out. That was obvious from what she told me the morning of the killing. Even more obvious from what she told me later."

Piper sits up. Lois is about to share the secrets that will decide Darlene Dowd's fate. "She told you different things at different times?"

"Not different, exactly. It's just that later, she filled in some details." Lois pauses and takes a long sip of iced tea. "The morning of the killing, it was about 6:00 a.m., a half hour after sunrise—I remember because I'd woken up at 5:15 and had gone to the bathroom and started the coffee. From the porch, I saw Darlene walking down the road past my house, toward the Dowd place, just like I'd seen her do before. She was wearing jeans and a shirt with a white jean jacket over it, and she was carrying a blanket. She didn't look to be in any type of hurry. Or upset, or anything. And she certainly didn't have any blood on her.

"Half an hour later, Cindy came rushing up to my porch in a panic, carrying something that turned out to be a hammer. She had blood all over her, and the hammer did, too. She started sobbing about how Lester had been molesting Darlene. She said she'd had a lot to drink that night and fell into a drunk sleep. When she woke up, she went downstairs and found Lester dead on the kitchen floor, beaten with the hammer. She begged me to hide the hammer. Bury it somewhere the police would never find it."

Piper leans back, feeling like she's been kicked in the gut. She tries to push out the question she already knows the answer to, but Susan beats her to it.

"She told you Darlene had killed her father," Susan says. "And she wanted you to hide the hammer to help Darlene."

"She didn't come out and say it was Darlene, but it seemed obvious."

"So you hid the hammer?" Tommy asks.

"Cindy asked me to keep it and preserve it. She watched me as I put it into a paper bag and sealed it shut with duct tape. She asked me where I was going to put it. I said I'd hide it in a metal locker my husband had in the back of our garage but never used."

"Why would she want you to keep it rather than toss it into a pond or lake where it would never be found?" Tommy asks.

"It didn't make sense to me, either. But I didn't pressure her to explain. She was so upset already. And I figured she'd tell me eventually."

"Did you hide the hammer while Cindy was there?"

"No, I told her to get back home and call the police. A little while later, I came down to the Dowd farm and pretended to be surprised by all the police cars out on the road. Cindy shouted to me that Lester had been killed and that there was blood everywhere—that way the police chief figured it was my first time hearing it. I told the chief I'd seen Darlene walking toward her house around six, and that she hadn't had any blood on her."

"You told this to Chief Foster, at the farm?" Susan asks.

"Yes, and I told him a second time when I went to his office a couple days later."

"But he threatened you," Piper says, repeating what Melvin Ott said. "He said he'd turn the FBI onto you."

"And with your background, that was a chance you couldn't take," Tommy says.

"I hated that man from the first time I met him. He'd just come back from the service. He was twenty-four, a year older than me. We were both putting gas in our cars down at the Gulf station, and he made a pass at me. I told him I was flattered, but that I was happily married. That didn't stop him. He kept on propositioning me for more than a year. Finally, I told Bobby about it. Bobby caught up with him, and that was the end of it. A few years later, Sonny joined the police department, and he started baiting Bobby to try and find some reason, I'm sure, to arrest him. Bobby didn't bite, but I was always afraid he was one step away from getting himself locked up."

"Locked up, and maybe having his past looked into," Tommy says.

Lois nods. "Sonny Foster was also an ultraconservative type, and he made it clear he didn't like 'hippies' like Bobby and me."

"How did he know to threaten you about your background?"

"He didn't. Not really. He always said he suspected Bobby and I were shady. We weren't locals. We didn't own our farm. Bobby never had a steady job with a local business. We held ourselves out as married but used different last names. He also didn't like the fact that, some years, Bobby grew cannabis on our farm—something Sonny could never prove but which everyone knew about." She takes a sip of iced tea. "Bobby said the whole township was situated in a microclimate perfect for growing pot, and we'd all get rich if it were ever legalized." Lois pauses and smiles. "Sonny also hated me for being an artsy type."

Piper looks confused, so Lois explains. "Allentown has its own playhouse, and I acted there for many years. Bobby and I fought about it more than once. He was afraid someone would recognize me and call the authorities. I told him acting was in my blood and that I'd explode if I had to give it up entirely. And I was careful. I cut my hair short and dyed it."

"So Sonny never knew anything specific—he just got lucky making his threat against you?" Tommy asks.

Lois shrugs. "I can't say for sure what Sonny knew, but he made the threat anyway. And he was not the type to bluff. So I sat quietly at Darlene's trial. The jury never heard I'd seen her that morning without a speck of blood on her."

"But what does it matter?" Piper says. "Darlene went home and killed her father. Cindy knew it, and you secreted the hammer away from the police in a failed effort to protect her."

She feels like crying—that's how much she'd wanted Darlene to be innocent.

Lois Beal looks directly at Piper. "That's what I thought, too," she says. "I figured that Darlene must have changed clothes, then left the farm after killing her father the night before. That when I'd seen her, she was returning home. But . . ."

Piper sits up. "But what?"

"I told you that Cindy later filled in some details that she didn't share that morning."

"Let me guess," Tommy says. "Cindy Dowd brought you the hammer to protect *herself*."

"She didn't admit it to me until five years later. It was right after Bobby died. I told Cindy I was moving to Georgia, to be near my sister." Lois pauses, shakes her head. Purses her lips. "If I'd have known at the time of the trial, I would have never let Darlene go to prison for Cindy, regardless of what it meant for me."

"Why do you think she told you after all that time?" Susan asks.

"Because she wanted me to go to the authorities with the hammer. When she died."

Susan's face can't hide her disdain. "And in the meantime, her daughter would keep rotting in jail?"

Her chest aching with rage, Piper says, "You're telling us that Cindy Dowd sat back and let her husband sexually abuse their daughter, and then essentially framed Darlene for murder? That's bad enough. But then you found out about it and did *nothing*?"

Lois Beal lowers her head and starts to cry. "I was afraid. That's no excuse. God forgive me."

"You're going to make this right," Piper says, pointing her finger, all her goodwill and empathy for Lois Beal gone.

"And when you're done testifying," Susan interjects, "we're—"

"We're going to decide whether to turn you in for the armored-truck killings," Tommy interjects.

Lois is crying so hard she's shaking.

Susan tells Piper, "I'll draft the 9453 motion as soon as we get back. We'll have it filed well within the sixty-day limit." She turns to Lois. "I'm going to draw up a certification for you to sign. It will include everything you told us about the day of Lester Dowd's killing and about what Cindy later admitted to you."

"Wait," Tommy says. "The hammer."

"I took it out of the locker and buried it before I moved. There's a small family cemetery on the farm. I buried it under one of the headstones."

"You're going to have to come back," Tommy says, "and unearth the hammer. On videotape. In the presence of law enforcement. We'll have the hammer examined for fingerprints, blood, and hair."

"I should have come forward years ago," Lois says, her voice raw and wet. "As soon as Bobby passed, I should have turned myself in for the robbery and come clean with what I knew about Lester Dowd. Darlene shouldn't have spent all these years in prison."

Piper sees Lois searching her eyes for some small measure of forgiveness.

She can offer none.

They're on I-95 South for forty minutes when Tommy says, "Why would she sit on it? Knowing Darlene didn't kill her father, and that Cindy did?"

"She was afraid of getting outed as Megan Corbett," Susan says.

"But she told the chief about seeing Darlene. She said she was ready to testify back then."

"Until Chief Foster said he'd look into her background," Susan says. "I think that sobered her up, made her realize she couldn't risk testifying."

"It just doesn't smell right," Tommy says. "She seemed like a decent person. I can't see her letting Darlene rot in prison for ten years after she found out it was Cindy all along. There has to be more to it."

"There always is," says Susan.

23

Sunday, May 26–Monday, May 27

Mick and Gabby are at the firepit on the far side of the great lawn. The temperature is sixty degrees, but there's a slight wind and moisture in the air that make it feel cooler. With sunset an hour behind them and the moon hidden by thick clouds, the fire is the only source of light.

Ten Adirondack chairs circle the fire, and eight of them are occupied: two by Mick and Gabby, two by the writer Alecia Stone and her husband, and four by the family Mick saw exit the Escalade the night before. The man, it turned out, is Jimmy Nunzio's brother, Stephen Nunzio, MD. He looks like Jimmy—fiftyish, trim and fit, with dark hair beginning to gray. The doctor's wife is considerably younger, in her midthirties, which would explain the twin boys, Gabby's age, and the newborn. The doctor's wife doesn't appear to be enjoying herself, but Dr. Steve is having a grand time, standing by the fire, joking with his boys, toasting marshmallows. Gabby is also toasting marshmallows and, Mick notices, glancing at each of the boys, then looking away when they catch her doing it.

A waiter from the lodge approaches and asks if anyone wants something to drink. The kids ask for hot chocolate, Alecia and her husband request wine. Mick orders a glass of Macallan 15.

"Make that two," says Dr. Steve as his wife—who wants nothing—rolls her eyes. "Maybe bring the bottle," he adds, winking at Mick.

Dinner was an interesting affair. All ten tables in the dining room were full. He and Gabby were seated at a table with Nunzio's accountant and his wife and daughter. Rachel, Christina, and Dr. Steve and his wife, sans children, were at their own table with the old guy who got off the helicopter with Christina.

The dining room featured a menu with everything one would expect at a four-star resort. Watching everyone eat and enjoy themselves at dinner, Mick wondered the same thing he's wondering now as Stephen Nunzio and Alecia Silver toast marshmallows around the firepit: *What the hell is going on here?*

The premise of this gathering, as he's been made to understand it, is that Nunzio's family and crew are under threat of imminent attack and have to circle their wagons. But the sense of menace he felt when he first arrived here last night seems to have existed only in his own mind. All the other guests are clearly on holiday. Or think they are. The image that comes to his mind is the scene in the old *Titanic* movie when the happy passengers frolic among the ice chunks that fall onto the deck when the ship strikes the iceberg.

"Having fun, Mick?"

He turns to see Rachel Nunzio coming up behind him, arm in arm with the old man.

"This is Mr. McFarland," she says. "Jimmy's attorney. Mick, this is my Uncle Ham."

He shakes hands with Rachel's uncle, finding his grip surprisingly strong for someone appearing so frail.

"I've heard good things about you," says Uncle Ham. His eyes twinkle, but Mick finds his smile less than benign.

"Everyone seems to be enjoying themselves," Mick says, "considering we're on the cusp of a mob war."

"Mob." Rachel spits out the word. "Little boys fighting in the backyard. There are much larger games afoot, Mr. McFarland."

He watches the old man, trying to gauge whether he knows what Rachel is talking about, but Uncle Ham's face is unreadable.

"When do you think we'll be able to leave?" he asks Rachel, who glances at Uncle Ham.

"When it's time," she says.

Her tone sends a clear message: *Drop it.*

He turns to the old man. "It was nice meeting you, Mr. . . ."

"It was good to meet you, too, Mr. McFarland," he says, offering his arm to Rachel, who takes it. "I hope everything turns out well with my nephew."

"James is your nephew? I thought you were Rachel's uncle."

Rachel smiles. "In our family, he's everyone's uncle."

Mick watches Rachel and the old man stroll across the great lawn toward the lodge, the hairs on the back of his neck at attention. Something's coming. He doesn't know what, but it's not going to turn out well. He turns to Gabby, now standing between the twins, the three of them holding their marshmallow sticks over the fire. He fights off the compulsion to throw her over his shoulder and run from this place as fast as he can. One glance toward the lodge, where he sees Johnny Giacobetti, his giant mastiffs, and half a dozen other soldiers pretending to lounge, tells him he'd never make it.

Angelo Valiante sits in the front passenger seat of the Ford Econoline van. Beside him, in the driver's seat, is Sal Tuscano, one of his brother Tony's closest friends. Behind them, on three rows of seats, are eight of the Valiante crew's toughest soldiers. Many of them served in the military, including two of the three men on the last seat, who were drummed out of Special Forces for being too violent. Five more identical vans, each with a driver and nine soldiers, are parked on the berm of River Birch Lane, the forest-lined private road leading to Nunzio's lodge.

The vans left Brooklyn earlier that evening, spaced roughly ten miles apart so as not to attract attention. They rendezvoused at the Rodeway Inn, a two-story motel in Milford, eighteen miles from the lodge. Other members of the crew rented rooms at the motel and stockpiled them with enough weaponry and rounds to invade a small country. They left an hour ago for the final push from Milford, up Routes 6 and 590.

Angelo was impressed with the vans as soon as he saw them. The glass is almost an inch thick. The armored chassis is so heavy the vans require special tires. Except for the front windows and windshield, the windows are tinted so dark as to be opaque from the outside. That was done because it's crucial that Nunzio's men believe the vans are loaded with Valiante's soldiers when they drive onto the property. Nunzio's men will burst from their little log huts and attack the vans, and that's when he and Sal and the rest of the soldiers will fire from the forest, tearing Nunzio's men to pieces.

"Nunzio's daughter," Sal says. "She's a looker. You gonna share?"

He considers this. "Why not? Let's pull a train. I'll be the engine, you follow right behind."

"Shit," one of the men on the seat behind them says. "I go after you two, I'll need a Kevlar condom."

Everyone laughs.

Gabby stirs in the bed, and Mick looks over at her. He's been awake for an hour now; before that, his sleep was fitful. After the firepit, he brought Gabby back to the room and put her to bed. They took turns reading from *Harry Potter and the Deathly Hallows.* Gabby fell asleep midway through the last chapter, "The Flaw in the Plan." True to form, she's been out cold ever since.

Mick waits another few minutes, then sits up in bed. He looks across the room, through the darkness, to the balcony. The night sky is black, telling him that the clouds have not moved out. He carefully stands, steps to the balcony, and looks out over the great lawn. The firepit is extinguished, and even the guards appear to have gone to bed. He closes his eyes, inhales the cool night air. When he opens them, he's struck by the sense that he's being watched. He scans the great lawn again, seeing no one. Then he glances below and sees her. Loki. The giant mastiff is sitting on the grass, staring up at him. His heart speeds up for a moment, until he wills it to slow.

"Just a dog," he murmurs as he turns away.

He decides to go out to the second-floor porch. He dresses in jeans and a black T-shirt. Flip-flops, because he doesn't feel like tying his sneakers.

The door to the porch is only a couple of doors down from his own. He opens it and steps outside. The roofed porch is furnished with outdoor couches and chairs. Walking toward the set closest to the railing, he feels her before he sees her. A warping of the darkness before him, the subtle scent of perfume.

The details become clearer as he moves closer. She's wearing an open robe over loose-fitting satin pajamas, emerald green. Her long, auburn hair caresses her shoulders.

She looks up at him from the couch. "Mick."

"Hi, Christina. Mind if I join you?"

"Couldn't sleep, either?" She nods toward the other end of the couch, and he takes a seat there. "Let me light a candle," she says, leaning over the coffee table and picking up a pack of matches. She strikes one and lights a white votive. In the candle's glow, the olive skin of her face looks smooth as porcelain.

"Tea?" she asks, and he notices a small clay pot and a cup and saucer. "I can go down to the kitchen and bring up another cup."

"Thank you, but no. The caffeine—I'd never get to sleep."

She refills her own cup.

"Your father won't tell me what happened that night, in the warehouse," he says, hoping Christina will open the door. "He says he's waiting until the time's right."

At the mention of her father, Christina purses her lips. She opens them but doesn't take the bait. "I've heard you're a good lawyer," she says. "I suppose you've heard things about me as well."

"A few things. I know you worked hard in college, graduated at the top of your class at Wharton. Since then . . ." His voice trails off.

"Since then," she repeats, nodding. She takes a sip of her tea, and they sit quietly for a while.

"What happened?" he asks.

"You mean, what made me turn from such a hard worker to a girl who jet-sets from one party to another?" She takes another sip of tea. "I've watched you playing with your daughter," she says. "It's obvious that you love her very much."

"More than anything in the world."

She turns to face him squarely. "Tell me, when your daughter talks to you, do you hear her?"

"Hear her?"

"Do you see her, Mick? Do you truly see your daughter?"

"Strange questions."

She smiles. "My father stopped hearing me, seeing me, a long time ago."

"So that's it? The partying, the waste of talent—you're just getting back at Daddy?"

His words seem to slap her, and her eyes fill with fury. She takes a deep, calming breath.

"There's a story in my family that my father killed his first man when he was twelve years old. His own father, and some of his men, marched my dad into a farm field, where they'd brought another man and put him on his knees. My grandfather told my father the man had wronged our family in some way. Then he gave my father a gun and told him to shoot. And he fired, shot the man dead."

He's not sure what to say.

"Some of the old guard say that's the day Jimmy Nunzio lost his soul." She waits a beat. Then: "But what if he hadn't?"

"Lost his soul?"

"Hadn't shot the man. I think most twelve-year-old boys wouldn't blow someone's brains out just because their father put a gun in their hand."

"I don't understand."

"Killing that man didn't make my father a killer. He was a killer to begin with." She turns away from him, stares through the railing. "You can't force someone to be something they're not. And it's not fair to try."

"Christina."

Mick recognizes the voice.

"You need to come inside," Rachel says, moving up to them. "You're too exposed."

"There's no moon, Mother. It's pitch-black," Christina says. "Even with the candle, no one out there could see us."

"That's not what I mean."

Christina stands and looks down at him. "It's been nice talking with you, Mick. Please remember what I said about your daughter."

He watches her turn away, walk with her mother across the porch, and disappear inside.

"I'll be back in a minute," Angelo tells Sal. They've been sitting in the vans for an hour, and he needs to stretch. He also needs to take a dump. His old man treated him and the other lieutenants to a big pasta dinner at Bamonte's, and he hasn't relieved himself since. He knows he should've used the toilet back at that motel.

He walks into the woods, far enough so he can't be seen by anyone in the vans, and drops his drawers. He squats, leaning against a tree. When he's done, he pulls out a handkerchief and wipes himself.

Crazy to think that human beings did this kind of thing for thousands of years, before someone dreamed up indoor plumbing.

On the way back to the vans, he glances at his watch. Three o'clock. Time to move in. When he gets back, he finds his door locked. He doesn't remember locking it, but maybe he did, or maybe Sal locked it after he left. Sal is asleep, so he knocks on the glass, first lightly.

"Come on, wake up."

But Sal doesn't wake up. He knocks harder.

Pissed, he looks through the front passenger window into the back of the van, and finds everyone else is asleep, too.

"The fuck?" he says, pounding on the side door. But nobody stirs. He looks at Sal again and notices for the first time that Sal's eyes are slightly open.

"Shit." He runs to the second van and finds the same thing. Everyone is unconscious, some of them with their eyes closed, some with eyes partially closed, and a few with their eyes wide open.

Dead.

He looks around in a panic, unsure which way to move. It's then that he notices the sickly sweet smell. They've been gassed.

It's a setup.

He reaches for his cell phone but remembers it's in the van. He left his pistol in the glove compartment, too. "Motherfu—"

In the distance, he sees headlights. He darts for the forest, pushing his way through the undergrowth, far enough away that he can hide but close enough that he can still see what's going on with the vans. After a moment, three big rigs pull ahead of the vans and stop. Men jump out of the trucks and make their way back to the vans. One of them is carrying some kind of device in his hand: a white plastic box with buttons and an antenna. The man moves up to the first van and does something with the box. All the doors to the van open.

He sees the man notice the empty front passenger seat—his seat—and hears the man shout at the row of semitrucks. A minute later, Giacobetti is with him, talking into a cell phone. The giant hangs up, shouts for some soldiers to join him by the van. At the same time, a man climbs into the driver's side of the first van, pushing Sal's body into the empty seat. The van starts, and the solider drives it up a ramp and into the back of one of the semitrailers.

Johnny Giacobetti turns toward the forest and peers through the trees. He pulls his gun and begins running in Angelo's direction.

Angelo leaps from his crouched position and races toward the lodge. He was a sprinter in high school and is still in great shape. He knows he can outrun Giacobetti and his men. He'll find a way into the lodge, find Nunzio's wife and daughter, and kill them. He doesn't have a gun, but he has his knife, a twin to the one his brother, Tony, always carried with him—the one Nunzio killed him with.

Mick is by the lake, rerunning his conversation with Christina Nunzio in his head. Still feeling wide awake, he's decided to walk the grounds. The beach curves the whole way around the lake, and he's on the far side now, standing in a fifty-yard clearing between the water and the trees. He looks back at the rear of the lodge. All the lights in the guest rooms are out, save for a few on the second floor. He wonders whether it's Christina who's still awake, or Rachel. Maybe it's the curious old man, Uncle Ham.

Without knowing why, his internal alarm goes off. A split second later, his mind registers the sound of labored breathing and heavy feet pounding on the grass, heading straight for him. He turns toward the trees to see the man coming at him, teeth bared, eyes blazing with rage.

"You're the lawyer!"

It takes Mick a moment to recognize Angelo Valiante in the dim light, to see the knife in Angelo's hand, to grasp that there's no time to react, to realize he's a dead man.

Then, in an instant, Angelo is gone in a blur of teeth and fur, jumped on and tackled by both of Giacobetti's beasts. The young gang leader hits the ground so fast it knocks the wind out of him, and he can't even scream.

Seconds later, Giacobetti bursts from the trees, half a dozen men behind him. "Settle! Settle!" he orders the dogs, who instantly lie down, one atop Valiante and one next to him.

Giacobetti clears the dogs away and roughly lifts Angelo to his feet.

"What the hell!" Mick shouts.

"Quiet," Giacobetti answers, his voice thick with menace. "You'll wake the guests."

"Are you kidding me?"

Giacobetti pulls a Taser from his coat pocket. "Don't make me put you down."

The giant drags Angelo Valiante around the lake toward the lodge, his men and dogs and Mick following behind. When they get to the side of the lake closest to the lodge, Rachel Nunzio approaches them.

"Are you all right?" she asks.

"This is crazy. I'm taking my daughter, and we're getting the hell out of here."

Two of the soldiers move on him, but Rachel calls them off.

"It's okay," she says. "He can leave. We can all leave. The war's over."

He looks at Rachel. "*This* was the war? One guy?" But he knows even as the words leave his mouth that it wasn't only Angelo. "Where are the rest of his men? What did you do to them?"

"Go back to your room, counselor. Pack up your things, and take your daughter to the porch. There'll be a car waiting for you."

He realizes he doesn't need Jimmy Nunzio's wife to tell him what happened to the rest of Valiante's men. "How many?" he asks. "How many were there?"

She takes a step toward him, her eyes black as coal. "Enough to kill us all, Mr. McFarland. If we hadn't stopped them."

When Angelo regains consciousness, he finds himself on his knees, his hands secured behind his back. He's on a concrete floor in a room of unpainted cinder block. There are no windows, and the wood beams and plumbing overhead tell him he's in the lodge's basement.

"Welcome back." A woman's voice. She approaches from a steel door, now open. Johnny Giacobetti, behind her, closes it.

"We chloroformed you," she says simply. "Didn't want to take a chance you'd wake our guests. We've gone to great pains to make their stay . . . unremarkable."

He struggles against the cuffs, the plastic digging into the skin on his wrists.

"I'm gonna kill you," he says. "I swear to God—"

"I think you overestimate your position."

"My *father*—"

"The poor man. I feel terribly for him. Antonio's death hit him so hard, I'm afraid he couldn't bear it. He took his own life." She looks at her watch. "In about ten minutes."

He screams, fights the cuffs again. He tries to get to his feet, but the giant, now behind him, presses on his shoulders, holds him down. He lowers his head, slumps.

"Any last words?" she asks as Johnny G. hands her a pistol.

Half choking, half crying, he says, "Fuck you, bitch."

She pulls the trigger.

24

Tuesday, May 28

Mick glances at the clock in the dashboard of his E350. It's 10:00 a.m. He's on the way to the prison to confront Nunzio. The ordeal that began with his and Gabby's abduction—and that's what it was—and ended with him watching Angelo Valiante being dragged away was among the most unsettling of his life. He wants answers. He would have paid a visit yesterday, but he wanted to spend the day at home, with his family. Piper, who returned from Georgia late Sunday evening, was a basket case. It took all his energy to keep her from calling the police on Nunzio.

Part of the difficulty, he realizes, is that he wasn't persuaded himself that not reporting Nunzio was the best course of action. Attorney-client privilege only extends so far. Certainly, it doesn't obligate him to shield Nunzio from what might be the ongoing kidnapping of Angelo Valiante. On the other hand, he's almost certain the young mobster is dead. The press is reporting that Angelo's father, Frank, was found dead of a supposedly self-inflicted gunshot wound to the head. The police want to question Angelo and Frank's other lieutenants and soldiers, but they can't be found—any of them. Mick believes that, like Angelo, the rest of Frank Valiante's army was at the lodge Sunday night or early Monday morning. And that's the strangest part of it. The two mob armies were in position to fight. But there was no fight. Or, more accurately, there was, but only Angelo showed up for it. What happened to the rest of Valiante's men? That's one question. The other thing troubling him is why Nunzio would have invited a celebrity writer and a movie producer to the lodge.

He parks the car, enters the prison, and makes his way through the tedious security procedures. The guard escorts him to the little room with the cinder-block walls and gray steel table and chairs.

"You son of a bitch." He's on his feet as soon as the door is closed behind Nunzio.

"You didn't like the salmon?"

"This is no joke."

The crime lord sits, waves his hand. "Okay, bring it on. Unload on me." He screws off the lid of a water bottle and takes a long swallow.

"You put my daughter in danger. You put me at risk, and if my wife had been home, you would have endangered her, too."

"You mean to say that I placed your family into the same situation as I placed my own—"

"Let's get to that. You hear Valiante is on the move against you for killing his son, so you bring your own wife and daughter and your brother's whole family to the same location. What were you thinking?"

Nunzio sighs, as if he must explain a simple concept to a child.

"Sun Tzu. When the enemy is at rest, make him move. Appear at places to which he must hasten."

Mick stares.

"If you know your enemy is going to attack you," Nunzio continues, "find a way to control where he attacks you. Set up a target he cannot resist."

"We were *bait*? My daughter, your own daughter and wife? My God, how low—"

"Enough!" Nunzio slams his palm on the table.

Startled, Mick pauses. Then he leans back. He is tired—and more than a little afraid—but he has to know the answers to the rest of his questions.

"The writer, Alecia Silver. The movie guy, Malcolm Crowe. Why have them there?"

Nunzio smiles. "You ever try to prove a negative, Mick?"

"A negative?"

"Like when the cops come to me and say, 'Hey, Mr. Nunzio. Frank Valiante's son and all of his men disappeared this weekend. We think you had something to do with it. Okay, maybe not you, because you're a guest of the state right now, but your men. Did your men make Valiante's guys disappear? No? Prove it.' And I say, 'I'm sorry, Mr. Federal Agent, I can't prove what my men were doing this weekend. I wasn't with them. But you know who was? My family and my defense lawyer. You say you don't believe them because they're biased? How about a famous writer and an even more famous movie producer? They were also with my men—all of my men—this weekend, in the Poconos.'"

"You had them there to be witnesses," Mick says. "To alibi your men."

Nunzio takes another drink of water, his cold black eyes locked on Mick's.

Mick thinks back to the crime for which Nunzio was originally arrested, suddenly seeing it from another vantage point. How spontaneous *was* Nunzio's murder of Christina's lover? Did Nunzio really race for his car, seemingly in a panic about his daughter, as the security guard portrayed it? It's hard to believe.

"That night, at the warehouse—"

Nunzio puts up his hand. "Not now."

He sighs. "What happened to Valiante's men?"

Nunzio shrugs. "It's dark in those mountains. Not like the city with all the streetlights and lights from buildings and cars and movie marquees. Plus, I'm told there was cloud cover. Maybe they lost their way and drove into a lake. There are more than a few up there."

Mick feels deflated. With the exception of the Hanson case, he's never felt so conflicted about his involvement in a case. He is truly in bed with the devil.

As if reading his mind, Nunzio says, "Why the frown, Mick? You've represented guys like me before."

"Have I, Jimmy? Are there other guys like you?"

Nunzio smiles. "Now you're making me blush."

It's almost midnight when they pull onto the small side street off Route 52 in Kennett Square. Directly to the north is the Chester County Prison. About a mile south and west is Longwood Gardens.

"Middle of nowhere," Mick says from the passenger seat of Tommy's F-150.

"Feels like it, but not really," Tommy says.

"I don't like it. Too much cloak-and-dagger."

"You want to talk to someone willing to give you the lowdown on Nunzio, this is what you're going to get."

The ordeal in the Poconos was making him more determined than ever to learn everything he could about James Frances Xavier Nunzio. He went back to Tommy about it and was happy to learn that his brother had been working on it all along. He'd already found someone with inside information who was willing to talk. When Mick asked Tommy how he persuaded the guy to open up, his brother said, "He owes me a favor. A huge favor."

Mick long ago accepted that Tommy spent a good part of his life in an underworld where favors and secrets were legal and illegal tender, traded on the full faith and credit of ex-cons, crooked cops, private investigators, and the more-than-occasional upstanding white-collar citizen caught doing less-than-upstanding things. In the case of Sid Haltzman, a retired reporter for the Philly *Inquirer*, the favor Tommy had bestowed involved rescuing Haltzman's young niece from an age-old profession. Tommy was short on the details, but from what he did share, Mick gathered that bones were broken in the process.

"We're here," Tommy says as they pull into a mud-rut driveway.

He narrows his eyes, looking for signs of life. All he sees is a beat-up old Airstream trailer sitting on cinder blocks at the end of the driveway.

"You're kidding me. This guy lives here?"

"No one lives here. His friend said he could use the place for a few hours."

They get out of the truck and walk up to the trailer. A pale-yellow light glows dimly behind a faded curtain. He stands back as Tommy knocks on the door. After a minute, it's opened slowly by a tall old man with a balding head and silver-framed glasses. He waves them inside.

The space is small and cramped. On the left wall is a cabinet with a sink and black Formica top. Beyond it, at the end of the trailer, is a fold-up table flanked by bench seats topped with rust-colored upholstery. The other end of the trailer holds the bedroom.

Sid leads them to the table, and they all sit.

"Isn't this a little over the top?" Mick says.

"You represent the man," the reporter says. "You tell me. Is there such a thing as 'too safe' when it comes to Jimmy Nutzo?"

"Good point," he says, glancing at Tommy.

"Let's go over the ground rules," Sid says. "First, whatever I tell you is only to be used for background information. You're not going public with any of it. Agreed?"

"Look, let's—"

"Agreed?"

"All right," he says. "Agreed. This is for my ears only."

"Second, my name is never to be mentioned by you with respect to anything having to do with Nunzio."

"I agree to that, too," he says. "Anything else?"

"No notes. And no tape. You're not taping me, right?"

He opens his jacket.

Sid Haltzman takes a deep breath, seems to relax a bit.

"I retired ten years ago, when I was fifty-five. A couple years before that, I found myself looking for a good story to wind up my career. I'd been a crime reporter for the *Bulletin* and then the *Inquirer* for almost thirty years. During that time, I'd broken some big stories. Shared a Pulitzer once for a series on the badlands in North Philly. But I'd gotten lazy in my old age and hadn't dug deep on anything for a long time. One day I heard something come across the police scanner about a guy found himself doing the face-float in the Schuylkill River. I did a little digging and heard the guy tried to double-cross Jimmy Nunzio. And I thought, *That's the story.* Not the floater, but Nunzio. Talk about a colorful character. Everybody in the city knows who he is, except they really don't."

"What do you mean?"

"You know where he lives?"

"South Philly, I expect," Tommy says.

"Oh, he has a row house there. A double house, actually. But where he really lives is on North Spring Mill Road in Villanova. You know, the Main Line's golden mile. His house is fifteen thousand square feet of stone and marble. Indoor and outdoor pools, fourteen-foot ceilings, eight-car garage. George Clooney doesn't live that well."

Mick remembers what Vaughn said about Nunzio having his own jet and suspecting he was more than just another South Philly mob boss. "So he's not what he seems to be."

"No. He's exactly what he seems to be. But he's a whole lot more. Starting with the fact that the Nunzios aren't just mafia, they're mafia *royalty*."

"I thought Nunzio's old man was just a midlevel lieutenant," Tommy says.

"I'm not talking Jimmy or his old man."

"You're saying Rachel is mafia, too?" Mick asks.

"I thought she was a Jewish girl from Penn who caught Nunzio's eye," Tommy says.

"That's the story," Haltzman says. "Nunzio met her at some campus bar he used to troll and fell hard. He married her, brought her into the life, her old man screaming the whole time."

"You're saying that's not true?"

Sid Haltzman smiles, and Mick can tell he's having a good time dragging out the tale.

"I feel like a marlin," Mick says. "You're pulling me in, letting me out, pulling me in."

"I've waited a long time to tell this story to someone. Indulge me." The reporter pulls out a pack of Camels and a lighter. "Mind if I smoke?" he asks, opening a small window.

"It's kind of close in here," Mick says as Haltzman lights up.

The reporter inhales, then blows a stream of smoke out the side of his mouth, toward the window. "Yep. Sorry."

In his peripheral vision, Mick can see Tommy smiling.

The reporter looks from Mick to Tommy. "If you ask most people who was the most successful crime boss in America, who do you think they'd answer with?"

"That's easy. Al Capone," Tommy says.

"Capone was convicted of tax evasion and spent seven years in prison, during which he became increasingly insane from neurosyphilis, which killed him when he was only forty-eight."

"Bugsy Siegel?"

"Shot down when he was forty-one."

"Dillinger?"

"A crook, not a crime boss. Shot dead at thirty-one."

"All right," Mick says. "Who was the most successful organized criminal?"

"Ever hear of Lenny Maher? His nickname was 'the mob's bookkeeper.'"

Mick had heard of Maher. "Didn't he work with Luciano?"

"They more than worked together. They ran the Jewish mob and formed the National Crime Syndicate with the Italians. Among all the bosses, Maher was the most successful. He owned points in casinos in Vegas, the Bahamas, Cuba, even London. Only spent a few years in jail. Died an old man, of natural causes, in his Miami mansion."

The reporter pauses, takes a deep drag of his cigarette. "In business, Lenny Maher was a ruthless killer. But in his personal life, he was a good family man. Three kids, lots of grandkids. Happily married until the day he died at age eighty-one in the mideighties. That's the official story, and it's all true."

"But in truth . . . ," Tommy leads him.

Sid Haltzman nods. "There's always a subtext. In Lenny's case, her name was Jade. Last name unknown. She was a dancer in a casino he owned, and by all accounts she was wild and gorgeous—dark hair, dark eyes, olive skin, and pouty lips. She was eighteen when they first met. Lenny Maher was thirty-nine. A year later, the dancer gave birth to a daughter. Miriam."

"And that was the end of Jade," Tommy guesses.

"Not at all. Maher was lost in that girl. But he did make her give up the daughter. Miriam was handed over to the wife of one of Maher's accountants, last name of Goldman."

He hears a buzzing sound and watches as Haltzman reaches into his jacket pocket and pulls out his cell phone. The reporter looks at the screen and says, "I have to take this."

"We'll go outside," Mick says, hurrying to stand and escape the smoke. He leads Tommy out, gulping deep breaths of the fresh night air.

"You wouldn't last very long in half the bars I go into," Tommy says.

He doesn't answer.

A few minutes later, the reporter calls them back inside, and he leads Tommy through the blue haze to the table.

"Okay," Mick says, bringing them back to where the reporter had left off. "So Lenny Maher has a secret daughter, Miriam Goldman . . ."

"And this is where the story starts to get interesting. Miriam wasn't Lenny Maher and Jade's only child. They had a son the following year. Maher placed him with another one of his associates, Phil Marx. The boy's name was Hiram."

Mick's hackles go up. "Hiram. Uncle Ham," he says, stopping the reporter cold.

"You know of him?"

"I'm pretty sure I just met him."

"Do the Nunzios know this?"

"They set it up. At least, they put us in the same place at the same time."

Haltzman studies Mick for a long minute, a strange look on his face.

"What?" Mick asks.

"Hiram Marx's connection to the Nunzios is one of that family's most closely guarded secrets."

"So, if they let me in on it . . ."

"They either trust you implicitly or they figure they have leverage against you that will keep you from sharing what you know."

Mick sits back. "Go on with the story."

"Miriam's adoptive father, Lev Goldman, died young. So her connection to the mob faded into the background. And when she was married off to a rabbi, her relation to Lenny Maher was forgotten completely."

"And Hiram?" Tommy asks.

"More complicated. Maher played no part in Hiram's life when he was younger. But at some point, Phil Marx revealed to the boy who his true parents were, and that he had a sister, placed with another family.

Hiram approached Maher, wanting in the life, but Maher wasn't having it. Hiram was stubborn and kept pushing. Maher got pissed off, and there was a big fight, after which the two men never spoke to each other."

"And Hiram and Miriam?"

"It's not clear when, but at some point after she was married, he approached her, revealed they were siblings. She told her husband, the rabbi, and he blew his top, forbade her to see her half brother. Then, the story goes, Hiram paid the rabbi a visit. He did or said something that scared the hell out of the man. From that point on, Miriam and Hiram were close—but never public about their connection, which remained a family secret."

"And Hiram Marx remains out of the life," Mick says. "Until Miriam has a daughter, Rachel, who marries Jimmy Nunzio."

The reporter nods. "And Hiram Marx finds an open door to the mob."

"So Hiram's in business with Nunzio," Tommy says.

Again Haltzman nods. "You ever hear of a transportation company called HML?"

"Sure," Mick says. "They're not as big as UPS or FedEx, but they've been around for a long time."

"If you asked your stockbroker to tell you who owns it, he'd dig and dig and get back to you in a week with the name of an offshore subsidiary. If you asked him who owns that subsidiary, he might get back to you in two weeks with the name of another subsidiary."

"Let me guess," Mick says. "The owners of the subsidiary that owns the subsidiary that owns the subsidiary that owns HML are Jimmy Nunzio and Hiram Marx. That explains where Nunzio's getting the money for the giant house in Villanova, and the jet. So does that mean Nunzio's playing the mobster role, but he's mostly legitimate?"

The reporter laughs so hard he starts to cough.

"Did I say something funny?"

"You ever hear of the dark web? Well, HML is to transportation what the dark web is to the internet."

"That's crazy," Mick says. "I see their trucks all over, delivering things to businesses, like any other delivery service. I've used them myself."

"HML is just the face of a much larger enterprise. Hiram founded HML twenty years ago, after working for a couple of bigger shipping companies and studying FedEx and UPS's business models. He started small and built the business over time as a legitimate enterprise. But Hiram has the blood, and he wanted to branch off into the under-the-table trade. He didn't get very far because he wasn't a made man and didn't have the connections. To put it simply, the bad guys didn't trust him. Then his niece marries Jimmy Nunzio, and in no time at all, trading on Nunzio's name, HML forms secret subsidiaries around the country, then the hemisphere, and then the world."

He recalls Rachel Nunzio's remark at the lodge: *There are much larger games afoot, Mr. McFarland.*

"What do they ship?" he asks.

"Word on the street? Anything and everything. Weapons, drugs, currency, gold, sophisticated electronics to enemy states. Humans. You name it."

"What's Hiram's relationship with Nunzio like?"

Haltzman smiles. "Let's just say when Rachel married Nunzio, she got a husband, but Hiram Marx got a soul mate. Talk about two sides of the same coin. Ambitious, avaricious, and Machiavellian."

"What about Rachel herself? Anything you can tell me about her?"

"Have you met her?"

"A couple times."

The reporter locks eyes with him but doesn't answer.

"Yeah," he says.

Rachel doesn't hide; she lets you see her coming. He asks the reporter what he knows about Christina.

"Not much. She was just a teenager when I stopped looking into the Nunzios. I do know," he says, "that Nunzio and Rachel's father, the rabbi, had words over her name. *Christina.*"

Mick sits back and waits for Haltzman to take a deep drag of his cigarette. "How did you find all this out?"

"It wasn't easy. Took me two years. Two years in the shadows—clandestine meetings, endless phone calls, weeks on the road, public records searches, trading favors, outright bribery. Quite a few times, I personally tailed Nunzio, Rachel, and Marx."

"The *Inquirer* paid for all this?" The newspaper has been strapped for cash for years.

"Are you kidding? My editor was ready to wring my neck after the first month. I paid for it all myself. Borrowed against my 401(k). Downsized my house. Why not? My wife had passed. My boy was grown. It became an obsession."

"Why haven't you gone public with it?"

The reporter's face darkens. He lights up another cigarette, waves the match out, takes a deep drag.

"About a week before I was ready to show the series to my editor—and that's what it was going to be, a ten-week series on the Nunzio family, going back to Lenny Maher—I got a call. It was Nunzio himself. He said he'd heard I was working on a story about him. Said he might have something to contribute."

"Where'd he have you meet him?" Tommy asks.

"Kelly Drive. A spot just west of the boathouses. There's a bench. You sit there and look out at the river."

"The Schuylkill," Tommy says, "right where they found the floater who'd pissed off Nunzio and started you looking into him."

"A message," Mick says. "The river."

"The river was part of the message." He pulls a small photograph from his jacket. It shows a young man in a suit and tie.

"Nunzio was at the bench, waiting for me. A couple of guys were with him. I was terrified. He motioned me to sit, and he sat down next to me. He told me my story was very good—"

"Wait," Mick says. "How would he know that? It hadn't been printed."

Haltzman looks down. Then after a moment, he looks back up at Mick. "I've no doubt he knew the whole time that I was looking into him, talking to people, searching records."

"But he waited until you were ready to publish to shut you down?" Tommy asks.

"I have a theory about that. I think he let me run loose to see what I'd come up with. What was out there that could be found out about him, his family."

The reporter pauses again, and Mick asks, "The photo?"

"My son. His graduation picture from Lower Merion. Nunzio told me he appreciated all the hard work I did for him. He told me I deserved to be fairly compensated and handed me an envelope with a check in it. Thanked me for selling him the story. Then he told me I was not permitted to publish it. 'Ever,' he said. Then"—Haltzman nods at the picture—"he handed me this."

"The other part of the message," Tommy says.

Haltzman nods. "The other part of the message."

Mick watches the older man stare at the photograph.

"Why are you doing this? Meeting with us?"

"Ask your brother."

25

Thursday, May 30

The cemetery on the farm Lois Beal used to rent from her sister is an overgrown field with a dozen or so granite headstones bordered in the back by a small forest. Some of the headstones are sunken almost fully into the ground. Some are chipped at the top. All are worn, most to the point that their carved lettering is indecipherable.

Tommy looks at his watch. It's just about 11:00 a.m. He glances to his right to see Piper and Susan huddled under the big golf umbrella he brought for them. The rain has been steady all night, turning the small field haunted by headstones into a swamp.

With them is Lois Beal, who flew up from Jacksonville the night before. Also present is Lance Newton, an FBI agent Susan knows from her days as a federal prosecutor, and another man he brought along to videotape the proceedings. Newton is going to take the hammer Lois claims is buried there for fingerprinting and DNA testing. The last two spectators are ex-chief of police Sonny Foster and his former officer, Melvin Ott. It was Susan's idea to invite them, her strategy being to call them as witnesses if the prosecutor in Darlene's retrial fights too hard against the admission of the hammer. Susan shared her plan with Ott, who is all for it, but kept it from Foster, who has made clear his view that what's happening is nothing more than a "stunt."

"There's no way a judge is going to buy this and grant you a retrial," Foster says.

"We'll just have to see," Tommy says.

"You're the guy who's been poking his nose into good people's business up here." The ex-chief takes a step closer to Tommy. "Not a smart idea."

Tommy leans in toward Foster, shovel in hand. "If they're such good people, why'd their noses get so out of joint just by me asking a few questions?"

Out of his peripheral vision, Tommy sees Piper shift on her feet.

"Let's get on with this," Piper says. "Lois, show us where the hammer's buried so Tommy can dig it up."

Tommy follows Lois to the two largest headstones, sitting side by side. Ephraim and Ruth, a man and his wife, dates of death: 1894 and 1910.

Lois inches closer to the headstones. He watches as she looks from one to the other, then back again.

"It's one of these two, but I'm not sure . . ." Her words trail off.

"No problem," Tommy says. "I'll dig in front of the one, and if it's not there, I'll dig down by the other—"

"No!"

The force of her injunction startles him.

What's the big deal? he wonders.

Lois Beal takes another full minute, then says, "It's that one. The one on the right that says 1910. That's the wife."

He positions himself in front of the stone, glances back at Lois to make sure. She nods, but the look on her face tells him she's terrified.

He starts digging in the muck. It doesn't take long before he feels the spade strike something solid. A metal box. He digs around it carefully, removing the heavy mud, then leans down, lifts out the box, and sets it on the ground. It's about a foot square and four inches deep. Rusted black metal.

"That's it." Lois's voice sounds behind him.

"Let me take it from here," Lance Newton says.

His videographer moves up, pointing his camera down at the box. Lance opens the box with gloved hands and lifts out a paper bag sealed with duct tape. He opens it to reveal a red-handled claw hammer.

"Is this it?" he asks Lois.

Tommy glances at Lois, who breathes a sigh of relief.

"Yes. Yes. That's it."

Tommy stares at Lois now, watching her chest rise and fall with her deep breaths.

The FBI agent places the hammer back into the bag and then the box. He stands and faces everyone. "What happens now is I send this to the lab. They'll test it, as we discussed. In addition to the DNA testing of any hair and tissue, the hammer will be tested for prints." At the time of the crime, given that the house was going to be dusted, Sonny Foster had asked Cindy Dowd to be fingerprinted so that her own prints could be discounted. Her prints were stored on IAFIS, the national automated fingerprint identification system maintained by the FBI.

"How long until we get the results?" Piper asks.

The agent glances at Susan, and Tommy sees warmth in his eyes. "Given your sixty-day deadline, I'll make this a priority. Two weeks."

"That'll give us just enough time to plug the results into our brief and get it filed with the court."

"And if it doesn't have the mother's prints on it?" asks Sonny Foster.

"It will," Lois says, her eyes boring into the former police chief.

"This is bullshit." Foster turns away.

Mel Ott nods to Piper and Susan, then follows his former boss down the field and past the barn to the driveway leading to the farmhouse. The FBI team leaves next, and after Tommy fills the hole back in, he, Piper, Susan, and Lois leave the old graveyard for their cars. Piper and Susan drove up together. Tommy picked up Lois from Philly International and met them at the farm.

"If no one minds," Tommy says, "I'm going to stay up in the area for a few more hours. Gotta see a man about a horse." He climbs into his truck's flatbed and places the shovel into a diamond-plate aluminum storage box in the back.

"That's fine," Piper says. "I can drive Lois back to the city. You're staying a few days, aren't you?"

"Yes," Lois says. "It's been a while since I've been back. I haven't seen the Barnes yet, or the Rodin Museum since it's been updated. And it's good to be away from Georgia for a few days."

Tommy gets into his truck and waits for them all to drive off. After they're gone, he waits a few minutes, then climbs back into the truck bed and removes the shovel from the storage box.

"I hope I'm wrong," he says as he trudges up the field to the little cemetery. Once there, he positions himself in front of the second headstone, the one dated 1894, and starts to dig. It takes only a few minutes before the shovel hits something solid. He sighs, keeps digging, and there it is. A second box. He lifts it, places it on the ground, and opens it.

"Shit."

A paper bag holding a second hammer—this one with a blue handle. The reason Lois Beal was so worried and had to make sure she had him dig in front of the correct headstone.

Shit.

26

Thursday, May 30, Continued

Mick looks up from his *Inquirer* to see Angie approaching his desk to drop off his mail. He can tell from her face she's frustrated about something.

"What's the matter?" he asks.

"Susan's father. Again. He's called three times this morning. I told him Susan was out of the office on a case, but I guess he doesn't believe me. Not that I blame him; she ducked his calls all morning yesterday, even though she was here. Then he caught her leaving the building to go to lunch, and they got into a big fight outside."

He sighs. "I'll talk to her. I don't want you put in the middle of this."

She thanks him and turns to leave. At the door, she turns back. "Is Susan working on the Nunzio case now?"

"No. Vaughn's still my second chair. Why?"

"Because that US Attorney Martin Brenner called here this morning. But he didn't ask for you, he asked for Susan."

"That shit. I told him Nunzio isn't going to deal with the government. I guess he thinks he can do an end run around me with Susan." She did say he was relentless. "Get him on the phone for me, please."

Angie leaves, and he returns his attention to the newspaper. Two stories are getting major play on the front page. The first is about the suicide of New York mob boss Frank Valiante and the disappearance of his son, his chief lieutenants, and most of his soldiers. According to the story, the Valiante crew vanished without a trace, almost as though they'd intended to cover their tracks so that no one would know where they were headed. Given the lack of mob violence since their departure, the feds think it likely they will all eventually resurface. But local mob boss Jimmy Nunzio isn't taking chances; fearful of retaliation against his family, he's requested police protection for his wife at their South Philly row house, where she is now holed up. Nunzio's daughter, Christina, the story says, remains out of the country, in treatment for post-traumatic stress disorder.

The second story, somewhat related, is about the upcoming election for district attorney, a close contest between the embattled incumbent Emlin Fellner and his first assistant, Devlin Walker. With four years of low conviction rates and an exploding opioid crisis, Fellner has been looking for something to run on and has all but promised a conviction in the Nunzio case. "The Philly mob, a century-long scourge of our city, will finally come to an end when this bloodthirsty gangster sees the inside of a prison," Fellner is quoted as saying. Yesterday, the story's reporter called Mick, asking for a quote. Given Nunzio's obvious guilt, he offered up his typical smorgasbord of banalities about the presumption of innocence, due process, and—what the guilty always say after they're charged and before they plead—that Nunzio is looking forward to his day in court, confident he'll be vindicated once all the facts are out.

He leans back in his chair, looks to the ceiling, and closes his eyes. Only two weeks from trial, and nothing in the case has gelled for him. All he sees is a tangle of strings. Nunzio and Giacobetti supposedly running from their building; the smashed-in warehouse door; Valiante's missing bodyguards; the plasticuff wounds on Tony Valiante's wrists and ankles; the arresting officer smelling pasta in the warehouse; Nunzio's decision to kill Valiante with his knife rather than his gun; Giacobetti gone from the warehouse when the police arrived. And then there's everything that has happened since. The bizarre scene at the lodge in the Poconos; Angelo's capture; Frank Valiante's "suicide" and his missing crew; Rachel Nunzio as the descendant of legendary mob boss Lenny Maher; brave Christina Nunzio, putting on a good face despite her broken heart; Uncle Ham and HML.

How to make sense of it all, for his own understanding? And how to arrange the mess into a pattern he can use to persuade the jury that Nunzio is . . . what? Innocent? Impossible. He was caught red-handed, the knife in his hand, the corpse bleeding out a few steps away. Sympathetic? No way—Nunzio murdered the guy in front of his own horrified daughter.

Maybe Vaughn can help him find some answers. He walks down the hall to the large conference room, where Vaughn and the team have been setting up to prepare for trial. He enters the room to see the conference table covered with case materials—police reports, photographs, the autopsy report, witness statements. Also on the table is a stack of newspaper clippings. Across the room, Vaughn has set up two easels with corkboards. At the top of the first, he has thumbtacked a label that reads "Prosecution's Witnesses." The first two names are Trumbull and Piccone, the police officers who first came to the warehouse. The third name is that of Mick's nemesis, the chief homicide detective who took over the case, John Tredesco. CSU lead investigator Matthew Stone is the fourth. Listed as number five is Deputy Chief Medical Examiner Ari Weintraub.

The second easel, "Defense Witnesses," has three names: 1. James Nunzio? 2. Christina Nunzio? 3. John Giacobetti? The list ends with "Other?" Below the names is written: "Defense Theory?"

Mick focuses on the question marks, then smiles at Vaughn, who's standing by the second easel. "I see you have it all worked out."

"Only thing left is our victory speech for the press." Vaughn slumps into a chair. "Seriously, Mick, who are we going to call? What's our story here? I'm stumped."

He sits across the table from Vaughn. "That makes two of us. I tried to bring it up when I saw Nunzio a couple days ago, but he shut me down again."

"Is he serious? Trial's in a few weeks!"

Mick shrugs.

"Did he say anything about pleading out?"

"No, and even if he does, Pagano's planning to try the case at this point." Mick points at the easels. "Why not, right, with the DA making the case a centerpiece of his campaign? There's not going to be a deal."

Vaughn chews on this. "Nunzio's sitting on something. An ace in the hole."

"What I'm thinking. But he's not ready to share it with me." Mick stands and retrieves a bottle of water from a silver serving tray on the cabinet beneath the audiovisual screen. When he turns back toward the table, Vaughn shifts gears.

"What do you think about this whole Valiante thing? The suicide? The disappearances?"

"I don't know what to make of it." He's told Vaughn all about the odyssey at the lodge—except for the likely fact that Nunzio wiped out Valiante's crew in the Poconos and used the gathering at the lodge to alibi his men. There's no way he's going to burden his team with that knowledge.

"Nunzio has to be breathing a sigh of relief that Frank Valiante's dead," Vaughn says. "Still, he has to worry about Angelo and the rest of Valiante's crew. You think they're still going to come after Nunzio, with Frank gone?"

Mick doesn't answer, unwilling to go further with it.

A moment later, his associate's face brightens. "That's great news about Darlene Dowd."

"I know," Mick says. "Piper's over the moon about it."

Vaughn shakes his head. "What a job we have, eh? On the one hand we get to right a terrible wrong, win freedom for someone like Darlene Dowd."

"And on the other hand, we have Jimmy Nutzo."

He stands as Angie calls on the conference-room phone. She tells Vaughn a client is calling with an emergency. Vaughn excuses himself to take the call in his office, and Mick walks to the easel with the list of prosecution witnesses. He scans the names.

"Which of you is Nunzio's ace in the hole?" he asks aloud.

And what could you possibly say that would save him from a guilty verdict?

It's close to 8:00 when Mick pulls into the garage. He pushes the button that automatically closes the garage door and gets out of the car. Even before he walks into the kitchen, he can smell that Piper is cooking dinner. He's surprised, given that she had a full day with the Lois Beal case. To celebrate the favorable developments, he'd planned to take her out to dinner at Nectar or Estia Taverna, spur of the moment.

"Hey," he says, entering the kitchen. Piper turns from the counter, her face aglow. Before she can say anything, he says, "You look happy."

"You should have been there! My heart was pounding a mile a minute when Tommy was digging up that grave. And then when he lifted out the metal box and opened it . . . The hammer was there, just like Lois said it would be . . . Darlene's going to get out, Mick. She never should have been imprisoned in the first place, and she's lost fifteen years of her life. But she's still young, and she'll be free."

"Congratulations, sweetheart." He puts his hands on her waist, kisses her, and envelops her in a long hug.

"Champagne?" she asks. "I have a Ruinart Brut. It's a blanc de blancs. It'll go well with the lobster."

He raises an eyebrow. "You know too much about wine."

She cocks her head, smiles. "Is that ever really possible?"

◆ ◆ ◆

It's a warm evening, and they eat on the back patio. Piper dishes the food onto their plates, then goes back inside and calls Gabby to join them.

"How was practice?" Mick asks when Gabby sits down.

"Nailed it," she answers. "Thanks to Christina. All those tips she gave me made me way better than everyone else."

He exchanges glances with Piper. Gabby has gushed almost non-stop about Christina Nunzio since she returned from the lodge. She's regaled them about Christina's beauty, her "amazing" skills at soccer, her helpfulness as a coach, and her overall excellence as a human being. Gabby even expressed her admiration for the graceful way Christina ate dinner—something she observed from across the dining room at the lodge.

The first night they were back together, Piper's patience with Gabby's hero worship quickly wore thin.

"I don't like our daughter idolizing the daughter of a vicious mob boss," she had told him later that night.

"The good news is, she'll be doing it from afar. She's seen her first and last of the Nunzios."

"That whole family is covered in blood," Piper said. "It pisses me off that she was even exposed to them."

Mick couldn't disagree.

"Coach is moving me forward," Gabby says.

"That's great," he says. Gabby had been practicing as a midfielder. Moving forward means her coach is looking at her as a striker.

"I know I can score at least one goal a game. At least."

"That's our girl." He smiles and winks at Piper, who narrows her eyes.

After dinner, he and Piper remain on the patio while Gabby goes inside to watch TV. It doesn't take long to finish the champagne, so he brings out a bottle of Chardonnay and two fresh glasses.

"I called Darlene again today, at the prison," Piper says.

He takes a sip of the wine, then raises something that's been troubling him since he found out about the new evidence.

"I'm sure she's happy she might get out," he says. "But how does she feel knowing it was her mother who killed her father, and that her mother kept it secret until she was on her deathbed? That she let Darlene rot in prison."

"I don't know. I haven't asked her, and she hasn't raised it. I'm guessing it must be too painful for her to talk about. Maybe even to think about. She could be holding back her feelings until after her trial. She knows she needs to focus."

He nods. "That makes sense. What about Lois Beal? Cindy told her she killed her husband, but Lois just sat back and let Darlene remain incarcerated?"

Piper frowns. "I'm not sure what to think about Lois. She seems like a decent person—"

"For an armored-car robber and fugitive."

"Right. Which explains why she didn't come forward, given the police chief's threat."

"But that was years before, when the crime had just been committed. Do you know whether the chief had retired by the time Cindy Dowd confessed to Lois?"

She doesn't answer. He knows by the look on her face not to press the point. In the law, victory can be fleeting, and it's important to savor your wins whenever they occur—and for as long as you can.

"Hey." He smiles and holds up his glass. "You're doing a great thing. Here's to you."

He waits for her to raise her own glass, and they toast.

It's close to midnight when Tommy knocks on the door to the large house on 108th Street in Stone Harbor, New Jersey. The two-story vacation home is a modern five-bedroom, four-bath property on a half acre of prime beachfront real estate. It is owned by Raymond Thorne, a former CIA agent now running his own security firm. Sometime ago, Tommy did freelance work for Thorne that worked out well. Thorne even offered to bring him on full-time. Tommy declined, but they remained friends.

As soon as he opened the second metal box and saw the blue-handled hammer, he knew Thorne was the man to bring it to. Thorne's forensic lab was top-shelf, and he could be trusted to keep their transaction secret.

Thorne answers the door. He's a sharp-looking man in his late fifties, clean-cut, with a square jaw and blue eyes. The perfect look for an agent of the CIA, which recruited him right out of college.

They shake hands, and Thorne leads him inside. The first floor is an open-design space with a large living room, kitchen, and bar. They walk up to the bar, and Tommy takes a seat. He sets the metal box on the floor. Thorne goes behind the bar, pulls out a bottle of Glenlivet XXV, and pours them each a couple of fingers. They clink tumblers and throw back the scotch. Thorne pours again, and then it's time for business.

When Tommy is done talking about the hammer, Thorne casts him a hard look.

"This is evidence in a murder case?"

He doesn't answer.

"You have an exemplar, for the prints?"

He nods. "Plastic water bottle. I put it in the box with the hammer."

It's Thorne's turn to stare.

"The subject was drinking out of the bottle. In my truck," Tommy says.

"You expect a match?"

"Oh yeah."

"Then what?"

He shrugs.

Thorne empties his glass, pours another one. "We find what you're expecting, you're not going to be able to use it in court. Big chain-of-custody issues here. But I guess you already know that."

He nods. "Whatever happens, this hammer's never going to see the inside of a courtroom."

"Uh-huh. Then why go through the exercise? Especially since you already know the answer, or think you do."

"Before I call her out on it, I want to be sure."

"This'll help your client?"

Tommy looks at him but doesn't answer.

"Not my business. I get it." Thorne pauses. "After I'm done testing it, you want me to lose it?"

"No need to lose what's never been found."

27

Friday, May 31

Mick leaves the courtroom following a suppression-of-evidence hearing in a narcotics case and finds John Tredesco waiting for him in the hallway. He grimaces as soon as he sees the lanky, pot-gut detective.

"It makes me happy to see you, too," Tredesco says.

"What can I do for you?" he asks, not slowing down.

"When can I talk to Giacobetti? And the daughter?"

Mick glances over his shoulder as he pushes the button for the elevator. "Flying pigs, Tredesco. Icebergs in Hades."

The doors open, and Tredesco follows him into the crammed elevator. Neither says anything on the ride down.

"See you later," Mick says, striding out of the elevator.

"Reason I ask is I had an interesting phone call today," Tredesco says, keeping close behind him. "From a US attorney, name of Martin Brenner?"

He stops and turns.

Tredesco smiles. "Got your attention."

"You're aware that your boss Pagano doesn't want the feds anywhere near this case."

"No shit. Nunzio's conviction is his ticket to the DA's desk. Least, that's what I'm thinking."

"What did Brenner want?"

"That's the funny thing. He wasn't real clear about it. He started out by saying he was looking for cooperation between the police and his office. Then he said something about convening a grand jury. Then he brought you up. Asked me all about you. What kind of lawyer you were, what kind of guy."

"What did he say about the grand jury, exactly? Is he going in that direction for sure?"

"You know, if Johnny G. and Christina came in, gave me statements, he might see no need for a grand jury."

"This is getting tiresome."

"I told him you were a good lawyer. Great, even. I didn't answer about what kind of person you were."

Mick turns to leave.

"Then he asked me about how you and Susan got along."

He turns back. "What? What did he ask?"

"He wanted to know, do you see eye to eye? Or are you like the '74 Oakland A's, always winning but cats and dogs in the locker room?"

Mick remembers Angie telling him that Brenner called the office yesterday, asking for Susan.

So he's trying to drive a wedge between us? Go behind my back and get Susan to talk to Nunzio about joining up with the feds?

But why? Brenner has to know that Nunzio will never turn state's evidence against his New York boss. Then he thinks about Uncle Ham and Nunzio's role in HML. If Nunzio's real game is shipping contraband internationally, as the reporter Haltzman claimed, maybe he *would* be willing to sell out the "little boys fighting in the backyard," as Rachel called them.

"You need to tell Pagano about the call," Mick says, turning away. "Have him fight Brenner on this."

"Talk about cats and dogs," Tredesco calls after him.

The detective's remark is the last thing he hears before he exits the building.

Out on Filbert Street, walking toward Broad, he dials the office.

"It's me," he says when Angie picks up. He'd asked her to get Brenner on the phone yesterday, but she'd told him she couldn't get past his voice mail. "Listen. That federal prosecutor who called yesterday. Brenner. If he calls—"

"Oh, we're way past calls. He's here now. With Susan. In her office. I don't think it's going well."

"I'll be there in three minutes," he says, picking up his pace.

"What the hell, Brenner?" he says, throwing open the door to Susan's office. Brenner is sitting in front of Susan's desk. Susan is standing behind it, her arms crossed.

Brenner turns and smiles. "Whoa, cowboy."

"I'm done," Susan says, walking from behind her desk and past Mick. In the doorway, she turns toward Mick. "You talk to him."

She leaves, and he closes the door behind her.

"What's going on?" Mick demands. "I've made my client's position very clear. He's not cooperating. Period. That's number one. Number two is that this is *my* case, not Susan's. Anything that has to do with Nunzio goes through me, not her. You get that?"

Brenner stands, the smile gone. They face off. Brenner is taller than Mick, and strongly built. He moves into Mick's space, pressing his physical advantage.

"Hey, Mick. I don't tell you how to do your job, you don't tell me how to do mine."

"You're crossing a line," Mick says, not backing away.

"A funny thing for someone with your reputation to say."

He feels the heat rising in his face. "And why were you asking a police detective about me? And my partner?"

"You don't do recon on your opponents?"

"We're not opponents, Brenner. You're not *in* the case, remember?"

"If that's what you think, you're not paying attention."

"You need to leave. Now."

Brenner's mouth smiles, but his blue eyes are cold. He walks to the door, then turns. "When the roof comes down on your client's head, don't say I didn't warn you."

Mick follows the prosecutor down the hall to the reception area. He opens the door and waves Brenner out. Halfway through the doorway, Brenner stops.

"Tell Susan I'll see her around."

It's close to 7:00 p.m. when Mick makes the turn from Kelly Drive to the Falls River Bridge, the halfway point of his run. After the bridge, he'll head east on Martin Luther King, past the Museum of Art onto Ben Franklin Parkway to Sixteenth Street. Eleven miles, round-trip. When the weather's good, he does the run two times a week. More if he's stressed out.

The day began badly—the encounter with Tredesco followed immediately by his run-in with Martin Brenner. And when he found Susan in the small conference room, things didn't go well with her, either.

"You said Brenner was relentless," he said, taking a seat at the conference table. "But this is something else."

"You're blaming me because *he's* acting like an asshole?"

The sharpness in her voice took him aback.

"Hey, I'm not blaming you for anything. You're not the bad guy here. But neither am I. I didn't invite Brenner to bring you into the Nunzio case."

"I want nothing to do with that case, or him."

He took a breath, tried to project calm. "I heard your father's still giving you a hard time."

"He's the least of my worries."

"Uh-huh. You ready to talk about whatever it is that's the worst of your worries?"

"Did I ask for your help, Mick?"

He didn't answer.

"I can handle it. I told you I could handle it, and I will."

With that, she stood and left the room.

Powered by sheer stress and anxiety, he races through the last five and a half miles and makes it back to the firm in thirty-five minutes. He cools his face, wipes off the sweat in the bathroom, then heads for his office and places a call. It's been a week and a half since he asked Tommy to look into Susan's boyfriend, the soccer player. He's seen Susan flustered before. It usually turned out to have something to do with some guy she was seeing. Tommy hasn't gotten back to him with any news, which must mean that his brother hasn't learned anything from Romero.

"Come on, Tommy," he says as the phone rings. "Let's get to the bottom of this."

28

Friday, June 7

Mick is in his office just before lunch when Angie rings through.

"Rachel Nunzio's on the phone for you. She sounds upset."

"I'll take it." He takes a deep breath, then picks up the receiver.

"We have a problem," she says. "A United States attorney just showed up at my home. He brought a subpoena. You need to get over here." She gives him an address on North Spring Mill Road in Villanova; then the line goes dead.

Angie was right. Rachel Nunzio is upset. Her sharp tone was a far cry from the air of calm nonchalance she affected at his office and at the lodge. Having a federal prosecutor on your doorstep serving subpoenas tends to have that effect on people.

Forty-five minutes later, he pulls his car onto a cobblestone driveway guarded by a black wrought-iron gate hung on two stone columns. He sees that the same fencing surrounds the entire perimeter of the front yard, which looks to be at least three acres. He's about to get out of the car and look for an intercom when the gate swings open on its own. The smooth driveway curves first to the right, then to the left, passing a stone wall backed by trees that hide the front of the house from anyone who might want to see it from the road. He stops beyond the wall and walks across a red-and-white brick patio that stretches the length of the house. The house itself is three stories of Old World stone topped by a red slate roof.

He rings the bell beside the ten-foot front door and is greeted by a middle-aged Hispanic woman in a maid's uniform, who directs him to follow her. She leads him through a marble foyer, down a long hall past rooms of rich, dark wood paneling, and stops before an arched doorway.

"Please make yourself at home," she says, extending her arm.

He passes through the doorway as she turns and walks away. The living room looks like pictures he's seen of European castles—almost large enough to accommodate a full-court basketball game; the floor covered by giant, plush Oriental rugs; the walls hung with tapestries and oil paintings. The space is filled with couches and high-backed chairs, giant coffee tables decorated with books and keepsakes, desks, and a game table. Unlike the rooms in Old World estate homes, however, this one doesn't feel heavy and worn, because the furniture is modern, all beiges and whites. The paintings are splashes of boldly colored paint—abstract expressionist and cubist works. Even the silk rugs are bright. The space is flooded with light from the floor-to-ceiling windows stretching the length of the back wall.

In the center of the wall adjacent to the hallway is a large white-marble fireplace, and he walks over to it. The mantel is covered with photographs. Jimmy and Rachel on their wedding day. Jimmy on a golf course with a group of men. Christina's college graduation picture, and an identical photograph of a young man, handsome and smiling in his cap and gown. Alexander, the son who perished in the train crash two years earlier. He thinks back to the criminal case that followed the crash, and Jimmy Nunzio's quest for vengeance against those responsible—a quest that imperiled both Vaughn and his cousin Eddy.

He leans into the mantel, studies a series of older photographs on the left-hand side. Some he doesn't recognize, though he can see Hiram Marx in the face of a younger man. In the back, he spots a photograph of Rachel Nunzio in an old-fashioned chorus girl's dancing costume.

But, of course, he realizes, it isn't Rachel. It's her grandmother, Jade. They could be twins, they look so much alike: the same olive skin, full lips, dark hair, and facial structure. It's the eyes that distinguish them. Jade's eyes smile, giving off a devilish gleam, but it is lighthearted, light-spirited. The luminosity in Rachel's eyes is darker, more malevolent than mischievous.

"The story goes that my grandfather fell for her the instant he first spotted her onstage."

He turns to find Rachel Nunzio behind him.

"Do you believe in love at first sight, Mick?"

He opens his mouth, but nothing comes out. His mind is brought to a halt by the madness of talking about love with someone like Rachel Nunzio.

"I wonder if that's what happened with Christina," she continues. "She hasn't opened up to me about Antonio yet. Maybe she never will. Perhaps she holds me to blame as much as she does my husband for what befell her lover."

"Befell? That's an interesting way to put it."

"Follow me," she says, ignoring him.

She leads him out of the room and down the hall to a back door that opens onto a courtyard complex adorned with plantings and trimmed hedges of various designs. He follows her through a second rear courtyard into a third area, where a large swimming pool is set into a spacious flagstone patio. On the other side of the pool, set back from it, are three canopied, double-chaise pool beds of the type he's seen at luxury hotels.

On the near side of the pool are tables and chairs. Rachel leads him to the farthest table, where Christina Nunzio sits with Hiram Marx. Johnny Giacobetti's mastiffs are lounging nearby, in the sun.

"Mick, you remember my uncle," Rachel says as Uncle Ham, now standing, extends his hand.

"Of course," he says, shaking hands with the old man. He greets Christina, and they all sit.

"Would you like some iced tea?" Christina asks, pouring.

He accepts the glass and takes a sip. "It's very good."

"I called Jimmy, told him what's going on," Rachel says.

Mick nods.

"He doesn't like it. And neither do I."

Rachel slides the subpoena across the table, along with two business cards. He reaches for the cards and sees that one is Martin Brenner's. The other belongs to an FBI special agent. Brenner probably brought the agent as a prop to increase the intimidation factor. Mick has seen the tactic before.

"Brenner did all the talking," Rachel says.

He nods. "What did Brenner say, exactly?"

"He said he was hauling Christina in front of a grand jury."

He turns to Christina and opens his mouth to address her. Before he gets the chance, Rachel turns to Christina herself.

"Christina," Rachel says, "I think this would be a good time for you to leave us."

Mick's on his feet as well. "You must be kidding. Your daughter is a material witness to what happened that night. I need to talk with her, find out what she would say if she were called to the stand. Or before a grand jury."

Her jaw clenched, Rachel says. "It's not time for you to know yet."

"We're two weeks from trial! And there's no telling how soon Brenner will put her before the grand jury."

"There's no need to raise our voices." Hiram Marx's own voice is quiet, but hard and unyielding as stone.

Mick sits again and exhales. Christina takes that as her cue to leave, and he watches her make her way past the pool through a stone archway leading toward the house. The hounds follow her.

"Mrs. Nunzio, I mean no disrespect. But if I'm going to have any chance of helping your husband at trial, someone's got to let me in on whatever story you all are planning on having me sell. And I have to know that story *before* Brenner tosses Christina to his own wolves."

In his peripheral vision, he sees Hiram smile at his use of the word "story."

"I don't even know who to call to testify on our behalf. Is your husband going to allow me to call Christina? Giacobetti? Is he hiding some other witness in his back pocket?"

"Why would you think there's another witness?" Hiram asks.

"Well, given that your . . . nephew-in-law refuses to plead, I have to think he has reason to believe he's going to win a verdict of not guilty. The only way that's going to happen is if he has an ace in the hole I don't know about."

A sliver of a smile spreads slowly across the old man's bloodless lips again. "That would make sense."

"So?"

"It's not time, Mr. McFarland," Rachel Nunzio repeats. With that, she stands. "I'll leave you two alone."

He watches her disappear through the stone archway, then turns toward Hiram Marx. They lock eyes, and he keeps his face expressionless, as does the old man. He wonders how he should play this, and decides to go on the offensive, see if he can rattle Marx.

"So," he says, "tell me about HML."

The old man's eyes widen, then narrow, and he presses his thin lips together. "Is it normal for a defense attorney to research his own client? Shouldn't you be focusing your efforts on the prosecution?"

"Nothing about this case is normal. And I already know the prosecution's take on the case, and what they intend to do about it."

"And what exactly is the prosecution's plan?"

"To take the case to trial and get a guilty verdict."

The old man's mouth twists into a smile, though his eyes remain cold. "You should have more faith in yourself, Mr. McFarland. My nephew has total confidence in you."

"Your nephew is playing me. I just haven't figured out how yet."

Hiram Marx takes a long sip of iced tea. "Cash, gold, weapons, and people."

"What?"

"In reverse order of importance, those are HML's most profitable payloads."

He considers this. "You're telling me that shipping people is your largest cash cow."

"Government leaders, corporate executives, Middle Eastern princes . . . It's amazing how powerful men so often feel compelled to be somewhere they're not supposed to be." He shakes his head, leans forward. "You want to know who are the worst? United States senators."

"And how much do you charge a senator?"

"Oh, the plane ride is free. Down the line, of course . . ."

"You blackmail them."

"We remind them how important their anonymity is. And we ask a favor."

"Is that why the US Attorney's Office in New York didn't move against your nephew?"

He shrugs, smiles.

"Couldn't you put the same pressure on our Pennsylvania senators to derail Martin Brenner?"

"I didn't say *all* senators availed themselves of our services."

They sit quietly for a few moments, both men swirling the ice in their glasses.

There's so much he wants to ask the old man about the Nunzios. What comes out is, "The story about Jimmy killing a man when he was twelve . . . is it true?"

"His bar mitzvah." The old man smiles, and this time it's genuine.

"You seriously call it that?"

"Just a joke. Jimmy doesn't like when I say it. He's a good Catholic, you know."

The old man waves away the topic and asks Mick why Brenner's so hot on the case.

"He wants your nephew to turn on his boss. That would be a huge feather in his cap. So he threatens Rachel with a grand jury subpoena, trying to get her to panic, to persuade Jimmy to cooperate."

"Rachel, panic?" He chuckles.

"She seemed pretty worried to me."

He leans forward. "She has no reason to worry. She knows that Jimmy and I would never let any harm come to her."

"Uh-huh. Speaking of which, let's talk about the lodge and what happened to Valiante's crew."

"Let's not."

"The six white vans I saw parked in the lot. Were those yours? HML's?"

"Those, and the other six you *didn't* see." Hiram Marx stands. "Thank you for coming, Mr. McFarland. I'll walk you out."

They retrace the route Rachel used to get him to the pool. Hiram Marx leads him to the front door, opens it, then pauses in the threshold, ushering him outside.

"It's been interesting speaking with you, Mr. McFarland. Thank you in advance for finding a way to keep Mr. Brenner at bay. I'm sure I don't need to tell you that neither Rachel nor Christina nor Mr. Giacobetti can be hauled before a grand jury."

"I can't control a federal prosecutor. And Martin Brenner seems hell-bent on co-opting your nephew."

"I think you'll find that you have more influence over Mr. Brenner than you think."

He's about to ask the old man what he means by that when Hiram Marx speaks again.

"Give my regards to your wife, Piper," says Hiram Marx, his face relaxing into a predatory smile. "And little Gabby, too. She made quite an impression on Christina."

A chill races up Mick's spine. The old man didn't even try to veil the threat. Mick stands frozen as the door closes in his face. After a few seconds, he turns and walks across the front patio to his car, parked where he left it.

He opens the driver's door and lifts his leg to climb in when he hears her moving up behind him.

"He made me laugh," she says.

He turns. "Christina."

They lock eyes for a long moment.

"Everyone asked me afterward what I saw in Antonio. Why I dated him when our families are so set against each other. And that's why. Tony made me laugh. He made me smile. His business, the same as my family's business, is so serious, so fraught with peril. But Tony was lighthearted, playful, even. With me, anyway. Being with him made me forget what I came from."

He closes the car door. "Please tell me what happened that night."

She closes her eyes, shakes her head. "There was going to be a war. Tony told me, and I overheard my parents saying the same thing. Tony's family was horning in on our territory, and my father and his boss weren't going to stand for it."

She looks away. He can see she's doing her best to gather herself for whatever is coming next.

"My father told me that he could stop the war if he could just sit down and talk with Tony, alone . . ."

His breath goes out of him, like he's been kicked in the gut.

"The call to your father, the one that brought him to the warehouse . . . it was *you*?"

"Tony didn't trust my father. He would never have agreed to meet with him alone. So my father persuaded me to wait until Tony and I were by ourselves and call him without Tony knowing so he could come and talk."

"I thought Tony never traveled without bodyguards. That he was very careful."

"That was his father's doing. Tony hated being shadowed like that, same as me. Sometimes we'd sneak away—to a hotel, or to that warehouse. Someone lived there full-time, to protect the drugs, but we'd chase him off for a few hours."

"So you called your father that night. And when he showed up . . ."

"He promised me he'd come alone. But he brought Johnny G. with him. They didn't knock. Just smashed the door in—I guess they wanted to take Tony by surprise. And once they were in—"

"Christina!"

He hears Rachel Nunzio's heels clicking swiftly across the brick behind him.

"What the hell are you *doing*?"

"You can't hide me forever!" Christina shouts back. "I'm not some doll you can put on a shelf to look pretty."

"Get in the house! Now!"

He sees something pass between the two women. Then Christina storms past him and flees into the house.

He turns on Rachel Nunzio.

"What kind of monsters are you? You and your husband? He used his own daughter as bait to set a trap for his enemy. Then he broke her heart by murdering the man she loved right in front of her. And *you* . . . you're helping him try to get away with it."

She throws her head back and laughs. Then she lowers her gaze, and her voice. With fire in her eyes, she says, "Who are you, little man, to judge my husband, or me? You scurry around at our heels, hoping . . ."

He sees her eyes flare as she catches herself.

"I think it's best you just leave now."

"You mean before you say something out of line?"

But she's already walking away.

Driving back to the office, Mick is furious with Jimmy Nunzio. He simply cannot comprehend how even a monster like that could use his own daughter as a pawn in a gangland war. *Unforgivable.* And Rachel Nunzio seems to be no better than her husband. He has no idea whether she knew beforehand about Nunzio's plan to use their daughter to isolate Valiante. But she sure as hell knows now, and she's keeping Christina's hands tied and mouth shut. And Rachel's ability to do so appears to be part of a pattern of total control over her daughter, he decides, recalling what Christina shouted to Rachel about being kept on the shelf like a doll. Is that why she's lost her ambition? Because her parents—*both* of her parents—are so domineering and want her to remain the proverbial child? Seen and not heard? No wonder she's given up.

Five more minutes. That's all it would have taken for Christina to tell him everything about what went down that night at the warehouse. Still, there'd been enough time for Christina to answer the key question of why Valiante's guards weren't with him. She also established the critical fact that the whole thing had been orchestrated by Jimmy Nunzio. Antonio Valiante's death was planned. It was only bad luck in the form of two cops deciding to investigate the Escalade parked in front of what they thought was an abandoned building that prevented Nunzio from getting away with it.

Christina also established that Giacobetti was with Nunzio when he showed up at the warehouse. That would explain why Christina's burner phone—the one she used to call Nunzio—hadn't been found by the police; Johnny G. took it with him when he left. But where did he go? How did he even leave, given that both Nunzio's Escalade and Antonio Valiante's Porsche were still parked outside the warehouse?

Those and a dozen other still-unanswered questions make his head spin. He takes some deep breaths, turns on the radio, and tries to relax. After a while, though, another question starts itching at the back of his head: Why didn't he get a call from Nunzio himself about Brenner showing up at his house? That's how it's been playing up until now.

Whenever something happens that bothers the mobster, he summons Mick to the prison. This time, though, Mick was ordered to the family home by Rachel even though she must have told Nunzio about Brenner's subpoenas.

Why?

There is only one logical answer: the Nunzios wanted him to talk to Rachel and Hiram rather than Jimmy. But what did they tell him that Nunzio couldn't have said himself? What did they really tell him at all, other than he needed to do something about Martin Brenner?

He lets the questions fade, but after a while, his mind wanders back to Christina Nunzio and Antonio Valiante. Two twentysomethings in love, seeing each other on the sly, their families at war. The press had it right, after all: it really was a Romeo-and-Juliet affair. Except in place of Capulets and Montagues, there were Nunzios and Valiantes.

29

Saturday, June 8

It's close to 5:00 p.m. when Tommy hears his cell phone ring. It's on the table next to the bed. Not his bed, Sharon's—the waitress he flirted with when he first came up to the Lehigh Valley a month earlier.

Visiting Lois Beal's farm last week got him thinking about the poker game at Elwood Stumpf's place the night Lester Dowd was killed. It got him to thinking, too, about how ol' Woody and Buck Forney gave him the cold shoulder, making it seem like maybe they were worried he'd uncover something they were up to now. And then Stumpf sending his grandson to run him down on the highway, removing the "maybe" from the equation. So he decided to come back a second time, shake the bushes, see if anything about the Dowd killing scurried out.

Elwood Stumpf had been even pricklier than the first time.

"I should never've sent Clem after you," Elwood said.

"You feeling guilty?"

"I shoulda sent Billy. That's my son, Clem's dad. Now there's a tough sombitch. You wouldn't'a walked away from that one."

"I'm going to find out what you're hiding one way or another. You may as well just tell me."

"I think he's around here somewhere. Hey, Billy!"

He put his hands up. "I get it. I'm leaving."

From Elwood's farm, he drove to Forney Chrysler/Dodge and read Buck as more scared than snappish.

"Dale told me you'd talked to him," Buck said of his son. "He had nothing to do with that girl."

"Not what he told me," Tommy said.

"A few dates. That was it."

"Why wasn't Dale at the card game that night?"

"The hell should I know? Maybe he was sick. There's a dozen reasons someone wouldn't show up to a card game."

"Well, when you talked to him after I did, which one did he offer up?"

Buck Forney glared. "You leave Dale out of this. Or you'll hear from my attorneys."

"Why is everyone so worried about Darlene Dowd? Elwood was ready to sic his son on me just for asking about her. Now you're calling out the lawyers?"

Forney stood, signaling that the meeting was over. "Look, no one's worried about Darlene or her father's killing. You're barking up the wrong tree."

"Are you going to answer it?" Sharon's lying on her side, propped up on her elbow. "Or is that your wife calling, and you don't want to talk to her in front of me?"

"You're the only one here that's married."

"I'm divorcing that bum. I told you."

The first time he met Sharon, Tommy made it clear that her jailed husband was a deal breaker for him. Today, she'd explained that her husband was in jail because he shot up a bank and sent a bullet into the abdomen of a pregnant woman, killing her baby. That was enough for Tommy to relax his rule.

He sits up in the bed, presses the "Answer" button, and lifts the iPhone to his ear.

"Tommy? It's Raymond Thorne. I got the results of the fingerprint analysis. They actually came back yesterday, but I was out of town."

"And?"

"What you thought. The prints on the hammer matched the ones on the water bottle."

He closes his eyes.

"You there?"

"Yeah," he says.

"Sounds like what you expected to hear isn't what you wanted to hear."

"Nope."

"You sure you don't want any testing of the blood? There's plenty of it. And hair. And very small pieces of bone."

"No. I know for sure who all that belonged to. The prints tell me what I needed to know."

"I'll have one of my guys deliver you the hammer and the box it was in. Plus, the report. You want it brought to your house?"

"That would be the best. Hey, thanks, Ray. I owe you one."

"I owe you more than one, so you're still ahead. And that job offer stands, as always."

"It's nice to know I have a place to land."

He places the cell phone back on the nightstand.

"What're you mixed up in?" Sharon asks. "Hammers and blood and hair . . . ?"

"You overheard all that?"

"I'm a foot away from you, dumbass." She eyes him and smiles. "You're not some kind of undercover cop, are you? Not that it would bother me. I've dated so many shitheads on the other side of the law, it might be a nice change."

He thinks. "Nah. More of a spy than a copper."

"Ooh, I like that." She tosses the sheets aside, straddles him. Her long brown hair flows over her generous breasts.

"I should've brought my little blue pills," he says.

"From what I seen, you don't need 'em."

It's close to 10:30 when Tommy parks his F-150 down the block from the house Armand Romero rents in Drexel Hill. He decided to scope out the soccer player's house on his way to his own place in Havertown, which is only about five miles away. Three times he's gone to soccer-boy's favorite watering hole and tried to get the guy to open up about Susan, or women in general, share some stories. Armand has been close-mouthed about his conquests. If Armand's cheating on Susan or abusing her, he isn't going to let Tommy know.

He isn't even sure at this point that Armand and Susan are still dating. Maybe it's some other guy who's causing Susan all her troubles.

He's about to start the truck when he sees headlights passing him on the left. It's a white BMW 335i. He knows the car.

He watches her turn the car into Armand's driveway. After a moment, the lights go off, and she exits the vehicle. Blonde hair over an athletic build. Susan. She walks onto the porch and knocks. The door opens, and she disappears inside.

"So they *are* still dating," he says aloud.

From behind him, he sees headlights on a vehicle slowly making its way up the street. The vehicle, large and black, parks just behind his truck. The lights go out, and the passenger-side door opens. He reaches to adjust his rearview to see whoever is approaching, but before he has time, his own passenger side door opens, and the giant climbs in beside him.

"The hell do you want?" he says. He reaches to his right for the pistol he keeps there but is stopped by an iron vice on his forearm.

"You don't pull back, this will go poorly for you," says Johnny Giacobetti.

"All right. Let go," he says as Giacobetti releases his grip.

"You're barking up the wrong tree," Nunzio's enforcer tells him.

"Second time today I heard that."

"So I'm told."

He does a double take. "How could you know about that?"

"Mr. Nunzio's business interests are widespread, and Lehigh County's not that far away."

"Nunzio's mixed up with Elwood Stumpf? Buck Forney?"

"We're working on something together. But they're not what I'm talking about when I'm telling you that you're looking in the wrong direction." Giacobetti nods toward Armand Romero's house.

"What's that supposed to mean?"

"It means that David Beckham there isn't your lady boss's problem."

"Then who is?"

"You'll find out soon enough."

"I'm starting to get pissed off here."

Giacobetti chuckles. Then his face turns serious. "Speaking of someone being pissed off, Mr. Nunzio isn't happy about you and your brother poking your noses into things that aren't your business."

He stares.

"Every family's got its skeletons. The Nunzios' bones need to stay buried."

"I don't know what you're talking about."

"I'm talking about a reporter who's been warned not to spread things around."

Sid Haltzman. "That was just a friendly conversation with your boss's lawyer. Everything to be kept confidential. Attorney-client privilege."

"The reporter was warned."

He doesn't like the tone in Giacobetti's voice. Nunzio's enforcer will be going after Haltzman unless he can think something up.

"I'd lay off him, I were you. Smart guy like that probably has a safe-deposit box with instructions to be opened in case something bad happens to him."

"That so? I'll pass it along."

"Back to Susan," Tommy says.

"I'll be calling you. When I do, you'll need to move fast."

"What—"

"Later," Johnny Giacobetti says, opening the door and climbing out.

As soon as the Escalade passes him, Tommy calls Sid Haltzman. When the reporter picks up, he identifies himself and gets right down to it.

"Do you have a safe-deposit box with your story about Nunzio in it?"

"No."

"Well, get one. In fact, get three or four. And be conspicuous about it."

"Nunzio found out? That we met?"

"I'm pretty damned sure." He explains about Giacobetti, and his planting the idea into the enforcer's mind that going after Haltzman might lead to the disclosure of the reporter's secret story on the Nunzios.

"You think it'll work? If I make copies and open safe-deposit boxes?"

"I think you have no choice but to try."

Silence at the other end. Then, "Fuckadoodledoo."

"Yep."

30

Monday, June 10

Piper's heart is pounding as she enters the conference room. She knows Susan is waiting for her. A few minutes earlier, Susan buzzed her to let her know a courier had just dropped off the results of the FBI's forensic testing of the hammer. Piper asked Susan on the phone whether Special Agent Lance Newton had called ahead of time to let her know what the results were, and Susan told her that Newton was out of the country but left instructions that the results be delivered when ready, whether he was back or not.

"Have you opened it yet?" she asks, sitting down next to Susan.

"Here," Susan says, handing her the envelope. "You do the honors."

"I feel like I did when I was opening college-acceptance letters," Piper says, carefully tearing the flap.

The envelope contains a cover letter on stationery identifying it as being sent from the FBI laboratory in Quantico, Virginia. Under the letter are two reports, one from the FBI's Latent Print Unit and one from its CODIS unit. The latter, she knows, manages the FBI's Combined DNA Index System (CODIS) and the National DNA Index System, or NDIS.

Taking the first report, the fingerprint analysis, she quickly scans past the details to the conclusion: "Conclusively matched to fingerprints stored in AFIS attributed to Cindy Dowd."

"It's her!" She waves the report in her hand. "Cindy was the killer!"

Susan smiles and takes the report, and Piper turns her attention to the report from the CODIS Unit. Piper learned from Melvin Ott that, at the time of Lester Dowd's murder, the district attorney and police chief were hopeful that the murder instrument would be found, and they wanted to be able to match any blood, tissue, and hair on the weapon to the decedent. At their direction, the pathologist swabbed Lester Dowd's cheeks to secure material for DNA testing, which was sent to the FBI lab for analysis and inputting into CODIS. The pathologist also ran the blood for blood type.

The CODIS report states that there was hair, blood, and brain tissue found on the hammer. The blood and brain evidence were too deteriorated to test, but the hair yielded a DNA match to Lester Dowd.

She reads the report twice, then uses it to fan herself. "This is it," she tells Susan. "Everything Lois said was true. Darlene is innocent."

Susan takes the report and is about to read it when Tommy walks in.

"Tommy!" Piper bolts from her chair. "We have the results from the FBI: Cindy Dowd *was* the killer, not Darlene!"

She runs to him and gives him a hug. Then she steps back. "Didn't you hear me? Darlene's innocent. She's going to go free."

She instantly sees through his forced smile. "What's the matter?"

"Nothing. That's great. I . . . something's up."

He turns and leaves the conference room.

"What was that all about?" she asks Susan.

"Don't ask me. I never got that guy."

Piper sits. She and Susan discuss the petition Susan's going to file under Pennsylvania's Post Conviction Relief Act. They're going to base their claim on the part of the law that allows for a new trial, in which a petitioner can prove the existence of newly discovered exculpatory evidence that was not available to the petitioner at the time of trial and that would have changed the outcome of the trial. A recently uncovered murder weapon bearing someone else's fingerprints certainly fits that definition. So does the existence of a witness turned away by law enforcement.

The law, though, requires the petition to be brought within sixty days of the date the claim could have been presented. And the state's conservative appellate courts interpret this time limit narrowly.

"If he wants to be aggressive," Susan explains, "the district attorney could argue that Darlene should have brought her claim as soon as she received her mother's deathbed letter."

"But we couldn't *prove* the hammer is exculpatory of Darlene until we received the test results, which is today," Piper says, her voice rising. "Same with Sonny Foster shutting down Lois Beal; we couldn't prove that until we met with Melvin Ott, which was toward the end of April, which is less than sixty days ago."

"I understand. Remember: I didn't say the prosecutor would win the argument, only that he could make it."

"Sorry. I just . . ."

"I know. I want to win this one, too. Which reminds me . . . I also received this today." Susan hands her a signed certification. Along with their petition, they have to provide the court with certifications of each witness who will attend the hearing, stating their backgrounds and the substance of their proposed testimony.

Piper scans it. "Hmm. Lois signed it as 'Megan Corbett.' Not that she had much choice."

"She had no choice at all, Piper. And I'm not going to apologize for that."

The most difficult part of all this for Piper has been Susan's refusal to overlook Lois Beal's role in the armored-truck heist. At the airport on their way home from Georgia, Susan made clear that she felt compelled to turn Lois in, even though it meant that Lois would likely face charges for murder in California.

Tommy had asked then, "So if some other lawyer had taken on Darlene's case, Lois would be in the clear? But since it's you, she's gotta go down?"

"Lois was going to have to face charges no matter *what* lawyer came on board, at least so long as she was planning to help Darlene. Look, when we file our petition asking for a new trial based on Lois's information, Lois will have to sign a certification with her name and date of birth. And she'll have to *testify* to who she is, too. No lawyer could submit a certification under a false name, let alone put her on the stand to perjure herself about her identity. It would cost the lawyer their license. Not to mention the fact that as an officer of the court, no honest attorney would do any of it."

"Then why should she help us?" Piper asked loudly enough that several of the other passengers turned toward them.

"Because it's the right thing to do," Susan answered. "And because if she doesn't, I can make the call right now rather than wait until after the hearing."

"That's what we're going to tell her?"

"It's what I'm going to tell her," Susan said. Then, softening, she added, "If Lois calls the authorities in California just before the hearing, tells them where she'll be, and then comes clean at the hearing about who she is, it'll help her. She'll be a lot better off than if I, or anyone else, makes the call."

Piper still doesn't think it seems fair, but Susan clearly hasn't changed her mind.

"Let's not forget what we're doing here," Susan tells Piper. "We're trying to save a young woman who was raped repeatedly by her own father and then tossed into prison. Lois Beal, a.k.a. Megan Corbett, has the chance to help us free this woman. That she's going to have to accept responsibility for some bad things she did when she was younger is . . .

Well, it's just something she's going to have to do. For Darlene's sake. Maybe even for her own sake. There's a part of each of us, I think, that wants to be held accountable, wants to be punished when we cross the line. I'd like to believe that's the better part of us."

Piper nods. She knows that part is a huge part of Tommy's history, the reason he spiraled into self-destructiveness. He had a drive to be punished for something he'd done that he'd felt was unforgivable. Ultimately, he bared his soul to her about it, and she helped him come to terms with the guilt.

"I know," she says. "I get it. I just think Lois is a good person, despite what she did as a nineteen-year-old. And it's not like she hasn't paid a price already. Having to live in constant fear of being caught. Never having children because she thought she might get dragged away to prison at any time."

"And never having closure," Susan said. "Which she will have now."

Down the hall in his office, Tommy sits back in his chair and rubs his eyes.

What in the hell am I going to do with the information about the second hammer?

Susan is already hell-bent on nailing Lois Beal. And Piper has so much emotionally invested in the case. He leans forward, his mind taking him back to the many nights he and Piper sat in her kitchen or on her back patio while he told her about the terrible things he had done in his life, including *the* terrible thing that sent him down the dark path in the first place. She listened and listened and never once judged him. Even more important, she tried to make him see that there was no need to punish himself. That he'd spent so many years of his life rushing to judgment for something that wasn't wrong. And then the Hanson case crashed down around all of them—Piper, him, and Mick—and he'd been forced to go down the dark path one more time to save them all. Since then, he's treated Piper like a jerk, which only makes him mad at himself. So far, he hasn't been able to find a way back to their friendship.

Now he might have to ruin the Dowd case for her.

"What am I going to do?"

31

Thursday, June 13

It's just before noon, and Mick and Vaughn are seated at the table in the conference room, which is now officially the firm's "war room" for the Nunzio case. The table is covered with legal pads, laptops, police reports, witness statements, and photographs. Scores of photographs: of the warehouse and Nunzio's Escalade, taken by the CSU team that managed the crime scene; of Christina Nunzio and Jimmy Nunzio, both covered in blood; of the knife used to kill Valiante, taken by CSU; and of Antonio Valiante's body, taken by the medical examiner. Enlargements of some of the photographs are pinned to the far wall on either side of the easels that still list the names of potential prosecution and defense witnesses.

"I've never entered a trial feeling less in control than I do with this case," Mick says.

"Nunzio still hasn't told you what happened at the warehouse?"

Mick shakes his head. "I still think he's sitting on an ace. But I can't figure out which of the witnesses it could be."

"My bet's on Giacobetti. Nunzio's going to have him take the fall. Say it was him who killed Valiante."

Mick doesn't share with Vaughn that Christina confirmed Giacobetti was at the warehouse. Nor does he tell them the whole thing was a trap Nunzio set for Antonio Valiante. He doesn't like keeping things from his team, but he's decided to play everything close to the vest on this one; he may have to suborn outright perjury, and he doesn't want Vaughn to be part of it.

"I've thought of that," Mick says. "But how would he explain Giacobetti's not being there when the cops showed up?"

"He darted out the back when the cops came," Vaughn says. "Nunzio's office is only a mile or so from the warehouse. He probably ran there."

"And Nunzio stayed because he wasn't going to leave Christina," Mick says. He chews on it a minute. "But if he were planning on pinning the murder on Giacobetti, why let Johnny G. leave at all? Why not throw him the knife as soon as they realized the cops were there?"

"I thought the cops surprised Nunzio. That he didn't know they were there until they came through the door. At least, that's how I envisioned it."

"We could go around and around on this," Mick says. "The bottom line is it's all speculation—not a defense. We won't know anything until Nunzio decides to let us in on what happened."

"Let us in on whatever bullshit he's baking, you mean," Vaughn says.

Mick nods. "So, for now, our strategy is simply to pick as many holes in the prosecution's case as we can find." He pauses a moment as Tommy enters the conference room. "Any idea what's happening at the DA's office?"

"My guess? Pagano's running everyone ragged. Every time the DA's poll numbers go down a little further, he goes on TV and promises Nunzio's gonna face jail time. So the pressure's on Pagano, and that means Max the Ax is probably swinging his blade like a madman. He has a reputation of bringing people onto his team, using them up, then throwing them out."

"And knowing Fellner, he'd be okay with that," Mick says.

"Are you kidding? Fellner's so panicked about the election, he's even offered to pay for a big-time jury consultant, but Pagano turned him down. Said he doesn't need a jury-whisperer, he can read jurors like books."

"Arrogant SOB," Mick says.

"Speaking of jury consultants," Vaughn says, "Lauren Zito sent over her draft jury questionnaires this morning."

Based in Los Angeles, Lauren Zito is considered one of the country's top jury consultants. A holder of doctorate and bachelor's degrees in psychology and a master's in education, she's worked on hundreds of cases around the country—and has actually developed much of the currently accepted methodology used by experts in jury selection. Nunzio insisted that Mick retain her firm for his trial. She flew in the night before for a meeting with the trial team.

"Good. I'll review them. What time is she coming to meet with us?"

"Three. In the meantime, I have a motion hearing set for this afternoon. You mind if I leave to get ready for it?"

Mick says, "Sure." He waits until Vaughn is gone. Then he turns to Tommy.

"Have you seen Susan yet?"

"She's in a mood today," Tommy says. "Gave me the cold shoulder. And Angie said she came in barking orders at Jill and Andrea."

He sighs. Susan continues to rebuff his invitations to open up to him about whoever's creating havoc in her personal life. Tommy told him that she's still seeing the soccer player but that Tommy's efforts to get the guy to talk to him about Susan haven't gone anywhere. More upsetting than any of that is the fact that—according to Tommy—Nunzio has Giacobetti spying on Susan for his own reasons. He can't believe Susan would be tied up with the Nunzios.

So why is Johnny G. following her around? And what did the giant mean by telling Tommy he's going to call, and that when he does, Tommy will have to move fast?

"I'll try to talk to her again," Mick says.

"You might want to bring up Giacobetti," Tommy says.

"That's the last thing I'd tell her about. She's rattled enough as it is."

"Maybe she already knows. Maybe that's why she's so upset."

At three o'clock sharp, Angie calls Mick to the conference room to meet Lauren Zito. This is the first time he's hired a jury consultant. He's not sure exactly how they work, or even convinced they really help. But Nunzio was adamant he hire Zito, and the money was there to do so.

Zito stands when he enters the room. She's an attractive woman in her midforties, petite and compact with toned arms and legs and a thick mane of dark hair. Her smile reveals perfect rows of white teeth. Her eyes are bright, but Mick sees something in them that gives him pause: an unpredictable intelligence he's encountered before—on both sides of the law.

Lauren offers her hand. They shake, and she introduces two of her assistants, Rob Sinnamon and Naumon Amjed. Everyone sits, and the meeting starts.

"This is your show," Mick begins, "but let me open it by telling you up front that I've never used a jury consultant before. I don't know much about what you do other than help the lawyers with the voir dire questions."

Zito smiles. "Then let me take a few minutes to give you a broad-brush view of what our role will be. First, we do draft the questions we think you should ask the prospective jurors. A lot of the questions you've probably seen before. As counsel for the defendant, you're looking for jurors whose background would cause them to mistrust the system, be skeptical of the police and the establishment in general—people at the bottom of the economic totem pole, or who have had run-ins with the police, or whose families and friends have been harassed.

The questions are designed to identify them. We have to be careful, of course, not to oversimplify based on neighborhood or race. Bad jurors for a defendant generally include people who are fearful of crime in their neighborhoods, though, of course, this isn't a case about someone being robbed on the street."

"Let's get to that," Mick says. "This isn't the usual situation where the jurors know nothing about the defendant. Everyone knows about Jimmy Nunzio. How do we exclude jurors who won't put his past aside?"

"You can't. No matter what the judge tells jurors about basing their decision only on the evidence presented in the courtroom, the fact is that everything the jurors know about Nunzio is 'evidence' they're going to bring with them to deliberations. And all of that evidence, as I'm sure you know, is bad. The fact is, the proverbial scales of justice are already tipped heavily against Nunzio."

Mick leans forward. "So how exactly are you going to help us level the field?"

"By helping you craft a compelling story, and by watching you and the jurors as you tell it."

"Watching me?"

"Yes. You, your client, and your witnesses. When people think of jury consultants, they picture someone sitting in court, laser-focused on the jury. We do, of course, watch the jurors, but we also watch the parties. A big part of my job will be scrutinizing the lawyers and witnesses for each side—how they move, how they talk, how they dress, how they behave—basically taking it in from the jurors' perspectives. That way I can tell you how you're coming across, and how to change it. Normally, though, I don't wait for the trial to get started. Before the first juror's picked, I meet with your witnesses."

"Meet with the witnesses before trial? Why?"

"I need to spend time with them, alone. I'll ask each of them to talk to me, tell me their story. When they're done, I'll say, 'Okay. Here's what I'm hearing. Here's where your story resonates with me. Here's where you're weak.'"

Mick shifts uncomfortably in his seat. "That's going to be a problem. I don't know who our witnesses are yet."

She stares at him. He can't read the look on her face.

"Nunzio won't let me in on what happened in the warehouse that led to the victim's death," he explains. "There were one, possibly two, witnesses—his daughter, Christina, and one of his henchmen. He won't tell me which, if either, he'll let me call to the stand. And there's no way I can call Nunzio. The prosecutor would crucify him."

"Seems like we're going to have to go into this with our hands tied," she says. "Partially tied, at least."

They stare at each other for a long minute; then he asks, "Tell me about the trial itself. What's your program?"

"Well, in addition to what I already told you, Rob, Naumon, and a third assistant will each have two shadow jurors with them—people we'll pick as demographic matches for the jurors. The shadow jurors will watch the trial and give their impressions of the lawyers and the witnesses—and of the real jurors—to my assistants, who will share it all with you and me."

"Sounds expensive."

Zito smiles broadly. "I drive a Lexus LS 460 and own two vacation homes. Most attorneys who hire me work for Fortune 500 companies that are defending multimillion-dollar civil suits."

He studies her. Notices for the first time how well dressed she is. Big corporations are smart with their money; they wouldn't lay out big bucks for jury consultants unless they felt it was worth it. He's about to say something when a light bulb goes off over his head.

He realizes he's found Nunzio's ace in the hole: the jury.

Nunzio believes Lauren Zito will be able to feed him the jury. He really believes *she's* going to pave the way for a defense verdict that will let him walk.

"My client has a lot of faith in you," he says. "I'm guessing he's more than just heard about you. I'm guessing you know each other."

A look crosses her face that tells him she's weighing how to answer. "Cards on the table? I live in California now, but I was raised in South Philly, not far from the Nunzios."

His chest tightens. "You grew up with Jimmy?"

"I was a few years younger."

He wonders whether he should probe more deeply, decides not to. "So you knew even before I told you that Nunzio's been holding back on his witnesses."

"We did talk, yes."

"I'm not sure I'm liking this."

"Shall we review the jury questionnaire?" She opens a folder and hands him the questionnaire.

Her message is clear: *What you like or don't like is irrelevant.*

It's just after 9:00 when Mick enters the kitchen. Piper is waiting for him, stirring something on the stove.

"Something smells good," he says.

"Nothing special," she answers. "Just some pasta with marinara sauce. You must be hungry."

"Starving," he says. "I can't wait. Is Gabby in bed?"

"Yes. And Franklin, too."

He pours two glasses of merlot, hands one to Piper, then sits at the island in the kitchen. After a few minutes, Piper hands him a plate full of the pasta and red sauce, and he digs in. She sits across from him, sipping her wine and flipping through this month's *Architectural Digest.* He's just finishing when his cell phone rings.

"It's Tommy," he tells Piper. Then, to Tommy, he says, "Hey, what's—"

"You need to come to Susan's place," Tommy says. "Now."

"Susan's? What's wrong?"

"I got the call from Giacobetti. I found out who's been bothering her."

"Is it someone we know?"

"Oh yeah."

He hears Tommy shout something on the other end of the phone; then he hangs up.

"What's wrong?" Piper asks as soon as he sets the phone down. "Is Tommy all right? What's going on with Susan?"

Up until now, Mick has honored Susan's request by not telling Piper, or anyone else, about going to Susan's apartment and finding it trashed. At this point, though, it seems that everything's going to come out, so he fills her in.

"Tommy's at Susan's place," he concludes. "And the guy's there, too."

He stands to leave.

"Be careful," says Piper. "Whoever it is could be dangerous. Shouldn't you call the police?"

He shakes his head. "I'm sure everything's under control. Tommy's there."

The Schuylkill is clear, but the drive to Center City seems to take forever. His mind spins with questions about what's going on in Susan's apartment.

Did Armand Romero—he has no doubt that's who the bad guy is—*hurt Susan? How badly has Tommy hurt the soccer player? And how the hell does Giacobetti fit into it?*

The clock in his car says 10:30 when he pulls in front of Susan's building. A moment later he's standing at the front desk. To his surprise, the front-desk clerk waves him up, doesn't even ask for ID.

"You're expected," the clerk says.

Getting off the elevator on the fourteenth floor, he races down the hall to Susan's apartment. He's about to knock on the door when it opens. Susan's on the other side, a sick look on her face. She glances down as he walks past, through the hall, and into the living room.

"Look what the cat dragged in," Tommy says.

"You're fucking kidding me," he says to the pathetic lump crumpled in the corner, his arms wrapped around his knees, which are drawn nearly to his chin. His eyes are blackened and swelling, his nose obviously busted.

Martin Brenner.

"He assaulted me," the federal prosecutor whines. "Your brother."

He ignores Brenner and motions for Susan to follow him into the bedroom. He closes the door behind them as Susan takes a seat on the bed.

"I'm so humiliated," she says, the tears starting to flow.

He pulls the chair from her makeup table and sits across from her.

"It's all right," he says. "Just tell me what's going on. We'll take care of it."

He leans back to give Susan space. After a moment, she tells him everything.

"Martin was seven years my senior and already a star at the US Attorney's Office when I joined up. Everyone seemed to defer to him. I was in my second year when he asked me to second-chair a big RICO case with him. I was thrilled. To be noticed by someone like Martin, let alone be asked to try a case with him, was an honor. We won, of course, thanks to Martin. He was a genius at trial. He shredded the defendants and all of their witnesses. The verdict came in late on a Friday. Afterward, Martin asked me to join him for a drink. But you know how it goes. One drink leads to two, and then three. We both got plastered, and I did something stupid. Martin was engaged, and I was seeing someone. We agreed it couldn't happen again. And both of us were good in honoring the agreement . . . until we weren't. We got together on and off for almost a year. Then Martin got married, and I told him we were done . . . but I let it go on for another few months.

Then his wife got pregnant, and I told him that was it. That time I meant it. We didn't see each other outside the office for half a year. Then one night he ran into me on the street, and we had a drink together. One drink. After which we left and went our separate ways.

"It was over for me. And I thought it was over for him. But a week later, Martin showed up at my place. I was renting a small house in South Philly then. He banged on the door until I let him in. He was plastered. He told me he loved me, was ready to leave his wife—who was eight months pregnant. It made me sick, what he was doing, what he was saying to me. I told him so. I told him to get the hell out of my house. He made a play, but I pushed him away. Jesus . . ."

Susan closes her eyes, clenches her fists.

He reaches out for her, but she slaps his hand away.

"Did you go to the police?" he asks. "Tell someone you worked with?"

"And admit what a moron I was? That I'd been sleeping with a colleague all during his engagement? And after he was married? While his wife was about to give birth? No fucking way."

He sits back and lets Susan gather herself. He's known for a long time that her romantic life was less balanced than her professional life, but he never guessed she would have let things get so out of hand.

"That's when I moved out of the house I was renting and bought a place here, at the Towers, where they have security. It's also when I announced I was leaving the US Attorney's Office, and when I came to work with you and Lou."

He nods, thinks about what she's told him. "That was five years ago. Why is he bothering you now?"

She lowers her head and closes her eyes for a long time. She exhales and looks up at him.

"I didn't hear from him again until about six months ago. He called me out of the blue, apologized for what an asshole he'd been to me. He asked if I'd meet him for lunch. I said no. He accepted my refusal, and we hung up on friendly terms. Over the next few days, I thought about his apology and how he didn't put up a fight when I turned him down for lunch. I called him back and said I'd changed my mind. I told him to meet me at Bank & Bourbon. He was friendly during lunch, but he seemed preoccupied. I asked him if something was the matter, and he told me that he and Heather were having troubles. That she'd told him she didn't want to be married to him anymore because he worked too hard and didn't pay enough attention to her and the girls."

Mick's chest tightens. He'd had the same conversation with Piper a few years back, when their own marriage had come perilously close to failing.

"I offered my sympathy and suggested they see a counselor."

She pauses and looks inward, a storm of emotions crashing behind her eyes.

"Let me guess," he says. "*You* became his counselor. His shoulder to cry on."

Her face now filled with rage, she says, "It was bullshit. All of it. His marriage wasn't on the rocks, at least as far as Heather knew. He made it all up to get back in with me."

She doesn't offer any more details, and he doesn't ask her to. He already knows what happened between them.

"At some point, you figured out he was lying and you tried to call things off, but he wouldn't have it. He started stalking you."

She exhales.

"How did he keep getting into the building?"

She lets out a bitter laugh. "He *moved* here, that's how. A few months ago. With his wife and his two daughters. He bought a two-bedroom apartment a couple of floors down. He comes up here first thing in the morning, or before he goes home from work. Knocks on the door, calls my name. He knows I won't let him in. I don't think he even cares anymore. I think he just wants to torture me for turning him down."

"How did he get in the other week? I assume he was the one who trashed your place."

"The prick called a locksmith to the building. He met the guy in the lobby and brought him up to my floor, pretended that my apartment was his. What am I going to do? I see his wife in the elevator, with their daughters. We make small talk. She has no idea."

Susan closes her eyes again, shakes her head.

"What happened tonight?"

"What happened is he's been coming up here every half an hour or so, knocking on my door, asking me to let him in. He's been calling, too. Apparently Heather is out of town with the girls. The last time, I opened the door a crack—it has a security chain—to tell him to get lost. He pushed the door, and the chain broke. At the same time, the elevator rang. The next thing I knew, Tommy rushed up and tackled him from behind." She pauses and stares at him, a confused look on her face. "How did Tommy know to be here?"

Mick weighs whether to tell her about Giacobetti. "We'll get to that. Just keep on with what happened after Tommy tackled him."

"Tommy asked if this was the guy who's been bothering me, and I told him yes. That's when Tommy clobbered him and threw him into the corner." She stops and stares at the floor.

"Come on," he says, standing and reaching down for her. She rejects his hand but follows him back out into the living room.

"I want to get up," Brenner says.

"Sure, we can go another round," Tommy says.

"Mick, please," Brenner pleads.

"Let him up," he says.

Tommy backs away, and Brenner slowly lifts himself to a standing position.

"Look at this, goddamn it. I'm dripping blood."

"You're breaking our hearts," Tommy says. Then he looks at Mick and asks, "What do you want me to do with him?"

Mick turns to Brenner. "It depends. How soon are you going to list your apartment?"

Brenner's eyes grow wide, then he slumps, resigned. "This week," he answers. "I'll call an agent this week."

"Not this week," he says. "Tomorrow. You'll hire an agent tomorrow, have the place listed the next day."

"And how am I going to explain that to my wife?"

"Tell her the neighborhood scares you," he says. "You're hearing things at work about a new crime wave in Society Hill."

Brenner is fuming now. "And this?" he says, pointing to his pulverized face. "What do I tell my wife about this?"

Tommy answers, "You were attacked on the way home from work. Fits in perfectly with the crime-wave story."

Mick and Tommy laugh. Even Susan cracks a smile.

"You're having a lot of fun with this, eh, Mick?"

Before he can answer, Tommy shoves the taller man against the wall, slaps his face with his left hand, grabs his throat with the right.

"Hey, asshole," Tommy hisses, "no one's having fun here. This is all fucked-up. What you've been doing to Susan. And for her, it's going to end *right now*. Or it's going to end very, very badly for you."

Brenner's wide eyes turn to Mick, pleading silently. Tommy tells him, "Look at me. From this minute on, and for the rest of your miserable life, I'm going to be looking for some reason, some excuse, hell, *any* excuse—to *end* you. You go near Susan again, knock on her door one more time, call her, or walk past her on the street, and I will find you. I will bash your brains in. Understand?"

The veins in Tommy's temple are throbbing now. His face is red.

Brenner's mouth is wide open, his eyes bulging. He nods his head, fast.

"Yes, yes," says courtroom lion Martin Brenner. "I get it. I get it."

Tommy releases Brenner and steps back.

Brenner stands frozen in place, his hands shaking.

"Now it's my turn, Martin," Mick says. "Two days from now, I'm going to pull up the multiple-listing service online. If I don't see your apartment for sale, I'm going to have a meeting with your boss. I'm going to tell him everything Susan has told me. And you're going to lose your job, your license, and maybe even go to jail. Unless, of course, I'm wrong and your boss decides I'm making the whole thing up. Which would not be good for you at all. Because if that happens, I'm going to call my brother. And Tommy will mete out *his* particular form of justice."

Brenner puts up his hand, extends his arm, and shakes his head. *No más.*

"Come on," Tommy says, taking Brenner by the arm and crossing the room. When they get to the doorway, Mick tells Tommy to wait a minute.

"I want to have a word alone with Martin before he leaves."

Tommy and Susan stay inside while he addresses Brenner in the hallway.

"What now?" Brenner asks when he closes the door.

"Nunzio," he says. "You're done with him. No more threats of convening a grand jury. No more harassing his family. And, of course, no more talking to Susan about it."

"But . . . just dropping the case out of nowhere? I'll look like an idiot!"

"You are an idiot."

He calls Tommy out to the hallway.

"Tommy, please take Martin into the stairwell. Martin, you're going to walk to your apartment. You're going to call the police and tell them you were mugged just outside your building. Right in the middle of the plaza. Undoubtedly by the guys perpetrating the crime wave you've learned about at work. You'll make sure your medical records are peppered with references to your having been assaulted outside."

He watches Tommy escort Martin into the stairwell. Then he returns to Susan's apartment. She's sitting on the couch, elbows on her knees, staring at the floor.

"I just don't get it, Susan. Why didn't you report Brenner to the police when he started in on you again a few months ago?"

"And say what? That I'm just some stupid girl who lets herself get played or bullied? I'm not a victim, Mick. I won't have people see me that way."

He wants to grab her and shout, "But you made yourself into a victim by not reaching out for help! By not calling the police or Brenner's bosses, your former colleagues, or me. You had resources, people who care about you, and you didn't reach out!"

Instead, he says, "Why didn't you at least tell Armand? He looks pretty tough. He could've straightened Brenner out."

"Armand was a . . . distraction. A pastime."

"Was?"

"It's over. I went to his house the other night and broke it off. For good, this time."

They sit quietly for a while, until Susan breaks the silence. "Your brother. The look on his face when he went after Martin . . ."

"Tommy's a scary guy when he wants to be."

"And loyal. To you. To Piper."

"To his friends, too."

Just then, the front door opens, and Tommy walks down the hall to the living room.

Susan stares up at him from the couch, and Mick can tell she's trying to make up her mind about something.

He gets up to leave.

"Come on," he says to Tommy. "Let's go."

"Wait," Susan says, standing. Then, to Tommy: "Could you stay for a while? In case he comes back?"

He looks at Tommy, seeing in his brother's eyes that they're sharing the same thought: *Martin Brenner isn't coming back, and Susan knows it.*

Mick exits the building. He spots the black Escalade parked behind his car and watches as the driver's window rolls down. He recognizes Giacobetti and walks up to him.

"I assume you took care of your problem," Johnny G. says. "Did you take care of ours, too?"

"There won't be a grand jury," he says flatly. "I don't like being played."

"Says the pipe organ."

"Fuck you," he says, and turns away. From behind him, he hears Nunzio's enforcer chuckling.

32

MONDAY, JUNE 17

It's just before 9:00, and Mick is in the holding cell adjacent to courtroom 1007, where Nunzio's trial will be held and where jury selection is about to start. He's making one final push to get Nunzio to let him in on the secret strategy the mobster has been holding back.

"I need to know where our defense is headed," Mick says. "Otherwise, Pagano's going to tell a story that I'll have no answer to."

"You can always wait until after the prosecution's case to give your opening," Nunzio says.

"Bad idea. Eighty percent of jurors make up their minds after openings. I need a speech that's just as persuasive as Pagano's if we're going to have any chance here. At the very least, I need enough information to offer up a theme for our case." Common themes for criminal defense counsel include the "rush to judgment" song and dance used in the OJ case—the idea that the police latched on to the first suspect and never bothered to undertake a full investigation. Another theme, particularly popular in Philly, is "The police are lying." Mick knows that neither theme will work in this case, though: Nunzio was caught at the crime scene with the murder weapon in hand.

"Why not just poke holes in the prosecution's case?" Nunzio says. "Bring up all the questions they can't answer."

Mick nods. "Throw everything against the wall and hope something sticks. That's what I'm planning to do because it's all I'm left with, but I can tell you it's nothing more than playing for fumbles, hoping the prosecution screws up. Problem is, Pagano's not going to screw this up. It's the biggest case of his career, and he's going to bring his A game. I need to know what our theme's going to be."

Nunzio leans back, looks at the ceiling, thinks for a few seconds. "How about, 'He hit me first'?"

He stares hard at Nunzio, unsure how to take the mobster's suggestion. Is he being serious or cute?

"You're planning on offering up a self-defense excuse?"

Nunzio shrugs, smiles.

He shoots to his feet, calls the guard to unlock the cell, then turns back to Nunzio.

"This is bullshit."

Mick and Pagano agreed to hold jury selection before a commissioner because the judge, Frances McCann, doesn't allow the lawyers to ask questions—she conducts the voir dire herself. Pagano refused to relinquish that amount of control to anyone, and Mick didn't want to lose his first chance to make a good impression on the jurors.

Mick stands and turns toward the benches as the panel of sixty prospective jurors is ushered in. They all have miserable looks on their faces, and why not? No one wants to serve on a jury. It's a week out of their lives, and they're not even being paid enough to cover parking. He looks down and sees that Nunzio is still facing the front of the courtroom. He leans down and whispers for Nunzio to stand and face the panel. It's a sign of respect every attorney has his client make. Nunzio does so, and the panel's demeanor is instantly transformed. Faces that were bored, annoyed, or half-asleep a second earlier are now wide with astonishment, alertness, and even fear.

The commissioner waits until everyone is seated, and then spends fifteen minutes explaining the process. In the meantime, Mick, Vaughn, Lauren Zito, and Max Pagano review court questionnaires that the jurors have completed. The top block of questions covers past and present occupations, marital status, education, and race. Below, another set of questions asks whether the prospective jurors have ever served on a jury before, have ever been the victim of a crime, witnessed a crime, or been arrested or charged with a crime themselves. The questions also ask whether the potential juror is more or less likely to believe a police officer because of his job and whether the juror could follow the instruction about the presumed innocence of the defendant. It also asks whether there is any reason the person could not be a fair juror. The questions are well known to the attorneys and jury consultant, and it takes little time for Mick and his team to identify potentially problematic panelists.

Before the attorneys get to their oral questioning, the commissioner runs through the tedious process of soliciting excuses from panel members who claim it would be a hardship to serve. The excuses run the gamut from the patently legitimate—*I have surgery tomorrow* or *My husband is coming back from a tour of duty in the Middle East*—to the patently frivolous—*I just got engaged and need to make wedding plans* or *The dog can't be left home by itself all day.* It takes about thirty minutes to address the hardship claims, after which the commissioner excuses twenty of the prospective jurors.

Once that is finished, the commissioner and attorneys question the prospective jurors who affirmatively answered questions on the questionnaires indicating that their beliefs would prevent them from sitting in judgment in a criminal case, or that they could not abide by the jury instructions or otherwise would not make fair jurors. This takes another hour, and fifteen more people are released.

With twenty-five panelists remaining, the commissioner calls for a midmorning break, after which the attorneys begin their own questioning. Pagano goes first. He begins by introducing himself and telling the panel that if they know him, or know of him, to raise their hands. No one does. He gives the same direction with regard to James Nunzio, and every hand goes up.

Mick and Vaughn exchange glances: this is going to be a long slog.

It's just after 11:00 when Piper checks into the Holiday Inn on Hamilton Street in Allentown. The hotel is only five blocks from the Lehigh County Courthouse, where the hearing on the petition for a new trial for Darlene Dowd will be held. Piper had expected it to take much longer to get the hearing, but the judge—the Honorable Katherine Iwicki—is new to the bench and eager to make a name for herself. Piper also suspects that the fact the judge is a woman helped move things along.

Piper checks her watch. Susan is due to arrive in an hour. They'll have lunch in the hotel restaurant, joined by Melvin Ott, whom Susan is planning on calling as a witness. Susan will use the time to prep him for his testimony. Judge Iwicki signed a transfer order, and Darlene Dowd was moved earlier that morning from the women's prison in Muncy to the Lehigh County Jail, where Piper and Susan are going to meet her later that afternoon to get her ready for the hearing. Around dinnertime, Special Agent Lance Newton will check in to the hotel, and the three of them will meet to go over his testimony. Last but not least, Susan and Piper are going to meet with Megan Corbett, a.k.a. Lois Beal, who is flying in today. Tommy is supposed to join them. Former police chief Sonny Foster has been subpoenaed, but they haven't heard from him.

Piper opens the door to her room. It has only one window, but it provides a lot of light. The white bedcover, light-cherry end tables and bureau, and beige-and-brown carpeting add to the room's cheeriness. The real lightness to her mood, though, of course, is that she's only hours away from winning freedom for an innocent young woman.

She unpacks her clothes and lies down on her back, her hands behind her head on the thick pillows. She takes a deep breath and closes her eyes. The Dowd case has been a roller-coaster ride like no other, from the mother's deathbed letter to Lois Beal's gravesite unearthing of the murder weapon.

All that remains is the hearing tomorrow. The current Lehigh County district attorney is fighting the petition for a new trial, but Susan believes he's doing it for form's sake rather than because he feels passionately about the case. Susan says the chances are excellent that Judge Iwicki will grant their petition.

As for Susan . . . Originally Piper assumed that they'd drive to Allentown together, but Susan said she wanted to come up a little later, claiming she had a motion that had to get filed in the morning. The real reason, Piper suspects, is that Susan doesn't want to talk about the Martin Brenner fiasco. Mick told Piper what happened in Susan's condo and about Susan's twisted history with Brenner. She was stunned that Susan—one of the strongest women she's known—allowed herself to be victimized for so long by Brenner, especially since her supposed reason was her desperate desire *not* to be seen as a victim.

Jesus, it's crazy how people can be so . . . crazy. More and more, it seems the "normal" ones turn out to be screwed up the most.

The thought causes her mind to skip to Darlene's parents. A father so evil he'd abuse his own daughter. A mother so weak and selfish she'd allow her daughter to be abused, and then let her daughter take the rap for a murder the mother committed herself. That Cindy Dowd opened the escape hatch from her grave does not, in Piper's mind, redeem her for sending Darlene to waste away in prison for fifteen years. Nor has she been able to find forgiveness for Lois Beal, who knew for years that Cindy was the real killer. With all the politically correct tripe the talking heads and politicians blare about the need for equality between the sexes, it's still a man's world. Men still get away with doing terrible things to women. Women have to protect each other, and yet those two women let down an innocent teen.

She gets out of bed and walks to the window.

"Well, it's my turn now," she says aloud, envisioning Darlene Dowd sitting in her jail cell. "And I won't let you down."

Tommy stands in the back of the courtroom, watching Mick and Pagano take turns questioning potential jurors. But his mind isn't on the Nunzio case. He's thinking about Darlene Dowd—about the suspicion that rose in his mind as he watched Lois Beal hesitate about which grave to dig. A suspicion confirmed when Ray Thorne called with the fingerprint results.

He's supposed to go to Allentown tonight to help Susan and Piper prepare Lois Beal for the hearing. Except . . . how can he do that without spilling the beans and wrecking everything for Piper?

Christ, what a schmuck I've been to her these past couple years.

And what about Darlene Dowd? She shouldn't be in prison; she deserves to be free, just as she deserved to have a normal childhood, go to college, get married, and have kids.

How can I fix this? he asks himself for the hundredth time. *How can I make this right?*

Jimmy Nunzio watches the two lawyers parry with the jury panel, each of them doing his best to slip subliminal cues into their questions consistent with the goods they plan to sell to the jury during trial. Pagano's questions seem designed to remind everyone how afraid they all are of the opioid crisis and resultant rise in the crime rate. He must use the phrase "organized crime" a dozen times. Mick's questions highlight the constitutional principles often cited as the bedrock of freedom, saying things like, "presumed innocent" and "prosecutor's burden" and "beyond a reasonable doubt." They're following the scripts used by all prosecutors and defense attorneys. McFarland's spiel, though, includes some pointed questions no doubt suggested by Lauren Zito. Once a cute little girl from his neighborhood, she's grown up into a beautiful, strong woman with a razor-sharp mind. A real asset to his trial team—more so than McFarland will ever know.

Lauren is the one who explained to Nunzio years ago what really goes on during jury selection: "Any experienced trial attorney would tell you that 'jury selection' is a misnomer. Lawyers aren't choosing jurors, they're rejecting them. It's really more like jury *deselection*."

Each attorney gets a certain number of "peremptory" strikes that they can use to boot someone for any reason at all, so long as it isn't based on race, while the judge has the unlimited authority to remove a juror "for cause" if they're convinced the person is strongly biased in some way.

Nunzio sits facing the panel, his hands folded on the table, his face a blank slate, as ordered by McFarland. He's bored by the process, though there are some amusing parts, like when one potential juror says she's clairvoyant. Max Pagano struggles with how to deal with her, not wanting to insult the woman in front of others but needing to get the loon out of the courtroom. McFarland, faster on his feet than the prosecutor, pretends to take the woman seriously and asks her, "If you were chosen for the jury, could you promise to base your decision solely on the *evidence* available to all of the other jurors as well?" She says no, she can't make that promise, and the commissioner banishes her.

On and on it drags—Pagano asking questions, McFarland asking questions. One panelist after another is told to leave the courtroom and return to the jurors' assembly room. Every now and then, he catches one of the panelists staring at him, trying to figure him out. They turn away as soon as they see he's looking back at them. Except for one woman in the first row, who holds his gaze. She looks to be in her early forties and is attractive—wide-set eyes, long dark hair, and a shapely figure. She's Italian, he can tell. He studies her as she does him, and he decides she could be an asset. He'll make sure McFarland doesn't give her the boot.

It's 8:00 p.m., and Mick is seated at the war-room conference table with Vaughn, Lauren Zito, and Rachel Nunzio, who insisted on being present to help review the jury-selection results thus far. As Mick and Vaughn predicted, picking a jury was proving to be a long process. The commissioner kept the pool past 5:00 p.m., and only five jurors were selected. Given the goal of twelve jurors and four alternates, that leaves eleven to go.

While jury selection went on in the courtroom, Lauren Zito had her team research the remaining panelists on various databases on the internet, giving the Nunzio trial team considerably more information about the panelists than was provided on their official jury questionnaires. Photographs of each of the remaining candidates, along with a detailed history—including where they were born and raised, job history, current address, and political affiliations—are spread out on the table.

Using this information, the trial team divides the remaining panelists into three piles: definitely, definitely not, and maybe. The only major argument involves Dianne Galante, the Italian American woman

Nunzio noticed sitting in the front row. Galante is well educated and holds a high-level administrative position with the University of Pennsylvania. During questioning, she came across as highly intelligent, well spoken, and strong-willed. Lauren pressed Mick to strike her but interestingly was overruled by Nunzio, who insisted he pass on her. Since Pagano didn't object, she made it onto the jury. But that hasn't ended it for Zito.

"I'm going to have my people keep looking into her," Lauren says.

"I think she's good," Rachel argues. "She'll be an asset because of her heritage; she'll identify with Jimmy and the rest of our family. She obviously identifies strongly as an Italian. Your team's research shows she belongs to two Italian American organizations. She'll be looking for a reason to acquit. If it's a close call, she'll come down on our side."

Lauren shakes her head. "It's not that simple, Rachel. Her high position, education, and personal strength mean she's going to be a leader on the jury. Her status as an Italian American—and Rachel, let's be frank, she looks more like a mobster's wife than you do—will give the other jurors another reason to follow her lead. Which means that if you're wrong and she comes down against you, she'll lead the rest of them straight to a guilty verdict."

Watching them argue, Mick believes he was right about the jury being Nunzio's ace in the hole. It's why he made Mick hire Lauren Zito and why Rachel is sitting in tonight as his proxy as they review the remaining panelists. As the evening progresses, the idea enters his mind that the Nunzios' focus on the jurors may not end with jury selection. Given the data Lauren's amassed on the remaining jurors, it would be a simple matter for Nunzio to have his henchmen approach the jurors or their families with threats, bribes, or both.

He glances at Rachel Nunzio as she studies the portfolio on panelist Kenneth Kraugh, a violinist with the Philadelphia Orchestra. Kraugh is a young, small-framed man with a high forehead and a soft voice. Mick can imagine a seemingly chance meeting on the street between

Kraugh and Johnny Giacobetti. Nunzio's enforcer bumps into the violinist, apologizes loudly enough for anyone nearby to hear, then leans in and curdles the juror's blood with a detailed description of how he'll lose his fingers and never play again unless he votes for an acquittal.

He's pulled from the vision by Rachel's dark eyes staring at him.

"Penny for your thoughts?" she says.

33

Monday, June 17–Tuesday, June 18

It's 10:00 p.m. Piper sits on the bed, enjoying an ice-cream sundae. The Holiday Inn has no room service, so she drove to Friendly's to pick up the dessert, rewarding herself because the witness preparations have gone so well.

Melvin Ott is ready to testify to Lois Beal's telling Chief Foster about seeing Darlene, unbloodied, walking toward her house the morning of the killing, as well as to Foster's threatening Lois away from court, the coercive nature of the confession wrung out of Darlene Dowd, and the poker game at which Lester was accused of cheating.

Lance Newton will testify to digging up the hammer and the test results showing it carried Cindy Dowd's fingerprints and Lester Dowd's DNA.

Lois Beal will testify to everything she shared with them in Georgia, including Cindy's bringing the hammer to her and Cindy's later admission that it was she who killed her husband.

Finally, Darlene herself will testify that she wasn't home the night her father was killed, and that the blood on her clothes was from tripping over him and slipping in the blood puddle on the kitchen floor.

The only thing missing is Tommy. She's called him half a dozen times, but has been put through to his voice mail. When she spoke to

Mick earlier in the evening, he told her that Tommy was present for jury selection until just before 5:00. He didn't show up for the meeting afterward and hasn't called in. As Mick said, "Tommy is Tommy. Who knows what the hell he's up to? He'll call or show up just in time, as always."

"Come on, Tommy," she says aloud. *"Just in time" is coming fast.*

Tommy paces his room. He knows what he has to do, but he just doesn't want to do it. "Fucking Lois," he says aloud. He paces some more, checks his email, sits on the bed, and runs his hand through his hair. Then he glances down at the canvas bag holding the metal box with the blue-handled hammer inside.

"To hell with it," he says, getting off the bed and reaching for the bag. He leaves his room, walks to the end of the hall, and knocks on the door. It's quiet on the other side; he expects she's sleeping. He knocks again, harder this time. After a few moments, the door slowly opens until the security chain is taut. Lois Beal peeks through the opening.

"It's Tommy," he says, seeing her trying to place his face. "I work with Piper and Susan."

"I already met with Piper and Susan. We went over everything." He sees her clutching the top of her robe.

"I know. But you and I have to talk, too."

"I wasn't told anything about having to meet with you."

He hesitates, not sure how to broach the subject. Then he steps back, lays the bag on the floor, unzips it, and lifts out the metal box.

She gasps and takes half a step back.

"Like I said, we have to talk."

Lois closes the door, and he hears her slide the security chain. Then she opens the door for him, and he follows her to a small round table.

She sits and waits as he lays the box on the table, opens it, and withdraws the hammer.

She stares at it for a long time, seemingly unable to lift her head and meet his gaze.

"Friend of mine runs a big security firm that has its own forensics lab. I asked him to test the prints against the prints on the water bottle you drank from in my truck." He doesn't have to tell her they were a match; she already knows.

They sit for a while until he says, "It never made sense to me—that Cindy Dowd would let her daughter take the rap for killing Lester when Cindy did it herself. You seemed like a decent person when we met, so it didn't make sense to me that you wouldn't come forward once Cindy confessed to you, even given the risk you'd be discovered."

She looks up at him now. "Please, can't you just stop there? You know what's at stake. You know what we have to do."

He shakes his head: he has to see this through. "There was only one way Cindy's silence and your own silence made sense." He sees a tear slide down Lois's face, and he gives her time to wipe it off. "You and Cindy didn't come forward with Cindy's guilt because she's *not* the one who killed Lester. It was Darlene who killed her father, after all."

Lois's eyes lock onto his now. "That *monster*. He got what he deserved. Why should that poor girl spend the rest of her life in prison when he drove her to . . . do what she did?"

He lets the words hang in the air. "Tell me what happened."

She closes her eyes, calms her breathing.

"Bobby, my husband, was away that weekend. I hated being alone on the farm overnight, so Cindy would come and stay with me sometimes. She was at my place that night. Around 5:00 or so, she got up and walked home. Our farms were only a quarter of a mile down the road from each other. It wasn't twenty minutes after she left that she came running back. She was crying and screaming and carrying the hammer. It took me a while to calm her down. When I did, she told me everything—about what Lester had been doing to Darlene. She said she didn't know at first but figured it out over time. I asked why she hadn't gone to the police, and she gave me her excuses—that she was afraid she'd end up with nothing, have to go back to where she'd come from. I had a thing or two to say to her. But this was about Darlene, so as quick as we could, we came up with the story about me seeing Darlene walking home that morning. We thought Darlene's lawyer could use that in court, help cast reasonable doubt. We didn't get far with it, though, thanks to Sonny Foster."

She pauses and purses her lips.

"Tell me about the hammers," he says.

She slowly nods. "That was Cindy's idea, to help Darlene down the road in case she did get sent to prison. Cindy brought the red-handled hammer, the one Darlene used on Lester. It was soaked with blood and hair and flesh. We unrolled some clear plastic wrap and used it to wipe as much of the blood off the handle as we could. Then we cleaned off the handle, to get rid of Darlene's fingerprints. Cindy put her palm onto the plastic wrap, let it get nice and bloody, and then gripped the hammer."

"To inculpate her down the line," Tommy says. "Once she was in the grave and safe from prosecution. The plan being that you would testify Cindy asked you to hide the hammer; then later she would confess to the killing."

"But that wasn't enough," Lois says. "Because if I died before her, there'd be no one to testify to her confession."

"So you pressed your own palm onto the plastic wrap and bloodied your hammer as well. To be used if *you* died first. In which case, what? Cindy couldn't very well say you had confessed to her—it wouldn't make any sense for her to have sat on the knowledge that you'd killed her husband and blamed it on her daughter."

"There's a safe-deposit box in my bank containing two letters, addressed to Cindy and to Darlene, in which I confess that it was I who killed Lester and hid the hammer to protect myself. The letters give the location of the blue hammer."

A frown appears on her face. "How did you know to look for it?" She indicates the blue-handled hammer on the table between them.

"That was your doing, in the graveyard. You stood before the two stones and hesitated. It was obvious you didn't know which one to point me to. But the tell wasn't in your hesitation; after so many years, it wouldn't be surprising that you'd forgotten which grave you buried the hammer in. The clue came in how sharply you told me to wait before I dug. I wondered why you cared so much if I started on the wrong grave. Why was it as important that I *not* dig the wrong grave as it was that I dig the right one? It seemed clear to me that something was buried in both graves. So when everyone left, I went back."

He sees her staring at the hammer, so he takes it from the table, puts it back into the metal box, and places the box into the canvas bag.

"That was some show you put on for us at your house," he says.

She smiles sadly. "I told you I was an actress."

"A damned good one." He exhales, thinks for a minute. "Someone not as smart as Cindy might have decided just to get rid of the hammer, thinking, *No weapon means no conviction.* But she knew the lack of a weapon wouldn't guarantee an acquittal, just make it harder for the prosecution. So she came up with the plan to hide it, for later. I get that. What I don't get is why, if she felt so guilty about her daughter's abuse, she didn't just confess to the crime and turn over the hammer with her own fingerprints on it."

"She wanted to," says Lois. "That was her plan when she brought me the hammer. But I talked her out of it. I said I understood why she felt she needed to take the blame, given that she'd let Lester's abuse of Darlene go on and on. But as bad as that was, she wasn't a murderer. She didn't deserve to go to prison for the rest of her life. The best we could do was set it up so that Darlene might be freed down the line after Cindy passed, or I did."

Lois pauses for a moment. "I have a question for you. When you found the second hammer, and your man found my prints on it, why didn't you conclude I was the killer? Or that Cindy was, based on the first hammer?"

"Because if it was you, Cindy would have turned you in to save her daughter. And if it was Cindy, she wouldn't have let Darlene take the fall. The only way the two hammers made sense was if Darlene killed Lester."

Lois nods. "I never told Cindy about my past. If I had, she'd never have trusted me to come forward to save Darlene in case Cindy passed first. Because of the risk I'd be taking that I'd be discovered. And to be honest," she says, "I was never sure myself that I'd be able to go through with it. But once I started talking with Piper and Susan . . ."

"You got into the role," he says. "And you thought you'd be able to get away with it. That you could come forward and testify, and no one would figure out the plan you and Cindy had hatched, or about your own criminal history."

"But I was wrong on both counts. Thanks to Susan and Piper, and you."

The words hang in the air.

After a while, he asks, "How much of this does Darlene know?"

"About my past? Nothing. As for what her mother and I did, Darlene had to know it all for it to work."

"What I thought."

His hands are resting on the table. She reaches out to grab them.

"Can't we keep this between us? Let the show go on tomorrow?"

A deep sadness wells up inside him. He's carried so many secrets in his life. The one about his father that almost destroyed him. The ones from the Hanson case. Secrets he kept from Mick. Secrets he still keeps from Piper. Too much weight to bear. He shakes his head.

"This isn't my call."

He watches as she lowers her head and tears slide down her cheeks. This time, she's not acting.

Piper takes a large bite of the chocolate-covered ice cream. She closes her eyes and smiles as the rich, cool combination slides down her throat.

She's pulled from her reverie by a knock at the door. She lifts herself off the bed, walks down the narrow hallway, and looks through the keyhole. She removes the security chain and opens the door.

"Tommy! Where have you been? I've been calling you all day. Tommy? What's wrong?"

It is 8:00 a.m. Piper sits at the gray metal table in the attorney meeting room of the Lehigh County Jail. Susan is beside her. Neither speaks. Piper glances at Susan, who stares straight ahead. Last night, once Tommy finished relating his conversation with Lois Beal, she went straight to Lois's room and confronted her. An hour of tears and anger and harsh words ensued, ending with her storming out of the room and slamming the door. She made it about ten feet before doubling over in the hallway and then sliding to the floor, her back against the wall. Lois must've known what was happening, because she walked into the hall and helped her up. They stood like that for a long moment, each staring into eyes filled with anguish.

She returned to her room and called Mick. She hated to do it, because he was already dealing with so much in the Nunzio case. But this was too big not to ask his advice. She laid it all out for him and waited, listening to him breathe and think and weigh his words. Unable to bear the silence, she spoke first.

"So what it all comes down to," she says, "is that the best that could happen here is that Susan and I put Lois Beal on the stand and let a fugitive killer lie under oath to spring another murderer."

"That's one way to look at it. The other way is that you're giving a woman who participated in a terrible crime the chance to redeem herself by winning freedom for another woman who was physically and psychologically tortured to the point that she committed an act of unspeakable violence, causing her to be locked away like an animal. In the end, all that happened was that she was moved from one hellish existence to another."

That's when she broke down completely. She wept and wailed and heaved until she was spent. She couldn't tell how much time passed, but when it was over, she realized she was still clutching her cell phone. And Mick was still on the line. He consoled her as best he could and promised that, whatever she decided, it would be the right choice, and he was behind her 100 percent.

It was only after she hung up that she realized she had no choice at all. Susan would never agree to move forward with the hearing. And Mick was firm that Susan had to be told.

We can't put Susan's license on the line by using her to suborn perjury to free a convicted killer.

The words remained unspoken by both of them, but they were thinking the same thing: how close they came to doing exactly that in the Hanson case.

She glances again at Susan as the door opens and the guard brings Darlene Dowd into the room. Darlene's eyes are aglow with hope and gratitude, much as they were when they met last evening.

"Sit," Susan says. Just one word.

Darlene slowly lowers herself into the chair, looking first at Susan then at Piper, then back to Susan. Piper sees that Darlene can tell something is wrong.

Piper is the first to speak. "Lois told us."

"Told you? What?"

Susan leans forward. "Everything."

Darlene's eyes grow wide. Her lower lip begins to quiver. She crosses her arms around her chest.

"Our firm's innocence project is just like the state's Innocence Project," Piper says. "It's only for people who did *not* commit the crime they were convicted of. People who are actually innocent. You knew that, Darlene."

"I *was* innocent! He stole that from me! He took everything. Everything!"

Piper can see that Darlene is struggling mightily not to cry. She succeeds in holding back the tears, but she can't hide the anguish and fear in her eyes.

"Tell us what happened that night," Piper says.

"It won't change anything," Susan says. "But we have a right to know."

Piper watches as Darlene's shoulders slump, and she shrinks into herself, resigned now to her fate.

"I was with Dale that night. Dale Forney. My mother was going to spend the night at Lois's house, because Lois's husband was away. And I knew my father was going to be at one of his poker games and wouldn't be home until early morning. So I knew there'd be time for me and Dale to be together. It would have been our first time. We'd only gone out a few times before that, and he'd kissed me, but that was it. I wouldn't let it go any further, and he respected that."

Darlene pauses here, and Piper can see that she's taking herself back fifteen years.

"I knew my parents would both be out of the house by 9:00, so I told Dale to come for me then. I walked to the end of our driveway, and he was waiting for me. He had one of those big pickup trucks they sell at the dealership. It was white, and I remember thinking, *Oh, there's Dale, my white knight*."

She smiles at this—a sad and pitiful sight that stabs Piper in the heart.

"Dale took me to a movie. It wasn't very good, but I didn't care; I was out on a date, like a normal girl. With a nice boy. I was having the time of my life. After the movie, Dale took me to a diner. He had a hamburger and fries, and a chocolate shake. I wasn't hungry, but I did have a shake of my own. Dale said things that were funny, and I remember laughing a lot. He laughed, too. And he held my hand across the table."

Piper listens to Darlene's story, thinking it sounds like something right out of Andy Griffith's Mayberry. She wonders whether it was as sweet as Darlene's telling, or whether she's idealizing it.

"After the diner, it was getting on to midnight, but I knew I had hours before my father got home. Dale knew it, too, because I'd told him. So he drove me down to a small lake at the end of a country road that was barely a road. He had one of those metal cabs over the bed of his pickup, and he led me to the back. We both got in. There was an air mattress with a comforter on it. I knew what he had in mind, and I wanted that, too. I really liked Dale, and I thought if I did it with a boy like him, it would help wipe away . . ."

Piper sees Darlene's breathing getting shallower, faster. She reaches across the table to where Darlene's hands are folded. Susan remains bolt upright in her seat.

"Take it slow," Piper says.

Darlene nods. "We started making out. Dale was very considerate—he took things very slowly. It was wonderful. And then, all of a sudden, it wasn't. I'm not sure how far things had gone—I think my shirt was off. Maybe he was, you know, feeling me. Something happened. It was like . . . all of a sudden it wasn't Dale's hands that were on me, but my father's. I flipped out. I started screaming and kicking and hitting Dale. I scratched his face. It was bleeding. He jumped off me and bolted from the truck."

Darlene stands, paces.

"I threw my shirt back on and climbed out of the truck, too. He was holding his face, wiping the blood off. He couldn't believe it. He started yelling at me, shouting that he didn't do anything I hadn't wanted him to. He called me a *freak.*" Darlene shouts the word, tears now flowing freely. "That's when I knew my father had ruined me. Ruined me forever."

Darlene closes her eyes and squeezes her fists, then slowly seats herself back at the table.

"Dale drove me home, but we didn't say a word to each other the whole way. I tried to say I was sorry, but I couldn't get the words out. I think I was afraid that if I started, I wouldn't be able to stop—that I'd tell him everything. And then he'd think I was even worse than a freak. I watched him drive away, and then I went inside. It was after 2:00 by then, and I went straight to bed.

"I cried myself to sleep. Then I heard my father come home. He moved around the kitchen for a while, then he came upstairs and stood in my doorway and stared at me. I pretended to be asleep, but, somehow, he knew I wasn't, and he told me so. He told me he was going to his workshop, and I needed to come up after him. 'Right quick,' he said. He left the house, and I forced myself to get out of bed. I went downstairs, but something came over me. Every step I took down the stairs, I felt more and more numb. He'd be coming back for me, I knew, once he realized I wasn't coming up to the shop. He would come in and grab me by the hair and drag me up there—he'd done that more than once before. But this time I wasn't going to let him. I searched the kitchen for something to wave in his face when he walked through the door. I found a pair of scissors in the drawer, but I knew that wouldn't scare him away. So I pulled out a big knife . . . but I was scared to use it. Finally, I found the hammer my mother used to hang pictures and such.

"It wasn't long before I saw him coming down the driveway from his workshop. The motion-detector lights outside our house turned on once he got close. I could see he was pissed that I hadn't come up, and I knew what that meant for how he was going to handle me that night. He opened the kitchen door and stepped inside. I went to wave the hammer at him, to scare him. But something happened, and I didn't just wave it—I hit him with it. He went down, and I went down after him. I don't know how many times I hit him, but I know it was a lot.

"I say it was me doing this, but it didn't feel like me. I was floating up by the ceiling, watching it happen."

"Can we take a break?" Piper says. "I need . . . I need a minute."

"Are you okay?" Susan asks once they're both in the hallway.

"It was awful reading about it in the trial transcript, but it's even worse hearing it from her."

"The thing about watching herself do it," Susan says. "She was in a dissociative state."

"I don't understand."

"I think Darlene suffered a complete psychotic break."

Piper doesn't know what to say.

"Darlene wasn't in her right mind. In a sense, it wasn't even she who was doing it."

"Does that matter?"

"At this stage, no. If Darlene had admitted to the killing when she was arrested, her attorney probably could have presented a strong case for legal insanity."

"You mean she would have gone free?"

"She would have been sent to a psychiatric facility for a period and treated. After a time, her doctors would have concluded she was sane enough to be released. There would have been a hearing . . ."

"And she would have gotten on with her life," Piper says. "My God."

They talk some more, then walk back into the interview room. Darlene is sitting at the table, motionless, her head hanging, all hope drained from her.

"What happened, after you hit your father?" Susan says.

Darlene shakes her head slowly. "It's all fuzzy. I know I let the hammer fall to the floor. I must've made my way to the workshop. Like I told you before, I don't know why I went there, of all places, but I did. Sometime later, I don't know how long, I heard my mother scream. She must have come home and seen my father. She started shouting my name while she was still inside the house, and then she came outside and ran up to the shop. She wouldn't come in, just like I told you before, but she talked to me through the window screen. She told me what she and Lois did with the hammers, and what Lois was going to say about seeing me walking toward the house with no blood on me. She said not to admit it was me—even to my lawyer—because even if I was convicted, I might get out of jail someday . . . if I insisted I was innocent. Because of the hammers."

Piper glances at Susan, and she knows they're both thinking the same thing: Cindy's advice not to come clean about the killing had shut down Darlene's chances at what would otherwise have been a compelling insanity defense.

The three of them sit in silence for a long moment, until Darlene looks up.

"That's it, then. It's over for me. I'm going back to Muncy, and that's where I'll stay."

Piper watches as Susan stands, walks to the door, nods for Piper to follow. When they're in the hallway again, Susan backs up against the wall, crosses her arms, and closes her eyes.

34

Tuesday, June 18

Facing the panelists for day two of jury selection, Mick and Vaughn flank Jimmy Nunzio at the counsel table. Lauren Zito sits at the end of the table, to Mick's right. From time to time, Mick surreptitiously checks his cell phone for word from Piper. She called him last night, terribly upset at having learned that Darlene Dowd did in fact kill her father and that Lois Beal and Darlene's mother concocted a plan to free her once one of them died. This morning, Mick spoke to Piper and Susan as they were headed to the prison to meet with Darlene. Piper was bereft, and Susan was steaming. He expects by now that Piper and Susan are almost back in Philadelphia, and Darlene Dowd is headed for the women's prison in Muncy, where she will end her days.

And here I sit, trying to free this monster by helping him stack a jury that'll swallow whatever line he's planning on feeding it.

The day started with an attack on Dianne Galante, the juror Lauren Zito had had such misgivings about the day before. Overnight, Zito's team tracked down Galante's social media accounts and discovered that one of the Italian American organizations she belonged to advocated strongly against movies and television shows that stereotyped Italian Americans as mobsters and thugs. And, true to her stripes, Galante tweeted into the late hours that she'd been chosen for the Nunzio jury, castigating Jimmy Nunzio as, among other things, "a stain" and "blight on all Italian Americans." She went so far as to predict that when the trial concluded, the Philadelphia Italian community would have one less "bosso-profundo" to be embarrassed about.

As soon as the commissioner took his seat, Mick was on his feet asking to approach the bench. He brought the printed tweets with him. Pagano fumed and gesticulated, but there was never any question that the commissioner would strike Dianne Galante from the jury panel. He had the court crier bring Galante into the courtroom while the rest of the panel remained outside. Then he chewed her out for fifteen minutes before banishing her from the jury.

That set them back to four jurors.

"Mr. McFarland?"

It's the commissioner, telling him it's his turn to question the panelists.

He rises, smiles at the panel members. He thanks them for their patience, repeats what he said yesterday about not wanting to embarrass anyone, tells them they should only raise their hands if their answer to one of his questions is yes. He promises to follow up for details privately, at sidebar with the commissioner and opposing counsel.

He reads through the short list of questions Zito prepared. Three or four jurors raise their hands at each question.

The first person to be called up to sidebar for private questioning is Malcom Dexter, a twentysomething African American. The traditional wisdom among Philly attorneys is that African Americans tend to be more forgiving of the mob. But Dexter raised his hand in response to the question about whether the panelists know anyone who may have been the victim of organized crime.

Mick watches him approach. He's well dressed and looks Mick in the eye as he approaches. Mick glances at Lauren Zito, who tilts her head, the signal that he should be careful with this panelist.

When Dexter is in position at sidebar, with Mick and Pagano on either side of him, the commissioner asks him which question he raised his hand about.

“It was the one about do I know anyone who may have been the victim of organized crime. I raised my hand because, well, I don’t know for sure, but there was a guy in my neighborhood who supposedly got on the wrong side of Johnny G. . . .”

Damn it. Mick does his best to keep his expression flat, but inside he’s roiling. There are more stories floating around about Nunzio’s enforcer than there are about Nunzio himself. Stories that end with someone beaten, dead, or missing.

When Malcom Dexter is finished, Pagano says, “But you don’t know for sure the story about Mr. Giacobetti is true, do you?”

“Well, I mean, I didn’t see it myself, no. But my friend Eugene, he was right there. He saw it.”

“Well, that’s what they call hearsay,” Pagano says. “Now, certainly, you can agree that if you’re on the jury, you’d base your decisions only on the evidence presented here in court, right?”

Mick shakes his head at Pagano’s leading questions. Pagano wants this man on the jury; Dexter would most certainly share with his fellow jurors the story he’s heard about Giacobetti, and hearsay or not, it would become de facto “evidence” against Nunzio.

Dexter wilts as Pagano stares. “Well, sure. Of course. I would only listen to the evidence.”

The commissioner turns to Mick. “Questions?”

“Just two. First, you know that Mr. Giacobetti works for Mr. Nunzio, don’t you?”

“Everyone knows that.”

“All right. Now, forget about words like ‘hearsay’ and ‘evidence’ for a minute. You believe in your heart that Johnny G., working for Mr. Nunzio, broke both of those man’s arms and then tossed him into the back of his SUV and drove away.” A statement, not a question.

"Absolutely."

Mick turns to the commissioner. He doesn't need to say anything.

"Mr. Dexter," the commissioner says, "thank you for answering truthfully. Please return to room 101. And don't talk to any other jurors before you leave."

"Nice try," Mick says to Pagano, who mouths a profane retort.

The commissioner tells them to knock it off and calls up the next panelist.

Mick takes a deep breath.

And the beat goes on.

Piper reaches to her right and squeezes Darlene's hand under the table. Darlene is still shaking from the hour she spent on the stand.

"You did great," Piper whispers in her ear.

Darlene was the third witness Susan presented, after Melvin Ott and Lance Newton. Both men did well on direct examination. Judge Iwicki paid close attention to what they had to say, and her eyes widened half a dozen times, including at the points when Ott discussed former police chief Sonny Foster threatening Megan Corbett and the coercive nature of Darlene's confession. She was equally impressed with Newton's testimony establishing that Cindy Dowd's prints were the ones on the hammer. What really seemed to have an impact on the judge, though, was Darlene's compelling testimony about the abuse she suffered at the hands of her father.

For his part, Assistant District Attorney Adam Tyson did a workmanlike job on cross, but Piper could tell his heart wasn't really in it. And the judge could tell, too.

As Susan rearranges her legal pads, Piper takes the time, once again, to take in the courtroom. It's a grand venue: a twenty-foot ceiling; chandeliers; recessed lighting; a long, elevated bench supporting four pillars topped by gold leaf, the woodwork an elegant white; three rows of pew seating for spectators. A far cry from the tiny courtrooms in Philadelphia's Criminal Justice Center, where Mick has tried most of his cases.

"For our last witness," Susan says, addressing the court, "we call Megan Corbett."

Piper turns to watch Lois Beal/Megan Corbett walk up the aisle. She sees a confused look cross Sonny Foster's angry face; he's never heard the name Megan Corbett. The hearing has been an ordeal for him, she knows. He has honored the subpoena and appeared, but he's grown steadily angrier as the proceedings continue. He's probably expecting to be called and given the chance to respond to the calumnies heaped on him, but Susan has no intention of putting him on the stand, and Piper doubts the ADA will risk doing so.

Megan takes the stand, places her hand on the Bible, and swears to tell the truth. At Susan's suggestion, Megan/Lois called the Philadelphia office of the FBI and dropped the proverbial dime herself. She told them who she was and that she'd be testifying at a hearing in Lehigh County. She also informed the person who took her call that there would be an FBI agent already in attendance, Special Agent Newton, who could take her into custody once it was over. That was an hour ago.

"Please tell the court your name," Susan says.

"My legal name is Megan Corbett."

"And what name have you been going by?"

"For the past few years, I've identified myself as Terri Petrini. Before that, for many years, I went by Lois Beal."

Sonny Foster is only a few rows behind her; Piper hears him take in a sharp breath.

"Why the aliases?" Susan asks.

Megan turns to face the judge. "Because I'm a fugitive from the law. I've been on the run since an armored truck was robbed in Palo

Alto, California, in 1969. The two men manning the truck were killed in that event."

Judge Iwicki's chiseled jaw drops to her chest. She looks around the courtroom.

"Bailiff . . . No, wait. Special Agent Newton—"

"I'm already on it, Your Honor," Newton interrupts her. "The witness called herself in to the Bureau. Two agents are on their way from Philadelphia. Until they arrive, she will be in my custody."

The judge takes a long, cold look at Megan Corbett. Then she turns to Susan.

"You may proceed. With caution."

Susan asks Megan Corbett to walk the judge through her history following the armored-truck heist. As she does so, Piper's mind drifts back to their meeting with Darlene this morning at the county jail. She sees herself and Susan standing in the hallway, sees Susan's back against the wall, her arms crossed. She hears herself thinking that this is where Susan tells her that Darlene Dowd is a criminal, and that she must return to prison. Then she sees Susan turn to face her.

"That poor girl's mother sat back for years while her father abused her," Susan said.

"Her mother tried to make up for it, in the end," Piper said. "Lois tried to help, too."

"And in trying to help her, they blew her only chance at freedom."

Susan unwrapped her arms, pushed herself from the wall. "Her only chance until now," she said. "Until us."

Piper watched as Susan turned back to the door, toward Darlene.

"Fuck it," Susan said. "Let's do this."

Watching Susan now as the lawyer forces herself to do something she hates in order to save their client, Piper holds her in greater esteem than ever before.

"Now, Ms. Corbett, tell us about the night Lester Dowd was killed."

Piper sees Megan steel herself. Their eyes lock, and for an instant, a look flashes across Megan's eyes that tells Piper they are thinking the same thing: this will be Megan Corbett's greatest performance as an actor.

For the next twenty minutes, Susan stands at the lectern as Megan lays it all out—the story as authored by her and Cindy Dowd fifteen years earlier. The tale in which Cindy was the villain and Megan her accomplice after the fact.

Judge Iwicki, a prodigious notetaker, doesn't even lift her pen, remaining laser-focused on Megan Corbett. Looking for the lie, the hole, or maybe something deeper: a way to reconcile the sweet seventy-year-old on the stand with the armored-car killer and accessory after the fact to a wife's murder of her husband.

When Megan Corbett is finished, Susan thanks her and turns her over for cross-examination. The young prosecutor opens his questioning with a knife to Megan Corbett's heart.

"You say Darlene's mother told you sometime after the murder that the prints on the hammer were hers? And yet you sat on this for years, allowing an innocent woman to pay for a crime she didn't commit? You were content to wait until the real murderer died until you came forward?"

Megan's face reddens with embarrassment. This will be the hardest part: her decision to sacrifice herself for Darlene—an act of pure heroism in Piper's eyes—depends, ironically, upon her allowing herself to be seen by the world as weak and selfish.

She lowers her head. "I will never forgive myself."

The look in Iwicki's ice-blue eyes tells Piper that the judge has no forgiveness in her heart for Megan Corbett, either.

The prosecutor lets the words hang in the air, then switches gears. "You said you have been on the run since an armored-truck robbery in which two men were killed. Were you, in fact, one of the people who robbed the armored truck?"

Piper holds her breath and watches as Megan does the same.

Kathryn Iwicki waits, then forces herself to throw Megan a lifeline. She'd clearly rather not but feels ethically obligated to do so.

"Ms. Corbett," the judge says, looking down at Megan from the bench, "you must either answer that question or invoke your Fifth Amendment right not to incriminate yourself."

"Oh, of course. Well, then, I'll take the Fifth. Is that how you say it?"

"Move on, Mr. Tyson," she tells the prosecutor.

The ADA flips through his legal pad and asks a dozen or so questions that appear designed to fill in gaps left by the witness rather than undermine Megan's credibility.

"I have nothing further," Tyson tells the court.

Judge Iwicki stares at Megan Corbett while the prosecutor takes his seat. Then she looks out into the courtroom.

"Mr. Newton?"

The FBI agent stands and walks up to the bar, where he waits for Megan Corbett. She crosses the well of the courtroom, opens the gate, and steps past the bar. There, she turns and puts her hands behind her back so smoothly that Piper thinks she's probably practiced the move a hundred times. Or had a hundred nightmares in which she was forced to do so.

Megan sighs deeply and steals a last glance at Darlene Dowd. Piper watches the two women hold each other's gaze. So much passes between them, it almost breaks her heart.

Lance Newton walks Megan Corbett to the back of the courtroom, where two grim-faced suit-and-tie types rise from their seats. Newton hands Megan off to them, and all four leave the courtroom.

The judge pauses. Then, to Susan: "Do you have any more witnesses?"

"No, Your Honor."

"Mr. Tyson?"

"The Commonwealth has no witnesses, Your Honor."

"What?"

Piper recognizes Sonny Foster's voice. She watches as Adam Tyson looks at the former police chief and slowly shakes his head. Sonny Foster's face is beet red.

"Does Your Honor need to hear argument?" asks Susan.

"Not unless you or Mr. Tyson feels a burning desire to explain the witnesses' testimony to me."

Susan and Tyson tell Judge Iwicki they are satisfied the court understands the evidence.

"Very well," the judge says, standing. "I will consider the motion and make my ruling."

The judge starts to turn away, then stops herself and looks down at their table.

"I won't take long, Ms. Dowd. You've waited far too long as it is."

Piper puts her hand to her chest. She turns to Darlene and sees tears in her eyes. They both know. Everyone knows.

She whispers to Susan, "She's getting a new trial."

"Maybe." Susan walks over to Adam Tyson. "Do we really need a second trial, Adam? You now know what happened fifteen years ago."

The young ADA exhales and nods his head. "I'll see what I can do."

The deputies allow Piper and Susan a few minutes to accept hugs from their client. Then they cuff Darlene and take her away.

Piper searches the courtroom for Sonny Foster, but he's long gone. The stenographer packs up her machine and exits through the judge's door behind the bench, leaving Piper and Susan alone in the courtroom.

"We did something good here," Piper says.

"No, Piper. We did something bad here. Very bad. We just did it for a good reason. Sometimes that has to be enough."

35

Friday, June 21

Everyone stands as the Honorable Frances McCann takes the bench. Her Honor is thin, with silver hair cut close to her head and steel-blue eyes set in a pale face. She was elected to the bench ten years earlier, after two decades as a career prosecutor. Mick has appeared before her half a dozen times and finds her to be a fair jurist.

Mick and Vaughn flank Jimmy Nunzio, as they did during jury selection, which took four full days. The first major difficulty was that everyone knew Nunzio. The second reason was that it's a capital case. Pagano is seeking the death penalty, and many potential jurors had to be stricken because they were frankly unwilling—or too willing—to send a defendant to the needle.

The final problem in selecting a jury was that on Wednesday and Thursday morning, Team Nunzio appeared in court with a motion to remove two or more of the already-chosen jurors, based on information gathered by Lauren Zito and her team. Pagano hadn't put up much of a fight when Mick requested the removal of Dianne Galante. But he fought hard against the other disqualifications, demanding the commissioner call each of the challenged jurors to the stand for detailed questioning. The result was that four jurors were removed and the process delayed.

No one was more frustrated than Mick himself. He'd fought with Zito over three of the jurors she targeted for removal. He believed she was seeing bias that wasn't there. But Zito was insistent. Rachel Nunzio, present every evening for the posttrial meeting as her husband's proxy, demanded that he abide by Zito's recommendations.

The ultimate result, he feels, is a jury no more or less fair than the one that would have been seated without all the ballyhoo. The twelve jurors and four alternates come from every area of the city. Some are professionals, some blue-collar workers, some students, some retirees. There are seven blacks, five whites, three Asians, and one Native American. The person sitting in the first seat of the first row, the presumptive foreman—Aaron Burnett—is a well-dressed, well-spoken African American. He's the CEO of a company that owns sixty-five Applebee's restaurants in Pennsylvania, New Jersey, Delaware, and Maryland. Freshly divorced from his wife, Burnett recently moved with his teenage daughter to the Ritz-Carlton condominiums, directly across from City Hall. Mick is terrified of him. Even if he hadn't ended up in the foreman's seat, Burnett would be a leader on the jury, a powerful voice that, if speaking against Nunzio, will carry the others along. Mick would have stricken Burnett, but Zito was adamant he not do so. She wouldn't explain her reasoning in the courtroom, but she did in the office afterward.

"Burnett is an alpha male," she told Mick after the rest of the staff had cleared out of the conference room. "He'll identify with Jimmy. He's also a father—"

"So am I! And I think a father who slays his daughter's lover right in front of her is beyond redemption."

"Really? Why did he do it, Mick?"

He stared at her, and then it hit him. "You know," he said. "You know what Nunzio's narrative is going to be."

"We all have our roles to play in this, Mick. We've been given the information we need to play them and no more."

"This is insane. I'm Nunzio's attorney. I have to know where the story is headed! *I'm* the one directing the show!"

She threw her head back and laughed. "You? You're just an actor reading his lines. We both are."

"So that's how it is? Nunzio is the Wizard of Oz, and the rest of us are just dancing down the Yellow Brick Road?" He was so angry he was pounding the table with his fists.

Lauren didn't rise to meet his ire. Instead, she lowered her voice, softened her eyes. "Oh, Mick," she said, "you have no idea what's going on here." She studied him, asked him to give her a minute, and left the conference room. A few minutes later, she returned and sat.

"All right, you want something to work with? Here it is. The theme of your opening, of your defense, is that the prosecution has no idea what happened in the warehouse leading up to Antonio Valiante's death, and no idea why Jimmy allegedly killed him."

He stared at her. "So this is what it's come to—my jury consultant is telling *me* what the case is about?"

She opened her palms.

"But it's not you telling me at all, is it? You went out into the hall to talk to Rachel, to get her permission."

Again, she didn't answer.

He sat back. "You want me to imply that the prosecution has it all wrong. But that only works if we come through with what *really* happened, and why. And only if the real scenario either clears Jimmy outright or provides a legal justification for the killing."

He waited.

Finally, she spoke. "When the time is right."

Thinking back on their discussion now, he is only a little less furious than he was at the time. He looks past Nunzio, who is seated to his right, to Vaughn. This morning he told Vaughn about his exchange with Lauren. Vaughn, an experienced trial attorney, feels as uncomfortable as Mick does going into a trial with only the vaguest idea of what the defense will be. He catches Vaughn's eye and follows it to Zito, seated just behind them in the first row. To the jury consultant's left is Rachel Nunzio, dressed conservatively in an off-white pantsuit with a white blouse and a string of small pearls. Gone are her five-carat engagement ring and diamond earrings from N D Reiff Company.

Behind them all sits a packed courtroom. The press is present in full force, along with a cabal of curious criminal-defense attorneys, mob-o-philes, and if the rumors are true, some Hollywood types scouting the trial as a possible basis for a future film. Mick also knows that three teams of shadow jurors are present—Lauren Zito's trial barometers, handpicked to hold demographic mirrors to the real jurors as the trial proceeds.

Mick casts a sidelong glance at Pagano. The DA's normal practice for a case of this significance would be to man the prosecution table with at least a second chair. But Pagano sits alone, sending the message that he doesn't need any help.

Shortly before the judge took the bench, Pagano approached the defense table and told Mick and Nunzio that he'd subpoenaed Christina for trial. "My detectives served the subpoenas at both of your houses," he told the mob boss.

"You're not getting Christina," said Nunzio.

Pagano smiled. "That's all I needed to know."

When he walked away, Mick whispered to Nunzio that he shouldn't have said that. "Now he knows he can paint the picture of what happened that night without fear of being contradicted by your daughter."

Nunzio didn't answer, only stared straight ahead.

Judge McCann finishes her initial instructions to the jury, then turns her attention to the prosecution table. "Mr. Pagano," she says.

Pagano rises and buttons his jacket. But instead of walking toward the jury, the bald, bowlegged bulldog walks away from them and positions himself directly in front of the defense table. Pagano stares at the jury for a long moment, then extends his left arm and points at Nunzio. "James F. X. Nunzio is a vicious, cold-blooded murderer."

Mick shoots to his feet. "Objection!"

"Counsel to the bench, *right now.*"

Once they are in position, Frances McCann leans down, her jaw clenched. *"No,"* she says quietly. "Not in my courtroom. This is going to be a trial, Mr. Pagano. Not a carnival. Do you hear me?"

Pagano grunts.

"Not good enough. I said, *Do you hear me?*"

"Yes."

McCann glares at Pagano. Then she sits back. "Proceed."

Mick returns to the defense table. He knows why Pagano started that way. He wanted to send a message to the jury: *I'm not afraid of this guy, and you shouldn't be, either.* Pagano sent the same message by packing the courtroom with uniformed police. Mick has never seen a larger law enforcement presence in a single courtroom. He wonders whether Pagano hasn't overplayed his hand, inadvertently sending the opposite message—Nunzio is so dangerous that it takes an army to guard against him.

Pagano positions himself in front of the jury box.

"This is a case about sending a message," Pagano begins. "You see, what you and I think of as the city of Philadelphia, the defendant thinks of as his personal territory. The mob has it all mapped out, this whole country of ours, and Philly belongs to Jimmy Nunzio."

Mick stands. "Objection. Speculation."

The court sustains the objection.

"The Commonwealth will present a witness, an FBI agent by the name of Ryan Wood, who will lay it all out for you—how the mob has divided the country into different turfs. And how, for the past few years, Frank Valiante of the New York–based Savonna crime family, through his son Antonio, has been making inroads into Philadelphia and South

Jersey, which have historically been run by the Giansante crime family, of which James Nunzio is a powerful underboss."

Mick glances at Nunzio. He'd told the mobster to keep his face free of expression, an easy task for Nunzio, who usually carries himself with features set in stone, except, of course, when he is seized by one of his legendary paroxysms of rage.

"What Agent Wood will tell you about the Valiantes' inroads into our city will be corroborated by the fact that Antonio Valiante's murder took place in a warehouse located on undeveloped grounds once part of the Naval Yard. A warehouse filled from floor to ceiling with heroin and fentanyl destined for our streets, key drugs in the opioid crisis claiming so many young lives."

Pagano's opening is laced with all the right buzzwords: *our* city, *our* streets, *opioid crisis.* He couldn't incite the Philadelphia jury any more skillfully than if he flashed pictures of Nunzio urinating on the Rocky statue.

"A message had to be sent, not just to the Valiantes, but to anyone who might think about horning in on Jimmy Nunzio's territory. But, of course, geography wasn't the only thing the Valiantes were horning in on."

Mick steels himself. *Here it comes.*

Pagano walks partway back to the defense table and half turns toward it. "Mr. Nunzio isn't just a crime lord, he's a father. His daughter's name is Christina Nunzio, laughingly referred to in our city as the Queen of Clubs—"

Mick clamps his right hand on Nunzio's forearm, but he is too late. The mobster is already up out of his chair. Pagano notices it and waits for Nunzio to sit back down, making sure the jury also catches Nunzio's emotional reaction to the derisive characterization of his daughter.

"So, you see, there were *two* messages Jimmy Nunzio had to send that night."

"Objection." Mick is on his feet again. "This is all wild speculation. And counsel's tone is more appropriate to closing argument than to opening statements."

"Sustained," the judge rules. "Mr. Pagano, these are opening statements. The place for facts, not conjecture. Statements, not speeches."

Pagano glares at the court. Then he forces a smile and turns to the jury.

"Fact: at exactly 9:22:15 p.m. on Wednesday, April tenth, of this year, James F. X. Nunzio received a call on his store-bought burner phone from another anonymous burner phone. Fact: a little more than two minutes later, at 9:25 p.m., he was seen racing from his office at the Naval Yard toward the parking lot, accompanied by his bodyguard, John Giacobetti. Fact: from exactly 9:58:22 to 10:02:28, defendant James Nunzio placed a call from his burner phone to another burner phone.

"Fact: at 10:05 p.m., two Philadelphia police officers, Jake Trumbull and Louis Piccone, having seen a car parked outside what was supposed to be an abandoned warehouse, approached the warehouse and heard a woman crying inside."

Mick's heart pounds as he listens to Pagano run down his list. Some trial attorneys persuade jurors by weaving seamless narratives around unspoken themes laced with argument inserted so cleverly that the jurors don't even know they are being persuaded of something. What Pagano is doing is the opposite: He's slapping everyone—judge, jurors, and Nunzio—in the face over and over again with the brutal realities of the case. He's playing the courtroom thug, the perfect counterpoint to Jimmy Nutzo.

It really was a brilliant move for Emlin Fellner to assign Pagano to this case.

"Fact," Pagano continues: "Officers Trumbull and Piccone entered the building, where they found Christina Nunzio on the floor, cradling the body of Antonio Valiante. Fact: the detectives also found plasticuffs that had been used to bind Valiante's hands and feet. Fact: Antonio Valiante's throat had been slashed by a knife. He'd bled to death through the gaping wound."

Pagano pauses and walks up to the jury box.

"Fact: not fifteen feet away from Valiante's bloody body, the police found James Nunzio hiding in the shadows, holding the knife. Fact: Christina Nunzio was so traumatized by what she'd seen that she had a complete mental breakdown. A breakdown so severe she had to be hospitalized and even now is not mentally competent to attend these proceedings and testify."

Pagano turns toward the bench, looks up at Judge McCann. "Facts, not conjecture. Statements, not a speech."

Pagano turns back to the jury and stands without speaking, giving them time for it all to sink in. Time to envision Jimmy Nunzio skulking in the shadows after slitting Tony Valiante's throat while his daughter wept. Time to look over at Nunzio and hate him.

Eventually, Pagano starts up again. He does his best to convince the jury that Nunzio went to the warehouse that night with premeditation—the specific intent to kill Antonio Valiante, justifying the death penalty. He downplays the many holes in the case, including why Nunzio killed Valiante with a knife rather than with the pistol he was carrying, what happened to Johnny Giacobetti, the identity of the person who called Nunzio's cell phone and that of the person Nunzio called from the warehouse. He characterizes these as "nothing more than typical examples of unanswered questions that exist in any homicide case."

Finally, he concludes: "There were at least three eyewitnesses to what went down in the warehouse that night. One of them is dead. One is mentally unable to talk to the police." He turns to Nunzio. "The other refused to talk to the police."

Mick sees Pagano glance at the defense table, mirth in his eyes. Pagano knows from Nunzio himself that Christina isn't going to appear as a witness. And there's no way Nunzio himself could take the stand.

The prosecutor would crucify him, not just about the crime at hand but about his nefarious history. The message the prosecutor's sending the jury is clear: Don't buy a pig in a poke. If the defense suggests there was a reason for what happened, make them prove it; if they can't, then there's no possible justification for what Nunzio did.

Pagano makes a few closing remarks, then takes his seat.

Judge McCann looks down from the bench. "Mr. McFarland."

He rises. "Thank you, Your Honor." He turns to his left, toward the jurors, and places his right hand on Jimmy Nunzio's shoulder. "I am proud today to be representing Mr. James Nunzio. Mr. Nunzio is a husband. His wife, Rachel, is sitting right behind us."

Rachel smiles at the jurors. It's a shy smile—demure, spiced with sadness and fear. They rehearsed it four times at the office this morning.

"Mr. Nunzio is also a father. You know about his daughter, Christina. You may also know he had a son, Alexander, who was killed in the tragic crash last year of Amtrak Train 174."

Mick pats Nunzio's shoulder. Then, the humanizing-of-the-client phase of his opening concluded, he walks to the jury box, stands before the jurors.

"Good morning, ladies and gentlemen."

He pauses, takes the time to look each juror in the eye.

"Things are not always as they appear. Anyone who reaches the age of adulthood knows this. And it is certainly true in this case. The prosecutor has described only the *aftermath* of what happened in the warehouse the night Antonio Valiante died. He said nothing about what led up to it, or why. That's because the prosecutor only knows half the story."

Pagano is on his feet.

"Objection. And *that's* because the defendant wouldn't talk to us!"

Judge McCann glares at Pagano. "No speaking objections, counselor. If you have an objection, simply say the word. I'll call counsel to the bench and hear you out."

Pagano glowers, takes his seat.

Mick continues. "There's a very good reason Mr. Nunzio wouldn't talk to the prosecutor, and I expect everyone in this town can guess what it is. There is only one place James Nunzio could ever hope to get a fair shake, and it's not at the Roundhouse. It's right here, in this courtroom. Rather than trusting his story to law enforcement, in whose eyes he's been guilty for years, Mr. Nunzio chose to share his truth with you, a panel of his peers who swore to listen to the evidence—*all* of the evidence—and reach a decision based on that evidence, rather than on preconceptions and prejudice.

"While we're on the subject of preconceptions and prejudice, let's talk about the victim, Antonio Valiante. Mr. Valiante was as well known to law enforcement as Mr. Nunzio. He was the reputed lieutenant and eldest son of New York crime boss Frank Valiante, and together they were making a huge play to become the largest sellers of illegal opioids in our city. But unlike those who would have you condemn Mr. Nunzio based on his alleged background, I'm not going to suggest that you acquit Mr. Nunzio just because every parent and member of law enforcement is happy that Antonio Valiante is off our streets."

"Objection," Pagano says. "It sounds like that's exactly what he's doing."

Of course it is.

Judge McCann looks down from the bench. "Mr. McFarland, you know better. Stay within the lines. First warning, and last."

Apologizing to the court, he steals a quick glance at the jurors. A few have their arms crossed, but others, he can tell, accepted his point. *What happened in the warehouse was something between mobsters. Who cares if one wiseguy offs another? The world's a better place for it.*

Foreman Aaron Burnett, however, is unreadable.

"Now, let's turn to what the evidence in this case will be. Or, more accurately, what it won't be. Question: Who placed the call to Mr. Nunzio's cell phone, and why? The prosecutor *implies* that it was someone tipping Mr. Nunzio off to the whereabouts of Antonio

Valiante. The reason the prosecutor implies this without saying it is that there is no evidence to support it. As to the call placed *from* Mr. Nunzio's cell phone, the prosecutor doesn't even venture an answer. The court has provided each of you with a yellow legal pad on which to make notes. I suggest you write the words *phone calls* and place a question mark next to them. If, by the end of the case, the prosecutor hasn't given you the information you need to cross off those critical questions, he will have failed to meet his burden of proof."

Mick's voice is confident, but inside he knows the jurors would never find against the prosecution because of its failure to resolve the phone mystery, for one simple reason: Nunzio knows the identities of the people who placed and received the calls. It's *his* burden—not in law, but in fact—to tell the jury if it helps exonerate him. Whether Nunzio will deign to explain the calls, including to his own lawyer, remains to be seen.

"This leads us to the next question the prosecution must answer: premeditation. The prosecutor would have you send Mr. Nunzio *to his death* based upon the prosecutor's assumption that Mr. Nunzio's intent in going to the warehouse was to kill Antonio Valiante. Question: What, in fact, was Mr. Nunzio's intent? Antonio Valiante was a dangerous organized-crime figure, and as both Mr. Pagano and I have told you, Mr. Nunzio is a father. Did Mr. Nunzio rush to the warehouse to harm Mr. Valiante, or did he race there to save his daughter? If, by the end of the case, the prosecutor hasn't given you the answer to this question, he will have failed to establish premeditation."

He's playing fast and loose here. Criminal premeditation—the intent to kill—can be formed in a matter of seconds, as the judge will instruct the jurors at the end of the trial. Mick wants to distract the jurors from that point from the outset—get them thinking that the key point at which to measure Nunzio's intent was when he left his office to go to the warehouse, not once he was there.

"The next question: If it really was Mr. Nunzio's intent from the outset to kill Antonio Valiante, why did he not run into the warehouse with his gun blazing? The evidence will be that Mr. Nunzio was carrying a pistol, a Sig Sauer P938. Yet Valiante died from a knife wound. When the police forensic experts tested the gun, they found it hadn't even been fired. Consistently, there was no gunshot residue on Mr. Nunzio's hands or arms. The police will admit all of this to you on the stand.

"Some more questions: Why the plasticuffs? Again, this is something the prosecution's own witnesses will admit to you. At some point that night, Valiante had been bound with plastic zip ties. When the patrolmen arrived that night, the cuffs had been cut off. Why were they cut off? Why was Valiante cuffed in the first place? How does any of this reconcile with the idea that Mr. Nunzio planned to kill Valiante? Additional questions the prosecutor must answer before you can fairly convict Mr. Nunzio of premeditated murder."

As he's speaking, he looks at each of the jurors in turn. They're doing their best not to reveal their thoughts, but he expects he's not convincing anyone of anything. And no wonder—he's not offering them an alternative narrative, a story counter to Pagano's highly believable tale of Mobster 1 executing Mobster 2. How could he? Nunzio has so far refused to give him the story.

He steals a quick glance at Lauren Zito and realizes that she's the key to salvaging the case. Surely, the Nunzios' trusted jury expert can see that he's not getting through to the jurors. After openings, he'll ask her to convince Nunzio that their defense lawyer needs to know their endgame.

He winds up his opening by hammering the same themes he touched on during jury selection: that all defendants are presumed innocent, and that it's the prosecutor's burden to prove a defendant guilty, not the defendant's burden to prove his innocence. He thanks the jury and sits. He takes a breath, then looks past Nunzio to Vaughn, who nods unconvincingly. It was a weak opening, and they both know it.

36

Friday, June 21, Continued

When Mick finishes, Judge McCann calls a midmorning bathroom break and tells everyone she wants them back in fifteen minutes. "Sharp."

The deputies take Nunzio to the holding cell off the courtroom, and Mick waves Lauren Zito and Rachel Nunzio to cross the bar and join Vaughn and him at the defense table.

"Your assessment of openings? The jury?" Mick asks Zito.

"Pagano is a brute, and that's how the jury sees him. You came off as a strident but sincere advocate. The jurors like you, and they don't like Pagano. But they believe what he's told them is the truth."

"Do you want to ask your shadow jurors what they saw?"

"They saw the same thing I did."

He furrows his brow. Zito remained seated as the jurors left the courtroom; she didn't go back to her team.

Apparently reading his confusion, she smiles, reaches up to her right ear, and removes an earbud.

"The shadow jurors slip notes to their handlers, and the handlers whisper to me."

He grimaces.

"Like it or not," she says, "the twenty-first century has found its way to the courtroom."

"Uh-huh. Is there something you'd like to say to Mrs. Nunzio?"

Zito looks confused. "Like what?"

"Like the reason the jurors are believing Pagano is that he's the only one offering up a story as to what happened in the warehouse. Like it's time the Nunzios armed me with the same power by sharing their narrative."

Rachel Nunzio merely offers him a sphinx's smile. "When the time is right."

Vaughn steps forward. "That's a nice saying, Mrs. Nunzio. Here's another one, given to me by your husband in the Amtrak 174 case, when he was poised to kill my cousin: 'Sometimes soon isn't soon enough.'"

Rachel's smile widens. "You *are* a clever one. Tell me, are you still driving the Porsche? I'm the one who picked that out for you."

Mick turns to Zito. "Lauren, this is crazy. Please get through to them on this."

But the jury-whisperer ignores him. "Come on," she tells Rachel. "Let's powder our noses. We only have five minutes left."

Mick watches the two women leave the courtroom.

"I can't believe how they're just laughing it all off," Vaughn says.

Mick nods. "Which tells me that I'm right: they have an ace in the hole. One or more of the jurors are in their pocket, or the Nunzios believe they are."

"You think Nunzio had his people approach them? Scare them?"

"The idea has crossed my mind."

"What should we do?"

"What can we do? Try the case, and hope that Nunzio's cards don't flip on him. If they do, the stink will attach as much to us as to him."

◆ ◆ ◆

Many of the spectators know that Frances McCann is a ruthless timekeeper, so almost everyone is back in their seats before she resumes the bench. Mick hears a stirring in the courtroom behind him and turns around. His attention is immediately drawn to a tall, well-dressed figure moving confidently down the center aisle. It's Emlin Fellner, the district attorney himself.

"I was wondering when he was going to make his appearance," Nunzio whispers to Mick.

Ever the politician, Fellner nods and smiles to people he knows in the benches. Then he walks up to Max Pagano, leans over the bar, and shakes his hand before sitting down. The show is Fellner's signal to the press that Pagano is "my guy," meaning that when Pagano sends Nunzio to prison, the credit belongs to Fellner.

The court crier announces the judge's return to the bench. Everyone stands.

After a few preliminaries, Frances McCann looks down to Pagano and says, "Call your first witness."

"The Commonwealth calls Matthew Arcangelo," Pagano announces.

Mick leans across Nunzio to Vaughn. "I don't recognize the name."

Vaughn begins leafing through the prosecution's witness list. "He's the junior medical examiner who helped Ari Weintraub perform the autopsy."

Normally, a prosecutor would start his case with the arresting officers, then move to the crime-scene guys, followed by the lead detective, who would give his opinion about the crime. Finally, he'd put on the ME and rub the gruesome body in the jurors' faces, get them good and sick at what the defendant's done. Pagano has apparently decided to *start* with the gore, helping the jurors hate Nunzio from the outset.

Mick takes his seat and watches Arcangelo pass through the bar and walk toward the witness stand. The pathologist looks to be in his early thirties, of middling height, but with thick arms, showing Mick that he works out. He has dark hair, swarthy skin, and a friendly face.

Something about him makes Mick uneasy, but he can't put his finger on it.

Pagano waits for the witness to be sworn in, then runs through his résumé. He has Arcangelo tell a quick story or two about his upbringing, and the young doctor's easygoing manner endears him to the jury. Once that's accomplished, Pagano asks him to relate the autopsy findings to the jury.

Arcangelo turns to the jury box.

"The postmortem examination was performed by the medical examiner, Dr. Weintraub, and I. The body was sixty-nine inches tall and weighed one hundred and eighty-five pounds. The decedent had dark hair and dark eyes."

Arcangelo discusses the weight and health of the internal organs, then raises a remote control that brings a photograph up on the large video screen Pagano has set up in the courtroom.

The jurors—and everyone else in the courtroom—visibly recoil at the picture, which is a close-up of Antonio Valiante's throat. Although the wound has been cleaned, it is still graphic, showing a gaping slash stretching from one side of the throat to the other. In pretrial motions, Mick objected to virtually all the autopsy and crime-scene photos of Tony Valiante's wounds. As expected, the court shot him down.

"What we're seeing," Arcangelo explains, "is a deep wound extending laterally the entire width of the throat. It severed the decedent's left sternomastoid muscle and partially severed the same muscle on the right. Also dissected completely were the left internal and external jugular veins and the left common carotid artery, as well as the same structures on the right."

"Can you show us where exactly on the victim's throat these wounds were?" Pagano asks.

Arcangelo raises his remote again, and the screen fills with a photograph taken from a little farther back. It shows not just the throat, but Antonio Valiante's whole neck and head and face. The head is tilted back, the jaw relaxed, the eyes open.

Studying the picture, Mick realizes what it is about the pathologist that made him uneasy: *He looks just like Valiante.*

"Your Honor, I'd like a sidebar," he says.

Once he, Pagano, and the court reporter are assembled on the side of the bench farthest from the jury, he tells the judge, "This is outrageous. The prosecutor's witness looks like he could be the decedent's twin."

Frances McCann turns and glances first at the video screen, then at the witness box.

"Dr. Arcangelo, please turn off the video while we're at sidebar," she says. Then, to Pagano: "Defense counsel has a point. Couldn't you have called Dr. Weintraub?"

"Your Honor, I was going to, but his calendar would not allow it."

She leans across the bench. "Dr. Weintraub's unavailability has nothing to do with the fact that his replacement is the decedent's doppelganger?"

"I don't think they look at all alike," Pagano says. "The doctor is taller, and—"

"Stop," she says. Then to Mick, "Mr. McFarland, do you have a motion to make?"

"I move for a mistrial," he says, his tone making it obvious that he doesn't really want one.

"Your record is protected for appeal. But I'm going to deny the motion. Mr. Pagano, you may proceed. And don't drag it out. Everyone's lunch is already ruined."

Mick turns away from the bench and catches Pagano smiling at him.

Once everyone is back in position, Pagano has the pathologist pull up the picture again. Mick catches several of the jurors looking from the photo to the pathologist, then back. There is no doubt in Mick's mind that the body the jurors see on the proverbial slab isn't that of a vicious wiseguy, but of the friendly doctor. He wonders whether Pagano knew about Arcangelo's resemblance to Valiante and somehow arranged to have him assist Weintraub, or whether it was merely dumb luck.

Pagano continues his direct examination.

"Doctor, were these wounds consistent with a quick slash or thrust of a knife?"

"Oh, no. That type of assault would have resulted in more superficial lacerations."

"So, what type of cutting would be consistent with these wounds?"

"These very deep and symmetrical wounds would have been caused by a slower, more methodical motion."

"Can you be more specific?"

Arcangelo pauses. "The attacker wasn't just lashing out or swinging from a distance, he was *sawing* at the decedent's throat, from very close."

Mick hears gasps and sees several of the jurors cover their mouths. One man, juror four, places his hand to his own throat.

Pagano slowly reaches to a pitcher on his table and pours himself a glass of water. Mick knows he's doing it to give the jurors plenty of time to consider the vision he's conjured up. When Pagano continues his questioning, he gives them something even more graphic to think about.

"Dr. Arcangelo, what is your opinion as to what caused the death of Antonio Valiante?"

"He died from massive exsanguination—blood loss—from the wound in his neck."

"What would have been the rate of the blood loss—how long would it have taken the victim to die?"

"Not long at all. The dissection of the carotid artery, in combination with a rapid heart rate and elevated blood pressure—which you'd expect given that the victim would have been terrified—would have resulted in arterial jetting. The blood would have literally been spraying out of the decedent."

Mick is on his feet before Arcangelo is even finished. "Objection."

"Sustained. Doctor, we can do without the commentary. You were asked how long it would have taken for death, nothing more."

"I'm sorry, Your Honor."

Pagano turns to the defense table, away from the court and jury, and winks at Mick. Then he turns back to the witness.

"Doctor, let's switch gears. Were there any wounds on the body other than those on the throat?"

Arcangelo uses his remote to pull up three photos, side by side, showing Valiante's ankles and each of his wrists.

"Yes. There were lacerations and bruising on both ankles and wrists."

Pagano lifts a clear bag, asks to approach the witness, and hands it to the pathologist.

"Doctor, I'm handing you Commonwealth Exhibit 17-A. This bag contains two zip ties. Have you seen these before?"

"Yes. I met with you yesterday evening and looked at them."

"Do you have an opinion whether the wounds you observed on the decedent's hands and wrists were consistent with having been restrained by zip ties?"

"Yes, and with trying to break them."

"Please explain."

"The lacerations—cuts—were very deep, and the bruising was extensive. The decedent was fighting to break free. Fighting hard."

Pagano turns toward the jury and looks from one to the next, nodding and making sure they're seeing what he wants them to see: Tony Valiante, on his knees, arms and legs bound behind him as Jimmy Nunzio stands over him, slowly sawing open his throat.

"A few more questions, Dr. Arcangelo," Pagano says, lifting the evidence bag containing the knife and walking it to the witness stand.

"Commonwealth Exhibit One—have you had a chance to see it before now?"

"Yes. You showed it to me last night, at your office."

"Could the decedent's throat wounds have been caused by this knife?"

"Yes. The length and thickness of the blade, and the serrated edge are consistent with the decedent's wounds."

"How does the serrated edge play into it?"

Arcangelo displays a close-up of the throat wounds on the video screen.

"The lacerations to the throat involved a lot of shredding, which I would expect, given the serrated edge. A knife with a straight blade would have produced a . . . a cleaner cut."

When it's Mick's turn to question Arcangelo, he sees Lauren Zito subtly signaling him. He stands and leans over the bar.

"Get in and out of cross as quickly as possible," she says. "Make your points and sit down."

He casts her a hard look. He was planning to do exactly that. He steps toward the witness stand.

"Doctor, you testified the decedent was cuffed at the wrists and ankles. Was the wound to the throat inflicted before the decedent was cuffed, while he was cuffed, or after the cuffs had been removed?"

"I don't know."

"So it's possible that the decedent was free of restraint when the wound to the throat was inflicted?"

"Yes."

"You testified that, at some point, the decedent was on his knees. Was he on his knees when the wound to the throat was inflicted?"

"I can't tell you that, either."

"So it's possible that the wound to the throat was inflicted while the decedent was on his feet."

"I guess so."

"Doctor, there's nothing from the autopsy that discounts the possibility that, when the wounds to the throat were inflicted, the decedent was on his feet and unbound, isn't that true?"

"That is true."

"And nothing from the autopsy to disprove that while the decedent was on his feet, unbound, he was fighting with whoever inflicted the throat wound."

"Well—"

"Objection." Pagano is on his feet. "Defense counsel is asking the witness to speculate."

"I'll sustain the objection, and I instruct the jury to disregard the last question."

Mick doesn't care whether the doctor answers the question or not. The jury has gotten the message.

"Doctor, isn't it true that the wounds you've shown the jury don't tell you who inflicted them?"

"That's true."

"They could have been inflicted by anyone with the knife."

"It would've taken some strength—"

"The strength of a giant mob enforcer?"

"Objection!" Pagano strides out from behind the prosecution table to stand beside Mick. "There's no evidence whatsoever that the wounds were inflicted by anyone other than Mr. Nunzio himself. Defense counsel's question is based on rank speculation."

The judge calls counsel to the bench. When they are in position, she addresses Mick.

"Mr. McFarland, do you have any evidence that the decedent was killed by Mr. Giacobetti? That is who you were referring to, isn't it?"

"I don't have any evidence as to who actually inflicted the fatal wounds, and neither does the prosecution. That's the point I'm trying to make, and it's a fair one."

The judge takes a minute. "I'm going to sustain the objection. And, Mr. McFarland, I'm instructing you not to ask questions for which there will be no evidence on the record."

"Yes, Your Honor," he says, wondering whether Nunzio is planning on throwing Johnny G. under the bus. If that turns out to be the case, the last series of questions will mesh perfectly with the Nunzios' endgame.

He walks back to counsel table as the judge tells the jury to disregard the last question. When she's done ruling, he addresses the bench.

"I have nothing further on cross, Your Honor."

"Redirect, Mr. Pagano?"

"No, Your Honor."

The court dismisses Arcangelo and tells Pagano to call his next witness.

"The Commonwealth calls Special Agent Ryan Wood of the Federal Bureau of Investigation."

Mick watches Wood take the stand. He's a tough-looking man in his midfifties with iron-gray hair and a pockmarked face.

Pagano leads the agent through his background, establishing Wood as an expert on organized crime. It quickly becomes clear to Mick that Wood is a "push-button expert," the type of witness with so much experience testifying that an attorney can simply push the button—ask an open-ended question—and let the witness run with it. Pagano does precisely that, and Wood expounds for twenty minutes on the history of organized crime in America, zeroing in on the rivalry between the Savonna and Giansante crime families and the bitter enmity between Jimmy Nunzio and Frank Valiante. Wood identifies both of them as top-tier underbosses in their respective families. Wood devotes the last five minutes of his speech to Nunzio's "ownership" of the Philadelphia and South Jersey territories and Valiante's invasion of those regions.

"That Valiante would set up a large drug-storage warehouse on the Naval Yard, just a mile from Nunzio's personal office, would have been a blatant affront to Mr. Nunzio," Wood says.

"You're referring to the warehouse where Antonio Valiante *hooked up* with Mr. Nunzio's *daughter*?" Pagano asks.

"Yes, I am."

Pagano doesn't ask whether Valiante's relationship with Nunzio's daughter would have been an even larger affront than the warehouse; everyone in the courtroom already gets that.

Pagano and Wood hit the ball back and forth a few more times; then the prosecutor walks back to his table and, with a smug look, tells the court he has no more questions on direct.

Judge McCann tells Mick he's up to bat, and he rises and walks toward the witness stand.

"So the Nunzios and the Valiantes were competitors?"

"More like blood enemies."

"*Blood enemies.* I like that. Did someone tell you to use that phrase?"

Wood glances at Pagano, and Mick sees the jury catch it.

"The Nunzios and the Valiantes aren't the only houses on the block, though, are they?" asks Mick.

"I don't understand."

"There are three other large organized-crime families besides the Giansantes and the Savonnas, and other underbosses working for them. And, of course, there's also the Russian mob, the Mexican cartels, and the Dominicans, right?"

"Okay."

"It would be to *all* of their benefit for Valiante or Nunzio, or both, to end up dead, wouldn't it?"

"Objection," Pagano announces. "Calls for speculation."

"Overruled. You presented Special Agent Wood as an expert on all things organized crime."

Wood looks up at the judge, then back at Mick, shifting in his seat. "I suppose."

"Did one of the rival mob families set the whole thing up? Or the Russians? Did they make the call to Nunzio, to make sure he and Valiante ended up in the same place at the same time? Hoping that one or both would end up on ice?"

"How could I know that?"

"You can't, can you?"

"No."

Mick walks back to the counsel table, takes a drink of water.

"Did you bother to investigate whether the other mob families were involved, or the Russians, or the Mexican cartels?"

"I didn't investigate anything. This wasn't a federal case. I was just brought in for background on the territorial divisions among the five families."

"Brought in by the DA?"

"Yes."

"Well, when Mr. Pagano brought you in to give the jury its history lesson, did he ask the FBI to get involved in the case?"

Wood shifts in his seat again. "Well, no. There's a jurisdictional issue."

"You mean the Philly police and the DA's office 'owned' the case and wanted to prosecute it by themselves, not let you have any of it?"

"Well . . ."

"The FBI's failure to get involved here was a 'turf' thing, like with the Nunzios and Valiantes?"

Wood's face turns red. Pagano is on his feet objecting. Mick turns away from the witness and smiles at the jury. Some smile back at him. Foreman Aaron Burnett is one of them.

Mick withdraws the question and tells the judge he is finished with the witness.

She calls to Pagano to do his redirect, but he says he has none. This surprises Mick. There were a couple of bits of his cross that he would have smoothed over if he were Pagano. And Pagano is the type to always want the last word.

Judge McCann glances at the clock on the rear wall.

"It's 12:30. We will take our lunch break now. I want everyone back in the courtroom at 1:45."

The reporters are the first to flee, wanting to get back to their offices and post the morning's developments to the online versions of their newspapers and television networks. The rest of the crowd takes its time, knowing the elevators will be jammed anyway. The deputies approach Nunzio to take him back to his holding cell. He winks at Mick, pats him on the shoulder.

"You're doing a good job," he says.

"All I'm doing is blowing smoke and hoping the jury will inhale it."

"Isn't that what reasonable doubt is all about?"

He shakes his head and watches the deputies take Nunzio out of the courtroom. Vaughn says he'll fetch Mick a hot dog and Pepsi and bring them back to the courtroom. Mick sits down to prep for the afternoon's lineup of witnesses. Once Vaughn leaves, Lauren Zito walks through the gate to the defense table. Rachel Nunzio stays back and waits.

Zito leans into Mick and speaks quietly. "That thing you did with Giacobetti and the knife—it got some interesting reactions with both our shadow jurors and the real jurors. See if you can develop that story line a little more in your cross-exams. We'll see how it plays."

He knows she's right about the Giacobetti narrative, and he's already decided to move forward with it. There are problems with that scenario, of course. Like, if Giacobetti were the killer, why did Nunzio have blood all over him? And why wasn't Johnny G. in the warehouse when the police arrived? He has to come up with answers to these and other questions to make the Giacobetti narrative fly with the jury.

"Mick, I'm not done talking," Zito says behind his back.

"Well, I'm done listening," he says over his shoulder.

He hears her huff and walk away.

This really is getting to be too much. Jury consultants telling me what roads to lead the jury down. My client sitting on the story that he'll ultimately demand I peddle to the jurors, giving me no chance to evaluate it for weaknesses.

Mick knows there's nothing reasonable about what's going on here. And there will be no doubt in anyone's mind, ever, that Jimmy Nunzio killed Tony Valiante.

37

Friday, June 21, Continued

Judge McCann retakes the bench at exactly 1:45 and tells Pagano to call his next witness. "The Commonwealth calls Rodger Carey."

Mick watches the man take the stand. He's short and wiry, and his blue security guard's uniform looks two sizes too big. Carey looks nervously around the courtroom as the bailiff administers the oath.

Pagano quickly establishes that Carey works as a second-shift security guard at the building next to the one in which Nunzio keeps his office, and that he was on duty the night of Antonio Valiante's murder. Carey testifies that he saw Nunzio running from his office building that night, at 9:25. He's sure of the time because he thought it odd to see James Nunzio running, so he made sure to glance at the clock. The whole direct examination takes just ten minutes. No doubt a deliberate choice by Pagano, based on Carey's nervousness.

When Pagano finishes, Mick begins his cross. He has only one point to make. He doesn't even bother standing in order to make it.

"Did you tell the police that you saw Mr. Nunzio running from the building?"

"Yes, I told the detective the same thing I just said here."

"But you told the detective there was someone running *with* Mr. Nunzio, didn't you?"

Carey glances at Nunzio, then out into the courtroom. "Yeah, the giant. Everyone knows who he is."

"State his name, please."

Carey mumbles the name. It's obvious to Mick that he's afraid.

"Louder, please."

Carey glances at the spectators' section. "Giacobetti."

"John Giacobetti?"

"Yes."

"Also known as Johnny G.?"

"Yes."

"He was running with Mr. Nunzio? Heading toward the parking lot?"

"Uh, yes."

"Why didn't you bring this up on direct examination?"

Mick already knows why: because Pagano told him not to. Carey glances at Pagano, broadcasting that very fact to the jury. Mick wonders why Pagano didn't bring it out on direct that Giacobetti was with Nunzio. His choice not to do so—and getting caught at it—only serves to emphasize the point, something that Pagano had to have foreseen. It's not like Pagano to make such a rookie mistake. Mick decides that Pagano's rushing the testimony wasn't only because of his nervous witness. Something else is going on.

The witness hedges, but Mick doesn't push him. His point has been made. Johnny Giacobetti is now in the case.

He tells the judge he's finished cross-examination, and Pagano declines the chance to redirect.

"We call Officer Jake Trumbull," Pagano says, summoning his next witness to the stand. Trumbull is in his twenties and just finishing up his first year as a patrolman. He has blond hair, blue eyes, and a friendly, clean-shaven face. The traditional all-American-boy look.

Mick sits back as Pagano begins his questioning. It's obvious to Mick that the young officer has little experience testifying. Pagano gives him space to work out his jitters, having the patrolman begin by telling the jury where he's from—Northeast Philly, where all the cops live—and describing his first year on the force. Once Trumbull's comfortable, Pagano turns to the meat and potatoes.

"Officer Trumbull, please tell the jury what you were doing on the night of April tenth, around 10:00 p.m."

"I was with my partner, Lou Piccone, in our patrol car. We were in a part of the Naval Yard that hasn't been developed yet. We were on Admiral Peary Way, and we had just passed that big airplane hangar—at least I think that's what the building is—and I saw there was a car parked outside this other building that was supposed to be vacant. I thought, *What's going on here?* and we turned onto the access road that led up to the building."

Trumbull describes pulling up, looking over the Escalade. "Then we noticed that the door to the building was smashed in. The doorframe was bent, and the door was splintered along the left side. Lou—Officer Piccone—said it looked like someone kicked the . . . kicked it in. There was light coming from inside the building, and we heard a woman crying.

"Officer Piccone took point and pushed the door open. I was right behind him, and we both had our weapons pulled."

"When you entered the building, what's the first thing that caught your attention?"

"It was a weird setup. The whole back of the building was filled with shelves stacked with plastic bags of white powder. The front part, though, was set up like an apartment. There was furniture and a kitchen and . . ."

The officer pauses in midsentence. Mick guesses that Pagano is sending him a signal—something trial attorneys do when a witness gets off track.

"But the first thing I noticed"—Trumbull corrects course—"was the woman. She was sitting on the carpet and was, like, rocking this dead guy. I mean, he turned out to be dead. She was crying and saying, 'Why, Daddy, why?' and 'I loved him.' I moved toward her, and out of the corner of my eye, I saw a guy. He was standing in the shadows with a knife in his hands. And I yelled to him to drop the knife. Officer Piccone saw him then, too, and shouted for him to drop the knife, kick it away, and put his hands behind his head."

"What did you and your partner do next?"

"Officer Piccone covered me while I holstered my weapon and went up to the guy, put his arms behind his back, and cuffed him. He had a gun tucked into the back of his pants, and I relieved him of it."

"What did you do with the weapon?"

"Since the perp was secured and the gun no longer posed a threat, I simply laid it on the ground so it could be retrieved and examined by CSU."

"Did Officer Piccone say anything to you at that point?"

"He told me to watch out for the blood, because the perp was covered in it. I mean, he was soaked."

"What happened next?"

"After the perp was cuffed, Officer Piccone came up to him and recognized who it was. I didn't know until then."

"Is the man you found holding the knife and covered in blood in the courtroom today?"

"Yes, he's right there," Piccone answers, pointing.

Pagano turns to the judge. "Let the record reflect that the witness has identified the defendant, James Nunzio."

Pagano has Trumbull describe walking Nunzio out to the patrol car as Piccone called it in to dispatch, asking for a CSU team and detectives and the medical examiner's office. Pagano then shows him the knife in the plastic bag, and Trumbull says it looks like the one Nunzio was holding.

"What about the woman? What happened with her?"

"She was a mess. Couldn't stop crying. We had to pry her from the body, lift her up. Some more squad cars had pulled up by then, and we were going to put her in one of them, but she collapsed on the ground as soon as we got her outside. We called for an ambulance, and I sat with her until it arrived. By then, she was just sitting on the ground, all spaced out. She'd stopped crying and I tried to talk to her, but I don't think she even heard me, she was so far away . . . mentally, I mean."

Pagano walks up to the witness stand and hands the patrolman a photograph. He asks if it depicts the woman in the warehouse. Trumbull says it does, and Pagano asks that the record reflect that the witness identified a photograph of Christina Nunzio.

"What, ultimately, was done with Mr. Nunzio?"

"The detectives arrived, Tredesco and his partner, and they took Nunzio from the patrol car and put him in their car and drove him away."

Pagano pauses to pour himself some water.

"Did you see anyone in the warehouse other than the defendant and Ms. Nunzio?"

"No."

"Did you see anyone holding a knife other than the defendant?"

"No."

"Thank you, Officer Trumbull. Nothing further, Your Honor."

"Mr. McFarland," the judge says. "Your witness."

In the month before trial, Mick had filed a pro forma motion asking the court to exclude all the evidence found inside the warehouse and dismiss the case on the grounds that there had been no probable cause. It was a no-chance motion, and the court denied it, as Mick had expected. For purposes of appeal, he has to revisit the issue at trial, and he does so now.

"Officer Trumbull, please explain to me why you felt you had probable cause to enter private property and drive up to the warehouse."

"There was a car parked outside the building."

"Have you never seen that before? A car parked outside a building?"

The question garners a few chuckles, but Trumbull ignores them.

"Not that building. It was supposed to be abandoned. I mean, we pass by there every night, and I never saw a car parked there, or lights on inside."

Mick knows why there would never appear to be lights inside; the factory windows had been painted black. As for the absence of obvious vehicles, the Valiantes would always park behind the building. That's where Antonio Valiante's Porsche was found. There was also a Chevy van backed up to a loading dock that ran into the back of the building.

Switching gears to rattle the young officer, Mick asks, "You say Mr. Nunzio had a gun?"

"Yes, tucked into the back of his pants."

Mick walks to the prosecution table and picks up a pistol with an evidence tag tied to the trigger guard.

"Is this the gun?"

"Looks like it."

"A Sig Sauer P938 Nitron?"

"I don't know the model."

"Didn't that seem strange to you? Mr. Nunzio had a gun, but the decedent was killed with a knife?"

"Well, he had the knife, too."

"But didn't that strike you as odd? Why kill someone with a knife if you have a gun?"

Trumbull shrugs, opens his palms. "I don't know. I mean, I don't run the mob. You'd have to ask *him*," he adds, nodding to Nunzio.

The chuckling this time is louder. To keep the jury from seeing his face redden, Mick turns back toward the counsel table and spies Lauren Zito signaling him to wrap it up. His embarrassment turns to anger.

"Just a few more questions. You said something about the door being smashed in?"

"Yes. The frame was made of metal, and it was dented, big-time. And the door, which was wood—the whole left side, the side where the doorknob was—was a mess."

"So it looked like someone had exerted a tremendous amount of force on the door?"

"Sure."

"Someone very, very strong."

Pagano is on his feet. "Objection, calls for speculation."

The judge sustains the objection, but Mick can tell that the jury gets the point.

"One final thing. You said you and Officer Piccone both went in the front door?"

"Yes."

"That meant that the back door was left unguarded."

"I guess so."

"So someone could have run out the back of the building when you and your partner entered in front, and you wouldn't have known."

"I guess so."

"Nothing further."

Pagano is on his feet before the judge turns the witness over to him for redirect.

"Did you see any bloody tracks leading from the decedent's body to the back of the building?"

"There was a lot of blood and footprints near the carpet. But I didn't see any running toward the back. No."

"Nothing further."

Mick is on his feet now.

"Did you look?"

"Uh—"

"Did you specifically look for bloody tracks leading toward the back?"

"That wasn't my job. You'd really have to talk to the CSU guys."

"Nothing further, Your Honor."

Mick sits, unhappy. The point about Trumbull not seeing any tracks because he didn't look is only a temporary victory. The CSU team certainly checked, and there were none. The bloody-footprints thing was a stupid move. Now he has no choice but to return to it with the CSU witness.

Trumbull's testimony takes only half an hour. It's 2:15 when Pagano calls his next witness. It's Lieutenant Matthew Stone, the lead investigator for the CSU assigned to the case. Mick knows Stone to be an honest cop, and thorough. His work at the warehouse crime scene will have been top-notch.

Stone takes the stand. He's forty-one but looks younger, with short blond hair and an honest face. Pagano takes him through his education, training, and experience with CSU, then has him run through the crime scene, using photographs to walk the jurors from the Escalade parked outside through the busted-up door and into the warehouse itself.

Using the same remote-control device used by the assistant medical examiner, Stone displays a medium-distance photograph of Valiante's body in situ. Even from a distance, it's a gruesome scene. Most of the jurors recoil and look away until they are able to steel themselves and study the photograph.

"Does this photograph depict the location where the body was found?"

"Yes. Of course, the body had been disturbed somewhat," Stone says, "when the patrolmen pulled the decedent away from Ms. Nunzio. But the photograph depicts where she and the decedent were positioned when the police entered the building."

"Based on the evidence, where do you believe the decedent was killed?"

"Oh, right here, where the body is lying. This is where the decedent bled out, and there was a vast swamp of blood soaked into the rug."

Extending his arm toward the defense table, Pagano says, "It has been suggested that perhaps the killer ran out the back after the murder. Did you find any evidence to support that notion? Any tracks, for example?"

"No. The only set of tracks—footprints—were those that led to where the patrolmen indicated they found the defendant, and then a second set of tracks from that spot out of the building to where I understand the defendant was placed into a squad car."

Stone pauses, then remembers something. "The defendant was still at the scene when I arrived, so I had the detectives, who arrived at about the same time, remove his shoes and put them into an evidence bag. The rest of the defendant's bloody clothes were removed and bagged at the Roundhouse."

"Did the footprints immediately around the murder site tell you anything about how the defendant moved?"

"Based on the spacing of the tracks and their configuration, it looks like he backed away from the murder site, slowly."

"Was there any sign of a struggle between Mr. Nunzio and the decedent?"

"Not that I saw. There was no upset furniture. The lamps were still sitting on the end tables."

Pagano moves to the defense table and retrieves some paper exhibits.

"As part of the CSU's investigation, did your forensics team perform DNA testing and fingerprint analysis?"

"Of course."

Pagano hands the witness the exhibits and has Stone identify them as the reports of the DNA and fingerprint analyses.

"Please tell the jury what the forensics team found."

Stone glances at the reports, then turns to the jury. "All of the blood was that of the decedent, and—"

"When you say 'all of the blood,' what do you mean?"

"The blood on the carpet, on the decedent, on Ms. Nunzio, who was cradling the body, on the knife, and on the defendant. And the footprints we spoke about earlier."

"And the results of the fingerprint analysis, focusing on the knife?"

"The only prints on the knife were those of the defendant."

"The defendant," Pagano repeats, letting the words hang in the air. "Sir, based on your analysis of the crime scene, the results of the forensics testing, and your experience as a police officer and CSU investigator, did you form a conclusion about the nature of the crime and how it was committed?"

"Yes. I concluded that the defendant used the knife, Exhibit 17-A, to cut the decedent's throat, and that the decedent bled out through the wounds. This happened on the carpet in the center of the living area of the warehouse. Then, with the knife in his hand, the defendant backed away from the murder site, twenty-one feet away, to be exact, to where he was standing when the police entered the building."

"Thank you, Lieutenant. Nothing further, Your Honor."

"Your witness, Mr. McFarland," the judge says.

He stands, buttons his coat, and walks toward the witness stand, pausing a respectful distance away.

"Lieutenant Stone, would you mind pulling up on the screen one of the pictures you took of the busted-in doorjamb and the door?"

Stone does so, and Mick gives the jury some time to study the photos, take in the extent of the damage.

"This was a warehouse, and the doorframe was steel."

"Yes."

"The door itself was a solid wood?"

"Yes."

Mick pauses, then walks to the evidence table.

"Commonwealth Exhibit 14," he says, lifting one of the bags and carrying it to the witness stand. "Are these the shoes you had removed from Mr. Nunzio?"

Stone studies the shoes through the clear plastic. "Yes."

"Italian loafers with thin soles?"

"I guess."

"Can you see the soles through the plastic? Does there appear to be any damage to the soles?"

Stone pulls the exhibit close to his face. "I don't see any."

"In fact, the soles are in pristine condition, wouldn't you agree?"

"There doesn't appear to be much wear on them."

"Do these look like shoes that kicked the warehouse door, bashed it with such force as to dent the steel frame and splinter the hardwood door itself?"

"Objection. Lack of foundation. How could the witness know that?"

"Sustained," the Judge McCann says. Then, leaning toward the witness, she asks, "Do you see any damage to the shoes or other markings indicative of sudden stress?"

"Just a lot of dried blood."

It's Mick's turn to object. Stone's a fair guy, but not above the occasional zinger on the witness stand.

"Sustained. Answer my question, Lieutenant."

"I apologize. There were no such markings."

Mick looks over at the jurors and sees that several of them are writing on their legal pads. He's convinced some of them, at least, that Nunzio isn't the one who kicked open the door.

"Moving on, Lieutenant Stone. Let's talk about the defendant's gun, the Sig Sauer P938 that Officer Trumbull testified he found on Mr. Nunzio's person."

He retrieves the gun from the evidence table and carries it to the witness stand.

"Did you observe the weapon on the warehouse floor, where it was left by Officer Trumbull?"

"I did."

"Do you recognize this gun, marked as Commonwealth Exhibit 2, as the one you observed that night at the warehouse?"

"Yes."

"Was the gun loaded? Did it have a clip containing nine-millimeter bullets?"

"It did."

"Had it been recently fired? I assume your team had it tested."

"We did, and the weapon had not been fired."

"And Mr. Nunzio had no gunshot residue on his hands or clothes?"

"That's correct."

"Tell me, did you come to a conclusion as to why Mr. Nunzio, if he wanted to kill the decedent, didn't simply use the gun?"

Pagano objects, but McCann overrules him.

"That wasn't part of my mission. My job was to observe, gather, and preserve the physical evidence to make a determination as to what *did* happen, not what the defendant *could* have chosen to do but didn't."

The perfect answer, and true, but Mick is fine with it. Some of the jurors are again writing on their legal pads.

"Let's turn to your testimony that there were no footprints, or tracks, leading from the murder scene to the back of the building."

Stone shrugs.

"Is the lack of footprints consistent with someone having come to the warehouse, killed Valiante just moments before Mr. Nunzio arrived, and then run out the back after removing his shoes—"

"Objection," Pagano calls out.

"You're grasping at straws," Stone says.

"Gentlemen! One at a time," the judge scolds them.

"I withdraw the question," Mick says. He looks at the jury and sees that only one juror is writing something down. Another seems to be thinking about it. The foreman stares at him.

"Lieutenant, when asked whether you saw any evidence of a struggle, your only answer was that the furniture didn't seem to be disturbed. Did you see any evidence conclusively establishing that the decedent was not engaged in a struggle in the open area of the warehouse, where there was no furniture?"

"I saw no evidence of that, either way."

"So it's possible that the decedent was engaged in a struggle with someone before the decedent ended up on the rug, where his throat wound was inflicted."

"If you're suggesting the decedent and the defendant were fighting—"

"I didn't say the defendant, I said someone—"

"The decedent's only injuries were to his throat, and to his wrists and ankles from the zip ties. There was no bruising or other injuries anywhere else on his body."

"People can wrestle without sustaining bruising, can't they?"

"Objection!" Pagano barks. "Lieutenant Stone is not a medical doctor. Defense counsel should have tossed up this round of speculation to Dr. Arcangelo."

"Sustained."

Mick concludes his questions by establishing that Stone can't say whether the victim was bound at the time he was murdered. The plasticuffs were splattered with blood, but they could have picked up the blood from the carpet, where they were found.

Again, Pagano does not engage in redirect. Again, it seems to Mick that the prosecutor is rushing his case. But why?

38

Friday, June 21, Continued

Matthew Stone's testimony takes a little more than an hour. The court calls for a short break at 3:30, with everyone to return at 3:45. Once the jury is out of the courtroom, Lauren Zito beckons Mick and Vaughn to join Rachel Nunzio and her on the other side of the bar.

"We like what you're doing with the Giacobetti thing," Lauren says. "The jurors and shadow jurors are responding to it. Is there a way you can work in a motive for Johnny to have been the killer?"

He glances at Vaughn, then Zito and Rachel.

"Does Giacobetti know we're taking this tack?" he asks Rachel.

She sighs. "Mick, please."

He can't tell from her tone whether she's saying, of course Johnny G. knows, or telling Mick that it's irrelevant whether he knows or not.

"You're missing the point," an exasperated Lauren explains. "Right now, we don't know for sure what's going to work with the jury. So far, your questions have opened the door to both a self-defense argument and a Giacobetti scenario. We need for you to run with both, see which one the jury's more open to."

"What kind of jury consultant are you that you're talking to me like this?"

"You mean saying out loud what it is you're already thinking as a defense attorney?"

He glares at Zito until Rachel breaks their standoff.

"Mick," Rachel says, gently reaching for his arms, "I understand your frustration. I do. And so does Jimmy. We haven't given you much to work with. But that's going to change, I promise. Please, just put up with it, and do what Lauren is asking a little bit longer."

He sees what appears to be genuine warmth in Rachel Nunzio's eyes. She's telling him she knows they're overstepping their bounds, and she's sorry for it.

"Stop playing me, Rachel."

As though a switch were turned off, her eyes instantly turn cold.

"I'll move forward with both lines of defense," he says. "I was going to anyway. But I don't like how this is going down. I've never worked with a jury-whisperer before, but I find it hard to accept that this is part of the normal program."

Rachel gives him a slight nod of acknowledgment. "Remember what I told you when I first came to your office? Mine is not a normal family."

"The Commonwealth calls Detective John Tredesco," Pagano says.

Mick watches as his nemesis from the police force makes his way to the stand. The detective limply raises his right arm and takes the oath with a bored look on his face. When he sits, Tredesco smooths his comb-over and focuses his narrow-set eyes on Pagano. From the outset, Mick can tell, the jurors are cool to him.

Pagano runs Tredesco through his tenure on the force—five years on patrol followed by eighteen years as a detective, thirteen being with the homicide unit—then takes him to the night of the murder.

"It was shortly after 10:00 when I received the call at home. There had been a killing at a warehouse off Admiral Peary Way. I got ahold of my partner at the time, Greg Lott. He lives about a mile from me, so I had him swing by and pick me up. We went right to the scene."

"What time did you arrive, and what did you do when you got there?"

"We arrived at 10:45, and the first thing we did was identify ourselves to the CSU lead, Lieutenant Stone. His people had just begun working the scene, so we weren't allowed inside. He did let us peek through the doorway, and we were able to see the murder site and the body."

"Were the defendant and his daughter still there?"

"The daughter had just been taken away by ambulance, I was told. The defendant was in the back of a patrol car, and I decided to take him back to the Roundhouse for interrogation."

"Would you describe the defendant's appearance?"

"He was drenched with blood. It was all over his shirt, his face, his hands. He had dark slacks on, and they were wet with blood, too."

Pagano thinks on this a minute. "If his slacks were dark, how could you tell the wetness was from blood?"

"It had to be either blood or urine, and I didn't think killing someone would make Jimmy Nunzio pee his pants."

"Detective!" The judge leans toward the witness box. "No more." She turns to the jury and tells them to disregard Tredesco's remark.

Mick studies the jurors; he can tell their distaste for Tredesco is growing.

"Please continue with what you did," Pagano says.

"Detective Lott and I put the defendant in our car and drove him to the station."

"How did he seem to you during the drive? What was his demeanor?"

"He seemed fine. Day at the beach."

Judge McCann glares at Tredesco but holds back.

"What happened in the interrogation room?"

"He asked for a lawyer as soon as he sat down."

"Mr. McFarland?"

"No. He didn't come into the picture until the next day. The lawyer who came that night was someone else."

"What did you do until the lawyer arrived?"

"We had the defendant change out of his bloody clothes. We placed them in an evidence bag for CSU and gave him an orange jumpsuit."

"And once the lawyer arrived?"

"That was it as far as getting any information from Nunzio. So Detective Lott and I went back to the crime scene. CSU was just finishing up, and we were allowed inside."

Pagano has Tredesco describe what he observed inside the warehouse—the shelves of drugs, the kitchenette, the living room furniture, and the blood-soaked rug. Then he takes the detective through his investigation over the next few weeks: his inability to speak with Christina Nunzio at HUP because she was heavily medicated and supposedly had suffered a mental breakdown; his interview with security guard Rodger Carey; his failed attempts afterward to locate and speak with Johnny Giacobetti; his failed attempts to get through to Frank Valiante once he learned that the victim was Valiante's son.

"Those mafia guys aren't keen on helping the police," he says. Then he mumbles under his breath, "Surprise, surprise."

Mick doesn't even bother to object.

"Did there come a point when you, as the lead detective on the case, learned the results of the analysis of Mr. Nunzio's phone?"

"Yes. A few days after the crime, I was provided a copy of the CSU report on it. The defendant received a call at 9:22 p.m. The call lasted about thirty seconds. A second call, lasting one minute and forty seconds, was placed from his phone at 9:58."

"Did you learn where the first call came from? Or to whom the second call was placed?"

"No, both involved burner phones. Nunzio's own phone was also a burner."

Pagano pauses. "Did you continue to try to speak with Mr. Giacobetti and Ms. Nunzio?"

"Yes. But the daughter disappeared from the hospital after about two days. And no one seemed to have any idea where Giacobetti was, at least until he was shot outside the defendant's office and taken to the hospital."

"Did you speak with him there?"

"Mr. McFarland had lawyers parked in his hospital room, and they wouldn't let us."

Pagano shakes his head disapprovingly. "How about Frank Valiante? Did he ever make himself available to speak with you about the enmity between him and the defendant?"

"He wouldn't talk to us any more than Nunzio would. Then he allegedly shot himself, right about the same time his younger son and his whole crew mysteriously disappeared."

Tredesco slowly turns his head toward Nunzio, and the jury follows with their eyes. The message is clear: Nunzio was somehow behind Frank Valiante's death and the disappearance and likely killing of his men.

Mick considers objecting but decides doing so would only make the point that much stronger.

"Detective, would you please summarize the results of your investigation, and place them in a timeline?"

"Sure. At 9:22 p.m., on the evening of April tenth, while at his office on Crescent Drive in the Naval Yard, the defendant received a call on his burner phone from another burner phone. Three minutes later, at approximately 9:25 p.m., the defendant and John Giacobetti were seen running from the building and toward the parking lot by the security guard in the building next door. At 9:58 p.m., the defendant placed a call from his burner phone to a third burner phone. Shortly after 10:00 p.m., patrolmen Piccone and Trumbull noticed a car parked outside a supposedly abandoned building off Admiral Peary Way and then drove up to investigate. When they arrived, they found a Cadillac Escalade, which turned out to be owned by a company registered with the Commonwealth of Pennsylvania Corporation Bureau as being owned by Modern Innovations, Inc., the same name on the door of Mr. Nunzio's office. While standing by the Escalade, Officers Piccone and Trumbull heard a woman crying inside the building, and they saw a light coming through a busted door and doorframe. They immediately entered the building and observed a young woman, who turned out to be Christina Nunzio, sitting on the floor and cradling the body of Antonio Valiante. They observed a large cut wound in Valiante's throat and fresh blood coming from that wound. They also observed cut wounds to the victim's wrists and ankles, and two sets of plasticuffs nearby on the floor. After a few seconds, they noticed the defendant, James Nunzio, standing twenty feet away, holding a knife and covered in blood. CSU forensics identified the blood on the knife, and on the defendant, and on the floor and carpet, as that of the decedent, Antonio Valiante. CSU forensics also determined that the only fingerprints on the knife belonged to the defendant.

"The forensic blood and DNA evidence, and the records of Nunzio's cell phone, of course, came in later, after the arrest."

"Once you obtained the phone records, what was your operating theory?"

"That Nunzio had one or more of his guys following Antonio Valiante, hoping to catch him when he was vulnerable. They tailed Valiante and Nunzio's daughter to the warehouse and called Nunzio, who raced there with the intent to kill Valiante. Based on that intent, the homicide charges were upgraded to murder one."

Mick takes note that Pagano doesn't bring up the second call on Nunzio's burner, the one he placed himself while he was at the warehouse. He thinks that's odd, given that Pagano mentioned the call in his opening statement.

"In your investigation, did you find any evidence to discount or disprove this?"

"No."

"Any evidence the call to Nunzio's cell phone came from someone other than an agent of James Nunzio?"

"No."

"Any evidence that Nunzio's purpose in going to the warehouse was anything other than to kill Valiante?"

Mick stands. "Objection. All of this is speculation—unsupported opinion disguised as questions pretending to inquire as to actual evidence."

"It's a close call, but I'll overrule the objection," says Judge McCann. "To be fair about it, you'll be allowed to engage in reciprocal questioning on cross-examination." Turning to Tredesco, she says, "The witness may answer the question."

"I uncovered no evidence that Nunzio's reason for going to the warehouse was to do anything else but take the life of the decedent."

The judge calls a quick break so she can take an important phone call, telling everyone to remain seated until she returns. Ten minutes later, she resumes the bench and tells Pagano to continue. He asks Tredesco a few more cleanup questions, then tells the judge he's finished.

Mick waits for Pagano to take his seat. Then he stands and walks toward the witness stand.

"Detective Tredesco, you testified that your partner in the investigation for this case was Greg Lott. Is he here today?"

"No. We're no longer partners."

"How long was he your partner?"

"About two months. Up to a few weeks ago."

"Who was your partner before Detective Lott?"

"That would've been Detective Smith. William."

"How long was he your partner?"

"About three months."

"And before Detective Smith?"

"Detective Milone. Stephen."

"How long did he last with you?"

Pagano is on his feet. "Objection, Your Honor."

"Sustained. Mr. McFarland, you know better."

He apologizes, then turns to the jury and smiles. They all smile back. He couldn't pull that type of move on a witness the jury liked, but there was no danger of that with Tredesco.

"You say that once Mr. Nunzio's lawyer arrived, you and Detective Lott returned to the crime scene? And CSU was already cleaning up?"

"Yes."

"How long did you have Mr. Nunzio wait in the interrogation room before you came in to talk to him and he told you he wanted a lawyer?"

"Well, I had a lot of paperwork to do, in opening the case, before I could talk to the defendant."

"How long?"

Tredesco's eyes narrow. "About three hours."

"So Mr. Nunzio sat in the little interrogation room in bloody clothes for three hours?"

"I suppose."

"Did you bring him any water? Ask him if he needed a bathroom break?"

"No, and I didn't call over to the Ritz to bring him room service, either."

The judge sighs and leans toward the witness. "Just answer the question."

"The answer is no. I didn't bring him water or let him go to the bathroom."

"And why should you, right? I mean, you'd already convicted him of first-degree murder, in your mind."

Tredesco crosses his arms and raises his chin in indignation. "I didn't convict him of anything. That's the jury's job."

"Detective Tredesco, you were asked on direct about your 'operating theory' about who placed the call to Mr. Nunzio's cell phone and what Mr. Nunzio's purpose was in going to the warehouse. And you said you found no evidence to contradict your theories. You remember those questions?"

"Yes."

"Did you find any evidence to support your theory about who it was that called Mr. Nunzio?"

"I mean, it's common sense. Whoever called him knew the number of his anonymous burner phone, so it had to be one of his guys."

"Which one?"

Tredesco shrugs.

"You don't know because you never connected the phone that placed the call with any specific person, did you?"

Tredesco shrugs again.

"Answer the question, Detective. Do you or do you not know the identity of the person who called Mr. Nunzio?"

Tredesco shifts on his seat. "I do not know the person by name, no."

Mick pauses, turns back to the counsel table, and pretends to look at his notes. Remembering what Christina told him outside the Nunzio mansion—about the bullshit her father fed her to get Valiante to the warehouse—he asks, "Is it possible that Mr. Nunzio's purpose in going to the warehouse was to make *peace* with Antonio Valiante?"

"You're kidding, right?"

"Answer the question."

Tredesco exhales loudly. "No, in my opinion, it is not possible."

"Did you interview any witness who told you that Mr. Nunzio had expressed a purpose that was something other than reaching an accord, making a deal, with Antonio Valiante?"

Tredesco stares. "I mean, the proof is in the pudding. He killed the guy. He didn't take him to The Hague and sign a treaty."

Mick hears the laughter from the gallery and sees some of the jurors chuckling, but he presses on.

"Just as things aren't always as they seem, things don't always turn out as you plan, right, Detective?"

"I don't understand what you're asking."

"In your so-called investigation, did you consider that Mr. Nunzio went to the warehouse with a hope to make peace but things didn't turn out as he'd planned?"

"Things turned out as he *made* them turn out."

Mick ignores the answer and says, "You're aware that Mr. Nunzio was in possession of the pistol when he went to the warehouse?"

"Absolutely."

"And yet, despite your theory that he went to the warehouse to kill Mr. Valiante, he obviously did not enter the warehouse with his gun blazing?"

"I don't know what he did."

"The gun had not been fired, there were no bullets found at the warehouse, and no powder residue on the defendant, isn't that true?"

"Sure, but so what?"

"If Mr. Nunzio had intended to kill Mr. Valiante, he certainly would have used his readily available gun, not a knife."

Tredesco scolds him with a shake of the head. "He brought the gun to subdue the victim. Then, once he was subdued and secured with the plasticuffs, he went to work with the knife."

Mick blinks. *That is a plausible answer to the gun issue. Damn.*

"Doesn't it seem more plausible that Nunzio brought the gun because he couldn't be certain what he was walking into? And that Valiante pulled the knife on him once he was there? That they fought and Valiante ended up dead?"

"What seems plausible to me, counselor, from everything I learned in my investigation, and from what I already knew about your client, is that Valiante was horning in on Nunzio's home turf and shtupping his daughter at the same time and had to be taught a lesson—up close and personal."

They go back and forth, neither giving an inch, until the judge tells Mick to move on.

"Let's talk for a few moments about John Giacobetti. Do you know who he is?"

"Everyone in law enforcement knows Johnny Giacobetti."

"He was at the warehouse with Mr. Nunzio, wasn't he?"

"We found no evidence of that. And since we couldn't talk to him—"

"You're referring to when he was in the hospital?"

"In the hospital and guarded by your associate there, Mr. Coburn, and your other associate, the woman."

"Guarded because he'd been *shot*. And heavily sedated."

"He wasn't sedated when he skipped out. And I assume he hasn't been sedated in all the weeks since. But I haven't seen him come to the station to tell us what happened that night."

Mick moves on. He lost the last point. Simple as that.

"If Mr. Giacobetti was at the warehouse that night, isn't it possible that *he* and Valiante got into a struggle?"

"No, it's not."

"How can you be sure of that?"

Tredesco leans forward and smiles. "I'm sure because Tony Valiante ended up cut, not broken into pieces and tied up like a soft pretzel."

The laughter is quite loud, and Mick can see that even the jury is laughing with, not at, Tredesco. The dirtbag detective is beating him. Badly.

"And," Tredesco continues, though there's no question, "only one person had blood on his shoes—the defendant. I just can't see Giacobetti taking off his shoes and tiptoeing through the tulips and out the back door."

He and Tredesco go at it for another fifteen minutes, during which he gets the detective to admit that he doesn't know the identity of the person to whom Nunzio placed the call from his burner phone. Apart from that, all Mick can do is score some minor points and get Tredesco to make some snide remarks that renew the jurors' distaste for him. But whether the jurors like Tredesco or not, Mick can see that he hasn't put any real cracks in the man's testimony or in the prosecution's case.

Mick finishes, and Pagano stands.

"Detective, you were asked about the second call, the four-minute call the defendant placed from his burner phone at the warehouse. You testified you don't know who was at the other end of that call."

"For the same reason I don't know who called the defendant: because Mr. Nunzio hasn't shared that little secret."

Mick is on his feet. "Objection—"

"Nothing further," Pagano says, turning away from the witness.

"Sustained," the judge rules.

"But I know why he called," Tredesco says, his voice rising. "He called for someone to come and clean up the mess."

"Objection!" Mick shouts so loudly his voice cracks.

He glares at Tredesco, who smiles back at him, his own eyes gleaming. Now he knows why Pagano hadn't brought up the second call on direct; he and Tredesco had worked out the "cleanup" scenario and decided to end the detective's testimony with it.

Judge McCann sustains the objection, but the damage has been done.

"Mr. Pagano," the judge says, turning toward the prosecutor, "it's 4:30. There's time to start your next witness."

"Your Honor, the Commonwealth rests."

This surprises Mick. Pagano is ending the week strong, and the jury will have all weekend to chew on the strengths of the prosecution's case. But the smart play for Pagano would be to present at least one final witness on Monday, to start next week strong as well, reinforce his bond with the jury. Keeping his case open would also force the defense to spend time—drain resources—preparing to cross-examine potential prosecution witnesses. By resting now, Pagano is freeing the defense to focus on its own case. And it defines the boundaries of the prosecution's evidence, giving the defense precise knowledge of the opposing evidence as it prepares over the weekend.

Once again, Mick can't help but suspect that Pagano's up to something. Most likely some surprise move that will catch the defense off guard and seal Nunzio's fate.

39

Friday, June 21–Sunday, June 23

Judge McCann calls it a day and has the jurors sent back to their hotel, where they will remain sequestered until the end of the trial. As the courtroom clears, Mick visits Nunzio in the holding cell.

"Your thoughts?" Nunzio asks. His tone is chipper, but Mick can see worry lurking behind his dark eyes.

"I'm thinking that all I did today was toss lobs for Pagano to hit out of the ballpark."

Nunzio doesn't respond.

"You ready to tell me our endgame yet?"

The crime lord takes a deep breath, studies Mick for a moment. "You familiar with the story of the rock and the water? There was a small pool of water at the top of a hill, held back by a rock. One day the rock gets dislodged, and it and the water start down the hill. The rock says to the water, 'Let's race,' and it then rolls on ahead, straight down, and fast. The water descends in a trickle, and along the way it goes around everything in its path. It goes around trees and boulders and debris. Halfway down, it sees the rock lodged against a fallen tree, unable to move. But the water goes around the fallen tree and keeps on moving down the hill, to the bottom."

Nunzio pauses, shrugs.

"The rock couldn't change its shape to adjust to its environment. Its shape was set in stone, so to speak. But the water was malleable. It accommodated itself to its environment. It yielded to everything and was therefore stopped by nothing."

"More of your Sun Tzu bullshit?"

They stare at each other until Mick gets it.

Of course.

"The reason you haven't told me your story is because you don't know what it is."

The mobster smiles. "So you *were* paying attention."

"What happens now?"

"We feed the data into the machine and see what it spits out."

"From rocks and water to computers . . . you got metaphors galore but not much of a defense."

Nunzio shrugs him off. "Talk to Rachel and Lauren. They'll give you the answer as soon as it's ready."

"The answer," Mick says flatly.

"The road map, down the hill."

Mick stands. "I figured the jury was your ace in the hole. But I thought you'd come at them along more traditional lines—bribes or threats. Not hire jury experts to read their minds and feed them a line they're hungry for."

"It's the twenty-first century, Mick. Get with the times."

The meeting with the trial team back at the office is a short one. Somehow, Rachel and Lauren know about his conversation with Nunzio, and they tell him to sit tight; they'll reach out when they're ready, give him his battle plan. They won't say what they'll be doing in the meantime, but he suspects their plan is to run a bunch of scenarios past a full mock jury. He wonders where they'll do it. Probably some hotel conference room.

That night, after Gabby goes to bed, he vents his frustrations to Piper.

"I know exactly what Rachel Nunzio and Lauren Zito are going to do. They'll write up a handful of fictional accounts that incorporate all the facts that have come out at trial so far and run them past some mock jury and see how the fake jurors react. Then they'll hand me whichever story works best and order me to run with it—or else."

"They're going to make you suborn perjury."

He sees that the perjury play makes Piper uncomfortable, and he knows why: That's what she and Susan just did in the Dowd case. They sold a frank lie to the court. Something Piper is exquisitely aware of.

"At least there was nobility in the Dowd case," Mick says. "You and Susan broke all the rules, but you did it to save someone deserving."

"There are probably a lot of people out there who'd disagree about how deserving Darlene was."

"Well, I'm not one of them. I don't think she deserves to be in prison."

She agrees and tells him that she, Susan, and Darlene are still waiting to hear back from the court. "Every day that passes makes me more nervous the judge will change her mind and deny our motion," she says.

He tells her that's not going to happen, and they switch topics and finish their wine. When they go upstairs for bed, Piper surprises him.

"I want to come in when you read to Gabby tonight," she says.

"I already read with her, when I put her to bed."

"But sometimes you read to her after she's asleep, too. Tonight, let's do it together."

They brush their teeth and change, then sit together on Gabrielle's bed. Mick reaches out for Piper's hand, and they watch Gabby breathe for a while.

"She's growing up so fast," Piper says.

He nods. "She'll be a teenager soon."

"She won't want to hear anything we have to say."

The remark causes his mind to jump back to the night he happened upon Christina Nunzio, sitting in the dark on the porch at the lodge.

He looks at Piper. "Probably. But let's make sure we hear what she says. Not close our ears to her, or our eyes."

Piper looks at him, confused.

"Never mind," he says. "I'm just tired."

He opens the Harry Potter book, hands it to her.

"Start here."

It's an unusually hot Sunday afternoon, temperatures hovering in the high eighties. Mick and Piper are sitting at the table on the back patio, drinking adult lemonades and watching Gabby dance circles around Tommy in their backyard. Tommy, sweating and breathing heavily, is positioned between Gabby and a soccer net. She glances up at Mick and Piper and winks, then dribbles the soccer ball past Tommy with ease and drills it into the net.

"You better take a break," Mick calls to his brother with a smile.

"Come up and have some lemonade," Piper says.

"Five more minutes," Tommy yells. "Forget the lemonade, though. I'll need a cold beer."

Piper goes inside to the refrigerator as Mick's cell phone rings.

"Mick." It's Rachel Nunzio. "Check your email."

He bolts out of his chair and races into the house, to his home office. He opens the laptop on his desk and boots it up. There's an email from Lauren Zito in his in-box. He clicks it open and finds a fifteen-page script—the questions he's to ask and the answers the witness will give.

"Christina." He says the name aloud.

Tommy and Piper both appear in the doorway.

"What's up?" Tommy asks as they enter and stand before his desk.

"The Nunzios finally figured out their play," he says. "I'm to call one witness: Christina."

"Damn," Tommy says. "I didn't think Jimmy would use her."

"Why? Because she's his daughter? The prick used her to lure Valiante to the warehouse, what started this whole thing. Now he's going to use her to try to save his ass from prison."

"I can't believe her mother doesn't put a stop to it," Piper says.

"Are you kidding? She's as bad as Nunzio. *This*," he adds, holding up the pages, "is her work. Her and that psycho jury-whisperer they hired."

"What are you going to do?" Tommy asks.

Mick glances at the photograph of Gabby on his desk. In a silver frame, it shows her in her soccer uniform, holding the ball, with a huge smile on her face. He closes his eyes.

This is so fucked-up.

"I'm going to play the only card the Nunzios gave me. The Queen of Clubs."

40

Monday, June 24

The courtroom is full, and Nunzio is already at the defense table when Mick enters and takes his seat. He's told Vaughn to sit in the spectators' gallery next to Rachel Nunzio and Lauren Zito and keep tabs on them.

He pulls his legal pad from his leather satchel and waits for the judge to take the bench. His hands folded in front of him, he stares straight ahead. He hasn't greeted his client. The judge is long in entering the courtroom, and he grows impatient. Finally, Mick turns slightly toward Nunzio and asks under his breath, "Are you sure you want to do this?"

Nunzio doesn't answer, just clenches his fists.

"She's your daughter, for God's sake. Not a sacrificial lamb."

Nunzio turns to him. There is death in his eyes. "You have no idea what sacrifices are being made here."

Mick doesn't know what to say.

Nunzio leans toward him, almost imperceptibly. "Just play your part."

He turns around, catches Rachel and Lauren Zito both staring at him. He narrows his eyes and turns back around. He hates them all.

Judge McCann appears from behind the bench, and the court crier announces her. Once the judge is seated, the bailiff brings in the jurors.

Mick watches them walk to the jury box and take their seats. Only a few of the jurors look back at him. None of them smiles. Aaron Burnett keeps his eyes on Nunzio.

"Mr. McFarland, call your first witness," the judge says from the bench.

"The defense calls Christina Nunzio."

"Objection! Objection!" Pagano is on his feet and racing toward the bench. "I'd like a sidebar."

McCann calls Mick up and asks Pagano what his objection is.

"I was told the daughter wouldn't be a witness! I expressly asked, and defense counsel told me he wasn't presenting her."

"Is that true, Mr. McFarland?"

"No. Mr. Pagano approached me and my client just before his opening on Friday and told Mr. Nunzio that he'd subpoenaed his daughter. Mr. Nunzio, as a father, was upset and simply said, 'You're not getting Christina.' At no point did I say that *I* wasn't going to present Christina Nunzio as a witness in my case in chief."

Pagano's face is red with rage. "But, but—"

"Mr. McFarland," the judge asks, "is Ms. Nunzio's name on your witness list?"

"Everyone and his brother is on the defendant's witness list!" says Pagano.

"Yes, Your Honor, Ms. Nunzio is on my list," Mick says.

"That's it, then. She can testify. Have her take the stand."

Mick and Pagano turn away from the bench.

"This is bullshit," Pagano mutters.

The door at the rear of the courtroom opens, and everyone turns to watch Christina make her appearance.

Mick takes her in as she passes by the jury box. She looks ghastly. Her face is pale and drawn with fatigue. She carries herself with the slow and careful gait of someone navigating a boat deck in rough seas.

So different from the sure-footed gazelle who schooled Gabby on soccer. Mick wonders whether she's on medication, or whether Rachel and Lauren Zito worked her to exhaustion as they drilled her on her lines. Or whether it's simply that it has all finally caught up with her: witnessing her father murder her lover; the pathological control both of her parents have exercised over her throughout her life; the gilded cage she's grown up in, paid for with blood spilled by generations of her mob family. He might have suspected it's all a performance, except that Christina's endured so much for so long that it only makes sense she'd be broken in the end.

"Would you like some water?" the judge asks solicitously after Christina assumes the stand and is sworn in.

"Yes, please, Your Honor," Christina says, her voice barely above a whisper.

The bailiff pours her a glass from a pitcher, and everyone waits for her to take a sip and ready herself.

"Mr. McFarland?"

"Thank you, Your Honor. Ms. Nunzio, are you the daughter of the defendant, James Nunzio?"

"Yes. I am. His daughter." Her words are halting and nervous.

"And how old are you?"

"I'm twenty-five."

"Christina, do you know what your father does for a living?"

She looks down, in embarrassment, and lowers her voice. "I think so. I know what I've read. And I've . . . I've overheard things."

"Did any of the things you read, or overheard, play a part in what happened on April tenth of this year?"

She takes a deep breath. "Yes."

"Tell us."

"I knew my father's . . . family . . . was at odds with another family, because of what Tony . . . what Antonio Valiante was doing."

"When you say your father's 'family,' do you mean the Giansante crime family? And the other family is the Savonna family?"

"Yes."

"What was your understanding of what Antonio Valiante was doing?"

"He was coming into my father's territory."

Mick pauses. "And what did you hear about how your father's 'family' was taking this?"

"Objection!" Pagano shouts. "This is all hearsay. Out-of-court statements."

"No, Your Honor," Mick says. "I'm not asking what she heard to determine truth, only to establish that she heard them and that they spoke to her motivation."

The judge overrules the objection, and Pagano throws down his pen.

"Mr. Pagano." It's the judge, leaning over the bench. "Pick up the pen."

"What?"

"Pick. Up. The. Pen."

Pagano's eyes flare as he does so.

"Now. Lay down the pen. Gently."

He complies, and Mick can see it takes all of Pagano's self-control not to throw it at the judge.

"Thank you. Now, Mr. McFarland, please proceed."

"Christina, what did you hear about how your father and his people felt about Mr. Valiante's invasion of their territory?"

"There was talk of a war. Not that my father wanted it, but that he was worried there would be one."

Mick nods. "Now, let's talk about Antonio Valiante."

At the mention of his name, Christina seems to shrink into herself, and Mick knows that everyone in the courtroom can see she's in pain. He alone knows that part of it must be her having to go along with the bullshit script she's being forced to act out.

"You knew who he was? That he was in the same line of work as your father?"

"Yes."

"And as you already testified, you knew about the enmity between Mr. Valiante's people and your father's?"

"Yes."

"And you knew about the personal enmity between Antonio and your father?"

She glances at Nunzio, her eyes filled with sadness. "Yes."

"And yet you were dating Antonio?"

She turns to her father again. "I fell in love with him."

Mick lets the words hang in the air.

"He made me laugh," Christina starts up again. "There was so always much stress, so much tension in my family. Everyone so serious. For as long as I could remember. But Tony was lighthearted. He joked around, made me laugh. And he listened to me. He understood me."

Mick follows Christina's eyes back to her father, and he sees Nunzio's face tighten.

Christina takes another sip of water.

"Now, Christina, please tell the jury what happened on the night of April tenth."

"A sidebar, please, Your Honor." It's Pagano.

Mick glances at the jury on the way to the bench. They know they're at the crux of the whole case, and they're not happy about Pagano's delays. He's surprised that Pagano is behaving this way; Christina's testimony will be all the more impactful for the delays. Pagano must really be sweating.

At sidebar, Pagano looks up at the judge and says, "Can defense counsel be told to stop calling her Christina? She's not ten."

Judge McCann nods. "He's right, Mr. McFarland. Don't refer to the witness by her first name."

Mick and the prosecutor return to their respective tables, and he continues his questioning.

"The night of April tenth. Tell the jury what happened."

"Like I said, I had heard talk of a war. I was afraid a lot of people would get hurt. That Tony would get hurt. Or my father. I thought . . . I thought if only I could bring my father and Tony together, they could work something out . . ." She lowers her head.

Mick lets the word hang for a moment, then asks, "What did you do?"

"Tony's father insisted he not go anywhere without bodyguards. But Tony hated it, and sometimes we would sneak away together for a few hours by ourselves. Tony convinced the bodyguards not to tell his father. That night was one of those times. Tony and I went to the warehouse to be alone." She takes a drink of water, and Mick can see that her hand is shaking.

"My father's office was only a mile away. I figured it was an opportunity to try to bring him and Tony together. So I called my father."

"The call to his cell phone that night, at 9:22—that was you?"

Christina nods, and the courtroom stirs. One of the central mysteries of the case has just been solved. Mick glances over at Pagano, who sits as still as a rock, paralyzed by fury.

"I told my father where I was, and that I was with Tony. I told him they should meet with no one else around, and this would be the perfect time. He was upset, but he said he'd come right over. He didn't tell me he was going to bring Johnny." She shakes her head. "The next thing I knew, Johnny came crashing through the front door, and my father came in through the back. Tony thought I'd set him up. He grabbed me and started cursing at me." Christina's eyes well up, and tears begin sliding down her face. "Johnny pulled Tony off me and tied him up with the plastic things—"

"The plasticuffs?"

She nods. "He gagged him, too. Then my father got in my face, and he started yelling. He said Tony was just using me. How could I be so naïve?"

Here, Christina looks at the defense table, where Jimmy sits with his head bowed and his eyes closed.

"I tried to get him to calm down. I explained again that I just wanted him and Tony to talk so they could find a way to prevent a war. But my father wasn't listening. He started pacing around the room, shaking his head, trying to figure out what to do. Johnny asked if he should *take care of* Tony, and I started crying because I knew what that meant. But my father said no. He wasn't to be harmed."

Christina starts to hyperventilate, and Judge McCann asks her if she'd like a minute. She nods, and everyone waits for her to regain her composure.

"What happened next?" Mick finally asks.

"My father told Johnny to leave, to go to 'our place' and call the men there, get ready in case something bad went down. There were vans parked out back, and my father must have seen them when he came in because he told Johnny to leave their car and take one of the vans. Johnny left, and my father came over and stood by Tony."

"What was Tony doing?"

"He was screaming through his gag and trying to break out of the restraints. My father told him to calm down. He said if he kept a cool head, everyone would get out of this okay. Then my father told me he was going to make a call."

"Did he say who he was going to call?"

Pagano objects on grounds of hearsay. The judge overrules him.

"He said he was going to call Tony's father, see if he could fix things so that no one got hurt."

Mick pauses to let the jury consider this. He hears murmuring in the courtroom. A second mystery of the case—who Nunzio called from the warehouse—has been solved.

"Tell us what happened next."

Christina takes a deep breath.

"My father went out back, and I sat on the couch near Tony. He was looking up at me, from the floor. There was so much pain in his eyes, and fear. He thought I'd betrayed him, and he thought my father was going to come back and kill him. I told him I just wanted peace, just wanted him and my father to talk, and that he would be all right. But then I thought about it and I . . . I wasn't sure what my father was going to do. I was afraid he'd kill Tony after all. Tony kept a small knife in his boot, and I pulled it out and told him I'd cut him free if he promised just to leave, to run away. He nodded, so I cut the cuffs."

Mick glances around. The courtroom is perfectly still. Everyone is sitting forward, motionless, hanging on Christina's words.

"Tony stood up just as my father came in through the front door. Tony grabbed the knife from me and ran at my father. My father grabbed Tony's knife arm, and Tony grabbed my father's other arm. They struggled like that, standing up. Tony was crazy by then. He kept telling my father, 'I'll kill you! I'll kill you!' And I knew he might if it went on long enough, because Tony was strong.

"They were moving as they were struggling, and they came to the carpet. They both went down, and I started screaming. I turned away and closed my eyes. And the next thing I heard was Tony choking. I opened my eyes and looked over and . . . and . . ."

Christina's face is white. She looks like she's ready to faint or throw up.

Mick steps back, gives her time to gather herself, exactly as the script instructed.

"What happened next?"

"My father stood up and kind of stumbled backward. He was out of breath, and he bent over. I ran to Tony and sat down on the floor, and I pulled him to me. I couldn't stop crying, shouting at my father. The next thing I knew, the police were there."

By this time, Mick has moved right up alongside the witness box. When Christina stops talking, he waits a moment, then reaches over and covers her hand with his own. He looks up at the judge.

"Nothing further."

The judge waits for Mick to sit, then looks at the prosecution table. Before she even says his name, Pagano is on his feet, marching toward the witness box, his face contorted in anger.

"So your father's completely innocent, and it's all *your* fault? That's the story you've come up with?"

"Objection!" Mick growls. "He's harassing the witness."

"Ramp it down, Mr. Pagano," the judge instructs.

Pagano stands still, his chest heaving. He asks his next question through his teeth. "There wasn't a mark on your father, do you know that?"

She shakes her head.

"No punch wounds or scratches or anything on the victim, either."

"They weren't hitting each other. They were, like, wrestling."

Pagano attacks for another five minutes, but all he accomplishes is to make Christina look more and more pathetic and reveal himself as a heartless bully. Finally, exasperated, he turns his back on her and sits.

"We're going to take a break now," the judge says. "I want everyone back in twenty minutes. The witness may leave the stand to use the restroom if she so desires."

Christina slowly rises, steps down from the witness stand, and walks out of the courtroom. No one moves until the courtroom door closes behind her.

The deputies move up to take Nunzio back to his holding cell.

"A minute, please, with my lawyer," Nunzio tells them. They stand back.

Mick knows that it's not him Nunzio really wants to talk to; together they wait for Rachel Nunzio and Lauren Zito to pass through the bar and gather around the defense table.

"Well?" Nunzio asks Zito.

She looks down, slowly shakes her head. "I'm sorry."

"They didn't buy it?" Nunzio asks.

"Not to the point that you can stake the next twenty years on it."

Nunzio turns away from the jury-whisperer. Mick watches the mobster and his wife stare at each other for a long moment. Then, Nunzio nods and moves toward the deputies, who take him to his holding cell.

When he's gone, Lauren Zito says, "The jury may not have fallen for it, but it sure seems like *he* did."

Mick follows her gaze to Max Pagano, who paces back and forth in front of the prosecutor's table.

"I think he believes it went down just like Christina testified," she says in a low voice. "I think he believes Jimmy killed Valiante in self-defense. It's why he's so pissed off. He knows he has to put Jimmy in jail—his career depends on it."

His eyes glued to Pagano, Mick says, "I don't get it. What the hell is he seeing that we're not seeing?"

Pagano turns and sees McFarland staring at him. Then he strides out of the courtroom and takes the stairs down to the ninth floor, where he pulls out his cell phone. He dials Emlin Fellner's cell number. When the district attorney answers, he lays it out.

"We're fucked."

"What?"

"The daughter testified, and we lost the fucking jury. They believe Nunzio killed Valiante in self-defense. Worse yet, I think it's true." He explains Christina's testimony, sensing Fellner's panic rise by the minute on the other end of the phone. "I think he's going to walk."

"Fuck that. I promised the whole city Nunzio was going to prison."

Pagano listens but doesn't answer.

"Get him to plead!"

"He'll never plead now. Not after what I just saw."

"He'll plead to something! He's facing the needle. Get it done!"

Pagano hears the phone go dead. He stands for a long moment, then walks back up the stairs and enters the courtroom. McFarland is behind the bar now, standing with his hard-case brother and his associate, Coburn. He approaches them and looks at Mick.

"Let's talk."

Two hours later, the news of Nunzio's plea to involuntary manslaughter sweeps the city. It's the top story on the local midday news programs, both cable and network, and the lead on Philly.com, the internet site of the *Inquirer* and *Daily News*. Trying to jump out ahead of the story, a pale Emlin Fellner holds a press conference, declaring that the eighteen-to-twenty-four-month sentence Nunzio will likely get is "the victory over organized crime our city has been waiting for." No one believes him, and his poll numbers drop precipitously.

It's 7:00 p.m. when Mick enters the Ranstead Room. It's light outside, but the upscale, speakeasy-style bar is dark, and it takes his eyes a while to adjust. It's early enough that the bar is almost empty, which adds to the sense that it's a real hideaway. He makes his way to one of the red-chaired booths and waits.

The courtroom thug enters at the same time the waiter brings Mick his tumbler of Macallan 18.

"Whatever he's having," Pagano tells the waiter as he walks up, "bring me something better."

Mick takes a sip of the single-malt scotch and waits.

"How did you know?" Pagano asks.

"After we were done with the judge, I saw you glance back at Rachel and Lauren, and something passed between the three of you. Then it hit me. *You* were Nunzio's ace. The whole thing with the jury consultant was a feint. Well, not a complete feint. The Nunzios hired Zito to tell them whether Christina's story worked with the jury. If it did—if they were *certain* it did—Jimmy would take the verdict. But if they weren't sure the jury bought it, you were in the wings, ready to tell Fellner you'd lost the jury, that the case was about to crash and burn. He'd panic and tell you to take a plea, any plea, that would get Jimmy jail time." Mick takes a sip. "Did I get it right?"

"Pretty close." Pagano smiles. "How'd you like my act on cross?"

"It was good. You seemed crazy, pissed off, scared. Lauren Zito said it looked like you actually believed Christina was telling the truth." He pauses. "I did some checking on you after the trial. You grew up in South Philly, same as Nunzio and Zito. But he's ten years older than you, and she's five. Any chance you knew them growing up?"

"I knew of Nunzio, of course." He smiles. "As for Lauren, she was the best babysitter I ever had. She let me sip my old man's booze. Even showed me her tits sometimes. All I had to do was keep quiet about her having her boyfriend over. Man, those two would screw for hours."

Mick shakes his head. "The story they finally came up with . . . ?"

"Took a lot of work, from what I understand. Lauren and Rachel flew Christina to the West Coast, where no one knows about the case.

Lauren ran a bunch of mock juries, had Christina up on the stand selling a bunch of different stories. There was a jealous-Giacobetti tale, and a version where Valiante set it all up as a trap for Nunzio. But the story that sold the best was the one you heard today: naïve Christina sues for peace."

"Meanwhile, the real story—that Nunzio used his daughter to lure Valiante into a trap—gets buried."

Pagano shrugs.

Mick shakes his head. "Christina . . ."

"I feel bad for her. I really do. Still . . ."

"A pit of fucking snakes I fell into," Mick says.

"You walked into it. Willingly. How much did the Nunzios lay out? A hundred K? Two hundred?"

"Nowhere near enough."

The waiter brings Pagano a glass of high-end scotch, and he takes a long swallow.

"Do the Nunzios know you figured it out?"

"No," Mick answers. "And I'd be grateful if you didn't tell them."

"That might be a problem. I just tendered my resignation to the DA. I'm one of Jimmy's lawyers now. I'll be on the QT about it for a while, of course."

"So that's what it was about for you? Money?"

"I have three daughters. Each one smarter than the next. You know what college costs these days?"

Mick stares at him.

Pagano takes another sip. Then: "It's been what, ten years since you switched sides, sold your soul?"

"I didn't lose my soul when I left the DA's office," Mick answers.

That came later.

They sit in silence until their glasses are empty. Mick tosses a fifty on the table and stands.

"Be careful, Mick," Pagano says, looking up at him.

"You're the one has to be careful. I'm done with the Nunzios."

Pagano smiles ruefully. "You're never done."

Mick can see from the look in Pagano's eyes that he knows the price he's going to pay for his daughters' education.

41

Friday, June 29

Tommy sits on his screened-in porch, throwing back a Budweiser. A storm is blowing in from the west, and the skies are growing darker. Earlier that morning, he spoke with Mick. The Nunzio thing is weighing heavily on his brother. He can't seem to get past what Jimmy Nunzio did to his own daughter. First subjecting her to the horror of Tony Valiante's murder, then throwing her under the bus at trial.

"He's a monster, and I let myself become his stooge," Mick said.

"You were his lawyer, and you did your job. That's all."

They went back and forth about it, but the call ended with Mick seeming to feel as bad as he had at the start.

Fortunately, Susan and Piper are another story. The Darlene Dowd ordeal has helped bridge the divide that opened between Piper and Tommy as a result of the David Hanson fiasco. He came clean to her about the anger he harbored and apologized for being such a jerk.

"It just got to the point for me that I didn't know how to come back to you," he told her. "Our friendship saved me when I was in prison and helped me rejoin the living once I got out, and I value it more than anything. I guess it's a sad testament to me that I was willing to throw it away the first time it was tested."

He asked for her forgiveness, and Piper granted it without hesitation.

He thinks about calling her now, but he knows she's on her way to the women's prison in Muncy with Susan, and that they probably need time together to talk about that mess. He wonders whether, as part of it, Susan will open up to Piper about her own issues, much as she did with Tommy in her apartment the night he and Mick confronted Martin Brenner.

Susan's life was defined by her father's abandonment when she was young. It left her feeling unprotected and unsafe, even as she despised her father's weakness. Apparently, Susan compensated for this by seeking out alpha males in relationships, which resulted in a long series of self-involved lovers who had little interest in anything but themselves.

They talked some more about it at the office, after the Darlene Dowd hearing. Susan told him about her decision to save Darlene even though she knew Darlene was guilty of killing her father. Even though it meant betraying her own principles by misleading the court.

"It's hard enough to do the right thing to save someone," she told him. "It's even harder to do the wrong thing to save them. It was for me, anyway."

"You certainly pay a high price for it," he said.

She waited for him to explain, but he didn't. She didn't press.

He empties his beer and shakes his head, thinking about the terrible things he's done for the people he loves. But maybe that's the test of love: that you care so much for someone you'll risk your very soul for them.

About 170 miles northwest, Piper and Susan are sitting in Piper's Range Rover, waiting for Darlene Dowd to walk through the gates of SCI

Muncy. It's pouring rain, and the wipers move noisily back and forth across the windshield.

Piper shipped a duffel bag with a change of clothes to the prison earlier in the week so Darlene would have something decent to wear. On the way to the prison, she and Susan stopped at the Lycoming Mall and bought her some more clothes, along with toiletries and a few pieces of inexpensive jewelry.

During their calls following the hearing, Piper offered to put Darlene up for a few weeks or more near Philadelphia, help her find a job, then an apartment. Darlene thanked her profusely but told Piper that she was going to make it on her own—all she wanted was a ride to the Greyhound bus station in Williamsport.

"There she is," Susan says.

Piper gets out and runs to Darlene. She covers them both with her umbrella. They walk back to the car, and Piper starts the sixteen-mile trip to Williamsport.

"The suitcase on the seat is for you," Susan says. "Some more clothes and personal items."

Darlene thanks them and they make small talk, Piper and Susan telling Darlene she looks great, Darlene saying she's been working hard to lose weight and is planning to join a gym when she settles down.

After a while, she says, "I feel terrible about Lois—I mean, Megan."

Megan Corbett, a.k.a. Lois Beal, a.k.a. Terri Petrini will likely spend the rest of her life in prison. Alan Kane, the United States attorney for the Central District of California, is a Bush II law-and-order appointee who made it clear to Megan that unless she quickly pled to one count of felony murder, he would try her on two counts and a dozen other offenses as well. She gave in and will formally plead and be sentenced a few weeks hence.

"I spoke with her by phone on Wednesday," Piper tells Darlene. "She told me she's at peace. She said for the first time in decades she feels like she's not living life as an impostor. That she's back to being Megan Corbett. That people can see her for who she is."

Darlene thinks this over, and they sit quietly for a few minutes. Then Piper pulls the car up to the bus-station underpass. All three get out. They hug, and Piper and Susan watch as Darlene turns away. She takes a couple of steps, then turns back.

"It's funny," Darlene says. "Megan is happy to finally be herself. What I want is just the opposite. I want to go someplace where no one knows who I am. Where I can look into someone's eyes and not see pity, or fear. Someplace where I can reinvent myself and leave Darlene Dowd and all of the rest of it behind me."

She thinks a minute, and it seems as if she's going to say something more, but she doesn't. Darlene Dowd simply turns, walks into the station, and disappears.

42

Friday, July 18; Wednesday, April 10

"I really don't feel comfortable with this," Piper says, glancing at Mick from the passenger seat. They're in his car, driving south on I-476.

"I don't, either," he says. "But I think we should just look and see what's out there."

They are on their way to a small gun shop located in Prospect Park, about twenty miles south of Mick and Piper's house in Wayne. Mick first brought up the idea of them arming themselves the week after the Nunzio trial. He was still unnerved by how easy it was for Nunzio's goons to waltz into his house the night they forced Gabby and him to go to the lodge in the Poconos.

They went around and around over the idea of bringing guns into their home. Neither felt good about it, but both thought that maybe it was time they opened their eyes. They knew that a fair number of their friends owned guns for self-protection, and many even had licenses to carry. In the end, they agreed to meet with someone knowledgeable about firearms who could fit them with the proper weapons in case they decided to move forward. Mick's former client has a brother, Butch, who owns a gun shop. Mick called him to set up a visit.

Mick pulls into a small space beside the gun store, which is housed in a white stucco building with a red door. Butch has the door open before they reach it. He's a large man in his fifties, with a ruddy face and a big smile. He shakes hands with Mick and Piper and welcomes them inside.

Mick already explained his situation over the phone, so Butch knows they may or may not actually buy any weapons. He tells them now that he's good with that and says, "This will be more of an educational session."

On the glass counter, Butch has already laid out two sets of weapons, one for Mick and one for Piper. He asks who he should start with, and Mick tells him to begin with Piper.

"Okay. Well, I've got four pieces here. There's the Glock 43, the Ruger LC9s, the Kahr CW9. And, my favorite for a woman, the Sig Sauer P938 Nitron."

The same gun found on Nunzio at the warehouse.

Butch lifts the Nitron and explains that it's the smallest .9 mm weapon Sig Sauer makes, perfect for a purse. He explains its features, but none of it is registering with Mick. His mind has carried him to the Nunzios' swimming pool, where Uncle Ham told him about Jimmy's "bar mitzvah," when his father put a gun into his hand and told him to kill a man. He sees Christina on the sofa at the lodge, telling him it's not fair to try to make someone into something they're not. And what she said about her father not "seeing" her. He remembers what he was told about Christina being the president of her sorority, then the head of all the sororities.

He knows now what Nunzio was hiding. What he didn't want him to see.

"Monster."

"Mick?" Piper grabs his hands. "Are you okay? What's wrong?"

"Come on," he tells Piper, grabbing her hand. "We have to go. Now."

He leads her to the car and races back home. On the way, she presses him to tell her what's going on, but all he says is, "I know what happened that night. What really happened at that warehouse."

He drops Piper off, then retraces his tracks down 476 toward the airport, turning onto I-95 North, toward the Naval Yard. An hour after leaving the gun shop, he's moving down the hallway toward the offices of Modern Innovations, Inc. Through the glass door, the pretty receptionist watches him, wide-eyed, the whole way.

"I'm here to see the boss," he tells her as Johnny Giacobetti strides into the reception area.

"The boss is in prison. Did you forget?"

"I think she's right here," he answers.

The giant's eyes open as wide as those of the young woman sitting at the desk.

Giacobetti stares at him for a long moment, then shakes his head and tells Mick to wait. Five minutes later, Johnny G. returns. He searches Mick, then leads him down the hallway. When Mick enters Nunzio's office, he finds Uncle Ham sitting in one of the guest chairs in front of the desk. Behind the desk sits Rachel Nunzio.

"Sit," Giacobetti says.

He lowers himself onto the seat, and Rachel Nunzio, pen in hand, looks up from a document on her desk.

"Give me a minute," she says. "I have to finish up a contract. You know, the problem with opioids is that the product actually reduces the client base—at least that's the case with heroin and fentanyl. Marijuana users, on the other hand, seem to be multiplying like rabbits, and they stick around forever. Medical marijuana's already being legalized everywhere and is vastly profitable. I'm told that in another decade or so, the law will yawn at recreational marijuana, too. Did you know that not an hour from this office there's a perfect microclimate for cannabis? We found out not too long ago, and we're working with some local businessmen to exploit those growing conditions. We can't let the state find out about our involvement, of course. Or let the regulators learn about Mr. Stumpf's colorful past."

She pauses and smiles. Then she looks back down at the papers and pretends to track the language with her pen, which, he notices, she doesn't use to make any changes. She turns the pages one by one, then looks up at him.

"I'm told you came here to see the boss. So, how can I help you?"

He leans forward. "You can get me the boss. At least, the interim boss for the next eighteen to twenty-four months."

Rachel Nunzio's face tightens, and he sees her glance at the old man to his left. Before she can think of how to answer him, a hidden doorway in the wood paneling behind her opens, and Christina Nunzio enters the room. Without words, Rachel rises and steps away.

Christina takes the throne. She stares at Mick, her face unreadable. "So . . ."

"The gun was yours," he says. "The warehouse—it was to be your bat mitzvah."

Uncle Ham sits up straight. "Ah, you remembered." He turns to Christina. "I told him about your father's bar mitzvah."

"I hate it when you call it that," says Rachel, now standing behind Christina.

"Loose lips, Uncle Ham," Christina says in a mock-scolding tone.

The old man shrugs, but Christina apparently sees something in his eyes. "My uncle's not happy about this turn of events, Mick. Nor is my mother." She looks from one to the other and tells them, "There's nothing to worry about; we have leverage against Mr. McFarland. Speaking of which . . ." She reaches beneath the desk and lifts out a white box with a pink ribbon, sets it on the desk. "I was going to mail this to Gabby. But since you're here, you can deliver it personally. It's a soccer ball. But it's not just any ball. It's the second ball Carli Lloyd kicked through the net against Japan to win the 2012 Olympic gold medal. Signed."

"I'll be damned if I'll give my daughter this ball, or anything else from you. And don't you dare try to come near her."

Christina shrugs. "I actually think the world of Gabby. She's going to grow up to be someone special. I saw it in her eyes."

"Stop talking about my daughter," he says through clenched jaws.

She looks at him for a long moment.

"All right, Mick. Let's get to it. Yes, the gun was mine, given to me by my mother when I turned eighteen. My father took it from me in the warehouse, after—"

"You were supposed to use the gun to kill Antonio."

"Right again. My father's plan—"

"Bullshit." His voice is flat.

She sits back and stares, her eyes cold.

"Fine," she says. "Tell me what *you* think happened at the warehouse that night."

Jimmy Nunzio sits behind his desk and smiles. The transportation side of the business is booming. In the past six months, he and Uncle Ham have opened six new dark hubs in Europe, offering regional air transport, eighteen-wheelers, and smaller trucks. Even at HML, the legitimate side of the business, profits are up. The smaller, traditional side of the family business—gambling, loan-sharking, and narcotics—is also flourishing. With his don spending his days drooling into a cup, James Nunzio is the de facto head of the family, the other underbosses—with various degrees of resentment—taking direction from him. The only fly in the ointment is Frank Valiante's incursion into his territory in an attempt to slice off a big part of the opioid trade. But Nunzio has been moving out of the opioid business anyway—it's starting to kill enough people that, sooner or later, the government's going to come down hard on the pushers. In another month or so, he'll reach out to Frank's boss and offer to strike a deal whereby Frank and his sons move the product, and he gets a cut. That'll leave him more time to focus on the burgeoning medical-marijuana business, which he's going to get into in a big way, starting with his partnership with the locals in the Lehigh Valley.

He looks at his watch. It's close to 9:30. He reaches for his cell phone to tell Johnny he can go home, but the burner rings as he lifts it. He recognizes the number of the burner on the other end.

"Hey." He tries to sound upbeat. They've been fighting so much lately. Practically anything he says sets her off.

"Daddy, I need you to pay attention to what I'm going to say. I'm at the Valiantes' warehouse, with Tony, and—"

He shoots out of his seat. *"What?"*

"Just listen! I'm tired of pretending. Tired of acting like I'm some kind of brainless party girl. I'm part of our family, and it's time you brought me into the business."

"No! That's not who you are—"

"Yes, it is! I'm just like you. Just like Uncle Ham. I belong in the family, and tonight I'm going to prove it to you."

His heart is pounding in his chest.

"What are you planning?"

"Tony's here. So are his bodyguards, or what's left of them."

"What did you *do*?"

"I poisoned them. They're dead. Tony's tied up, and I'm going to do for you what you did for your father. Prove myself the same way. Tonight's my bat mitzvah, and you're invited."

"Christina!"

"What's the matter?" It's Johnny G., in the doorway.

"Come on!" He pushes the giant out of the way and races down the hall to the emergency stairs. He's out of breath by the time he and Giacobetti reach the Escalade. He orders Johnny to give him the keys, and he climbs into the driver's seat as his enforcer takes shotgun. He puts the pedal to the floor. They arrive at the warehouse in minutes. He shuts off the lights as they make the turnoff to the service road, not sure what he'll find and not wanting to alert anyone inside of their arrival.

"I'll go around back; you count to twenty and bust in the front."

He runs to the rear of the building, climbs onto the loading dock, and enters through an unlocked back door. Pulling his Glock, he quietly makes his way through the darkened rear of the building, navigating through the shelves of white powder standing like canyon walls from floor to ceiling. He sees Christina standing by a couch in the front of the space. Antonio Valiante is on the floor, his hands zip-tied behind him, his ankles bound as well. He's shaking his head like he's groggy and just coming to.

Johnny bursts through the front door. This startles Christina. It only takes her a second to put her hand on the Sig Sauer tucked in her waistband, but Johnny's on top of her before she can get it. He grabs the gun and pushes her down onto the couch.

Tony's fully awake now, and cursing.

"Shut him up," Nunzio tells Johnny G., who pulls a handkerchief out of his pocket and uses it as a gag.

He holds out his hand and has Giacobetti give him Christina's gun, which he tucks into the back of his pants. "Here," he says to Johnny, handing him his own gun, "take this."

He takes a deep breath, and it's then that he notices the bodies on the floor. He turns to Christina. "What the hell have you done?"

"I told you, I poisoned them. I put up with their leers and their snide remarks for months. And then, tonight, I cooked them a big pasta dinner, and they died. Tony's food had something else in it—something that would knock him out but not kill him."

He paces the floor, literally pulling at his hair, trying to process what he's seeing. He stops and tells Johnny, "There're vans in back. Load the bodies into one of them."

He looks down at Valiante, who's raging through the gag.

"You have no idea what you've done," Nunzio tells his daughter, who shouts back at him.

Johnny finishes loading the bodies and approaches him, waiting for orders.

"Drive the van to one of our dark hubs, park it with the other vans. Call Uncle Ham, tell him what's up. He'll take care of the rest."

"Should I come back here then?"

"No. I'll take care of this myself."

Johnny leaves, and Nunzio orders Christina to sit on the couch and wait for him. Then he walks out the back and calls Frank Valiante.

"I have your boy," he says when Frank answers. "Tony."

Valiante goes crazy, but after a while, he settles down and asks him what he wants.

"I want to make a deal," he answers. "You want the opioid business, it's yours, starting now. You run it and give me a cut, twenty percent. That's part one. Part two is you and I both agree that our kids are off-limits. I'll let Tony go. You promise not to harm my daughter."

Frank Valiante accepts immediately, and they hang up. He realizes that he's walked around the building, so he reenters the warehouse through the front door. And there she is, standing over Antonio Valiante with a knife in her hand. She has removed Valiante's gag, and he's raging at the top of his lungs.

"See me!" she screams. Then she leans down, and saws through Valiante's throat.

Blood sprays everywhere.

"No. *No!*" But he's too late.

Valiante's body slumps, and his blood jets ten feet into the air, coating Christina from waist to forehead.

That's when he notices the lights. He races to the door, peers through the space between it and the doorjamb, spotting the patrol car slowly making its way up the service road. His head clears in an instant, and he races to Christina.

"It's the cops." He gently pulls the knife from her hand and cuts the zip cuffs off Valiante's wrists and ankles.

Christina stares at him, panic growing in her eyes.

Nunzio thinks for a nanosecond. "Romeo and Juliet!"

She slides onto the floor and pulls Antonio on top of her, a ready explanation for the blood covering her. He gets onto his knees, hugs them both, covering himself in Valiante's blood. He wipes the knife handle, clearing it of Christina's prints. Then he looks into her eyes, and in that instant, they both know he's going to take the fall.

"You hesitated when Johnny broke down the door. You want to be a leader in this family? Never hesitate."

He watches as her eyes well up. She understands what he's just told her. He sees her for who she is now, and he accepts her.

He slowly backs into the shadows.

The police rush in, guns drawn.

43

Friday, July 18

Having come directly home from his audience with Christina Nunzio, Mick sits with Piper on the patio as he tells the tale. It's an unusually beautiful day in July. The sky is bright blue, the temperature in the low eighties, humidity at 10 percent. Inside, however, Mick's mind is mired in darkness.

"She asked me what I thought went down at the warehouse, and I laid it out for her. When I finished, she told me I got some of the details wrong but got the gist of it right. She asked me how I figured it out; she said the gun couldn't have been all there was to it. I told her she was right. The gun was just the hook that pulled down the veil. After it was gone, I could see clearly. I realized that her work leading the Greek system at Penn wasn't simply her volunteering, helping out, or being a party girl; it was her taking over everything she touched. Same thing with the soccer team in college. Captain Christina. I also figured out that when her cheating college boyfriend was beaten half to death, it wasn't Jimmy who had it done, but Christina. What her roommates thought was her yelling at Jimmy for the assault was actually Jimmy yelling at her. I told her that her history was probably littered with many more markers of what she was that I didn't know about."

Piper waits as he stares across their backyard for a few minutes, then looks back at her.

"The worst part was when I asked her what happened to Valiante's men. The ones who disappeared. I figured they came to the lodge with Angelo."

He shares what Christina told him about the vans and the poison gas. When he's finished, he sees horror on Piper's face.

"She killed sixty men?"

He nods.

"And then she executed Valiante himself. She laid it out for me like she was explaining how she'd done her laundry. It meant nothing to her."

In fact, Christina had sat back and smiled, her face changing before his eyes. All the softness drained out of her skin, all the youth. Her eyes grew black as coal. He knew it had to be his imagination, but it seemed as if she transformed from a beautiful young woman into something very, very old and evil.

He shares some more details of his meeting with Christina Nunzio, and Piper listens patiently, letting him vent. When he's finished, she leaves him alone; she knows him well enough to understand that's what he needs.

He putters around the garage for an hour, then goes to his home office, shuffles some papers, makes some calls. The hours drag on, and at some point, Piper pulls him from his thoughts with a call to dinner. They eat quietly. Gabby notices and is quiet, too, upset. He can tell. He forces himself to smile, tell a joke, but she isn't buying it. He sinks back into himself.

The evening passes slowly, but it passes, and eventually Gabby goes to bed, and then Piper, and Mick is left alone.

He sits behind his desk, nursing his scotch. The only light in the room comes from the green banker's light on the desk. He hears the grandfather clock in the hallway chime half past midnight, and he takes it as a signal to empty his glass and pour another.

His mind takes him to what Christina Nunzio said when he asked her why her father chose him to be his trial lawyer. She said it was because he was smart and slick and had a reputation for doing anything necessary to win.

"Then why didn't he tell me the truth about you and what really happened?"

"Because he was shielding me, protecting me. As a father. And that's the other reason he hired you."

He tilted his head.

"You're blind. You have a great big daughter-shaped splinter in your eye. Just like he had."

"He was counting on me not being able to see you."

"It worked. You looked at me and saw Gabby. Isn't that true?"

It is.

"That day I was at your house . . . you told me that your father played you."

"Misdirection. That was my mother's idea—to call you to the house and have me feed you that line to reinforce that it was all my father's doing."

He nods. "I thought your father was a monster who had fed you to the wolves. Twice."

But you were the monster all along.

He takes another sip of the scotch, and his mind drifts back to the morning after the murder, when he was in the kitchen with Piper and Gabby and he saw the video replay of Jimmy Nunzio's perp-walk from the police car to the station. The crime lord had an odd look on his face. Mick couldn't place it then, but now he realizes what it was: Jimmy Nunzio had finally seen his daughter, and it haunted him.

For a long time, he sits motionless. Then he leans forward and lifts the picture of Gabby off his desk. It's the photo of her in her soccer uniform, taken the year before. He stares at it and remembers how angry he was when Gabby was accused of tripping another girl on the soccer field. Then he recalls Christina telling him that she saw something special in Gabby, and it makes him shudder.

He brings the photo closer to his face, his heart breaking as he studies his daughter in her soccer uniform at nine years old, her smiling face open, her eyes wide with wonder and joy. A fat tear slides down the side of his face and splashes onto the glass. More follow, until Jimmy Nunzio is weeping openly.

"Christina."

ACKNOWLEDGMENTS

As with all my works, this book was a team effort. I have a lot of people to thank, starting with my wife, Lisa Chalmers, whose support, motivation, and advice are the fuel that move me forward in all things, including my writing. Thanks also to my early readers—Jill Reiff, Alan Sandman, Ellie Moffat, and Courtney Johnson—I am indebted to you for your suggestions and feedback.

Special thanks to Greg Pagano, a great Philadelphia criminal-defense attorney, for your advice and help with issues of criminal procedure. Thank you, too, for agreeing to let me use your last name for one of the characters. The Pagano in this book is tough like you, though not as smart.

My continuing gratitude goes to my editor, Ed Stackler. You return each of my manuscripts with more red marks than all my elementary, middle school, and high school teachers combined. I pull out my hair, but always end up thanking you in the end.

Cynthia Manson, my agent and mentor, thank you for guiding me through the wilderness. This is quite an adventure.

Finally, thank you, Gracie Doyle and your team at Thomas & Mercer. Writing a book is like building a race car: without someone great to drive it, it goes nowhere. So thank you, Jeffrey Belle, Mikyla Bruder, Galen Maynard, Clint Singley, Sarah Shaw, Dennelle Catlett, Ashley Vanicek, Gabrielle Guarnero, Laura Constantino, and Laura Barrett.

ABOUT THE AUTHOR

Photo © Todd Rothstein

William L. Myers, Jr., is the author of the bestselling Philadelphia Legal series, which includes the #1 Kindle bestseller *A Criminal Defense*, *An Engineered Injustice*, and *A Killer's Alibi*. A Philadelphia lawyer with thirty years of trial experience in state and federal courts up and down the East Coast, Myers has argued before the United States Supreme Court and still actively practices law. Myers was born into a proud working-class family; graduated from the University of Pennsylvania School of Law; and now lives with his wife, Lisa, in the western suburbs of Philadelphia.